A Chronicle
*"Men are not prisoners of fate, bu minds.*
– Franklin D. Roosevelt

# Ashes of Empires

This is a work of fiction. Similarities to real people, places, or events are entirely coincidental.

ASHES OF EMPIRES

**First edition. December 2, 2024.**

Copyright © 2024 Sebastian Crowe.

ISBN: 979-8230512356

Written by Sebastian Crowe.

# Table of Contents

Ashes of Empires ............... 1
1. Ashes in the Wind ............... 2
2. Echoes of Greed ............... 23
3. The Tipping Point ............... 43
4. Whispers of Revolution ............... 60
5. Trials of Trust ............... 84
6. Fortress of Fear ............... 187
7. Chains of the Past ............... 213
8. A World in Flames ............... 238
9. The Last Stand ............... 266
   - A New Threat Emerges ............... 287
10. The Price of Innovation ............... 290
11. Ashes of Empires ............... 414
12. The Fragile Future ............... 440
Epilogue ............... 478

# Act 1: The Catalyst

# 1. Ashes in the Wind

## ○ A Ruined Cityscape

The wind carried a biting chill, sweeping through the skeletal remains of what was once a thriving metropolis. Shattered glass crunched underfoot as Alex Novak carefully navigated the crumbling pavement, his every step echoing in the eerie silence. The city, once alive with the hum of traffic and laughter of its inhabitants, now lay in ruin—a graveyard of twisted steel and concrete monuments to humanity's ambition and its folly.

The sky above was a sullen gray, the sun hidden behind a perpetual haze of smoke and ash. Buildings leaned precariously, their facades scarred by fire and time. A billboard, its once-bright advertisement now faded and torn, fluttered weakly in the breeze. "A brighter tomorrow," it promised in bold letters, a cruel reminder of promises long broken.

Alex tightened his grip on the rifle slung over his shoulder. The weight of it was both a comfort and a burden. In this world, survival meant vigilance, and vigilance meant always being ready to act. His sharp eyes scanned the rubble-strewn street ahead, looking for signs of movement. There were no guarantees in the wasteland—only the ever-present threat of marauders or worse.

Behind him, Sophia Alvarez lagged slightly, her breath visible in the frigid air. She clutched a small satchel close to her chest, its contents more valuable than gold in this broken world. Alex didn't know exactly what was in it, but he knew it mattered. Sophia's work was their fragile hope, and hope was in short supply.

"Do you think they're still following us?" Sophia's voice broke the silence, trembling with fatigue and fear.

Alex glanced back at her, his expression unreadable. "Probably," he said curtly. "But they won't risk coming into the city center. Too exposed. Too dangerous." His gaze shifted to the jagged horizon, where the remains of a skyscraper stood like a jagged tombstone against the murky sky. "We'll rest when we reach cover."

Sophia nodded, though her steps faltered. She was not built for this kind of journey. The scientist who once lectured in air-conditioned halls now found herself navigating a world stripped of reason, clinging to Alex's quiet strength as her anchor.

They pressed forward, weaving through the maze of debris. The air smelled of decay and something acrid—chemicals, perhaps, leaching from the gutted factories that lined the industrial quarter. A toppled lamppost blocked their path, its base torn from the ground as though by some immense force. Alex helped Sophia climb over it, his calloused hands steadying her as she struggled to keep her footing.

"Careful," he muttered. "One wrong move out here, and—"

A distant clatter cut him off, the sound of metal striking stone. Both froze, their breaths caught in their throats. Alex's hand instinctively went to his rifle, his eyes narrowing as he scanned the shadows. He motioned for Sophia to stay behind him.

"Stay low," he whispered, his voice barely audible.

The sound came again, closer this time. Alex crouched, raising the rifle to his shoulder. His heart thudded in his chest, not with fear but with the grim resolve that had kept him alive this long. Whatever—or whoever—was out there wouldn't catch him unprepared.

Sophia crouched behind a slab of concrete, her wide eyes fixed on Alex. Her fingers dug into the satchel, as if clutching it tightly would ward off whatever danger loomed.

Alex peered around a corner, his finger hovering over the trigger. The street ahead was empty, save for the rubble and the skeletal remains of abandoned vehicles. But he knew better than to trust appearances. The wasteland thrived on deception.

A soft rustling reached his ears, followed by a shadow flickering at the edge of his vision. It wasn't the marauders; they were louder, cruder. This was something else—something calculating. He steadied his breathing, his senses razor-sharp.

The silence stretched, oppressive and suffocating. Then, with a sudden burst of motion, the source of the noise revealed itself.

A lean, emaciated figure darted from the cover of a crumbled wall, moving with the desperation of the starving. It wasn't a marauder or a soldier but a scavenger—a survivor like them, dressed in tattered rags with eyes hollowed by hunger. The scavenger froze when they spotted Alex, their hands raised instinctively in a gesture of surrender.

"Don't shoot!" the scavenger croaked, their voice hoarse from disuse. "I'm just looking for scraps. Please!"

Alex didn't lower his rifle immediately. He studied the stranger, his sharp gaze searching for any hidden weapons or signs of deceit. The scavenger was unarmed, their bony fingers trembling in the cold. Still, trust was a luxury Alex couldn't afford.

Sophia, watching from her hiding spot, hesitated before stepping out into view. "Alex," she said softly, her voice carrying a note of compassion. "He's harmless."

"He's desperate," Alex corrected, his rifle unwavering. "Desperation makes people dangerous."

The scavenger took a cautious step back, their hands still raised. "I don't want trouble," they said. "I swear. Just let me go, and you'll never see me again."

Sophia moved closer to Alex, her expression pleading. "We can't keep treating everyone like an enemy. Not if we want to rebuild anything worth saving."

Alex's jaw tightened, but after a tense moment, he lowered the rifle. "Fine," he muttered. "But if you try anything—"

"I won't," the scavenger interrupted quickly, their voice cracking with relief. "Thank you."

The stranger turned and disappeared into the maze of rubble, their figure quickly swallowed by the desolation. Alex watched them go, his grip on the rifle still firm.

"You're too soft," he said, glancing at Sophia.

"And you're too hard," she replied, her tone gentle but firm. "There has to be a balance, Alex. Otherwise, what are we even fighting for?"

Alex didn't respond, but her words lingered as they resumed their journey.

The landscape grew even more treacherous as they pressed deeper into the city's heart. Sophia stumbled over loose stones, exhaustion etched into every line of her face. Alex paused to help her up, his expression softening for the briefest moment.

"We're close," he said. "Just a little further."

Finally, they reached what had once been a public library—a grand building, now reduced to a crumbling shell. Its marble columns lay shattered on the ground, and the roof had caved in, but the basement was still intact, offering a rare refuge.

Alex led the way inside, his rifle at the ready. The air was heavy with dust and mildew, but it was warmer than the open streets. Sophia collapsed onto a broken chair, clutching her satchel protectively.

"We'll rest here for the night," Alex said, his tone leaving no room for argument. He began barricading the entrance with fallen debris, his movements precise and practiced.

Sophia pulled a notebook from her satchel, flipping through pages filled with sketches and equations. Despite the weariness in her eyes, a spark of determination remained.

"What you're working on," Alex said after a moment, his voice quieter now. "Is it really worth all this?"

Sophia looked up, meeting his gaze. "It's not just worth it," she said firmly. "It's everything."

Alex nodded, his expression unreadable. He didn't fully understand what drove her, but he knew one thing for certain: her belief in this project, whatever it was, was the only thing keeping her going. And for now, that was enough.

Outside, the wind howled, carrying with it the mournful echoes of a city that refused to be forgotten.

## ○ Shadows of the Past

THE STORM RAGED OUTSIDE, its fury battering against the crumbling walls of the library as Alex sat by the flickering fire. The wind howled through the shattered windows, sending sheets of rain in all directions. But the warmth of the fire did little to chase the chill that had settled deep within him.

Sophia was lost in her thoughts, her notebook spread out before her, the dim glow of the fire casting long shadows across her tired face. Her fingers trembled slightly as she scribbled down calculations, her brow furrowed in concentration, but Alex could see the exhaustion in her eyes.

The fire crackled, breaking the silence. Alex leaned back against the wall, his gaze drifting toward the remnants of the once-grand library that had now become their refuge. A place of knowledge, once brimming with ideas and the wisdom of the past, now reduced to dust and decay, much like the world outside.

"Do you ever wonder," Alex's voice broke through the quiet, his words coming slowly, as if weighing each one, "how we got here?"

Sophia looked up, her eyes meeting his. For a moment, there was something in her expression—something dark and distant. It was as if the storm outside had somehow found its way into her heart.

"We didn't just wake up here," she said softly, her voice almost lost in the wind. "It didn't happen overnight."

Alex stared at her, the weight of her words sinking in. He had been so focused on survival, on the next step, the next shelter, the next move, that he had never fully allowed himself to stop and consider how the world had fallen into such ruin. He knew the basics—the wars, the betrayals, the collapse of governments, the rise of new powers—but there was more to it than that. There was a story behind the destruction, a story that hadn't been told.

Sophia shifted in her seat, her eyes distant. "I remember the old days," she said, her voice barely above a whisper. "I remember when the world was whole... or at least, we thought it was. We lived in a time where history was something we learned from books, not something we were living through."

Alex didn't speak immediately. He could see the sadness in her eyes, a kind of nostalgia for a past she could never reclaim. He knew that feeling—he had seen too many good people vanish, too many cities fall to the tide of violence and despair. The world they had once known was gone, and in its place, only memories lingered like fragile ghosts.

"Do you ever think about your family?" Alex asked, his voice rough. The question was sudden, but the curiosity had always been there, hidden beneath the layers of their survival routine.

Sophia's hands stilled, and she looked down at her notebook. "They were lost long ago," she said, her voice tight, as if the mention of them brought a flood of grief she had long buried. "When the war began, they... they were among the first to disappear." She hesitated, then added, "I never got to say goodbye."

Alex didn't push her further. He understood that pain—he had his own ghosts, his own shadows of the past that he never spoke of. There were things too painful, too raw to relive. But there was something about the storm, the fire, the emptiness of the world around them that made it feel harder to ignore the past.

The fire crackled again, sending a shower of sparks into the darkened room. Outside, the storm seemed to intensify, as if the heavens themselves were mourning for the lost world.

"Sophia," Alex said after a long pause. "We can't keep running from it forever."

She looked up at him, her expression guarded. "From what?"

"From the past," he said, his voice soft but firm. "From everything that led us here. We need to understand it. We need to know why it happened. Otherwise, how can we ever rebuild? How can we ever make sure it doesn't happen again?"

Sophia's gaze softened, and for the first time in a long while, there was a flicker of something other than fear or exhaustion in her eyes. "Maybe you're right," she said quietly. "Maybe understanding the past is the only way we'll know how to move forward."

Alex stood up slowly, the weight of his words hanging in the air like a storm cloud. He didn't have all the answers, but for the first time in a long time, he felt like they were on the right path. They had survived the collapse of the world, but survival wasn't enough. They needed meaning. They needed purpose. And that, perhaps, lay in the shadows of the past.

Sophia closed her notebook and stood beside him, her face set with quiet resolve. "Then let's uncover it," she said. "Together."

The wind howled outside, but inside, for a moment, there was peace. Not of certainty or security, but of shared determination. They would face the ghosts of the past—no matter how dark or painful they might be—because only by understanding them could they hope to carve a future from the ashes.

## ○ An Uneasy Alliance

THE NEXT MORNING, THE remnants of the storm hung in the air, a thick mist blanketing the ruined city. The fire had burned down to embers, casting only a faint glow in the corner of the library. Alex and Sophia were already packed, ready to continue their journey deeper into the heart of the city. But today, something felt different.

Sophia paused, her hand resting on the cracked edge of the stone table as she scanned the city outside the broken window. The city, once vibrant, now felt like a graveyard—streets where the living fought for scraps, where the dead whispered through the ruins. But there was a strange energy in the air, a shifting tide of something greater than just survival.

"We're going to need help," Alex's voice interrupted her thoughts. "If we're going to uncover what's left of the old world, we can't do it alone."

Sophia turned toward him, her eyes narrowed. She had been bracing herself for this. She'd seen it coming in his silence, in his hesitant decisions. He was right, of course. Their journey would be perilous, and while they had each other, that wouldn't be enough to face the world they now lived in.

"Help?" she asked cautiously, unsure of where he was going with this.

Alex's jaw tightened, his gaze distant. "We'll need allies. People who know the city, its hidden paths, its dangers. We can't fight every battle on our own."

Sophia raised an eyebrow. She'd known him long enough to understand that trusting others wasn't something Alex did easily. He had always been a lone wolf, a survivor in the truest sense of the word. But the world had changed, and even the most solitary of men couldn't fight the storm alone.

"You're right," she said softly, though a lingering sense of unease curled in her stomach. "But who can we trust?"

Alex was silent for a moment, his gaze shifting toward the doorway. His thoughts seemed to be locked in a battle, the weight of a thousand decisions pulling him in different directions. Finally, he spoke, his voice low and filled with a mixture of reluctance and necessity.

"There's a group. They call themselves the Ashen Covenant. They're a faction of survivors, ruthless but organized. They know the city better than anyone. And they have resources. But they don't trust outsiders, especially not ones who don't share their... goals."

Sophia felt a wave of discomfort wash over her. The Ashen Covenant. The name was whispered with fear and suspicion among the few survivors still clinging to life in the city. They were known for their harsh methods, their ruthless pursuit of power, and their willingness to manipulate anyone who crossed their path. They weren't the kind of people Alex usually worked with—or anyone, for that matter. But in this new world, the line between right and wrong had blurred. Survival was the only rule.

"And you think they'll help us?" Sophia asked, her voice laced with doubt.

Alex's eyes flickered, the weight of his next words pressing heavily on his shoulders. "They will, but at a cost. They don't do favors without expecting something in return. And their price... well, it's not something anyone would willingly pay."

Sophia took a deep breath. She had seen too much darkness in the last few years to be surprised by what Alex was saying. But there was still a part of her that hesitated. A part that wanted to believe in something better, something that wasn't rooted in manipulation and survival at any cost.

"I don't like it," she admitted. "But I don't see another option."

Alex nodded slowly, a flicker of understanding passing between them. They were both caught in the same bind. Trusting the Ashen Covenant was dangerous. But trusting anyone at all in this fractured world was dangerous. There were no easy choices, only the ones they had to make to keep moving forward.

"I'll make contact," Alex said, as if making a final decision. "But you need to stay alert. Don't trust them—don't trust anyone in this city. Not even me, if it comes down to it."

Sophia's heart skipped a beat at the finality of his words. She had known he was a survivor, but the depth of his cynicism never failed to unnerve her. Still, she understood the weight of what he was saying. She didn't trust anyone, not really. Not anymore.

The two of them left the library in silence, stepping into the wreckage of the city that had once been a place of life and vibrancy. Now, it was a battleground, a maze of crumbling buildings and desperate souls.

They moved cautiously through the streets, avoiding the snipers and scouts that had become a constant threat. Every corner held danger, every shadow masked a potential enemy. They didn't speak much, knowing that the few words they exchanged were too important to waste.

As they approached the outskirts of the city, the ruins grew more desolate. The Ashen Covenant's stronghold was nestled in the heart of what had once been a vibrant neighborhood, now reduced to a fortress of scrap metal and barricades. It was a place of power, and no one got in without permission.

Alex took a deep breath, then nodded to Sophia. "Stay close," he whispered. "And remember—this is an uneasy alliance. We don't owe them anything. Don't forget that."

Sophia didn't need any more reminders. The Ashen Covenant had their own agenda, and they would do anything to achieve it. But they were their best hope, for now. She followed Alex toward the gates, her hand on the hilt of her knife, ready for whatever lay ahead.

## ○ Scarcity Breeds Desperation

THE GATES OF THE ASHEN Covenant's stronghold loomed before them, a towering structure of rusted metal and broken concrete. It was a monument to desperation, a physical manifestation of everything the world had become—a place where the desperate sought refuge, and the powerful controlled what little remained of civilization. Alex and Sophia approached slowly, the crunch of their boots on the broken asphalt the only sound breaking the eerie silence around them.

The city had been without resources for years. Water was rationed, food was scarce, and the air itself felt heavy with the weight of unspoken fears. People fought for scraps, clawing at any remnants of a life that had once been normal. What few supplies remained were hoarded by the powerful factions that had risen in the ashes of the old world. And the Ashen Covenant, with its ruthless grip on the city's lifeblood, was at the top of that pyramid.

"Keep your guard up," Alex muttered as they neared the entrance. His voice was low, but there was a note of tension beneath it. "They're not interested in charity. They don't give without taking something in return. And I have no idea what they want from us yet."

Sophia nodded, her hand gripping the edge of her weapon, the weight of its handle grounding her in the moment. They had already encountered the Covenant's scouts—their eyes sharp, their movements calculated. She could feel the undercurrent of danger in the air, the heavy realization that trust in this place was a luxury they could not afford.

As they approached the gates, two guards stepped forward, their faces hidden behind cracked visors, their expressions unreadable. One of them held a rifle loosely in his hands, the other a baton, his fingers resting near the trigger of a hidden weapon. They both surveyed Alex and Sophia with calculating eyes, as if weighing whether these two would bring value or danger to their enclave.

"What do you want?" the guard on the left spoke first, his voice rough, like it had been scraped raw from years of shouting orders.

"We need to speak to your leader," Alex replied, his tone steady but edged with the urgency of the moment. "We have information. Information that could be useful. But we need protection in return."

The guard on the right grunted, his eyes narrowing. "Protection? From what?" he demanded.

"The city. The factions," Alex answered, choosing his words carefully. He could already feel the weight of the lie on his tongue. They didn't have valuable information—not yet, anyway. But this was a game of survival, and desperation made people say things they didn't believe. If they could gain entry, it might be enough to learn what they needed.

"We don't trade for information," the first guard responded curtly. "But we might be willing to strike a deal." His voice dropped, as if sharing a secret. "The world's running dry. Supplies are limited, and even the strongest among us are feeling the pressure. People are desperate... and desperate people do desperate things."

Sophia stiffened, the implications clear. Resources were at a premium, and the Covenant wasn't just protecting its own—they were hoarding what little the world had left. Everyone here had something to sell, whether it was their labor, their loyalty, or their bodies. The air was thick with the scent of desperation, and it made her stomach twist.

Alex's gaze flickered toward the guard, meeting his eyes with an intensity that seemed to pierce through the masked indifference.

"We're not here to beg for charity," he said, his voice low but resolute. "We can offer something in exchange. We need to get inside."

The guard studied him for a moment, then turned to his companion. They exchanged a look, a silent conversation passing between them. After what seemed like an eternity, the guard nodded, his decision made.

"You'll get in," the guard said finally. "But you'll have to prove your worth. You'll do something for us first. A job, so to speak. Then, and only then, will we discuss your 'protection.'"

Sophia felt her stomach tighten. Nothing came for free, and nothing was ever simple. The Ashen Covenant's reputation wasn't one of kindness or fairness. If they wanted something in exchange, it would likely be dangerous—and it would come at a cost they weren't prepared to pay. But they had little choice.

"What kind of job?" Alex asked, his voice level, but his eyes flickering with suspicion.

"There's a convoy, moving through the western sector. We need it intercepted. Whatever's in it, we want it. You take care of it, and we'll consider your request," the guard answered, a cold edge in his voice.

Alex and Sophia exchanged a brief look. It wasn't ideal. Taking down a convoy in the western sector meant getting into the heart of another faction's territory. The risks were immense—hostile forces, traps, and potentially an all-out fight. But they had no better options. They needed to make it inside the Covenant's walls, and this was their ticket.

"I'm not promising anything more than that," Alex said carefully. "But we'll do it. For now."

The guards stepped back, nodding. "Then you'll follow us." The heavy gates began to creak open, and a wave of tension washed over both Alex and Sophia. What they would face inside the Covenant's stronghold, they didn't know. But the uneasy alliance had been forged.

Desperation had its price, and the two of them had just begun to pay it.

## ○ Sophia's Discovery

THE HOURS DRAGGED BY as Alex and Sophia trudged through the crumbling streets, their steps taking them deeper into the heart of the Ashen Covenant's stronghold. The compound was a fortress of rusted metal and fractured stone, the remnants of a city once alive with the hum of industry and the pulse of human ambition. Now, it was little more than a graveyard of broken dreams, an echo of a time long gone.

Sophia's mind raced. The job, the convoy—they had no choice but to follow through, but there was a growing sense of unease gnawing at her. The guards had been vague, only promising a meeting with the Covenant's leader if they succeeded. But something felt wrong. The faction had a reputation for cruelty and manipulation, and their promises never came without strings attached.

She was snapped from her thoughts as Alex turned to her, his face grim in the dim light. "We'll need to stay sharp. Don't trust anyone in there," he muttered, his eyes scanning their surroundings.

Sophia nodded, but her thoughts were elsewhere. Her eyes scanned the compound as they made their way through it—fences, watchtowers, armed sentries at every corner. It was a fortress in every sense of the word. But even amid the decaying walls and rotting structures, Sophia couldn't shake the feeling that something was hidden beneath the surface.

A movement caught her eye. Across the compound, she saw something she hadn't expected—a small, unmarked door tucked away behind a rusted supply shed. It was the kind of door that wasn't meant to be noticed, the kind that only the most observant would pick out from the clutter. There was a faint light coming from inside, a glow that seemed out of place in the otherwise oppressive darkness.

Without thinking, she pulled Alex to a stop, her voice barely above a whisper. "Wait," she said, her eyes locked on the door. "Something's off. I need to check something."

Alex followed her gaze, his brow furrowing. "What is it?"

"Just a feeling," she muttered. "Stay here. Keep watch."

Before Alex could protest, she slipped away, moving swiftly and silently through the shadows. The door was close now, just a few steps away. Her heart pounded in her chest as she reached out, her fingers brushing the cold, rusted handle. For a moment, she hesitated, knowing that every step they took in this place was dangerous, every action carrying weight. But curiosity and caution fought inside her, and she knew she couldn't ignore this feeling.

She twisted the handle, and the door creaked open with a hesitant groan. The light inside was brighter now, a steady, artificial glow that seemed to beckon her in. Sophia stepped into the room cautiously, her eyes adjusting to the sudden brightness.

What she found inside was not what she expected.

The room was small, almost like a storage closet, but it was clean—too clean for the rest of the compound. The walls were lined with crates, some marked with symbols she didn't recognize, others with simple black ink scrawls. But what caught her attention were the tables—several of them, each covered with strange devices, mechanical parts, and maps. A map of the city, meticulously detailed, with notes scribbled in several languages she didn't understand.

But there was something else, something that sent a chill down her spine: a series of photographs pinned to the wall, each one showing various people, men and women, children—civilians, seemingly. But each one had a red X marked through their face, as if they were targets.

Sophia's breath caught in her throat as she recognized the faces in the photographs. They weren't random civilians. They were people she knew—people from the outskirts of the city, people who had vanished in the chaos of the past few months. Families, neighbors, and friends. All of them were gone now, their fates unknown. The Covenant had been tracking them, hunting them.

She felt her hands shake as she stepped closer to the wall, her eyes darting over the photos, trying to make sense of it all. But the more she looked, the more the realization hit her like a slap across the face: the Covenant wasn't just hoarding resources. They were systematically hunting people, using them for something—maybe experiments, maybe for something darker.

Her mind raced, piecing together the information she had. The convoy they had been assigned to intercept—could it be related to this? Was it carrying more people, more "targets" for the Covenant's operations? She had to find out more, but the danger was becoming too real, too immediate. She couldn't stay here much longer.

Just as she was about to turn and leave, the faint sound of footsteps echoed from the corridor outside the room. Panic surged through her. She didn't have time to think. With a glance at the photographs once more, she knew she couldn't leave without taking something—proof of what she had just discovered.

She grabbed one of the maps, shoving it into her pack, and then moved quickly toward the door. Her heart pounded in her chest, her breath coming in short, quiet bursts. She had to get back to Alex, had to tell him what she had found.

But as she reached for the door, the creak of the floorboards froze her in place. A voice—low, cold—sounded from the hallway.

"Who's there?"

Sophia's blood ran cold. She turned, every muscle in her body tensed for flight, but the door was too far, and the footsteps were too close. She pressed herself against the wall, trying to make herself as invisible as possible, praying that she wouldn't be seen.

The seconds felt like an eternity. Then, just as the footsteps passed by the door, she exhaled in relief. She held her breath for another moment, then slipped out of the room as quietly as possible, her heart racing in her chest.

She met Alex at the corner of the compound, her face pale and her movements sharp with urgency.

"We need to talk," she said, her voice low but filled with a new kind of fear. "What we're dealing with here—this place isn't just a stronghold. It's a hunting ground. And they've been tracking people—people we know."

Alex's brow furrowed as he listened, but there was no time for more explanation. Their mission had just taken a darker turn, and now, more than ever, they couldn't trust anyone—not even the very faction they had come to bargain with.

## ○ A Glimpse of Hope

THE WORLD OUTSIDE HAD already given up on hope. Cities crumbled, governments collapsed, and the survival of the human race seemed a fragile, fleeting thing. Yet in the shadow of the devastation, where nothing but ashes and whispers of the past remained, there were still pockets of life that refused to surrender to despair.

Sophia and Alex moved cautiously through the wasteland, their eyes scanning the horizon, alert to every sound, every movement. The sun hung low in the sky, casting a dim, reddish glow over the fractured world. The winds carried dust and ash, and the air smelled faintly of burning. Yet even in the suffocating silence of the desolate landscape, there was something stirring—something just beyond their reach, like a faint pulse in the deadened heart of the world.

They had spent months traveling through the ruins, scavenging what little they could, avoiding factions like the Ashen Covenant that would rather exploit them than offer help. But now, as they neared the outskirts of what had once been a thriving community, a sense of something more lingered in the air.

Sophia's eyes caught sight of a structure ahead—a small building, half-buried in rubble, but with a faint light flickering through the cracks in its walls. It was a place that shouldn't have been there, not in this world, where every corner seemed to swallow hope. The building was untouched by time, its silhouette sharp against the horizon, standing tall amidst the chaos.

She turned to Alex, her voice barely a whisper. "Do you see that?"

Alex squinted into the distance, then nodded. "I see it. But it's not on any map I know."

They approached cautiously, their footsteps muffled by the thick dust underfoot. The closer they got, the more they could feel the weight of the place—the feeling that they were walking into something far older, far more significant than they could comprehend.

As they neared the door, the light inside flickered once more, and Sophia could feel a strange pull in her chest. There was a flicker of something here, something they hadn't seen in months—a spark of life that seemed almost too good to be true.

"Stay alert," Alex muttered. "We don't know what this is."

Sophia nodded, her hand resting lightly on the handle of her rifle, though she hadn't had to use it in days. The light spilling through the cracks in the door seemed warmer now, more inviting, and her pulse quickened.

With a deep breath, she pushed the door open.

Inside, they were greeted with the soft murmur of voices—laughter, low and careful, as though they didn't want to disturb the fragile peace that hung in the air. The room was small, lit by flickering lanterns and the glow of old, mismatched candles. But it was alive. There were people here, sitting around a table, talking quietly among themselves. They were huddled together, their clothes worn but clean, their faces tired but full of purpose.

Sophia's eyes scanned the room, her instincts telling her that this was something different. It was a small community, hidden away from the chaos outside, a place that had managed to survive by retreating into the shadows of the old world. A family, perhaps, or a collective—living on the fringes, avoiding the war and the politics that had torn the world apart.

A woman in the corner looked up, her face warm with a quiet smile, as though they had been expected.

"You're the ones from the convoy," she said, her voice soft but carrying an air of certainty. "We've been waiting for you."

Sophia stepped forward, confusion creeping into her mind. "How did you—?"

"We knew you would come," the woman interrupted gently. "When the time was right, when the stars aligned, you would find us. We are the last of the resistance."

Alex glanced at Sophia, his brow furrowed. Resistance to what? They had heard whispers of resistance movements—groups who had fought back against the factions like the Ashen Covenant, but they had all disappeared over time, either destroyed or absorbed into the larger powers that controlled the new world order.

But this was different. This wasn't a group hiding out in a cave, or a guerrilla movement on the run. There was something about the way the woman spoke, the way she looked at them, that made Sophia pause.

"What is this place?" Sophia asked, her voice quiet but edged with disbelief. "How have you survived?"

The woman smiled again, standing slowly and walking toward a map pinned on the wall. It was a map of the old world, much like the one they had seen before, but there were markings all over it—dots, lines, and symbols that none of them recognized.

"This is our sanctuary," the woman said. "This is the last place that remains untouched by the war. The Covenant and the other factions don't know we exist. We've been hiding here, waiting for the right moment to act. We've been preparing."

Sophia exchanged a look with Alex. "Preparing for what?"

The woman's eyes sparkled with a quiet intensity, and her voice dropped to a near whisper. "For the return of hope."

Sophia's heart skipped a beat. The woman's words hung in the air, heavy with meaning. The return of hope—what did that even mean? Was it just a metaphor, a hopeful vision of a better future? Or was it something more tangible? Was it a weapon? A strategy?

Alex moved closer, his tone guarded. "What are you saying? How can you fight back against all of this? You're just a few people. The Ashen Covenant, the other factions—they're too strong."

The woman met his gaze steadily. "We're not just a few people. We are the last of something much older, much stronger than what the Covenant has become. We carry the knowledge of the old world. The knowledge of how to rebuild."

Sophia's mind reeled. It was impossible to believe, yet she couldn't ignore the glimmer of something inside her—something long forgotten, a feeling she hadn't allowed herself to acknowledge in months. The idea that the world could still be saved, that there could be a way out of the nightmare they were trapped in.

Could it be true? Was this the glimmer of hope they had been waiting for, or was it just another cruel illusion?

She didn't know, but for the first time in a long time, she allowed herself to wonder.

The woman gestured to the group gathered around the table. "We are more than just survivors. We are the custodians of the old world's knowledge. And we have a plan—one that can change everything."

Sophia felt her pulse quicken, her breath shallow as she stood on the precipice of something huge. Something that could reshape the course of their fractured world.

Alex looked at her, his gaze unreadable. "What do we have to do?"

The woman's smile deepened, and for the first time, there was a flicker of something dangerous in her eyes. "First, you must decide if you're willing to fight for it."

And that was when Sophia realized: this was no longer just about survival. This was about reclaiming the future—if they could find a way to fight back against the chaos that had torn everything apart.

There was hope, and it was fragile. But it was a start. And that was more than they had had in a long time.

# 2. Echoes of Greed

## ○ Victor Lynn's Empire

Victor Lynn had always been a man of contrasts. From the outside, he appeared to be the epitome of control and power—tall, imposing, with sharp features that exuded authority. His empire, a sprawling network of companies, financial institutions, and hidden alliances, was an invisible force that had shaped the world for years. Yet, for all his power, there was something deeply unsettling about Victor's rise to the top. He wasn't just a man; he was a symbol—a figure whose name carried both fear and admiration in equal measure.

The roots of his empire stretched back long before the fall of the old world. Victor had been a businessman at the heart of the international financial system, a master of leveraging chaos for personal gain. But as the global order began to crumble, he adapted—quickly, ruthlessly. The very systems that once served to destabilize economies became the tools with which he would reshape the future. Governments had fallen, cities had burned, and yet Victor's empire remained untouched, flourishing in the dark corners of the new world.

Sophia and Alex, after their unexpected encounter with the resistance, had learned of Victor's name. The woman, who had introduced herself as Elena, had spoken of him with an unmistakable sense of reverence. "Victor Lynn controls everything," she had said, her voice quiet but laced with fear. "He is the one who has the power to bring the world to its knees—and he is the one who holds the key to rebuilding it."

Sophia didn't understand it at first. How could one man hold so much influence over the fractured remnants of the world? But as Elena explained, Victor had seized control of not just the resources that were essential to survival—water, food, and medicine—but also the most advanced technologies left in the wake of the collapse. His empire was built not just on wealth, but on knowledge, and in the new world, knowledge was as valuable as gold.

"He has a network of loyalists everywhere," Elena continued. "People who do his bidding without question. He's untouchable. And if you want to survive in this world, you will eventually have to make a choice: ally with him, or fall under his shadow."

The idea of aligning with someone like Victor Lynn was anathema to everything Sophia and Alex had fought for. They had seen the destruction wrought by the likes of the Ashen Covenant and the other warlords who sought to impose their will through force and manipulation. Victor, they knew, was no different. He would use anyone, anything, to further his agenda.

But the resistance was in a precarious position. They had no resources, no army, no weapons to match the power of Victor's empire. Sophia understood this as she and Alex listened intently to Elena's words. The world outside was brutal, unforgiving. To survive, they would need allies—powerful ones. And as much as it pained them to admit it, Victor Lynn's empire was the only viable option.

"The choice is simple," Elena concluded, her eyes darkening with a sense of inevitability. "You either join him, or you fight him. And if you fight him, you may very well lose everything."

As the days passed, Sophia and Alex wrestled with the dilemma. The idea of serving someone like Victor was repulsive. They had seen enough of his kind to last a lifetime. But the stakes had never been higher. With every passing day, the world they knew seemed to inch closer to total destruction. They couldn't afford to be idealists anymore. The time for fighting for a better world had passed—now, the fight was simply for survival.

Victor Lynn's empire had become a beacon in the darkness, and in this world, it was the only light left.

Sophia couldn't help but wonder, though, if they were truly joining to survive, or if they were slowly becoming part of the very machine they had once sought to destroy.

Victor's private estate was a fortress, a sprawling complex hidden deep within the wasteland. Sophia and Alex arrived under cover of darkness, their faces obscured by masks and cloaks. The air felt heavy, thick with tension, as they made their way toward the gates. They had been briefed on the protocols—how to behave, what to say, what not to say. In this place, there was no room for mistakes.

The guards at the gate were armed to the teeth, their eyes scanning every movement with the cold precision of people who had learned the hard way not to trust anyone. They were, in a sense, the first line of defense against the chaos that Victor had carefully constructed around himself. The rest of the world might have descended into madness, but here, in this isolated sanctuary, Victor's empire held firm.

Sophia's pulse quickened as they approached the entrance, the weight of the decision settling heavily on her shoulders. She had never imagined herself in a place like this—entering the lair of the very man whose name had haunted the world's most powerful figures. But this was it. The only choice they had left.

The door swung open, and they were ushered inside by a silent servant, who led them through marble halls adorned with intricate paintings and sculptures—each piece reflecting the grandeur of a world long lost. There were no signs of decay here, no remnants of the war that had ravaged the outside world. It was as if time had stood still in this place, and it only made the reality of their situation more surreal.

They were taken to a large, dimly lit room, where Victor awaited them. He stood at the center, his silhouette framed by the massive windows that looked out over the horizon. The room was silent, save for the soft hum of machines in the background. Victor didn't speak immediately. Instead, he regarded them with a quiet intensity, his gaze sharp and calculating, as if he were assessing their every move.

"You've made the right choice," he said finally, his voice low but commanding. "You understand that, don't you?"

Sophia's throat tightened, but she nodded. "We understand."

Victor smiled, the expression cold but satisfied. "Good. Because in this world, you either adapt, or you perish. I've adapted."

The words hung in the air like a challenge, and for a moment, Sophia and Alex found themselves staring at him, unsure of what to say next.

"I'll give you what you need," Victor continued, his tone softer now. "But understand this—there are no favors in my world. Everything comes at a cost. Everything."

Sophia swallowed hard, her mind racing. The cost of survival. The price of hope. She had a feeling that whatever they did next, the price would be steep. But it was a price they would have to pay if they were to change the world—or simply survive it.

Victor Lynn's empire had no room for innocence. Only the ruthless need apply. And as they stepped deeper into his world, Sophia knew that nothing would ever be the same again.

## ○ The Price of Progress

THE HUM OF MACHINES and the sterile coldness of the underground facility were a constant reminder of what Victor Lynn had achieved. Progress. It was a word that had been bandied about by every politician, every leader, every self-proclaimed visionary throughout history. But in Victor's world, progress wasn't about lifting humanity to new heights. It was about control, consolidation, and the relentless march toward power. The price of progress was steep—too steep for most to comprehend.

Sophia and Alex stood in the vast command center, surrounded by monitors displaying streams of data, flickering images of global hotspots, and maps littered with the red marks of territories under Victor's influence. The sprawling network of satellites, drones, and surveillance systems painted a picture of a man who had harnessed the tools of modern civilization to create a global empire that extended far beyond the borders of any nation. In his world, progress didn't just mean innovation—it meant dominance.

Victor stepped beside them, his presence more imposing than the machines surrounding them. He seemed to own the very space they occupied, his every movement calculated, deliberate. "This is the future," he said, voice laced with pride. "A world where information is power, where technology is the key to survival, and where I hold the keys to it all."

Sophia couldn't help but shudder. She had seen glimpses of the past—a world teetering on the brink of collapse—and now, she saw a future shaped by one man's vision. It wasn't a future of equality or freedom. It was a future where the few had all the power, and the many were left to beg for scraps.

"Victor," she began, her voice measured but with an edge of defiance, "what exactly are you offering? Security, survival? Or are we just pawns in your game, held hostage by your technology?"

Victor didn't flinch at her words. Instead, he turned slowly, his eyes narrowing as if weighing her sincerity. "Pawns?" he repeated, as though tasting the word on his tongue. "No, Sophia. You are not pawns. You are... partners. For now."

His smile didn't reach his eyes. "Progress doesn't come free, though. Every advancement, every step forward, requires sacrifice.

You think the world can simply pick itself up from the ashes without paying a price? You're wrong. I've learned that the hard way." He gestured to the room around them, to the machines humming in the background. "All this—what you see—costs more than you can imagine. People. Lives. Resources. And I don't have the luxury of thinking in terms of idealism. In the new world, there's only one currency that matters: power."

Alex, who had been silently absorbing the conversation, stepped forward, his voice low but firm. "You're not wrong about the price, but the way you see the world, Victor... it's broken. This isn't progress—it's tyranny. You can't control everything and expect it to end well."

Victor laughed, a sound that was sharp and cold. "I don't expect it to end well. I expect it to endure. That's what I've built—a system that will last beyond this world's collapse. You think the chaos will end? No. It will continue. I'm simply ensuring that my empire survives the storm."

Sophia felt a tightness in her chest. She had spent so long fighting against forces like Victor's—people who sought to rule through fear, control, and manipulation. And yet, here she was, standing at the crossroads of survival. She had no illusions that joining Victor would lead to peace. But perhaps it was the only way forward. The only way to ensure that the resistance didn't simply fade into the annals of history as another failed cause.

"What's the cost, then?" she asked, her voice barely above a whisper, though her words carried the weight of a decision that would change everything.

Victor's smile deepened, his eyes gleaming with something cold and knowing. "The cost is loyalty. Absolute loyalty. In exchange, I'll provide you with resources, technology, and the protection of my empire. But you will serve me. You will follow my rules, and you will never question my authority. If you can accept that, then the price is one you can afford."

Loyalty. It was a word that had so often been twisted by men like Victor, used as a leash to bind others to their will. But it was also a word that, in a fractured world, could mean the difference between survival and death. Sophia exchanged a look with Alex. There was no easy choice here—no righteous answer. The path ahead was murky, and the cost would only reveal itself in time.

Victor turned back to the monitors, his gaze sweeping over the world he controlled, as if taking inventory of his dominion. "I've made my choice," he said quietly. "And now, you will make yours."

The weight of the decision pressed down on them, suffocating and inevitable. Sophia knew that aligning with Victor would come at a cost far greater than just their loyalty. It would demand their very souls.

"Remember," Victor continued, his voice echoing in the sterile room, "the price of progress is never as simple as it seems. There are always those who are willing to pay the price—and those who aren't. The question is, which side are you on?"

As the words hung in the air, Sophia couldn't help but wonder if they were already too far gone to turn back. The road ahead was fraught with peril, and in Victor's empire, there was no place for second chances.

---

Later that evening, as they sat in a small, dimly lit room, the weight of the decision settled over Sophia and Alex like a shroud. The quiet between them was deafening, each lost in their own thoughts, the gravity of what had just transpired hanging in the air.

"I don't know if we can do this," Alex muttered, his hands clenching the edge of the table. "Victor... he's not someone we can control. He'll use us until we're no longer useful, and then—" He shook his head, unable to finish the thought.

Sophia looked at him, her eyes filled with the same uncertainty. "I know. But what other choice do we have? This isn't just about us anymore. It's about the people who are still out there, the ones who have no hope. Maybe we can change things from the inside. Maybe we can take him down from within."

Alex met her gaze, his expression softening, though doubt still lingered in his eyes. "And maybe we'll become just another cog in his machine."

Sophia didn't have an answer. She didn't know what the future held or whether they had made the right choice. But she did know one thing: the world had changed, and they had to change with it. Whether that meant sacrificing their ideals or finding a way to bend the system to their will, the price of progress was one they would have to pay.

And in that moment, as the shadows of the past loomed large, Sophia realized that no matter the path they chose, the price would always be the same. Progress came at a cost—and they were paying it with their lives.

## ○ Emma's Hidden Truth

EMMA SAT IN THE DIMLY lit room, the only light coming from the flickering screen of her terminal. The glow cast long shadows on her face, making her look like a ghost of the woman she once was. She had always been careful, meticulous, always playing the game from the sidelines, hidden in the shadows where she couldn't be seen. But now, as the walls seemed to close in around her, she couldn't ignore the gnawing truth any longer: everything she had built was teetering on the edge of collapse.

Her fingers hovered over the keys, hesitating. She had been tracking the global networks for weeks now, piecing together fragments of information, following the whispers that had led her to this dark corner of the world. It wasn't supposed to happen this way. She was supposed to stay invisible, a silent observer, never the one pulling the strings. Yet here she was, on the precipice of exposing something far darker than she could have ever imagined.

Emma's breath caught as she stared at the encrypted files on her screen. Each one contained a piece of the puzzle, a glimpse into the hidden depths of Victor Lynn's empire. She had known about his rise to power—everyone did. His empire stretched across continents, a well-oiled machine of technology, manipulation, and cold calculation. But what she had uncovered was something much more sinister. Something that could unravel everything, not just his empire, but the very fabric of what remained of society.

She leaned back in her chair, a wave of nausea sweeping over her. She had known there were secrets, things that people like Victor were willing to do to maintain control, but she hadn't anticipated this. No one had. The files contained names—people she had worked with, people she had trusted. And beneath their names were coded messages, encrypted transactions, and hints of betrayals that went far beyond mere politics or power struggles.

Emma's hands shook as she clicked open one of the files. The data was undeniable. She had seen the patterns before—small discrepancies in financial reports, whispers of covert operations, but now, it all made sense. Victor's network wasn't just a web of influence; it was a living organism, its tendrils embedded in every corner of the world. And Emma was about to learn just how far those tendrils reached.

She scrolled down through the document, each word feeling like a blow to her chest. It wasn't just Victor who had been hiding the truth. She had, too. She had been part of it, unknowingly at first, but now she could see the full picture. She had helped create this monstrous system, had been complicit in its growth, its expansion. She had turned a blind eye to the cost, to the lives destroyed in the pursuit of progress, thinking it was for the greater good.

But now, the truth was inescapable.

Victor wasn't just using technology to control people. He had been manipulating them on a much deeper level, using bioengineering, mind control techniques, and even psychological warfare to keep his empire in check. Emma knew that his reach went far beyond what most people understood. But what terrified her more than anything was the realization that she, too, had been part of the machine. Every step she had taken, every decision she had made had only served to strengthen his grip.

The sound of footsteps behind her pulled Emma from her thoughts, and she quickly minimized the files, her heart pounding in her chest. She didn't need to turn around to know who it was. Alex had arrived, as he always did, right when she was on the verge of something important. They had worked together for years, but she had never told him the full extent of her involvement in Victor's empire.

He stood in the doorway, silhouetted by the weak light filtering through the hallway. His voice was low, calm, but she could hear the tension in it. "You've been quiet tonight," he said, his eyes scanning the room, landing briefly on the faint glow of her terminal before meeting her gaze. "Is something wrong?"

Emma swallowed, her mouth dry. "No. Just... thinking."

Alex stepped into the room, his eyes narrowing slightly as he took in her posture, the way she was sitting so stiffly, her hands clenched in her lap. He could always tell when something was off, and Emma wasn't exactly known for her honesty. She had spent too many years hiding her true thoughts, pretending to be a part of something bigger than herself. But now, she could feel the weight of her own secrets threatening to suffocate her.

"You don't have to keep hiding it," Alex said softly, taking a few steps closer. "I know you, Emma. I can see when something's wrong. Whatever it is, you don't have to bear it alone."

For a moment, Emma considered telling him everything. The files. The truth. The horrifying realization that she had been complicit in the rise of Victor's empire. But the words caught in her throat. She had worked so hard to build this life, to distance herself from the shadows of her past, and now she wasn't sure if she could face the truth without losing everything she had worked for.

"I'm not hiding anything," she said finally, her voice cold, but betraying a flicker of guilt. "I'm just... trying to make sense of everything."

Alex didn't press. Instead, he just nodded, his eyes lingering on her for a moment longer before he turned to leave. But just as he reached the door, he stopped. "Whatever you're holding back, Emma, you don't have to face it alone. I'm here."

As the door clicked shut behind him, Emma was left alone in the silence, the weight of his words heavy on her shoulders. Could she really keep hiding? Could she continue to live with the secret, the truth that would shatter everything she had ever believed in?

She looked back at the terminal, her fingers itching to open the files again. But this time, she didn't. She couldn't. The truth was no longer something she could bury. It was there, in front of her, undeniable and unavoidable. The question was, what would she do with it?

The empire that Victor had built wasn't just built on power—it was built on lies. And now, Emma realized, she had a choice. She could continue to play the role she had always played, keeping the truth hidden, or she could expose it all, risking everything in the process.

Either way, she knew one thing for certain: the truth had a way of coming out, no matter how deeply it was buried. And when it did, there would be no going back.

## ○ Danny's War Scars

DANNY STOOD AT THE window, the glass cool beneath his fingertips, staring out at the sprawling city below. It had been weeks since he returned, but every time he looked out at the city, he felt like a stranger. The streets he once knew so well, the places he had walked in and out of without a second thought, now seemed alien to him. The war had taken more than his innocence. It had taken his sense of belonging, his understanding of himself, and the world around him.

The scars from the war weren't just on his body, though they were there too, the faint outline of burns on his arms, the twisted joints that never fully healed. No, the real scars were the ones inside. The ones that no one could see, the ones that tore at him every day, made sleep impossible, and brought him to the edge of madness. Each night, the memories came back with cruel clarity—the explosion that sent him flying across the ground, the faces of friends turned to ash, the screams that echoed in his ears long after the sound had faded.

He rubbed a hand over his face, trying to push away the images, but they wouldn't go. They never did. The flashes of gunfire. The crumbling buildings. The desperate eyes of civilians who saw more than just soldiers—saw ghosts of the past in every uniform, in every soldier who had walked through their city.

But the worst part? The worst part was the quiet. The emptiness that followed him everywhere, even in the midst of a crowd. The silent scream in his mind that no one else seemed to hear. He had thought that coming home would be the end of it. That the war would be over, and with it, his suffering. But it wasn't.

Home wasn't home anymore. It was just a place, a building with walls and windows that felt too close, too suffocating. And no matter how many people surrounded him, he was still alone.

"Danny?"

He turned at the sound of her voice. Emma stood in the doorway, her face drawn with concern. She had been his friend before the war, his anchor when everything else seemed to be falling apart. But even she couldn't understand what he was going through. No one could. How could they? The war had changed him in ways that couldn't be put into words.

"You've been quiet," Emma said, stepping into the room, her eyes searching his face. "I haven't seen you smile in weeks."

Danny gave her a small, tight smile. It didn't reach his eyes. "I'm just... trying to figure things out."

"Trying to figure things out?" she repeated, walking closer. "Danny, you don't have to figure this out alone."

He shook his head, feeling a lump form in his throat. "I don't know how to explain it. I don't know how to make you understand."

Emma sat down beside him, her presence warm and steady. "Try," she said softly. "You've always told me everything."

Danny looked away, his eyes focusing on the skyline in the distance. The world seemed so distant now, as though it was a place that didn't belong to him. He had been fighting for so long, had been consumed by survival for so long, that he didn't know how to live without it.

"It's not the same," he said finally, his voice raw. "I used to think that if I just made it out, if I just survived, it would all get better. That I could put everything behind me and start fresh. But I can't. I can't shake the feeling that I'm still there, still fighting. That the war... it didn't end when I left the battlefield. It's still inside me. It's in my head. In my chest. In my bones."

Emma didn't speak for a long moment. She simply sat there, her eyes focused on him with understanding. "I can't imagine what you've been through, Danny," she said, her voice gentle but firm. "But I know you're not alone. I'm here. We're all here."

Danny looked at her then, really looked at her, and for the first time in weeks, he felt something stir inside him. It wasn't hope, not exactly, but it was the faintest glimmer of connection. Maybe he wasn't as alone as he thought.

"I don't know how to stop it," he confessed. "I don't know how to stop being at war with myself."

"You don't have to stop it all at once," Emma said, her hand reaching out to touch his arm. "But you do need to let people help. You don't have to carry all of this by yourself."

Danny stared at her hand, then up at her face, and for a moment, the world seemed to fall away. The war, the scars, the loneliness—they all seemed distant. He was still broken, still haunted by what had happened, but maybe, just maybe, he could begin to heal.

"I'm not sure I'm ready for that," he said quietly.

Emma squeezed his arm gently. "That's okay. But when you are, we'll be here. All of us. No one expects you to be okay overnight. It's going to take time. But you don't have to face it alone."

Danny nodded, but the doubt still lingered in his chest. He didn't know how to fix himself. He didn't know if he could. But for the first time since he came home, he didn't feel entirely hopeless.

Maybe it would take time. Maybe it would take years. But there was something inside him—a small, fragile thread—that whispered that maybe, just maybe, he could start living again.

## ○ A Plan in Motion

VICTOR LYNN STOOD AT the edge of the map, his fingers tracing the lines of territories that had once been his empire. The walls of his office were adorned with old photographs of victories—battles he had won, deals he had brokered, and the unyielding rise of his power. Now, those victories seemed like distant memories, each one a stepping stone toward the larger, more elusive goal that consumed him. His eyes flickered to the digital clock on his desk, counting the seconds, the minutes. Time was running out.

The war had turned the world upside down, and with it, his position. Power, in this new age, was fleeting. Victor knew better than anyone that empires did not last forever. They were built on unstable ground, and in times like these, they crumbled quickly. His once unassailable grip on the city's finances, its commerce, its politics—everything he had fought for—was beginning to slip.

But Victor wasn't one to wait for fate. He never had been. If there was one thing he understood, it was the need for control. And so, with the weight of the world pressing down on him, he had decided to act.

The room around him felt colder, the air thicker, as he considered the task ahead. The first step was simple enough: secure the resources. Without them, there was no power to wield. Without them, he was just another man in a crumbling city, fighting to survive. But securing the resources wasn't the hard part. The hard part was securing the right allies—people who would understand his vision, people who would do whatever it took to ensure that he stayed at the top.

His phone buzzed. He didn't have to look at it to know who it was. Lena's name flashed on the screen. She had been his right hand for years, a woman as ruthless as she was brilliant. If anyone could help him navigate the treacherous waters of the new world, it was her.

Victor answered the call.

"We're in position," Lena's voice crackled through the speaker. "The shipment is ready. It'll be in your hands within the next twenty-four hours."

Victor allowed himself a brief, tight smile. The plan was coming together. But Lena's words also reminded him of the danger. He had to move fast. The political alliances were shifting like sand, and the people in charge now were not the same ones he had negotiated with in the past. The new power brokers were far less predictable.

"I want everything covered," he said, his voice low and firm. "No mistakes. We can't afford a single slip-up. The moment we make a wrong move, it's over."

Lena was silent for a moment, but Victor knew she understood. She always did. "Understood," she replied finally. "And what about Emma?"

Victor paused. Emma. She had become more of a problem than he'd originally anticipated. While she was loyal to him, she also had a sense of morality that often complicated things. Her position in the underground resistance was valuable, but her hesitation to act outside her moral code could jeopardize everything.

"She stays in the shadows for now," he said, his voice cold. "She's too close to the revolutionaries. I need her to be where she belongs—silent and unseen. Don't give her any reason to believe she's in control. This is bigger than her."

There was a brief silence on the other end, and Victor could almost hear Lena's sigh. But, as always, she complied.

"Understood," she said, her voice unwavering. "I'll make sure she's out of the loop."

Victor disconnected the call and leaned back in his chair, staring at the map once more. The plan was set in motion, but there was still so much to do. The coming days would be crucial. If they were successful, Victor would have the leverage to force the government's hand, securing a position of influence that could not be contested. If they failed... well, failure wasn't an option. Not for him.

He turned his attention to the city outside, the ruins of what was once a thriving, prosperous place. Now, it was a battleground, a reflection of everything that had been lost in the wake of the war. But Victor Lynn wasn't one to dwell on the past. He had always believed that the future was his to shape—and he would do whatever it took to ensure that it was shaped in his image.

The clock ticked down. The plan was in motion. And the world, as always, would bend to his will.

## ○ The Enemy Within

THE SUN HAD BARELY set, casting a soft, amber glow over the city as Sophia walked briskly through the streets, her mind a whirl of conflicting thoughts. The weight of the discovery she had stumbled upon weighed heavily on her shoulders. For weeks, she had quietly observed, listened, and pieced together fragments of conversations. She had been careful, biding her time, and now—finally—she had the evidence she needed.

Her phone buzzed again. She glanced at it, the screen illuminating her face in the dimming light. Another message from Danny. It was brief, but it sent a chill down her spine:

*We need to talk. Urgently.*

She hesitated for a moment, then quickened her pace. She had suspected that Danny was involved, but she had no idea how deep it ran. The fact that he had reached out now meant one of two things: either he had discovered she was onto him, or he had finally realized the gravity of the situation. Either way, she needed to meet him. It was the only way to uncover the full extent of what was happening.

Sophia arrived at the abandoned warehouse on the edge of the city, where they had agreed to meet. The place was eerily quiet, the sounds of the world outside muffled by the thick concrete walls. She stepped inside, her heart pounding in her chest. The darkness seemed to swallow her whole as she moved deeper into the warehouse.

A figure emerged from the shadows. It was Danny.

He looked different—more worn, his face gaunt, eyes hollow as though sleep had long since abandoned him. The last time she had seen him, he had been a different person: confident, assertive, and full of fire. Now, he seemed to be carrying the weight of the world on his shoulders.

"You shouldn't have come here, Sophia," he said, his voice tinged with regret.

Her breath hitched in her throat. She had expected a confrontation, but not this. "I had no choice, Danny. I found out what you've been hiding. What we've both been hiding. This isn't just about survival anymore. It's about betrayal."

He shifted uncomfortably, his gaze avoiding hers. "I didn't want you to find out. I was trying to protect you... to protect us. But now... now it's too late."

Sophia took a step closer, refusing to let his evasiveness throw her off track. "What's going on, Danny? Who's pulling the strings? You've been working with the enemy, haven't you?"

His eyes flickered with panic. She had hit the mark.

"I didn't have a choice," he murmured, his voice cracking. "The resources, the connections—they were too valuable. The resistance... the truth is, they never stood a chance without Victor Lynn. Without him, we wouldn't have made it this far. I tried to shield you, to keep you out of it. But I was wrong. I should've told you."

Sophia took a step back, her mind racing as the realization settled over her like a blanket of cold dread. Danny, her ally, her closest friend—he had been working with the very man they had been fighting against. Victor Lynn, the ruthless businessman who had orchestrated the fall of the city, the very person she had vowed to bring down.

"You sold us out," she said quietly, her voice barely above a whisper. It felt like the ground was shifting beneath her, the walls closing in. The air felt thick with betrayal.

"I didn't sell you out!" Danny's voice was louder now, desperate. "I didn't have a choice. You think the resistance would have lasted without Lynn's support? He's been feeding us information, providing us with weapons, but I couldn't let you know. You wouldn't understand."

"I understand enough," Sophia replied, her voice steady despite the storm raging inside her. "You've made a deal with the devil, and now we're all going to pay for it."

Danny's face twisted in anguish. "You don't know what it's like. You don't know the pressure he put on me. I did what I had to do to survive. I did it for us, Sophia."

"For us?" She felt a bitter laugh bubbling in her throat. "This isn't about survival anymore. This is about power. This is about him using you as a pawn in his game."

The silence between them was thick, filled with the weight of their unspoken words. Sophia could see it now—the fear in Danny's eyes, the way he had become trapped in a web of manipulation and deceit. And she knew, deep down, that the enemy wasn't just Victor Lynn. It was also Danny. He had become part of the system they had once fought against. His loyalty had been corrupted, and now, she didn't know who he was anymore.

"I don't know what to do," Danny admitted quietly, his voice broken. "I've already gone too far. The enemy isn't just out there,

Sophia. It's inside us, inside our own ranks. And I don't know if we can fight it anymore."

Sophia's heart clenched. She wanted to believe him, to offer him a way out, but the reality was too harsh. The trust they had once shared had been shattered. The line between right and wrong had become blurred, and now, there was no way to turn back.

"You've made your choice, Danny," she said, her voice firm. "And now, we'll have to live with the consequences."

As she turned to leave, the echo of her footsteps felt like the final nail in the coffin of their broken alliance. The enemy within was far more dangerous than any external force, and the war they were fighting had become one of survival, not just against the people who held power, but against the darkness that had taken root in their very souls.

# 3. The Tipping Point

## ○ Rising Tensions

The air was thick with tension as the city seemed to hold its breath. Sophia stood at the window of the makeshift command center, staring out over the skyline. The once bustling metropolis now felt like a shadow of its former self—buildings that once symbolized prosperity were now hollowed-out shells, looming like silent sentinels over the ruin. The world outside seemed to be teetering on the edge, much like the fragile coalition she was trying to hold together.

Her mind raced, replaying the conversation with Danny earlier. The reality of his betrayal hung over her like a dark cloud. But there was no time to dwell on the personal cost of their shattered trust. The larger battle was intensifying. Victor Lynn's forces were on the move, his empire expanding ever outward as he consolidated power in the aftermath of the initial conflict. Lynn wasn't just a businessman anymore. He was a warlord, pulling the strings from behind the scenes, turning the city into a personal kingdom.

And yet, the resistance—the fractured alliance of survivors, militants, and former allies—was far from beaten. In fact, it had begun to stir again, their movements growing bolder. Sophia could feel the undercurrent of a new resolve, like a spark ready to ignite into a full-scale rebellion. But with that rising resistance came greater danger. The enemy had its eyes on them, and it was only a matter of time before Lynn's forces moved in for the kill.

"Sophia, we need to talk," Danny's voice broke through her thoughts. He had entered the room without her noticing, his presence heavy with a mixture of guilt and urgency.

She turned to face him, her expression unreadable. "About what?" she asked, trying to keep the bitterness from creeping into her tone. She could feel the weight of his eyes on her, but it didn't matter. She had more pressing concerns now.

Danny stepped closer, glancing around as if ensuring no one was listening. "Lynn knows. He knows about the operation. We've been compromised."

Her pulse quickened, her mind spinning. "What do you mean, compromised?"

"The message we sent out last night. It didn't stay encrypted. There was a leak." He paused, eyes darting to the door. "And someone inside the resistance is working for Lynn. We have a mole."

Sophia's blood ran cold. A mole. This wasn't just a setback—it was a catastrophe. Lynn's network of spies had infiltrated deeper than they thought. The very people they had trusted with their lives could be working against them, feeding information straight to their enemies.

"Who?" she asked, her voice barely above a whisper.

"I don't know yet," Danny admitted. "But it's someone high up. Someone with access to sensitive intel. They're watching us, waiting for the right moment to strike."

Sophia clenched her fists. "We can't afford to wait, Danny. We can't let this go on. We have to act now."

He nodded grimly. "I agree. But it's going to take time to identify who it is. We can't make any moves until we're sure."

She turned back to the window, her eyes scanning the horizon as the weight of the situation settled in. Time was something they didn't have. The enemy was closing in, and every hour that passed without a plan put them at greater risk.

"Then we move in silence," she said finally, her voice firm with resolve. "We go underground. We shut down all comms for now. If we can't trust our own people, we'll have to rely on ourselves. No more leaks. No more mistakes."

Danny hesitated. "And what about the rest of the resistance? We can't afford to isolate ourselves from them."

"We'll keep them in the dark," she replied, turning to face him fully. "For now, we operate on a need-to-know basis. They don't need to know everything. If we can uncover the mole, we can make our move before Lynn does."

He met her gaze, his expression torn. "You're asking us to trust no one. Not even our own people."

"Trust is a luxury we can't afford anymore," Sophia said, her voice hardening. "Lynn is a master manipulator. He's had years to build this empire, and he's not going to stop until he has complete control. If we don't act quickly, we'll be the ones in chains."

The silence between them was heavy, laden with the weight of their shared responsibility. The stakes were higher than ever, and every decision they made from this point forward could be their last.

But one thing was certain—if they were going to survive, they couldn't trust anyone outside their inner circle. Rising tensions in the city were only a reflection of the storm that was brewing within the resistance itself. The war wasn't just against Lynn's forces. It was also a war for the soul of the movement, and Sophia had to decide who would survive it—and who would fall.

## ○ A Deadly Encounter

THE DIM LIGHT OF DUSK filtered through the cracked windows of the abandoned warehouse, casting long, sharp shadows across the cold concrete floor. Sophia stood motionless, her breath shallow as she scanned the room. The air smelled of dust and rust, mingled with a faint metallic scent—blood, perhaps, or something worse. Her fingers tightened around the hilt of her pistol, the cool metal grounding her in the present, in the danger that lay ahead.

The plan had been simple: intercept the supply convoy that was scheduled to arrive at this location, seize the weapons, and vanish into the night. But nothing was ever simple anymore. From the moment they had arrived, a nagging sense of unease had settled over her, and it hadn't taken long for that feeling to grow into something darker.

She wasn't alone. Behind her, Danny kept to the shadows, his body tense, his hand resting on the grip of his own weapon. The rest of their small squad had fanned out, securing the perimeter, but even as they moved in the shadows, their presence felt exposed. It was as if the very walls of the warehouse were watching, waiting for something—anything—that would break the stillness.

Suddenly, a noise. A faint scrape of metal against stone, followed by the unmistakable sound of boots on the ground.

Sophia's heart quickened. "Get into position," she whispered, her voice low, steady, as she slid into the nearest alcove, the shadows swallowing her whole.

There was a rustling sound to her left, then a soft thud as Danny crouched beside her. He looked at her with a grim expression, his eyes betraying none of the tension he was feeling. "This feels wrong," he muttered under his breath. "We've got company. And they're not who we're expecting."

Sophia didn't respond immediately, her mind racing through a dozen possibilities. If the convoy had been compromised, it could mean they were walking into a trap. But who else would be here? The enemy had become adept at setting up ambushes, using the wreckage of the city and the crumbling infrastructure as their cover. And there were whispers of a new force emerging, a faction with its own agenda, operating outside of Victor Lynn's control. She had to know who they were—before they knew her.

The sound of footsteps grew louder, closer. Too close. In a matter of seconds, a figure emerged from the shadows, tall and imposing, a silhouette against the fading light. Sophia's breath caught in her throat.

It wasn't one of their own.

The man's face was partially obscured by a scarf, but the glint of steel in his hand was unmistakable. His eyes, cold and calculating, scanned the warehouse, flicking over the abandoned crates and machinery, before settling on Sophia. He was a hunter, and she had just been marked as prey.

A flicker of recognition passed through her, but it was gone before she could place it. Who was he? What did he want?

The man took a step forward, his voice low but edged with a warning. "I wouldn't make a move if I were you."

Sophia's heart hammered in her chest. She couldn't afford to be captured. She needed information, and she needed it now. She reached for the comm device at her side, ready to signal Danny to prepare for an escape, but before she could, the man raised his hand, stopping her in her tracks.

"You're not going anywhere," he said, a chilling calmness in his tone. "Not unless you want to find out just how dangerous your little resistance really is."

The words sent a shiver down her spine. Whoever he was, he was not just a mercenary or a rogue soldier. He was part of something much larger.

Suddenly, there was a movement behind her, and before she could react, a second figure emerged from the shadows. This one was smaller, more agile, but just as deadly. She recognized the gleam of a knife in the second figure's hand and cursed under her breath. They were surrounded.

Danny's voice crackled through her earpiece. "Sophia, get out of there now! It's a trap!"

She didn't have time to respond. Without warning, the man in front of her lunged, his hand shooting out to grab her by the arm.

He was fast, too fast. But she had been trained for this. With a swift twist, she pulled free, aiming a quick kick to his chest. He staggered back but recovered quickly, a smirk tugging at the corner of his lips.

"You're good," he said, his voice laced with admiration. "But not good enough."

Sophia's mind raced as she calculated her next move. There was no room for hesitation now. With one swift motion, she drew her pistol and aimed it at the man's head, her finger poised on the trigger. The warehouse was silent, save for the rapid beating of her heart.

And then, just as quickly, the sound of a gunshot shattered the tension, but not from her weapon.

A new figure stepped into the fray, a third adversary, this one with a calm precision that made Sophia pause. The bullet had grazed the man in front of her, sending him to the ground in a spray of blood.

The newcomer, a woman with a scarred face and a hardened look in her eyes, lowered her weapon and smiled grimly. "I don't think you two are ready for this fight."

Sophia's mind spun with the implications. Allies? Enemies? In this world, it was hard to tell the difference anymore. But one thing was certain—this deadly encounter was far from over.

## ○ A Betrayal Revealed

THE CHILL OF THE NIGHT air seeped into the marrow of Sophia's bones as she stood at the edge of the crumbling building, gazing out over the devastated cityscape. The flickering lights in the distance were like tiny embers in a sea of darkness, a city struggling to breathe under the weight of its own destruction. She could feel the tension in the air, thick and suffocating, as though the very earth was holding its breath.

She hadn't expected this. She hadn't expected betrayal to come from within their ranks.

The thought gnawed at her, its sharp edges biting deeper with each passing second. Her mind replayed the events of the last few hours, the moments that had led her here, to this cold, desolate rooftop, as she tried to make sense of it all. She'd known something was off, but the truth had been buried beneath layers of deception, hidden in plain sight.

Victor Lynn. The man she had trusted, the man who had promised to lead them to victory, had betrayed them all.

A soft click broke the silence, and she turned to face Danny, who had approached silently, his expression grim. His eyes, usually sharp with determination, were now clouded with uncertainty.

"Did you know?" she asked, her voice barely above a whisper.

Danny shook his head, his jaw clenched. "I should have. But I didn't want to believe it. I couldn't."

Sophia took a deep breath, steadying herself against the flood of emotions threatening to overwhelm her. She had always known that loyalty was a fragile thing, easily shattered in the wake of war. But she had never imagined that someone so close to them, someone they had fought beside, would be the one to pull the trigger.

"We've been feeding him intel," Sophia continued, her voice cold as ice. "All this time, thinking we were working together, trying to weaken the enemy, to end this war. And all along, he's been playing us."

Danny looked away, his gaze distant as if he were trying to will the reality of it all to disappear. "We never stood a chance, did we? Lynn's been two steps ahead the entire time."

A wave of anger surged through Sophia, the betrayal stinging like salt in an open wound. She had given everything to the cause, sacrificed her own humanity to fight for a future that now seemed impossible. And for what? So that Victor Lynn could profit from their bloodshed, strengthening his grip on the power he'd coveted from the beginning?

"I should have known," she muttered, more to herself than to Danny. "The way he moved in the shadows, the way he manipulated every situation to his advantage. I thought he was just playing the game. But now…" Her voice trailed off as the full weight of the betrayal settled over her like a suffocating blanket.

"We can still stop him," Danny said, his voice filled with a new resolve. "We know his plan now. We can take him down, take back what he's stolen from us."

Sophia turned to him, her eyes narrowed, her mind already racing through the possibilities. He was right. They could still stop him. But it wasn't going to be easy. Victor Lynn had built an empire on lies and manipulation, and tearing it down would require more than just firepower. It would take precision, patience, and a willingness to sacrifice everything.

"We'll have to move fast," she said, her tone hardening with determination. "The longer we wait, the more people he'll hurt. He's already got the upper hand, but we know his weaknesses. We'll use that against him."

Danny nodded, his eyes alight with the fire of battle. "What's the plan?"

Sophia glanced over at the shattered skyline, her mind calculating every move. She could feel the weight of the decision pressing down on her. This wasn't just about stopping Lynn anymore. It was about reclaiming the future, about making sure that their struggle wasn't in vain.

"First," she said, her voice steady despite the chaos swirling inside her, "we need to find out where he's hiding. We'll need to get close, find out who's still loyal to him and who's willing to turn against him. Once we have that intel, we strike fast, strike hard."

"And then?"

"And then we make him pay," she said, her words sharp and filled with a cold promise. "For every life he's destroyed. For every lie he's told. We'll expose him for the coward he is."

Danny met her gaze, his expression resolute. "We'll do it together."

Sophia didn't answer immediately. Instead, she took a deep breath, gathering her thoughts. This was it. The moment where everything changed. They were no longer fighting for the same cause they once believed in. They were fighting for something much more personal: justice.

"We'll do it together," she finally said, her voice steady. "But make no mistake, Danny. When this is over, there will be no going back."

And in the silence that followed, they both understood that this battle—against Victor Lynn and everything he represented—would be the last war they ever fought.

## ○ The Burden of Leadership

SOPHIA STARED OUT OF the narrow, dust-coated window in the makeshift command center, the weight of leadership pressing heavily on her shoulders. The dim light of the fading day cast long shadows across the room, the same shadows that seemed to stretch endlessly in her mind. She had never imagined that leading would feel like this—a constant balance between hope and despair, action and inaction, between doing what was right and what was necessary.

A soft knock on the door interrupted her thoughts, and Danny stepped inside, his face lined with exhaustion. His eyes, once so sharp and focused, now appeared clouded, burdened by the same weight she carried.

"We need to talk," he said quietly, his voice betraying the tension in the air.

Sophia didn't turn around. She knew what he was going to say. They had been dancing around the topic for days, but now it was inevitable. She had known from the moment she assumed command that the choices would become harder, the consequences more dire. And yet, even as the cost of leadership grew steeper with each decision, she had hoped—hoped that they would find a way to avoid this.

"I know," she replied, her voice flat. "It's about the attack."

Danny nodded. "We lost a lot of good people. And not just that. It's the fallout. Our support is slipping. The people are scared. The factions are growing restless. We're not just fighting Victor anymore, we're fighting ourselves. Every decision we make seems to push us further into a corner."

Sophia's chest tightened. She had never been prepared for this part—the burden of not just the battle, but the moral weight of leadership. In war, the lines were never clear. The good, the bad, the right, the wrong—all of it blurred into shades of gray. And every move she made now seemed to tighten the noose around them all.

"I know," she said again, her voice cracking slightly this time. "I never thought it would be this way. I thought—" She paused, struggling to find the words. "I thought we could unite them. That they would follow us because of our cause. But it's not that simple. People are scared. They don't trust me. And they don't trust each other."

Danny took a step closer, his gaze softening with understanding. "You can't control how they feel, Sophia. You can't carry all their burdens on your shoulders. You're doing what you can."

Sophia turned away from the window, finally facing him. Her eyes were tired, bloodshot from sleepless nights spent calculating risks and second-guessing every decision she made. "But I *am* carrying their burdens. Every life that's lost, every mistake, every compromise... it's on me. It always will be."

Danny took a deep breath, as if weighing his next words carefully. "You're not alone in this. We're all here with you. But you can't do it all by yourself. There has to be a limit. We're fighting for something bigger than ourselves, but if we don't have each other, what's the point?"

His words lingered in the air, a quiet reminder that leadership, while solitary, didn't have to be isolating. But it was hard. Every command she gave, every life she risked, it felt like another layer added to the already crushing weight on her shoulders. She had been forced to make decisions that shattered parts of her soul—sacrifices she had never imagined she would have to make.

"I should have been more decisive," she whispered, more to herself than to him. "I should have acted sooner. Maybe we could have saved more. Maybe we wouldn't be in this mess at all."

Danny placed a hand on her shoulder, steady and firm. "Sophia, you're doing the best you can. The decisions you've made, even the hard ones, were made with the right intentions. You can't blame yourself for things beyond your control."

But that was the problem. Everything felt beyond her control. Every plan that had seemed so perfect in theory unraveled at the slightest misstep. Each betrayal, each failure, had rippled outward in ways she hadn't predicted. She had once believed that if they fought hard enough, they could reclaim their future. But now, the future felt more elusive than ever.

"We can still turn this around," Danny said, his voice resolute, though she could see the cracks in his own composure. "We just need to refocus. We need to remind people what we're fighting for, what we stand for. You're not just a leader to them. You're a symbol. But that symbol has to believe in itself first."

Sophia looked into his eyes, searching for the hope she had once carried so easily. She saw it there—a glimmer of the same unwavering determination that had first drawn her to this fight. And she knew, in that moment, that she couldn't give up. She couldn't let the weight of her own doubts, the burden of her choices, pull her down.

"I won't quit," she said, her voice firmer now. "I can't. Not now. Not after everything we've lost. We've come too far, Danny. We have to finish this. We owe it to those we've lost."

Danny nodded, his expression softened by respect. "And we'll do it together. We'll see this through. You're not alone in this, Sophia. We're all in this fight. All of us."

For a long moment, neither of them spoke. The silence hung heavy between them, not of defeat, but of understanding. They both knew the road ahead would be even harder than what they had already endured. But in that moment, as Sophia looked into Danny's eyes, she found something more valuable than any strategy, any battle plan—she found the strength to keep going, the strength to lead.

And though the burden of leadership would never truly lighten, she understood now that it wasn't something she had to carry alone.

## ○ Sophia's Dilemma

SOPHIA SAT ALONE IN the dimly lit war room, the hum of the generator providing the only sound in the stillness. A map of the city was spread out on the table before her, dotted with makeshift markers representing her forces and Victor Lynn's empire. Her fingers traced the lines of the streets she had once walked freely, streets now turned into battle zones. Every decision she made would shape not only the lives of her people but also the future of the city itself. And tonight, the weight of it all felt unbearable.

The dilemma had been brewing for weeks, festering like an open wound. Intelligence reports confirmed that a shipment of supplies vital to Victor's operations was scheduled to pass through the eastern corridor at dawn. Taking it out could cripple his forces and buy Sophia's side much-needed time. But the route ran through a heavily populated civilian district—a district already battered by war. An attack would surely lead to collateral damage, and the thought of more innocent lives lost gnawed at her conscience.

Her team had argued about it earlier that evening, voices rising in a heated debate that left no room for resolution.

"We can't afford to miss this chance," Danny had said, slamming his hand on the table. "If we don't stop that shipment, Victor gains the upper hand. We're already on the back foot, Sophia."

Emma, always the voice of caution, had countered, "And at what cost? Those are families out there, Danny. Kids. Elderly. If we hit that convoy, we're no better than him."

The arguments had swirled around Sophia like a storm, each side pulling her in a different direction. But in the end, the decision rested with her. Now, in the quiet of the night, she was left with nothing but her thoughts and the crushing weight of responsibility.

Her mind drifted to her parents, who had raised her in this city before it became a wasteland. Her mother's laughter in the kitchen, her father's firm but gentle guidance—they had always taught her to do what was right, no matter how hard. But what was *right* in a world like this? Was it right to risk civilian lives for the greater good? Or was it right to hold back, knowing it could mean the death of her own people in the long run?

The door creaked open, breaking her reverie. Emma stepped inside, her expression a mix of concern and exhaustion.

"You're still here," Emma said softly, pulling up a chair next to her. "I figured you'd be wrestling with it."

Sophia offered a weak smile. "I can't stop wrestling with it. No matter which way I look at it, people will suffer. And I'm the one who has to choose."

Emma placed a reassuring hand on Sophia's arm. "No one said this would be easy. But whatever you decide, we'll stand by you. That's what leaders do—they carry the burden so the rest of us don't have to."

"That doesn't make it any easier," Sophia replied, her voice barely above a whisper. "If I choose to attack, those people out there... they'll hate me. They'll never forgive me. And if I don't, Danny's right—Victor will only get stronger."

Emma leaned back, her gaze thoughtful. "It's not about who forgives you, Sophia. It's about what you can live with. The choices we make in this war will haunt us no matter what. The question is, which choice lets you keep fighting for what matters?"

Sophia looked at Emma, her heart heavy with gratitude for the support, even as doubt clawed at her resolve. She thought of the people she was trying to protect, of the hope she was trying to keep alive in a city that had forgotten what hope looked like. And she thought of the faces of those who had already been lost—their sacrifices demanding that she make every choice count.

"I need more time," she said finally, though she knew time was a luxury they didn't have.

Emma nodded, rising from her chair. "Just remember, whatever you decide, we're with you. You're not in this alone."

As the door clicked shut behind Emma, Sophia turned back to the map. The markers seemed to mock her indecision, each one representing a life, a hope, a future. She closed her eyes, letting the weight of the moment wash over her.

Tomorrow, the sun would rise on a city still teetering on the edge of ruin. And by then, Sophia would have to make her choice—a choice that could either turn the tide of their struggle or shatter what little remained of the fragile trust holding her people together.

## ○ **Into the Unknown**

THE HORIZON LOOMED like a smudged watercolor painting, streaked with shades of gray and burnt amber from the endless smoke that hung in the air. The city's outskirts were a no-man's land, an expanse of rubble, cracked highways, and skeletal remains of once-bustling industrial parks. Beyond it lay the Unknown—uncharted territories where the rule of law and even the illusion of order dissolved entirely. Few who ventured there returned, and those who did came back changed, their eyes haunted by what they had seen.

Sophia tightened the straps on her weathered backpack, her gaze fixed on the road ahead. This journey wasn't one she wanted to take, but the situation left no choice. Intelligence suggested that Victor Lynn's most closely guarded operation—a potential game-changer in their conflict—was concealed in the wilderness outside the city limits. If she could uncover its secrets, it might be the leverage her people needed to turn the tide.

"You're sure about this?" Danny's voice broke her concentration. He stood a few paces away, his rifle slung over one shoulder. His usual bravado was tempered by concern as he glanced between her and the desolate expanse.

"No," Sophia admitted, her voice calm but firm. "But I'm going anyway. We can't afford not to."

Danny nodded, though the unease in his eyes didn't fade. Behind him, Emma busied herself checking their gear, her movements precise and deliberate, a reflection of her need to control what little she could in an uncontrollable world. The team had been stripped to its essentials—Sophia, Danny, Emma, and a young scout named Milo, whose knowledge of the outskirts had earned him a place on the mission. It wasn't much, but any more people would draw attention, and stealth was their only advantage.

Milo spoke up, his voice barely audible over the distant wind. "The terrain gets tricky once we clear the industrial zone. Lots of sinkholes and collapsed tunnels. And the gangs out there... they don't take kindly to visitors."

Sophia met his gaze. He was barely twenty, yet his face carried the scars of someone who had seen too much. "That's why we stick together. No detours, no heroics. We get in, find what we need, and get out."

The plan sounded simple, but everyone knew better. Simplicity was a luxury long lost to the war and the decay it had wrought. Still, no one voiced their doubts. They couldn't afford the cracks that fear would bring.

As they set out, the city fell away behind them, its broken skyline shrinking into the haze. The transition to the outskirts was gradual but unmistakable. The remnants of civilization—graffiti-tagged walls, burnt-out vehicles, forgotten storefronts—gave way to barren landscapes of ash and twisted metal. The air grew heavier, the silence more oppressive. Every sound—each crunch of rubble underfoot, every distant creak of shifting debris—seemed magnified, a constant reminder of how exposed they were.

Hours passed in tense quiet, the group navigating the treacherous terrain with deliberate care. Sophia's mind churned as she led the way, her thoughts split between the mission and the unknown dangers they were walking into. Her instincts screamed that something was wrong, that they were being watched, but the desolation around them offered no clues.

"Hold up," Milo whispered suddenly, raising a hand. The group froze, weapons instinctively at the ready.

"What is it?" Danny asked, scanning the horizon.

"Over there," Milo said, nodding toward a distant structure. It was barely visible through the haze—a crumbling tower that might once have been part of a factory or power plant. "That's new."

Sophia squinted, her heart pounding. "You're sure?"

Milo nodded. "It wasn't there last time I came this way. And look—tracks." He pointed to a faint trail in the dirt, evidence of vehicles moving through the area.

Emma knelt to inspect the tracks, her brow furrowing. "Heavy machinery. Recent, too. Victor's men?"

"Most likely," Sophia replied, her mind racing. "If they're moving equipment this far out, it's got to be important."

Danny glanced at her. "So, what's the play?"

Sophia hesitated for only a moment. "We investigate. But carefully. Milo, you take point."

The young scout nodded, leading them toward the structure with practiced ease. As they approached, the air grew colder, and an unnatural stillness seemed to settle over the area. The tower loomed larger, its jagged edges silhouetted against the murky sky. It was a grim monument to the world's decay, yet it pulsed with the faint promise of discovery.

Sophia's hand tightened on her weapon as they neared the base of the tower. Shadows danced in the corners of her vision, flickers of movement that her rational mind dismissed as tricks of the light. But her gut told her otherwise. Whatever lay within the Unknown, it wasn't just Victor's secrets waiting for them. Something far older, far darker, lurked in the ruins—and it had noticed their presence.

# 4. Whispers of Revolution

## ○ Gathering Allies

The room buzzed with the low murmur of conversations, tense yet restrained. It was the kind of gathering that only desperation could summon, a mix of unlikely allies brought together by a common enemy. Sophia scanned the faces before her—a patchwork of humanity that spanned former city officials, hardened resistance fighters, and scavengers who had survived by wit and sheer luck. Each carried their own scars, their own grudges, but for this moment, their differences had to be set aside.

The gathering was held in the basement of a bombed-out library, the walls still adorned with charred remnants of bookshelves. A single lantern illuminated the space, casting flickering shadows that seemed to mirror the unease of those present.

Sophia stood at the center, her voice steady but her heart pounding. "You've all seen what Victor Lynn's empire has done. Entire communities swallowed, lives destroyed for the sake of his power. Alone, we're just pieces for him to crush. Together, we're the storm he can't control."

Murmurs rippled through the crowd, some nodding in agreement while others exchanged skeptical glances.

A gruff voice broke through the din. "And what's to say we can trust you?" The speaker, a burly man with a jagged scar running down his face, crossed his arms and leaned against the wall. "You come from the same city that let him rise. Why should we believe you're any different?"

Sophia met his gaze without flinching. "Because I've fought against him from the start. I've lost friends, family—everything.

I'm not here to save myself; I'm here to finish what they started. But I can't do it alone. None of us can."

The man didn't respond immediately, his eyes narrowing as he studied her. Finally, he gave a reluctant nod. "Fair enough. But talk won't win this war. What's your plan?"

Danny stepped forward, his presence a reassuring counterpoint to the tension in the room. "We hit him where it hurts—his supply lines, his outposts. But that's just the start. We've got intel on a facility he's guarding like it holds the crown jewels. Whatever's in there, it's important enough to risk everything to keep secret. We take it, and we take away his edge."

Another voice chimed in, this one softer but no less determined. "And what about the civilians caught in the crossfire? Victor's men don't hesitate to use them as shields." The speaker, a woman with tired eyes and a bandage wrapped around her arm, spoke with the weariness of someone who had seen too much but refused to give up.

Emma stepped in, her voice calm but firm. "We don't abandon them. That's non-negotiable. But if we don't act, more people will suffer in the long run. We can't let fear paralyze us."

The room fell silent, the weight of the decision settling over everyone. It was Milo who finally broke the quiet, his youthful voice carrying a surprising steadiness. "I'm in. If there's even a chance we can stop him, it's worth it."

One by one, the others began to speak up, their assent cautious but resolute. The scarred man who had questioned Sophia earlier gave her a grudging nod. "You've got my men. Just don't make me regret it."

Sophia felt a surge of relief, though she kept her expression measured. The hardest part was yet to come, but this was a start. She stepped forward, her voice carrying over the crowd. "We move at dawn. Gather what you can—supplies, weapons, anything useful. And remember, this isn't just a fight for survival. It's a fight for the future. Let's make sure it's one worth living in."

As the group began to disperse, whispers of strategy and preparation filling the air, Sophia allowed herself a moment to breathe. Danny approached her, his usual smirk softened into something resembling pride.

"You're a natural at this," he said, leaning against a crumbling column. "Convincing people to risk everything."

Sophia shot him a wry look. "Let's hope I'm convincing enough to keep them alive."

Danny nodded, his expression growing serious. "We'll get through this. One way or another."

She hoped he was right. But as she watched the makeshift alliance take shape, she couldn't shake the feeling that their unity was as fragile as the world around them, and the price of failure would be too high to bear.

## ○ The Seeds of Rebellion

THE NIGHT WAS EERILY quiet, the kind of silence that pressed against the ears and heightened every flicker of movement. Sophia crouched behind the skeletal remains of what was once a thriving marketplace, her breath shallow as she scanned the desolate square. The seeds of rebellion were fragile things, and tonight was the first test of whether they would grow or be trampled underfoot.

Beside her, Danny adjusted the strap of his scavenged rifle, his expression a mix of grim determination and nervous energy. "You sure this is the right spot?" he murmured, his voice barely audible.

Sophia nodded, her eyes fixed on the warehouse across the square. The building, though outwardly decrepit, had become a fortress for Victor Lynn's supply operations. Taking it down wasn't just about crippling his resources—it was about sending a message. The rebellion wasn't just whispers in the shadows anymore.

"It's the right spot," Sophia whispered back. "The question is whether they'll come."

"They'll come," Emma's voice cut through the dark as she appeared from the shadows, her movements smooth and deliberate. She carried a makeshift satchel slung over one shoulder, its contents clinking faintly. "The ones who are tired of running always do."

The plan was simple in theory: rally those brave or desperate enough to strike a blow against Victor's empire. The warehouse was their first target, a calculated risk to test their strength and ignite a movement. Sophia had sent word through the resistance's fractured networks, each message a promise and a challenge: *The time to fight is now.*

As if on cue, figures began to emerge from the darkness, hesitant at first but gradually forming a loose circle around Sophia and her group. They were a motley crew—former factory workers, scavengers, even a few teenagers clutching makeshift weapons with trembling hands. Each face bore the weight of loss, yet in their eyes flickered a glimmer of defiance.

Sophia stepped forward, her voice low but firm. "Thank you for coming. I know what it took for you to be here, and I won't ask for more than you can give. But tonight, we take back a piece of what was stolen from us. Are you with me?"

The murmurs of assent were quiet but steady. One man, his face lined with exhaustion and resolve, spoke up. "We've been waiting for someone to lead. Just tell us what to do."

Sophia nodded, her heart heavy with the responsibility she had taken on. "We split into three groups. Emma and Milo will handle the explosives. Danny and I will lead the assault team. The rest of you, focus on securing the perimeter and keeping watch. We need to be fast and precise."

The group began to move, their unease tempered by purpose. Emma knelt near the building's foundation, her hands deftly working to set the charges. Milo hovered nearby, his youthful enthusiasm tempered by the seriousness of the task.

Danny, meanwhile, positioned their team at the warehouse's main entrance. He exchanged a glance with Sophia, his usual humor replaced by grim focus. "This better work."

"It will," Sophia said, more for her own benefit than his. Failure wasn't an option—not tonight.

The signal came as a sharp whistle, cutting through the stillness. In an instant, the rebellion sprang to life. Emma's charges detonated with a muffled *boom*, and chaos erupted. The rebels surged forward, their shouts mingling with the sounds of gunfire and clashing metal.

Sophia moved with purpose, her weapon steady as she led the charge. Each step forward felt like reclaiming a piece of herself, of the world she refused to let Victor destroy. Around her, the rebels fought with the desperation of those who had nothing left to lose and everything to gain.

The battle was short but brutal. By the time the last of Victor's guards were subdued or fled, the warehouse was theirs. The rebels stood amidst the wreckage, their faces etched with exhaustion but also a cautious pride.

Sophia climbed onto a broken crate, her voice rising above the din. "This is just the beginning. Tonight, we showed Victor that we won't be silenced. But the fight ahead won't be easy. If you're with me, we'll take this rebellion to every corner of his empire. We'll remind him that this world belongs to all of us."

A cheer erupted from the crowd, raw and defiant. For the first time in what felt like an eternity, hope was no longer a distant memory but a living, breathing force. The seeds of rebellion had taken root, and Sophia vowed to nurture them until they blossomed into something unstoppable.

## ○ A Fractured Team

THE AIR IN THE ABANDONED factory was thick with tension, the silence punctuated by the occasional clink of metal or scrape of boots on concrete. The team had gathered in what once might have been an assembly line room, now a makeshift base. But there was no sense of unity here. The fractures within the group were becoming too glaring to ignore.

Sophia leaned against a rusted pillar, her arms crossed and her jaw tight. Across from her, Danny paced, his movements restless and agitated. Emma sat on an overturned crate, sharpening her blade with deliberate focus, her expression unreadable. Milo stood near a shattered window, pretending to keep watch but clearly avoiding eye contact with anyone.

"This isn't working," Danny said finally, his voice sharp as he stopped mid-step. "We're barely holding it together, and now you're talking about taking on Victor's main operations? It's suicide."

Sophia exhaled slowly, keeping her tone measured. "We've already made progress. The warehouse was a victory—"

"A *small* victory," Danny interrupted, turning to face her. "And we paid for it. Two of our people didn't come back. How many more are you willing to lose for this crusade?"

Emma's blade paused mid-sharpening. "It's a rebellion, Danny. Losses are inevitable. Or did you think we'd overthrow Victor with hugs and heartfelt speeches?"

Danny shot her a glare. "I'm just saying we need to be smarter. This isn't just about guts; it's about strategy. And right now, I don't see one."

Milo shifted uneasily, his voice hesitant. "Maybe Danny has a point. We're all angry, but if we keep rushing into things..."

Sophia straightened, her gaze moving from Danny to Milo. "So what's your suggestion? That we sit here and wait for Victor's men to find us? Because that's the alternative. He won't stop hunting us."

The room fell silent again, the weight of her words settling over them. Emma broke the tension with a dry laugh. "You know what the real problem is? None of us trust each other anymore. Danny thinks Sophia's too reckless, Milo's too scared to take a stand, and I'm—what was it you called me, Danny? A loose cannon?"

Danny's jaw tightened, but he didn't deny it.

Emma shrugged, turning her attention back to her blade. "Face it. We're a mess."

"Then we fix it," Sophia said firmly. She stepped forward, her voice steady despite the turmoil brewing inside her. "None of us can do this alone, and we're fooling ourselves if we think otherwise. If we're going to have any chance against Victor, we need to stop fighting each other and start fighting *him*."

Danny crossed his arms, his expression skeptical. "And how do you suggest we do that?"

"By remembering why we're here," Sophia said, her voice rising slightly. "Each of us has lost something—or someone—because of Victor. That's what unites us. Not our trust, not our loyalty to each other. Our pain. And we can either let it tear us apart, or we can use it to bring him down."

Milo glanced at her, his expression softening slightly. "You make it sound simple."

"It's not simple," Sophia admitted. "It's messy, and it's hard, and there's no guarantee we'll succeed. But if we don't even try, then what's the point?"

Emma let out a long sigh, standing and slipping her blade into its sheath. "Fine. I'm in. But if Danny keeps whining, I might accidentally stab him."

Danny gave her a withering look but said nothing. Instead, he turned to Sophia. "Alright. I'll stay. For now. But you'd better have a solid plan, or this whole thing is going to blow up in our faces."

Sophia nodded, relief washing over her despite the tension still lingering in the room. "We start planning tonight. No more impulsive moves. We do this right."

The uneasy truce held as the group began to gather around a makeshift map spread across a broken table. The fractures in their team hadn't disappeared, but they were temporarily mended by a shared purpose. For now, it was enough.

But as Sophia glanced around at their wary faces, she couldn't shake the feeling that the greatest battles weren't the ones they fought against Victor—they were the ones they fought within themselves.

## ○ Emma's Gamble

EMMA ADJUSTED THE STRAP of her backpack and checked the small recorder tucked into the inner pocket of her jacket. It was a relic of the old world, battered and scratched, but it worked—mostly. The weight of it felt oddly reassuring, a tether to her former life as an investigative journalist. Now, in this crumbling world where survival often trumped truth, it served as both a tool and a reminder of who she used to be.

The night was uncomfortably still, the kind of silence that amplified every creak of a rusty gate or crunch of gravel underfoot. She crouched low behind a rusted-out vehicle, her eyes scanning the perimeter of Victor Lynn's compound. The sprawling estate was an anomaly in the wasteland—high walls, electrified fencing, and armed guards patrolling in disciplined formations. Floodlights swept across the barren land like accusatory fingers, ensuring no one could approach unseen.

Emma's heart pounded against her ribcage as she whispered into her handheld communicator.

"Alex, I'm in position. Do you copy?"

Static hissed in response before Alex's voice came through, strained but clear.

"Loud and clear. You've got ten minutes before the patrol circles back. Make it count."

"Roger that." Emma inhaled sharply, steeling herself. This was insanity, she thought. But insanity and courage often shared a thin line, and tonight she would walk it.

The plan was simple in theory and treacherous in execution. Emma would infiltrate the compound, plant a small transmitter in Victor's private quarters, and retrieve any evidence of his exploitation of survivors. The recordings could expose his black-market dealings and shift the balance of power in the wasteland. But it wasn't just about toppling Victor—it was about hope. Hope that truth still mattered, even in this broken world.

Emma slipped through a gap in the fencing that Danny had painstakingly scouted earlier. The edges of the wire snagged at her jacket, but she pushed forward, her movements careful and deliberate. The guards were predictable, their routines meticulously timed. She ducked behind a stack of crates as two figures passed, their boots crunching on gravel. Their muffled conversation drifted toward her.

"...heard he's testing it again tomorrow. Another village wiped out, probably."

Emma clenched her fists. She didn't need to hear more to know what they were referring to—Victor's experiments, the ones that turned entire towns into ghostly ruins.

The air felt heavier as she approached the main building. Inside, the compound was a stark contrast to the wasteland beyond its walls. Polished marble floors gleamed under harsh fluorescent lights, and expensive art adorned the walls, remnants of a world Victor had plundered for his own gain.

Emma moved swiftly, her footsteps muffled by the thick carpet as she navigated the labyrinthine halls. Every turn felt like a gamble—one misstep, and she'd lose everything. She reached Victor's office, a massive door flanked by two surveillance cameras. From her backpack, she pulled out a compact device that Sophia had crafted—a signal jammer. With a flick of a switch, the cameras blinked off.

She slipped inside and immediately felt the weight of the room's oppressive luxury. A massive oak desk dominated the space, and behind it, a wall of screens displayed live feeds from the compound's security system. Emma's eyes darted to a small safe tucked into the corner.

Her fingers trembled as she worked to plant the transmitter beneath the desk, securing it to the underside with a piece of adhesive. The device emitted a faint green glow, signaling it was active.

Just as she turned to leave, the door handle rattled.

Her heart lurched.

## ○ The Call to Action

THE MORNING AIR CARRIED the sharp scent of decay and ash, a constant reminder of what the world had become. Alex stood at the edge of the crumbled overpass, surveying the distant remnants of the city. Concrete spires once stood tall as symbols of human achievement, but now they jutted into the gray sky like jagged bones of a long-dead beast. The wind tugged at his tattered coat, but he hardly noticed. His mind raced with the implications of Sophia's revelation the night before.

"Alex, we can't wait any longer," Emma's voice broke through his thoughts. She approached him cautiously, her boots crunching against the brittle remains of the asphalt. Her face was etched with the weight of sleepless nights and unspoken fears. "If we sit on this, Victor's people will catch wind of it. They'll destroy her work—or worse, use it for their own gain."

Alex turned to her, his eyes heavy with the burden of leadership. "And what would you have us do, Emma? March straight into Victor's stronghold with nothing but our ideals to shield us? We don't even know if the stabilizer will work. It could be a death sentence."

Emma crossed her arms, her expression hardening. "It's already a death sentence out here. We've seen what happens when people cling to survival without purpose. Sophia's invention—it's more than hope. It's a chance to give humanity a future. But that means nothing if we let fear dictate our actions."

From behind them, Danny emerged, his hulking frame casting a long shadow in the dim morning light. His rifle was slung across his back, and his expression was grim. "Emma's right," he said, his voice low but steady. "Waiting won't make us any safer. We've already lost too much. If there's even a chance we can turn the tide, we have to take it."

Alex sighed deeply, running a hand through his unruly hair. His gaze shifted to Sophia, who was hunched over a makeshift workbench nearby, tinkering with the stabilizer's prototype. The device was a patchwork of wires and salvaged metal, its design both intricate and fragile. Sophia's hands moved with precision, her brow furrowed in concentration, as though she could block out the world's chaos through sheer focus.

He approached her, his steps hesitant. "Sophia," he said gently, "what are the odds this thing will work?"

She didn't look up, her voice clipped and efficient. "It's not about odds, Alex. It's about necessity. The stabilizer can repair critical ecosystems, jumpstarting the planet's recovery. But it needs to be deployed on a large scale—and soon. Every day we delay, the damage compounds. You know that."

Alex clenched his fists, the weight of her words pressing down on him. He thought of the children they'd passed in the last settlement—hollow-eyed, malnourished, their laughter extinguished before it could take root. He thought of the barren fields stretching endlessly under the poisoned sky. This wasn't just about survival anymore; it was about redemption.

"All right," he said finally, his voice firm. "We move forward. But this isn't just a mission—it's war. We need allies, resources, a plan that doesn't get us all killed. Emma, I want you to connect with anyone who still has a shred of influence or firepower. Danny, scout ahead and map out a route to Victor's territory. And Sophia..." He hesitated. "You need to prepare for the worst. If this stabilizer is as powerful as you say, Victor won't stop until he has it—or you."

Sophia straightened, meeting his gaze with unwavering determination. "I've prepared for the worst since the first day of the collapse, Alex. This won't be any different."

As the group dispersed to carry out their tasks, Alex lingered, his eyes fixed on the horizon. The weight of their mission settled squarely on his shoulders, but for the first time in years, there was a flicker of something more—a belief that the ashes of empires could still nurture the seeds of something new.

The call to action had been made. There was no turning back.

○ **No Turning Back**

THE SUN DIPPED BELOW the jagged horizon, painting the ruined city in hues of deep crimson and gold. It was a fleeting moment of beauty in a world marred by devastation, a brief reminder of what had been lost. Alex stood atop the crumbling overpass, the wind whipping at his tattered coat as he scanned the barren streets below. The remnants of society sprawled in chaotic clusters—makeshift camps, smoldering fires, and the occasional distant cry of desperation.

Behind him, the group gathered in uneasy silence. Sophia clutched her satchel tightly, its contents the hope of a dying planet. Her face, though streaked with dirt, held an expression of fierce determination. Danny leaned against the rusted railing, his rifle slung over one shoulder, eyes scanning for threats in the growing shadows. Emma sat cross-legged on a piece of broken concrete, scribbling notes into a battered journal, her pen moving with the urgency of someone chronicling the end of the world.

"We've got no choice," Alex said, breaking the silence. His voice carried a weight that silenced even the wind. "If we don't move now, we lose everything."

Danny scoffed, pushing off the railing. "And if we do? You think Victor's just going to let us waltz in and take what we need? His men will gut us before we even reach the gates."

Emma glanced up from her journal. "So what's the alternative? Stay here? Wait for his scouts to find us and do the job anyway?" Her tone was sharp, but her gaze softened when it met Alex's. "You know she's right," she added, gesturing toward Sophia.

Sophia took a cautious step forward. "This isn't just about us. It's about everyone out there who still has a chance. If we succeed, we can—"

"If," Danny interrupted. He turned to Alex, his expression hard. "This isn't a plan; it's a suicide mission. You're asking us to follow you into a fight we can't win."

Alex met his gaze, unwavering. "I'm asking you to believe that we can make a difference. That what Sophia has in that bag is worth fighting for. Worth dying for, if it comes to that."

The words hung in the air, heavy and unrelenting.

Emma stood, dusting off her hands. "He's right. We've come too far to turn back now. We either move forward or we die here, waiting for the inevitable."

Danny exhaled sharply, running a hand through his hair. "Damn it, Alex. Fine. But don't think I'm going to play hero for you."

"No one's asking you to," Alex replied. "Just do what you do best. Keep us alive."

Sophia stepped closer to Alex, her voice soft but resolute. "Thank you," she said, her eyes searching his for a moment.

He nodded, then turned back toward the edge of the overpass, where the city stretched out like a graveyard of dreams. "We leave at first light," he said, his tone leaving no room for argument.

As the group dispersed to prepare, Alex lingered, staring into the distance. The path ahead was fraught with danger, and the weight of their mission pressed down on him like an iron shroud. But deep within, a spark of hope flickered, fragile but unyielding.

There was no turning back.

The night settled over the city like a suffocating blanket. The air was thick with the acrid smell of burning refuse, mingled with the metallic tang of decay. Alex sat alone by a small fire, its flickering light casting shadows that danced across his face. The others had retreated into their makeshift shelters, catching what little rest they could before the perilous journey ahead.

Sophia approached quietly, her footsteps muffled by the cracked asphalt. She carried a battered tin cup, steam rising from its contents. Without a word, she handed it to Alex and sat beside him, her knees drawn to her chest.

"Thanks," he said, taking a cautious sip. The liquid was bitter, but its warmth was a small comfort in the chill of the night.

Sophia studied him for a moment, her gaze steady. "You don't have to carry this alone, you know."

Alex didn't respond immediately. He stared into the fire, watching the embers dance and fade. "I can't afford to think about that," he said finally. "If I start leaning on anyone, what happens when I fall?"

"You think strength means doing everything by yourself?" she asked, her tone gentle but firm. "That's not leadership, Alex. That's isolation."

He turned to her, his expression guarded. "And what happens when I make the wrong call? When people die because of me?"

Sophia's eyes softened. "People are going to die, Alex. That's the reality we're living in. But you're giving them a reason to fight, a chance to believe in something bigger than survival. That's worth the risk."

Her words lingered in the silence between them, as heavy as the night itself. Alex didn't reply, but a flicker of gratitude crossed his face. He took another sip from the cup, letting the bitterness settle in his chest.

In the distance, a faint sound broke through the stillness—a low, rhythmic thrum that sent a shiver down Sophia's spine.

"Drones," she whispered, her voice tight with fear.

Alex was already on his feet, his senses on high alert. "Wake the others," he said, his voice a sharp command. "We need to move now."

Sophia bolted toward the shelters, her heart pounding. Within moments, the camp erupted into controlled chaos. Danny emerged, weapon in hand, his expression grim. "What's happening?"

"Victor's men," Alex said, strapping on his gear. "They've found us."

Emma appeared, clutching her journal and a small pack of supplies. "How? We've been careful—"

"Doesn't matter now," Alex cut her off. "We head for the tunnels. It's our only chance."

The group moved quickly, their movements honed by necessity. The thrum of the drones grew louder, an ominous hum that seemed to echo the pounding of their hearts.

As they descended into the shadows of the abandoned subway, Alex glanced back one last time. The overpass, their temporary refuge, was already bathed in the harsh glow of searchlights.

"Keep moving," he urged, his voice steady despite the fear coiling in his chest.

The tunnels enveloped them in darkness, the air damp and stale. Their footsteps echoed off the walls, a haunting reminder of the emptiness surrounding them. For now, they were safe. But Alex knew the reprieve was temporary. The path ahead was fraught with danger, and every step brought them closer to the heart of the storm.

There was no turning back.

The subway tunnels stretched endlessly before them, a labyrinth of darkness and decay. Their flashlights carved narrow paths of light through the gloom, illuminating graffiti-scrawled walls and the occasional scuttle of rodents. The air was heavy, thick with the stench of mold and stagnant water. Every sound seemed amplified—the drip of water from rusted pipes, the crunch of gravel underfoot, the labored breathing of the group.

Danny took point, his rifle at the ready. Behind him, Emma clutched her journal tightly, her other hand gripping a crowbar scavenged from their last supply run. Alex walked in the center, his eyes scanning the walls for signs of danger, while Sophia brought up the rear, her satchel secured across her body.

"Are you sure this leads out?" Danny asked, his voice low but sharp. He paused to shine his flashlight ahead, revealing an endless corridor of darkness.

"There's a maintenance exit about two miles in," Alex replied. "It should bring us out near the industrial district. From there, we head north."

"Should?" Danny muttered, shaking his head. "Great. Real reassuring."

Sophia's voice cut through the tension. "Do you have a better idea, Danny? Because if you do, now's the time."

Danny glanced back, his face illuminated in the harsh light of his flashlight. For a moment, he seemed on the verge of retorting, but instead, he turned and kept walking.

"Thought so," Sophia murmured under her breath.

The group trudged on in uneasy silence, the oppressive darkness gnawing at their nerves. Emma, struggling to maintain composure, broke the quiet. "Do you think he's sending scouts down here too? Or is this just drones and foot soldiers topside?"

Alex didn't answer immediately. His focus was on the faint noise ahead—a soft, almost imperceptible hum that seemed to grow louder with every step.

"Stop," he said suddenly, raising a hand. The group halted, their flashlights swinging toward him.

"What is it?" Sophia asked, her voice barely above a whisper.

Alex gestured for silence, tilting his head toward the sound. It was no longer faint—there was a distinct mechanical edge to it now, like the whirring of gears and the faint hiss of pressurized air.

"Drones," Alex muttered, his jaw tightening. "Victor's tech isn't limited to the surface."

Danny cursed under his breath. "Fantastic. And here I was thinking underground meant safe."

Sophia tightened her grip on her satchel, her eyes darting around the tunnel. "We need to find a side passage. Somewhere to hide."

"There," Emma said, pointing to a rusted door partially obscured by debris. Without waiting for confirmation, she sprinted toward it, the others close behind.

Alex yanked the door open, revealing a narrow maintenance room filled with abandoned tools and machinery. They crowded inside, slamming the door shut just as the hum reached its crescendo. The walls vibrated faintly as the drones passed overhead, their searchlights visible through the gaps in the rusted door.

The group held their breath, the tension in the room palpable. Seconds stretched into minutes as the drones lingered, their mechanical movements punctuated by the occasional burst of static.

Finally, the hum began to fade, the drones moving further down the tunnel.

Alex exhaled, his shoulders relaxing slightly. "They're gone. For now."

Danny slumped against the wall, wiping sweat from his brow. "This just keeps getting better and better."

Emma leaned against a workbench, her hands trembling as she tried to steady her breathing. "How does he know where we are? It's like he's always one step ahead."

"Maybe we have a mole," Danny said darkly, his eyes narrowing as they flicked between the others.

"Enough," Alex said firmly. "Paranoia won't help us survive. We stick together, or we don't make it at all."

Sophia glanced at him, her expression unreadable. "And if they come back?"

"Then we fight," Alex replied, his voice steady. "But not until we've exhausted every other option."

The group fell silent, the weight of his words settling over them. They had chosen this path knowing the risks, but in the suffocating darkness of the tunnels, the stakes felt higher than ever.

No turning back. Not now. Not ever.

The room was cramped, the air thick with the smell of rust and mold. Each of them found a place to settle for a moment, their minds racing even as their bodies sought the briefest respite. The distant hum of the drones faded into the background, replaced by the rhythmic sound of their own breathing, the only comfort in a world that had become host

Alex's mind churned as he surveyed the group. They were good people, strong in their own ways, but they were still human—vulnerable, scared, and unprepared for the full weight of what they faced. He had to keep them focused, had to make them believe that survival was possible, that they could reclaim a world that see

"We wait here for a few hours," he said, breaking the silence. "We move at first light. No more distractions, no more detours. We stick to the plan."

Sophia met his eyes, her expression determined, but with an underlying exhaustion that she couldn't hide. "And if Victor finds the tunnels? What's our fallback?"

"There's no fallback," Alex said, his voice cold with resolve. "We don't get caught. We don't give them a reason to chase us. If it comes to that..." His voice trailed off as he thought about what lay ahead. He couldn't afford to dwell on worst-case scenarios, but he knew that nothing could be taken for granted anymore.

The silence stretched between them again, heavy with the weight of uncertainty. It was Emma who finally broke it, her voice small but laced with unyielding conviction.

"We'll make it," she said, her eyes flicking from one to the next. "We have to. For those we've lost."

Alex gave her a small, fleeting nod. Her words stung, not because they weren't true, but because they underscored how much was at stake—not just for them, but for everyone who had been left behind.

They spent the next few hours in quiet preparation. Each person checked their gear, made sure they had enough supplies, and steeled themselves for what lay ahead. There was no room for fear. No room for doubt.

But as the time dragged on, the weight of their situation pressed harder. They had crossed a point of no return, a threshold from which there was no guarantee of survival. The path ahead was treacherous, and every decision they made could be their last.

Sophia moved toward the back of the room, kneeling beside her pack. "We have a few options," she said, her tone softer now, thoughtful. "We can keep pushing through the tunnels, but if Victor's men are as thorough as I think, they'll be hunting us through every inch of this underground maze. There's no real safe route."

Alex looked over at her, his eyes narrowing as he weighed the risk. "What are you suggesting?"

"I've heard rumors," she said, hesitating for a moment. "There's an old network of underground bunkers—abandoned military facilities. If we can find one of them, we might be able to lay low long enough to figure out our next move. It's not much, but it's something."

Alex's mind raced. They didn't have the luxury of time, and yet they couldn't afford to rush blindly into the unknown. He thought back to the plan they'd originally laid out: get out of the city, make their way north, and find shelter. But things were different now. Victor's men were everywhere, and the possibility of being ambushed in these tunnels was high.

After a long pause, Alex made his decision.

"We take the risk," he said, standing up. "But we move quickly. No delays. We don't know how much time we have before they catch onto our trail."

Danny shot him a look, one that was part disbelief and part reluctant understanding. "You think it's worth it, risking getting lost in these damn tunnels?"

"It's our best chance," Alex replied. "And right now, it's the only chance we've got."

Without another word, they gathered their things and moved out, the weight of their decision hanging over them like a shadow. The tunnels felt colder now, the silence deeper. Every step forward was a step into the unknown, each turn a new gamble.

The sound of their footsteps echoed ominously, a reminder of how exposed they were. Alex's mind remained sharp, focused on the task at hand, but he couldn't shake the feeling that they were being watched. Every flicker of movement, every distant echo, made his heart race faster.

They moved in tight formation, using the shadows to their advantage, their senses heightened by the knowledge that danger was always just a step behind. Every sound felt like a warning.

The hours stretched on, and they began to feel the strain of their journey. Hunger gnawed at their stomachs, exhaustion weighed on their limbs, but still, they pressed on. They had no other choice.

Then, as they rounded a corner, the faintest glimmer of light pierced the darkness ahead.

"That's it," Alex said, his voice barely a whisper. "We're close."

Sophia's eyes lit up with a mixture of hope and apprehension. "It's the bunker, isn't it?"

Alex nodded. "Let's move."

They moved quickly, their footsteps echoing softly against the damp walls as they approached the faint light. Alex felt a surge of relief, but it was quickly replaced by caution. The closer they got, the more the light seemed to warp, as though the shadows around it were thickening, obscuring whatever lay beyond.

When they reached the entrance, Alex's hand hovered over the door, his fingers brushing the cold metal. The structure looked old—rusted hinges, peeling paint—but there was something about it that felt different. Solid. Safe, maybe, but that was a feeling Alex wasn't ready to trust yet.

"Do we go in?" Danny asked, his voice low, his eyes scanning the dark passageway behind them.

Alex turned to him, his face grim. "We don't have a choice. But keep your guard up. This could be a trap, or worse."

Sophia stepped forward, her face pale but determined. "If anyone's watching us, they're probably already on their way. We need to get inside, now."

With a slow, deliberate motion, Alex turned the handle and pushed the door open. A gust of stale air hit them, the smell of old machinery and dust mixing with the sharper scent of decay. They stepped inside cautiously, their eyes adjusting to the dim interior.

The bunker was cold, and the walls seemed to close in on them as they moved deeper into the building. It was mostly abandoned, but there were signs that someone—something—had been here recently. Old crates were stacked haphazardly, and empty shelves lined the walls. In one corner, a flickering lightbulb buzzed faintly, casting eerie shadows across the room.

Sophia walked ahead, her steps quick and purposeful. "We need to find a secure room, somewhere we can rest and plan our next move."

Alex nodded, but something nagged at him. The feeling of being watched hadn't gone away, and now, more than ever, it seemed like they were being lured into a trap. His gut twisted with unease, but he pushed the feeling aside. They couldn't afford to turn back now.

The group moved further into the bunker, their footsteps muffled by the thick dust on the floor. It felt as though the place had been abandoned for years, but the stillness was oppressive, like the silence before a storm.

They came to a set of stairs leading deeper underground, a faint humming sound emanating from below. Alex hesitated, glancing at the others. "This doesn't feel right," he said, his voice barely above a whisper. "Something's off."

Danny was the first to speak up. "We can't just sit here, waiting for them to find us. We need to move, get further down. The deeper we go, the safer we'll be."

Sophia shot him a pointed look. "And if it's a dead end? We'll be trapped."

Alex stared at the stairs, his mind racing. He had to make a decision, and fast. Time was slipping away, the tension in the air thickening with each passing second.

"Let's check it out," he said finally, gripping his gun tighter. "But stay alert. If anything goes wrong, we pull out immediately."

They made their way down the stairs, the hum of the machinery growing louder with each step. The atmosphere in the bunker felt more oppressive the deeper they went, the air heavier, colder. It was as though they were entering the belly of something alive, something that could swallow them whole without a second thought.

At the bottom of the stairs, they found a large, open room filled with old equipment, generators, and what looked like rows of computers, all powered down and covered in dust. A central control station stood at the far end of the room, its screen flickering erratically, as if it were waiting for something—or someone.

"This is it," Sophia said, her voice tense. "If we're going to hide, we need to secure this room first."

Alex nodded and motioned for the others to take up positions. They were vulnerable here, and if they were going to stay, they needed to make sure no one could get in without them knowing.

The minutes dragged by, each one stretching into an eternity. Alex paced the room, his mind constantly on edge. He couldn't shake the feeling that they were being drawn into a web, that every move they made was part of someone else's plan. Victor had eyes everywhere. He had to know they were here.

And yet, nothing happened. No sounds. No voices. Only the hum of the machines that seemed to mock their silence.

Suddenly, the ground beneath them trembled, the hum of the machinery intensifying to a low, vibrating thrum. Alex's heart skipped a beat, and he rushed to the central console, flipping switches in a desperate attempt to understand what was happening.

"What the hell is this?" Danny shouted, his voice laced with panic.

Sophia was already on her feet, scanning the room. "It's some kind of power surge, but from where? There's no way the grid's still active."

The lights flickered overhead, and then, with a deafening crash, the doors to the room slammed shut, locking them inside.

"Trap," Alex whispered, his eyes wide with realization. "It's a trap. We've walked right into it."

# Act 2: The Descent

# 5. Trials of Trust

## ○ A Treacherous Path

The sun hung low in the sky, casting long shadows over the barren landscape. Alex stared ahead, his eyes narrowed against the setting light, trying to make sense of the rocky, desolate terrain that stretched endlessly before them. The wind howled through the ruins, a cold, biting reminder of the world they once knew, now nothing more than a graveyard of empires and broken promises. Each step felt heavier than the last, the weight of leadership pressing down on him, demanding decisions that no man should ever have to make.

Beside him, Danny moved with a practiced caution, his hand always near the grip of his rifle. There was a tension in the air, thick and palpable, as though even the earth itself held its breath, waiting for something to snap. Emma walked slightly behind, her gaze sharp, constantly scanning their surroundings, a woman who had learned the hard way to never let her guard down. Sophia, in contrast, seemed oblivious to the danger, her eyes locked on the horizon, her mind a million miles away in thoughts of the technology that could save—or doom—the world.

The path ahead was treacherous, a narrow strip of dirt cutting through the wilderness, flanked by jagged rocks and overgrown vegetation. It had been days since they had left the relative safety of the last settlement, and the further they traveled, the more the terrain seemed to shift, growing more hostile with each passing mile. It wasn't just the environment that made this journey dangerous, though—it was the people who watched them from the shadows, waiting for any sign of weakness.

"This place gives me the creeps," Danny muttered under his breath, glancing over his shoulder. His voice was low, but there was a thread of unease in it that Alex didn't miss. The soldier had been through hell, yet something about this stretch of land unsettled him.

"It's the silence," Alex replied, his voice steady but laced with the same tension Danny had spoken of. "The calm before the storm. We're too close to Victor's territory. He won't let us pass without a fight."

Emma shook her head, her expression hardening. "Victor won't fight us. He'll do worse than that. He'll make sure we don't make it to the other side."

Alex felt a chill at her words. She was right. Victor Lynn was a man who didn't play by the rules. His empire wasn't built on strength alone—it was built on manipulation, on fear, on cutting people down before they even realized what was happening. If they weren't careful, they would walk right into a trap.

They had no choice, though. They had to keep moving. Sophia's invention, the stabilizer, was their only hope. Without it, the war-torn world would continue its downward spiral, and no amount of hope or good intentions would be enough to turn it around. But to reach it, they had to cross through Victor's stronghold—an area now so heavily fortified, it was rumored that even the most seasoned soldiers had disappeared without a trace.

"We'll make it through," Alex said, though his voice held little conviction. He had no illusions about the danger ahead. He had seen too much to think otherwise. But for Sophia's sake, for the sake of whatever future there might be, they had to try.

A sudden noise made them freeze in place. It wasn't the usual sound of wildlife, nor the wind whistling through the dead trees—it was the unmistakable sound of footsteps. Heavy, deliberate, and close.

"Get down," Alex ordered, his voice low but urgent.

They ducked behind the nearest rock formation, the echo of their movements muted by the surrounding rubble. Alex held his breath, straining his ears, hoping to catch any sign of what was approaching. He could feel his heart pounding in his chest, each beat reminding him of the stakes. If they were discovered now, it would be over.

Minutes passed, and the sound of footsteps grew louder, then stopped entirely. Alex risked a glance around the edge of the rock, his eyes scanning the distance. Figures appeared from the shadows, a group of soldiers dressed in the unmistakable black uniforms of Victor's personal militia. They moved with precision, as though they had been trained to track anyone who dared to cross into their domain.

Alex's mind raced. If they were spotted, a firefight would be inevitable. But if they stayed hidden, they risked being cornered. There was no perfect solution. Only survival.

"Move back," he whispered, his voice steady despite the chaos swirling in his mind. They had to find another way around—anything to avoid a confrontation.

Slowly, they crept backward, making their way further into the treacherous path. The soldiers were too close now. They couldn't afford to make any noise. Every step felt like an eternity.

As they retreated, the land seemed to close in on them, the rocks and debris offering little protection from the eyes of their would-be pursuers. Alex's mind whirled with possibilities, none of them good. There was no doubt in his mind that Victor's men were closing in. And the path ahead? It was more treacherous than any of them had realized.

Time was running out.

They moved cautiously, their footsteps muffled by the loose gravel and dust beneath them. The sun had dipped further, casting an eerie twilight over the landscape. Shadows stretched long, their edges becoming indistinct as the sky darkened, making it harder to distinguish friend from foe. Alex's heart thudded in his chest, the rhythm of it blending with the sounds of the distant soldiers as they continued their search.

Sophia was the first to break the silence. "We can't keep running forever," she whispered, her voice tight with frustration. "If we don't get to the stabilizer soon, all of this—this whole journey—will have been for nothing."

Her words struck him like a blow. The weight of their mission pressed down on him again, suffocating in its urgency. They couldn't afford to waste any more time. Yet, every step forward felt like it was leading them deeper into enemy territory. He glanced at her, seeing the determined glint in her eyes. She wasn't just concerned about their safety; she was fixated on the technology that could either save or doom them all.

"Trust me, we're getting there," Alex said, though the words tasted hollow in his mouth. "We just need to outlast them."

Danny shot him a look, his expression hard as stone. "Outlast them?" he muttered, his voice barely audible. "How do you plan on doing that when we're walking straight into a trap? We need a plan, not just hope."

Alex didn't have an answer. Hope wasn't a strategy, but it was all they had left. Victor's men were ruthless, and the terrain only made their movements more perilous. But there was one thing Alex had learned over the years—when there's no way out, sometimes the best option is to keep moving forward, even if you don't know where the next step will land.

They pushed on in silence, their senses heightened, aware of every rustling leaf and shifting stone. The tension between them was palpable, the unspoken fear that gnawed at each of their souls. Every now and then, they would catch a glimpse of movement in the distance, or hear the faint echo of boots on gravel, reminding them that they were being hunted.

It wasn't until they reached the narrow gorge that Alex began to feel the first stirrings of hope. The jagged cliffs on either side of them created a natural funnel, a narrow pass that led toward a series of caves rumored to be hidden deep in the mountains. The caves weren't much, but they would offer cover, a place to regroup, and perhaps even a chance to lay low while they figured out their next move.

"We're almost there," Alex said, his voice firm now, filled with a sense of resolve that he hadn't felt in hours. He glanced at Danny and Emma, both of whom had fallen into a tense, wary silence. Sophia, however, remained focused, her eyes scanning the gorge ahead, already calculating their path.

The wind had picked up, howling through the gorge and sending clouds of dust into their faces. The air was thick with the scent of earth and decay, the remnants of a world that had once thrived but was now slowly being eaten away by time and conflict.

They passed through the narrow pass, the cliffs rising ominously on either side, closing in on them like the walls of a tomb. As they approached the caves, Alex's mind raced with the next steps. They couldn't stay there long. The soldiers would track them, and the longer they lingered, the more likely they were to be discovered.

"I'll take the first watch," Danny said abruptly, breaking the silence. He had already begun to settle in near the entrance of one of the caves, his rifle at the ready.

Sophia nodded. "We need to make sure they don't see us coming. Victor's men will be relentless."

Emma pulled her jacket tighter around her, trying to block out the chill that had settled in the air. "And if they do find us?"

"We fight," Alex replied, his voice hard. "We fight, and we don't stop. Whatever it takes."

They made camp in the dark cave, the shadows swallowing them whole as they huddled together, trying to find a moment's respite. The crackle of a small fire broke the stillness, casting flickering shadows on the cave walls. It was hard to tell how much time had passed—hours, maybe more—but the sense of urgency was never far from his thoughts. The weight of their mission, the knowledge of what was at stake, pressed down on him with every breath.

Alex found it hard to sleep, his mind racing with possibilities, scenarios he couldn't control. Every plan they'd made felt fragile, each step they took more dangerous than the last. But as he stared into the fire, watching the flames flicker and dance, he realized there was no turning back. The path ahead was treacherous, yes. But it was the only path they had.

Suddenly, a noise broke the stillness—a faint crack of a twig. Alex's head snapped up, his senses alert. He held his breath, listening intently. The sound came again, closer this time.

He motioned for the others to stay quiet, his hand gripping the handle of his gun. His eyes darted toward the entrance of the cave, where the shadows shifted unnervingly. The soldiers. They were here.

Alex's pulse quickened as he signaled to the others, his eyes never leaving the shadowy mouth of the cave. The wind howled louder, masking any other noise, but the sharp crack of a twig underfoot betrayed their enemies' presence. Slowly, silently, the group positioned themselves, each person taking cover in the darkness.

"Stay low," Alex whispered, his voice barely audible against the wind.

Sophia's eyes were wide with tension as she pressed herself against the rocky wall. Danny, ever the pragmatist, adjusted his grip on his rifle, his face a mask of concentration. Emma, though clearly nervous, held her ground.

The sound grew nearer, and Alex could feel the weight of the moment settle on him. They weren't just running away anymore; they were fighting to survive.

A figure emerged from the shadows, silhouetted by the dim glow of the fire. It was just one man, but that didn't mean they were alone. More would follow soon. Alex's heart raced as he crouched, trying to remain as still as possible, knowing that even the slightest movement could give them away.

The man stopped at the cave's entrance, pausing to scan the area. His back was turned, but Alex knew better than to assume they were safe. His instincts screamed that danger was just moments away.

Then, the man spoke—a low murmur carried by the wind. "They couldn't have gone far. Spread out."

The words sent a chill down Alex's spine. The soldiers were already moving in on them, and there was no way to avoid a confrontation.

"On my mark," Alex murmured to the group. He saw the nods of understanding from Sophia, Danny, and Emma.

The next few moments felt like they stretched on forever. The soldier took another step forward, his attention momentarily distracted by a shift in the wind. The others were likely closer now, making their approach, unaware that Alex and his group had already spotted them.

Alex's hand tightened around his gun. The time had come. He glanced at Danny, who gave him a brief nod, signaling he was ready. Then, without a second thought, Alex sprang into action.

"Now!" he hissed.

In one fluid motion, they erupted from their hiding spots. Danny's rifle cracked through the silence first, the sound echoing off the cave walls as he took out the nearest soldier. Sophia and Emma moved like shadows, flanking the second man who was still trying to adjust to the sudden chaos. Emma's shot was quick and clean, silencing him before he could raise an alarm.

But it wasn't over. As soon as the gunfire echoed, more soldiers came running toward the noise. Alex could see them, just silhouettes in the darkness, but there were too many. He grabbed Sophia's arm, pulling her deeper into the cave.

"Fall back!" Alex shouted.

They scrambled, adrenaline pumping through their veins. They couldn't afford to stand and fight. Not here. Not with so many enemies closing in.

The narrow passages of the cave twisted and turned, a labyrinth that had once been an escape route but was now a death trap. The sound of boots grew louder behind them. The soldiers were relentless, closing the distance with every passing second.

Alex's mind raced. They needed a way out. A way to lose the soldiers in this maze of stone. His gaze flickered to the walls, to the sharp turns and hidden crevices. The answer hit him like a flash of lightning.

"Up ahead," Alex muttered to the group, his eyes locking onto a narrow, barely visible passage in the rock. "Through there."

Without waiting for a response, he moved toward it, hoping the others would follow. Sophia and Emma were right behind him, and Danny stayed close, covering their retreat as they sprinted down the narrow tunnel. The soldiers' shouts grew fainter, their pursuit slowing as they struggled to navigate the twisting passageways.

Alex's breath came in ragged gasps as he led them deeper into the cave system, the weight of the mission still pressing on him.

They couldn't stay here long. The soldiers would regroup, and the last thing they needed was to be cornered.

Finally, they reached a small, hidden chamber deep within the cave. It was a dead end, but one that could offer them a moment's respite. They collapsed against the cool stone, gasping for air, their hearts still racing from the close call.

"We need to rest," Sophia said, her voice shaky. "Just for a moment. I don't know how much longer we can keep this up."

Alex nodded, though he wasn't sure they had much time. His mind spun with possibilities, each one darker than the last. They had barely escaped this time. How many more times could they dodge death?

"We rest for a moment," he said, his voice steady despite the storm raging in his mind. "But we keep moving as soon as we can. They'll be on us again before long."

As they settled into the cave's cramped corners, Alex's thoughts wandered back to the mission, to the high-tech stabilizer that was their last hope. The group's survival depended on it.

But it was more than that. The world outside, the one they'd left behind, was crumbling faster than they could comprehend. Each choice they made now could mean the difference between life and death—not just for them, but for everyone.

And in the silence of the cave, with the sounds of the soldiers' pursuit still ringing in his ears, Alex knew one thing for sure: The path ahead was only going to get more treacherous from here. But he couldn't turn back. There was no going back now.

The silence in the cave was deafening, only the sound of heavy breathing and the occasional scrape of stone against gear breaking through the stillness. Alex couldn't shake the feeling of being hunted. It was the way the soldiers moved, too coordinated, too relentless. This was no random search; they were after something, something Alex and his team had stumbled into. He wasn't sure what yet, but he had a growing suspicion that the stakes were much higher than they could imagine.

"We can't stay here long," Danny murmured, his voice cutting through the tension. "They'll find this place eventually. We need to move."

Alex nodded, wiping the sweat from his brow. He could feel the weight of his decisions pressing down on him, but there was no time for second-guessing. They couldn't afford to stop now, not with so much on the line.

"Yeah, but we need to figure out where they're coming from," Alex said, his voice low and sharp. "If we don't know where they're positioning themselves, we're running blind."

Sophia shifted uneasily. "We don't have that kind of intel, Alex. We can't just go in blind."

He didn't need to look at her to feel her doubt. Sophia had always been the voice of reason, the one who kept them grounded. But this was different. The world outside was crumbling, and they had no choice but to push forward. They had to survive, not just for themselves, but for everything they were fighting for.

"We won't be blind for long," Alex replied, his voice growing more determined. "We find a way to move forward. We track them. Get in, get the stabilizer, and get out."

"Get out?" Emma's voice broke through the gloom. She was sitting against the far wall, arms wrapped around her knees, eyes distant. "And what then? Where do we go? Do you really think we can just escape once we have it?"

Alex took a deep breath, frustration flickering in his chest. "We don't have a choice, Emma. The world's falling apart out there. If we don't get that stabilizer, it's over. For everyone."

There was a long pause before Danny spoke again, his voice gruff but tinged with an understanding that cut through the tension.

"If we're going to keep going, we need a plan," Danny said. "We can't afford to keep reacting. We need to take control."

Alex turned to face him, meeting his eyes. Danny had a point. Up until now, everything had been about survival, about evading the threat. But they were losing control. The soldiers were one step ahead of them, and without intel, they'd be trapped in the same cycle.

"We need to find their command post," Alex said, the idea forming in his mind. "That's where the real answers are. If we can take that down, we take away their advantage."

Sophia raised an eyebrow. "And how exactly do you plan to find their command post? We've barely managed to evade them this far."

Alex was already moving, his mind racing through the possibilities. "We've seen their patrols. We know they're not working alone. Someone's orchestrating this."

Danny stood up, dusting himself off. "And if we find this 'someone,' we can turn the tables on them. I like that."

The air was thick with tension, but the spark of hope had ignited in Alex's chest. This wasn't over. He knew they could do this, but only if they stayed ahead of the soldiers. They needed information. They needed to find out who was pulling the strings.

"Alright," Alex said, his voice calm but firm. "We move out at first light. We'll track the patrols and figure out where they're coming from. We hit their command post and take it down. Then we get the stabilizer, and we get the hell out."

Sophia nodded, though her face was still lined with worry. "You know this is going to be dangerous, right?"

Alex met her gaze. "It's always dangerous. But right now, it's our only option."

---

The night passed slowly, and Alex could feel the weight of his thoughts pressing in on him. He couldn't afford to make any more mistakes. The stakes had never been higher, and failure was not an option. The world outside the cave was slowly falling apart, and if they didn't act soon, it would be too late to save anything.

He leaned against the cold stone, eyes closed, listening to the sounds of the cave around him. It was hard to remember what peace had felt like. The days before everything changed, before the war had turned the world into this fractured, desperate place. He didn't have the luxury of nostalgia anymore. He had a mission to finish, and it was all-consuming.

In the distance, the sounds of the soldiers' movements still echoed through the night, but Alex didn't let himself dwell on them. They were a constant now, always present, always pushing. But he would push back. He would keep moving forward, no matter the cost.

As the first light of dawn began to filter into the cave, the team gathered their equipment and prepared to move. The air was thick with anticipation, the tension palpable in the stillness of the early morning. The shadows of the night seemed to cling to them, unwilling to release their grip as they stepped into the harsh daylight outside.

Alex scanned the landscape, his eyes darting over the rugged terrain. The soldiers would be moving soon, just as they had every day for the past week. They needed to be ahead of them, to get in position before the patrols had a chance to spot them. It wasn't just a matter of survival anymore; it was a race to prevent something far worse from happening.

"Alright, everyone," Alex said, his voice steady despite the weight of the situation. "We stay low, keep to the hills. We'll head northeast for the first few kilometers, then cut west to avoid the main route. We'll track the patrols from there."

Sophia nodded, though her brow furrowed with concern. "And if they're already waiting for us?"

"We won't give them the chance," Alex replied, his jaw tightening. "We're not sitting ducks anymore. They won't expect us to hit their command post. Not yet."

With a final glance toward the cave, Alex turned and began to lead the group. The day was beginning to heat up, and the rough, unforgiving landscape stretched out before them. The terrain was a mix of rocky outcrops, sparse vegetation, and jagged hills that offered little shelter. They would need to move quickly, stay hidden, and pray the soldiers weren't already ahead of them.

As they moved through the brush, the team kept their steps light, aware of every sound. Alex felt the weight of the map in his pocket, the only tool they had that might guide them to the command post. The maps were outdated, but they'd learned to use them to their advantage. They had to.

Hours passed, and the tension never eased. The farther they moved from the cave, the more exposed they felt. Every rustling of the wind, every creak of the ground beneath their feet, made Alex's heart race. They were being hunted, and every instinct told him that the soldiers were close. He couldn't shake the feeling that the stakes were shifting—if they didn't act quickly, they would be cornered.

"Stay alert," he said, his voice low. "We're getting close. They'll have eyes on us if we aren't careful."

Danny was at the front now, his sharp eyes scanning the horizon for any signs of movement. "There's something up ahead," he whispered, pointing toward a narrow valley that split the hills. "We need to check it out."

Alex motioned for the group to halt. They took cover behind the rocks, peering into the valley. It was eerily quiet, the air heavy with the scent of dust and dry earth. But something about it felt wrong—too quiet, like the calm before a storm.

After a few tense moments, Alex nodded. "We move in slowly. Check every corner. If they're here, they won't show themselves easily."

They moved as one, cautious and silent. As they descended into the valley, Alex felt the weight of every step. He knew they were close—closer than he wanted to be. There was no room for error.

And then, as they rounded a bend in the valley, they saw it.

A group of soldiers—three or four—crouched behind some rocks, watching the valley's entrance. They were alert, their rifles at the ready, scanning the area for anything out of place. Alex's stomach churned. They had been spotted—or worse, they had walked right into a trap.

His heart pounded in his chest. This was it. The moment of truth.

"Back. We need to retreat," Alex whispered, urgency lacing his voice.

But Danny was already moving, a glint of determination in his eyes. "No. We hit them now, before they realize we're here."

Before Alex could protest, Danny had already darted forward, using the terrain to his advantage. The others followed, moving in a tight formation. There was no time to think, no time to hesitate. It was all or nothing now.

As they closed in on the soldiers, Alex's mind raced. They had to take them down quickly. If the soldiers called for reinforcements, they were done. But if they could neutralize the threat, they might just have a chance.

The first soldier fell silently, a quick strike to the neck. The second was down in a flash, Danny's hands swift and sure as he disabled the enemy. The third soldier didn't even see them coming, caught off guard by the sudden assault.

For a moment, everything went still. The valley seemed to hold its breath, and Alex could feel the adrenaline surge through his veins. They had done it. The soldiers were down. But this wasn't over.

"Keep moving!" Alex ordered, his voice urgent. "They'll come looking for us. We don't have time to waste."

They had a narrow window. The soldiers might not have known they were here, but that wouldn't last long. Alex's mind was already working, calculating the next move.

The map. They needed to find the command post, and fast.

"Danny, lead the way," Alex said. "We're not stopping until we get to their command center. That's our only shot."

The team moved on, their pace quickening, the danger at their backs pushing them forward. Alex's thoughts kept racing as they moved deeper into the valley. The soldiers had been a small obstacle, but it was only a matter of time before the real fight began. He didn't know how much longer they could keep running, how much longer they could survive. But one thing was certain: they couldn't turn back now.

They were too far in. And if they didn't get to that command post, the world as they knew it would fall apart.

The sun was beginning to dip below the horizon, casting long shadows across the jagged landscape. The valley was becoming a maze of darkness and uncertainty. Alex's senses were on high alert, every rustle of the wind or crack of a twig setting his heart racing. The command post was close. He could feel it. But with each step, the threat grew. They were entering enemy territory—territory that had swallowed whole battalions before.

Danny led the way, his silhouette barely visible in the dimming light. He was moving with the confidence of someone who had been in this situation before. But Alex knew that even Danny's experience couldn't predict everything. They had already crossed one line by ambushing the soldiers. Now, the risks were multiplied.

The enemy would be watching for them, waiting for the slightest mistake.

As they descended further into the valley, Alex slowed his pace, motioning for the team to do the same. He needed to think. They had no backup, no way to call for reinforcements. If anything went wrong, it would be the end of their mission—and probably their lives.

"We've got to make it through the next ridge," Alex whispered, his voice barely audible above the whisper of the wind. "From there, it's only another few kilometers to the command post. We need to be quick."

Sophia, who had been walking silently at the rear, stepped up beside him. Her face was streaked with dirt, but her eyes remained focused. "What if they've already moved? What if it's a trap?"

"We can't afford to think like that," Alex replied, his gaze fixed ahead. "We have to trust the intel we have. And even if they've moved, we'll adapt. We don't have another choice."

Sophia nodded, though the unease in her expression remained.

"Let's move," Alex ordered.

The group pressed on, their footsteps barely making a sound as they advanced. The night air grew colder, and the valley seemed to close in around them. The oppressive silence was broken only by the occasional scuff of boots on gravel or the whisper of breath between the team members.

As they neared the ridge, Alex's pulse quickened. The shadows of the hills ahead seemed to loom larger with every step, and the hairs on the back of his neck stood on end. They were close now, dangerously close. If they didn't make it through the ridge undetected, the mission would be over. He could already picture the soldiers—sharp-eyed, calculating—waiting for them.

But just as the ridge came into view, a low rumble broke the silence. A distant sound, like the growl of an engine, echoed through the valley. It was faint, but unmistakable.

"Vehicles," Danny muttered, his voice tight.

Alex cursed under his breath. "We need to move, now. They're getting closer. We don't have time to wait."

They scrambled up the ridge, climbing over jagged rocks and uneven ground. The sound of the vehicles grew louder, and the tension escalated with each passing moment. The enemy was near. They had no idea where the patrols were or how many vehicles were moving through the area, but Alex knew they had to get to the command post before it was too late.

At the top of the ridge, they paused. The valley stretched out before them, but the terrain was more open now. There were fewer places to hide, fewer places to make a stand if they were spotted. The vehicles were getting closer, and Alex could almost feel the weight of the decision pressing down on him. They couldn't afford to be seen.

"Danny, take the lead," Alex whispered. "Sophia, you're with me. Keep your heads down."

Danny gave a quick nod and dropped into a crouch, moving stealthily ahead. The others followed suit, their movements fluid and coordinated. Every muscle in Alex's body was taut, his mind racing. The vehicles were too close for comfort. If they didn't make it to cover soon, they would be in plain sight.

The valley ahead offered a brief moment of concealment—rocks and low brush—just enough to break up their silhouette. They moved quickly, their hearts pounding in their chests as they navigated the treacherous terrain. The vehicles were now less than a kilometer away, and Alex could feel the heat of the danger mounting. The slightest misstep, the smallest sound, and they would be discovered.

They reached the cover just as the vehicles came into view—a convoy of military trucks, their engines roaring as they rumbled through the valley. Alex held his breath, praying they wouldn't stop, praying they wouldn't notice the dust rising from the ridge.

For what felt like an eternity, they lay there, barely breathing, watching as the convoy passed. The tension in the air was so thick, Alex felt it might suffocate him. He could see the soldiers inside the trucks, their faces unreadable, but he knew they were just a few seconds from spotting them. They had to move—quickly.

Once the last truck had passed, Alex exhaled sharply, signaling for the team to advance. "Now," he muttered. "Let's go."

They surged forward, moving faster now, using the cover of the valley walls to shield them as much as possible. With every step, Alex's mind raced ahead to the command post, where their mission would either succeed or fail. The soldiers were close, but they were too focused on the convoy ahead of them to notice a small group moving in the opposite direction.

As they neared the final stretch before the command post, the landscape began to change again. The terrain grew more treacherous, with cliffs on either side and no easy way to navigate through the rocks. The valley was narrowing, forcing them into a bottleneck. They couldn't go back now. They had come too far.

And then, just as they were about to round the last bend, they saw it: the dim outline of a fortified structure in the distance, its dark silhouette against the evening sky. The command post. It was closer than Alex had imagined, and yet, a part of him wanted to turn back. This was it—the final confrontation.

"Ready," he said to the team, his voice steady but filled with the weight of what was to come. "Let's finish this."

The night was growing colder, and the air felt heavier as they crept closer to the command post. The structure ahead, once a simple outpost, now loomed like a fortress, its walls jagged and reinforced. Alex's heart pounded with anticipation, but he kept his pace steady, focusing on the task at hand. This wasn't just about survival—it was about sending a message.

Danny, moving ahead cautiously, signaled to stop. They were just beyond the last stretch of open ground, now within a few hundred meters of the perimeter. Alex's eyes scanned the darkened walls, the faint outline of armed guards visible against the dim light. They couldn't afford to make any mistakes now.

"We can't get too close," Danny whispered, his voice barely audible. "The guards will spot us. We need to find another way in."

Alex nodded, his mind already calculating the best route. There was a small section of the perimeter that appeared less guarded, a gap between two concrete barriers. If they could reach it without being detected, it might offer a path inside.

"Sophia, you and I will take the left side," Alex said. "Danny, you stay behind and cover us. We'll move fast."

Sophia nodded, her face set in grim determination. She knew the stakes. There was no turning back now.

They crept along the shadows, moving swiftly and silently through the sparse cover of brush and rocks. The sounds of the guards patrolling grew louder as they neared the gap in the wall. Alex's senses were on high alert, and every nerve in his body screamed for him to move faster, but he knew they had to remain as silent as possible.

A faint light from a guard's flashlight flickered across the open space, and Alex froze, holding his breath. The guard paused, scanning the area, and Alex's heart seemed to stop in his chest. He motioned for Sophia to crouch lower, her back pressed flat against the cold stone. They waited, tense and unmoving, as the light swept past them, never once reaching their hiding place.

After what felt like an eternity, the guard continued on his patrol, and Alex exhaled slowly. "Move," he whispered.

They crossed the last stretch of open ground in a blur, reaching the gap between the barriers. Alex pushed through first, his heart pounding as he squeezed between the concrete walls. The air inside was still, and the faint hum of machinery echoed through the cold night. They had made it in undetected.

"Keep low," Alex muttered. "Stay close."

The command post was massive, sprawling with several connected buildings and fortified positions. Alex's mind raced, trying to calculate their next move. They had to locate the intel—fast—and get out before the enemy realized they had breached the perimeter.

They moved through the shadows of the complex, avoiding the few remaining guards. Every step seemed to reverberate in the silence, and Alex felt the weight of every decision pressing down on him. One wrong move, and they would be swarmed.

They reached the main building, a large structure at the center of the compound. Alex motioned for Sophia to cover the door while he scanned the windows. It was dark inside, but the faint glow of a desk lamp filtered through a cracked blind. It was a long shot, but Alex was certain that was where the intel was kept.

He pushed the door open slowly, the creaking of the hinges sending a jolt through his body. Inside, the room was dimly lit, with papers scattered across the desk and a large map pinned to the wall. Alex moved quickly, scanning the room for anything that looked out of place.

"Over there," Sophia whispered, pointing to a file on the desk.

Alex grabbed it, flipping it open. It was filled with encrypted military reports, but it was the last page that caught his attention. A list of locations—some of which matched the coordinates they had intercepted earlier.

"We've got it," Alex said, his voice low with a mixture of relief and disbelief. "We need to go now."

Sophia nodded, her eyes scanning the room for any signs of danger. Alex folded the paper carefully, slipping it into his jacket pocket. But before they could leave, the sound of footsteps echoed down the hallway.

"Shit," Alex muttered, motioning for Sophia to stay quiet. They couldn't afford to be caught now. They needed to get out—and fast.

The footsteps grew louder, and Alex's mind raced. He knew they couldn't make it back the way they came. They had to find another exit.

"Follow me," he whispered urgently, grabbing Sophia's arm.

They bolted for the back of the room, where a narrow hallway led to a small storage area. Alex pushed open a door to reveal a small courtyard behind the building. The moonlight barely illuminated the space, but it was enough. They were close to freedom—just a few more meters, and they could disappear into the shadows.

But as they reached the door, a voice rang out from behind them.

"Stop right there!"

Alex spun around, heart racing. Two guards appeared at the far end of the hallway, guns drawn. There was no way out. No way but forward.

He pushed Sophia back, positioning himself between her and the guards. "Run," he hissed, his voice steady despite the panic rising in his chest.

Sophia hesitated, her gaze locked with his. "No, Alex. We can't—"

"Now!" Alex shouted.

Without another word, she sprinted toward the courtyard. Alex turned to face the guards, drawing his weapon. The first guard fired, the bullet slamming into the wall beside him. Alex dove to the side, firing back in quick succession. His heart raced, but his aim was true. The first guard collapsed, but the second one was still advancing.

There was no time to waste. Alex sprinted toward the courtyard, just as the remaining guard's shots missed him by inches. He heard the guard yell for reinforcements, but by then, Alex and Sophia were already climbing the wall that separated the courtyard from the rest of the complex.

They dropped down the other side and ran, not daring to look back. The sound of alarms blared in the distance, signaling that the breach had been discovered. But it didn't matter. They had what they came for.

And now, it was time to finish what they started.

The cold wind bit at their faces as they sprinted through the dark streets, the night air sharp with tension. Behind them, the sounds of chaos echoed—guards scrambling, alarms blaring, but Alex and Sophia didn't stop. They couldn't afford to.

The map and documents were now in their hands, but they knew that the real challenge was just beginning. The path ahead would be perilous, fraught with danger and uncertainty. Alex's mind was already shifting gears, calculating their next move. They had to contact their team, but the enemy would be hunting them down. They needed to vanish before their pursuers had a chance to regroup.

"We're too exposed out here," Sophia said, breathless as they turned a corner into a narrow alley. "We need cover. Now."

Alex nodded, scanning the dark buildings around them. There was an abandoned warehouse up ahead—its rusted doors hanging ajar. It wasn't much, but it was better than nothing. They darted inside, crouching low as they moved through the shadows.

The warehouse was dimly lit by the flickering light from a broken bulb overhead. Dust and debris littered the floor, the remnants of forgotten crates and machinery scattered around them. Alex motioned for Sophia to stay low while he checked the perimeter. They couldn't stay here long.

"Anything?" Sophia whispered, her eyes wide with urgency.

Alex shook his head. "We wait. We'll get a signal from the others soon."

Minutes passed like hours. The only sounds were the distant city noises—sirens, the rumble of traffic, and the occasional distant shout. Alex's fingers tapped restlessly on the map. The enemy would be combing the area, trying to track them down. It wouldn't be long before they realized which direction Alex and Sophia had gone.

Suddenly, his earpiece crackled to life.

"Alex, do you copy?" It was Danny's voice, sharp and urgent.

"Loud and clear," Alex responded, his voice low.

"We've got movement," Danny continued. "They're closing in on your location. You've got maybe twenty minutes before they have the whole block surrounded."

Alex cursed under his breath. "Understood. We'll be moving out soon. Meet us at the rendezvous point."

"Negative. They've got eyes on it. You'll need to reroute."

Alex felt a cold knot form in his stomach. They were running out of options. The rendezvous point had been their only safe spot, but it was compromised.

"Any suggestions, Danny?" Alex asked, his mind racing for alternatives.

"Head towards the old dockyards. It's a maze of warehouses. You'll lose them there. I'll keep them distracted. Just get there, and we'll figure out the rest."

Alex nodded. "Copy that. We'll move out in five."

He turned to Sophia. "We need to move. Now."

She nodded, already on her feet, her eyes scanning the room for anything useful. They couldn't waste any more time. They slipped out of the warehouse and into the street, moving quickly but quietly through the dark alleys. The tension was palpable, each step bringing them closer to their goal but also deeper into the unknown.

As they neared the outskirts of the city, the streets grew emptier, the buildings more dilapidated. The dockyards loomed ahead, the rusting skeletons of ships and cranes visible in the distance. It was a desolate place—perfect for losing their pursuers.

The sound of footsteps behind them made Alex freeze. He signaled to Sophia to take cover behind a pile of crates. They crouched low, holding their breath as two enemy soldiers passed by, unaware of their presence. It was a close call, but they managed to stay undetected.

"Keep moving," Alex whispered. "The dockyards are just ahead."

They made their way into the maze of abandoned warehouses, the air thick with salt and decay. The towering structures blocked out most of the moonlight, casting long shadows that stretched across the cracked pavement. The echo of their footsteps seemed to reverberate endlessly as they moved deeper into the industrial wasteland.

But even here, in the relative safety of the dockyards, Alex couldn't shake the feeling that they were being watched. The hairs on the back of his neck stood on end, and his senses were on high alert.

"Stay sharp," he whispered to Sophia. "We don't know how much time we've got."

They reached an old warehouse at the far end of the dockyards, the door hanging open as if inviting them in. Alex peered inside, his eyes adjusting to the darkness. There was no sign of life, but that didn't mean they were alone.

"We'll hold up here for a while," he said. "Wait for Danny's signal."

Sophia nodded, but her eyes were filled with unease. "I don't like this place."

"Neither do I," Alex admitted, but there was no other choice. They had to wait. And in a place like this, they had to be ready for anything.

Minutes passed. The silence in the warehouse was oppressive, broken only by the occasional creak of the building settling. Alex couldn't keep still. He paced back and forth, trying to remain calm, trying to think. He could feel the weight of the documents in his jacket pocket, the gravity of their mission weighing heavily on him.

Suddenly, his earpiece crackled again.

"Alex, you there?" It was Danny again.

"Go ahead," Alex replied, his voice tight.

"We've got company. A lot more than we anticipated. They're closing in on your position. You're not going to be able to wait this out. You need to move—now."

Alex's pulse quickened. The situation was rapidly deteriorating. They were running out of time and options.

"Where's the backup?" Alex demanded.

"En route, but you need to buy time. Head for the old factory complex near the river. It's your best bet to lose them."

"Understood." Alex turned to Sophia. "We've got to move again. They're coming."

She nodded, grabbing her gear as they quickly slipped out of the warehouse. Their brief moment of respite was over.

The night had just begun. And with every step, they knew the treacherous path ahead would only grow more dangerous.

They moved swiftly through the labyrinth of warehouses, their eyes scanning every corner and shadow. The silence around them was suffocating, broken only by their hurried breaths and the distant, almost imperceptible hum of the city beyond.

Sophia led the way, her instincts sharp, knowing they needed to keep moving and not risk stopping for too long. Alex followed close behind, his mind calculating their every step, considering every possible outcome. The factory complex near the river was their last hope, and they had to make it there before their enemies closed in.

As they approached the edge of the dockyards, the faint sound of footsteps echoed from behind them. Alex tensed, signaling for them to stop. They crouched low behind an overturned shipping crate, listening. The footsteps were getting closer, and their pursuers were no longer trying to hide their presence.

"We can't outrun them anymore," Alex murmured, his voice barely a whisper. "We need a plan."

Sophia's eyes narrowed. She was always the one thinking quickly on her feet. "We'll have to double back," she said, her hand tightening on the grip of her gun. "There's a side alley we can take, cuts through the old coal yard. We'll be hidden until we can circle around."

Alex considered it for a moment. It wasn't a perfect plan, but it was their only option. They could make it to the factory complex if they could just buy themselves a little more time.

"Alright, we move fast," he said, his voice steady despite the rising tension.

They sprinted through the shadows, making their way towards the side alley. The sound of their pursuers was growing louder, and Alex could feel the hairs on the back of his neck standing up. The narrow passageways of the coal yard offered some cover, but the sense of being trapped was unmistakable. They were running out of room, and every turn felt like they were only getting deeper into enemy territory.

The cold, damp air hung heavy around them as they slipped into the alley, their footsteps echoing off the brick walls. The sound of their breathing was the only thing they could hear now, and Alex's thoughts raced. Time was running out. They had to keep moving, keep ahead of the enemy.

The alley opened up into a small, forgotten courtyard, the remains of old machinery scattered across the ground like abandoned relics. There was no sign of their pursuers—yet. Alex took a deep breath and motioned for Sophia to follow.

They moved through the courtyard, keeping to the shadows, their senses on high alert. Alex could feel his heart pounding in his chest, his mind calculating their next move. They were close now. Just a few more turns, and they'd be able to make it to the factory.

Suddenly, a voice rang out, sharp and unmistakable.

"There they are!"

The sound of footsteps grew louder, followed by the unmistakable snap of a rifle being cocked. The enemy had caught up with them.

"Run!" Alex shouted, his voice cutting through the air.

They dashed toward the factory, but their path was blocked by a group of armed soldiers, their faces hidden behind masks. Alex's heart raced as he scanned for an escape route, but the factory gates were locked, and there was no other way out.

Sophia didn't hesitate. She pulled out a small explosive charge from her bag and pressed it against the factory's metal gates.

"Stand back," she said, her voice cool under pressure.

The explosion rang out, deafening in the still night air. The metal gates buckled, giving way as the force of the blast sent debris flying. Alex's mind spun with the chaos, but there was no time to think. He grabbed Sophia's arm and pulled her through the gap in the gates.

"Go!" he urged.

They raced through the factory complex, weaving through the maze of rusted pipes and crumbling concrete walls. The night was filled with the sound of their footsteps, the distant shouts of their enemies, and the rapid crackle of gunfire.

They were almost there. The river was within sight—just a few more steps, and they could disappear into the night.

But just as they reached the riverbank, a shot rang out, striking the ground just inches from Alex's feet.

"Down!" he shouted, pulling Sophia behind a rusted shipping container.

The sound of approaching soldiers was getting louder. They were almost surrounded. Alex's pulse raced, and he could feel the cold sweat on his brow. They couldn't keep running. They had to make a stand, and they had to do it now.

Sophia glanced at him, her eyes hard with determination. "What's the plan?"

Alex's mind raced. There was no backup, no escape route. Only one thing remained.

He reached into his bag and pulled out a small detonator. A grin tugged at his lips despite the danger.

"I think it's time we sent them a message," he said.

Sophia's eyes widened, understanding the gravity of the situation. "Are you sure?"

Alex nodded grimly. "If we're going down, we're taking them with us."

He pressed the button, and the ground beneath their feet shook as a massive explosion erupted in the distance, sending a plume of smoke into the sky. The shockwave rippled through the air, knocking both of them to the ground.

For a moment, everything was still. The dust settled, and the sound of the river rushing by seemed louder than ever.

Sophia scrambled to her feet, pulling Alex up with her. "Did you—"

Alex nodded, his expression hard. "We've bought ourselves some time. Now let's finish this."

They sprinted toward the river, the chaos of the explosion still echoing in their ears. The water ahead was their only chance to escape.

But as they reached the river's edge, Alex stopped, his eyes narrowing as he scanned the area. Something wasn't right.

Suddenly, a voice broke the silence.

"You can't escape, Alex."

Alex froze. The voice was familiar—too familiar.

He turned slowly, his hand instinctively reaching for his gun.

From the shadows, a figure stepped forward.

It was Eva.

And she wasn't alone.

Eva stood there, her silhouette framed by the dim glow of the fire still burning in the distance. She wore a cold expression, her face partially obscured by the darkness. Behind her, two armed men emerged from the shadows, their weapons pointed directly at Alex and Sophia.

"Eva," Alex said, his voice barely a whisper. His mind raced as he tried to process the situation. "What are you doing here? I thought you were—"

"Dead?" Eva finished for him, her lips curling into a bitter smile. "I'm very much alive, Alex. And I'm here because you have something I want."

Sophia's hand shifted to her gun, her stance defensive. "You won't get away with this. There's no way out for you now."

Eva's eyes flicked to Sophia, a sharp glint of amusement in her gaze. "You think you're in control of this situation? I think you're mistaken." She stepped closer, the sound of her boots crunching on the gravel echoing in the silence. "You've made a mess of things, Alex. But it doesn't have to end like this."

Alex's heart pounded in his chest. The last few days, the betrayals, the lies, the constant sense of being hunted—it all led to this moment. Eva. He had thought she was on his side, but in the end, it had always been about power. About survival.

"You've always been good at playing both sides," Alex said, his voice laced with venom. "But this? This is a new low, even for you."

Eva's lips twisted into a cruel smile. "I don't care for your moral judgments, Alex. In the end, it's about who survives. And it won't be you."

Sophia's eyes flickered to Alex, a silent question passing between them. It was clear that they were trapped. They couldn't run. Not anymore.

"What do you want, Eva?" Alex demanded, trying to buy time, his fingers flexing around the grip of his weapon.

"The same thing I've always wanted," she said, her tone almost playful. "Power. Control. And now, you've handed it to me on a silver platter. All I need is the data you've been carrying. The one thing that will finally ensure my position."

Alex's mind raced. The data. The information they had gathered over the last few weeks was a ticking time bomb—too dangerous in the wrong hands. If Eva got her hands on it, everything they had fought for, every sacrifice made, would be for nothing.

"You won't get it," he said firmly, his voice steady despite the tension in the air.

Eva raised an eyebrow. "You think I'm just going to let you walk away after all this? You know too much. You've already seen too much. No, Alex. You're not walking away."

There was no hesitation in her voice, no doubt. She had already made her decision.

Before Alex could react, she gestured to the men behind her. They advanced, their weapons aimed directly at him and Sophia.

In that moment, everything slowed. Alex's mind clicked into overdrive, each possibility unfolding in rapid succession. There was no time to strategize, no room for negotiation. They were past that point.

"We're not dying here," Alex said, his voice firm. "Not like this."

Without warning, he lunged to the side, pushing Sophia down to the ground as the first shot rang out. The bullet whizzed past them, missing by inches. The second shot followed, but Alex was already moving, rolling behind the nearest shipping container for cover. Sophia scrambled to her feet, her gun drawn.

"Keep moving!" Alex shouted.

They didn't have the luxury of thinking things through. They had to act, and they had to act fast. They couldn't afford another mistake.

From behind their cover, Alex and Sophia fired back, aiming for the two armed men with Eva. The shots were quick, controlled, and sharp—targeting their weapons, disabling them. It wasn't enough to take them down completely, but it gave them a moment to regain control of the situation.

Eva, still standing calmly, surveyed the chaos unfolding before her. "You're not fast enough, Alex," she called out, her voice cutting through the noise. "This is the end of the road for you."

With a sudden movement, she disappeared into the shadows, her footsteps silent but purposeful. Alex's pulse quickened. Where was she going?

"Watch the flanks!" he yelled at Sophia, his eyes darting around as he tried to locate Eva's position.

But it was too late.

A sudden explosion shook the ground beneath them, the shockwave sending debris flying through the air. Alex barely had time to react as the world around him erupted in a blinding burst of light and sound. The explosion was close—too close—and the force of it knocked him to the ground, his vision spinning.

"Alex!" Sophia shouted, scrambling to his side.

He could hear the sounds of soldiers approaching, the sound of boots pounding against the earth. They didn't have much time.

"Move!" Alex grunted, pushing himself up with difficulty. His head was spinning, and his ears were ringing, but there was no time to recover.

They sprinted toward the river's edge once more, but the explosion had scattered their attackers, creating a brief moment of chaos they could exploit.

The water loomed ahead, a dark, cold abyss that seemed to promise escape but also threatened to swallow them whole.

Alex's mind raced. There had to be another way. They couldn't just dive into the river and hope to survive. They needed a plan—a way to get the upper hand before Eva and her men closed in again.

"We'll have to use the boat," Sophia said, her voice urgent. "The one docked on the far side. It's the only way we'll get out of here."

Alex nodded. His heart hammered in his chest as they pushed forward. Their last chance of survival was fading fast.

But the moment they reached the riverbank, a voice rang out, cold and mocking.

"You really thought you could escape, Alex?"

Eva stepped forward from the shadows, her eyes gleaming with satisfaction.

Alex froze for a split second, his heart pounding in his chest. He could feel the weight of their situation sinking in, the ever-present threat of failure closing in around them. Eva was right there, no longer the ally he had once believed her to be. She had outmaneuvered them every step of the way.

"We've been down this road before, Alex," Eva's voice sliced through the air like a razor. "You've made your choice, and I've made mine."

Sophia was already moving again, her steps quick and decisive. She darted to the side, taking cover behind a stack of wooden crates, her gun trained on Eva's position. Alex followed suit, instinctively drawing his weapon.

"You can't control everything, Eva," Alex called out, his voice low but firm, trying to regain some sense of control. "This game isn't over. Not yet."

Eva laughed, a cold, calculating sound. "I don't need to control everything. I just need to control you. And I'm doing that quite well, don't you think?"

She stepped forward again, her posture unbothered, like she had already won. But Alex could see the flicker of impatience in her eyes. She wasn't as certain as she pretended to be. There was a moment, a sliver of hesitation, that might just be their chance.

The tension in the air was palpable, thick enough to suffocate them. Every sound, every movement felt like it could tip the scale. The distant hum of the river, the rustle of the wind through the trees, the soft hiss of their breath—it all felt amplified, as if the world itself was holding its breath.

Sophia glanced at Alex, their eyes locking for a brief moment. They didn't need words; they knew what had to be done.

Alex was the first to move, pushing himself up from behind the cover, his weapon raised. He didn't wait for Eva to react—he fired first, aiming for her men. The shot rang out, sharp and loud, and one of the men fell to the ground, clutching his leg. The other reacted too slowly, raising his weapon just in time to be met by a well-placed shot from Sophia.

Eva didn't flinch. Her gaze never wavered, even as her men went down. She was calculating, always a step ahead, and Alex knew it. But in that moment, she hesitated, just enough to give them a sliver of hope.

"Don't make this harder than it needs to be," she said coldly, her voice quiet but fierce. "You've lost, Alex. This is your final warning."

But Alex wasn't ready to back down. Not yet.

"This isn't the end," he shot back, narrowing his eyes. "You can't just erase everything that's happened."

Without warning, he bolted toward the riverbank, making a break for the boat that awaited them. Sophia followed closely behind, her boots pounding against the dirt, but she kept her eyes on Eva.

The seconds stretched into eternity as Alex's legs burned, the distance between them and the boat seeming to grow with each passing moment. But the sound of gunfire echoed through the night, and Alex felt the sharp sting of a bullet graze his shoulder.

"Alex!" Sophia shouted, her voice full of alarm.

He stumbled but kept moving, adrenaline coursing through him. They had no choice now. They couldn't stop. Not now.

He reached the edge of the river and dove into the boat, pulling himself up onto the deck. Sophia followed, jumping into the boat just as the next bullet whizzed past them.

"Go!" Alex barked, gripping the oars. "We're not out of this yet."

Sophia wasted no time, grabbing the other set of oars and beginning to row as fast as she could. The boat lurched forward, its engine sputtering to life in the cold night air.

But just as they thought they might make it—just as the river stretched out before them, a path to freedom—a burst of gunfire tore through the air. Eva wasn't going to let them escape so easily.

They both ducked instinctively, the sound of the bullets splashing in the water around them. Alex's heart raced as he frantically looked around. The shore was too far to reach quickly, and there were no cover points in sight.

"We need to lose her," he muttered, his mind scrambling for a plan. The current was swift, and the river was dark, but it could work to their advantage.

Sophia glanced back at the shoreline, her eyes hard with determination. "If we go farther downstream, there's a series of rapids up ahead. We can use it to get away, but we have to be quick."

Alex nodded, trusting her instinct. "Then let's move. Full speed."

They pushed the boat harder, their strokes synchronized, the water rushing beneath them as they fought to get as far downstream as possible before Eva could get close enough to take another shot.

But the tension never eased. The sound of the pursuit lingered in the distance, and Alex knew they weren't safe—not yet.

The night seemed endless, the only sounds the rush of the river and the pounding of their hearts.

And then, through the darkness ahead, they saw it.

The rapids.

The water churned, frothing violently as it rushed over jagged rocks. It would be treacherous, but it was their best shot.

"Hold on!" Alex shouted as he gripped the oars with all his strength.

Sophia braced herself, her eyes wide, but there was no turning back now.

Together, they plunged into the rapids.

The boat lurched violently as the water swallowed them, twisting and tossing them in every direction. They struggled to keep control, but the force of the current was too strong. The boat hit a rock, and for a moment, Alex feared it would capsize. But with one final, desperate push, they were carried through the worst of it, the boat somehow staying afloat as they were thrown toward calmer waters.

They didn't stop to look back. They couldn't afford to.

The shore was still a ways off, but they were free. For now.

But as they rowed into the night, Alex couldn't shake the feeling that Eva was still out there, somewhere in the shadows, waiting for the right moment to strike.

The hours dragged on, the night sky above them slowly transitioning from inky black to a muted shade of gray as dawn began to break. The boat bobbed gently on the now calmer waters, but Alex felt no sense of relief. He kept his eyes on the distant shore, knowing that even though they had escaped the immediate danger, they were far from safe.

Sophia was silent beside him, her face drawn, the weight of their escape settling over her like a heavy cloak. The adrenaline had begun to wear off, leaving a cold exhaustion in its place. Yet there was something in her eyes—determination, steel—that told Alex she wasn't ready to give up.

"We can't stop now," she finally said, breaking the silence. "If Eva's after us, we need to keep moving."

Alex nodded, though his muscles screamed for rest. "Agreed. But we need to think this through. She's not going to stop. She's playing a long game, and we've just entered the next phase."

Sophia glanced at him, her brow furrowed. "What do you mean?"

"She's calculated," Alex said, his voice steady despite the weariness creeping in. "She won't waste resources chasing us down without a plan. We've probably already been marked. But if we can get ahead of her—get to the right place—we might be able to turn the tide."

The river, though more peaceful now, stretched on endlessly before them. Alex could feel the weight of the journey ahead pressing down on him. Every decision mattered. Every move counted. They couldn't afford another misstep.

Sophia adjusted her position, turning to face him with a sharp look in her eyes. "Where do we go from here?"

Alex hesitated for a moment. He knew the only place they might find refuge—and answers—was in the city of Belgrade. The chaos of the recent years had turned it into a hotbed of resistance, a place where those who sought to topple the established order had gathered. It was a city of rebellion and unrest, but it was also one of the few places left where they might find allies, where they could regroup and plan their next move.

"We head to Belgrade," Alex said firmly. "It's a long shot, but it's our best option."

Sophia didn't argue. She simply nodded, her face hardening with the resolve that had become a trademark of their survival. They both understood that the road ahead would be fraught with danger, but there was no other choice.

They turned the boat toward the distant horizon, the city of Belgrade now their only hope. As they rowed, the sun slowly rose above them, casting long shadows over the river's surface, a reminder of the dark world they were trapped in.

The next several days blurred together in a haze of exhaustion and danger. The river had become their lifeline, but it also made them vulnerable, exposed to anyone with the means to track them. They avoided major towns, steering clear of any signs of civilization that might give away their position.

On the fourth day, as they neared the outskirts of Belgrade, the tension in the air became almost unbearable. Alex could feel the eyes of unseen enemies on them, his instincts screaming that they were being watched.

"We're close," Sophia said, her voice low but firm. "We need to get off the water. Now."

Alex didn't need any further convincing. They had come this far, but the city loomed ahead like a beast waiting to devour them. They needed to disappear into its labyrinthine streets, to find the people who might still be loyal to the cause.

They made landfall in the early morning hours, the sun just beginning to rise as they pulled the boat into a small, secluded dock hidden by a grove of trees. Alex scanned the surroundings, his hand resting on the grip of his gun. The silence was deafening, broken only by the occasional rustle of leaves in the wind.

"Stay sharp," he murmured to Sophia as they made their way through the overgrown paths toward the heart of the city.

The streets of Belgrade had changed since Alex had last seen them. They were a mixture of the familiar and the foreign, the old city now overrun by the remnants of the war—buildings half-collapsed, windows shattered, graffiti scrawled on every surface. It was a city in transition, a place of chaos, but beneath that chaos lay a quiet undercurrent of defiance.

As they moved deeper into the city, Alex's mind raced. They were entering enemy territory now. Eva's reach had likely extended here, and the stakes were higher than ever.

They made their way to a nondescript building on the edge of the city, its exterior weathered but solid. A safehouse, a place where they could lay low and figure out their next move. It was a known location among the resistance, a meeting point for those who wished to remain out of the enemy's sight.

Sophia knocked once, sharply, on the door. A moment passed before a voice called from inside.

"Who's there?"

"It's us," Sophia replied, her voice steady despite the tension in the air. "Alex and Sophia."

There was a brief pause before the door creaked open, revealing a tall, wiry man with dark, calculating eyes. He didn't smile, but there was recognition in his gaze.

"Come in," he said, stepping aside to allow them inside.

They entered quickly, their movements practiced, and the door shut behind them with a soft click.

Inside, the room was dimly lit, the air thick with the scent of dust and old wood. The furnishings were simple—wooden tables, mismatched chairs, a few candles flickering in the corners. A small fire burned in the hearth, casting a warm glow on the walls.

"We thought you wouldn't make it," the man said, his voice quiet but tinged with relief. "It's getting harder to stay out of sight."

Alex nodded, glancing around the room. There were others here, faces familiar and unfamiliar alike, all hardened by the war, all with their own stories of survival and loss.

"We need to know what's going on," Alex said. "Is there anything new? Any sign of Eva or her people here?"

The man, whose name was Viktor, shook his head. "Not yet. But you're right to be cautious. They're closing in, and they'll be looking for you. We've heard whispers of something bigger brewing. The power struggle's intensifying. Eva's connections are growing."

Alex's stomach churned at the thought. They had been running from one danger to the next, but the true battle—what was coming next—was something far more insidious.

He glanced at Sophia, their silent agreement clear. They weren't just fighting for survival anymore. They were fighting for the future.

And that fight was only just beginning.

As the door shut behind them, the weight of the moment settled over Alex and Sophia. The safehouse felt like a temporary reprieve, but both knew it wouldn't be long before the city's undercurrents of danger would find them again. The room was dim, lit only by the flickering firelight and a few candles that cast erratic shadows on the cracked walls. Despite the sense of safety here, Alex's instincts remained sharp, ever alert to any sign of the enemy.

Viktor led them to a table where a map of Belgrade was spread out, littered with notes and markings, a visual representation of the city's fragile power balance. The map seemed to pulse with potential, but also with the risk of exposure. Alex took a seat at the table, pulling it closer to examine the points of interest marked on it.

"Do you trust anyone here?" Alex asked, his voice low, his gaze never leaving the map.

Sophia studied the room, then glanced at Viktor, who was now busy adding a few new notations to the map. "We have to trust someone, or we're dead," she replied quietly.

Alex's fingers hovered over a cluster of markings near the eastern edge of the city. There was one that stood out—a symbol that didn't belong to any faction he recognized. He leaned in closer.

"What's this?" he asked, pointing at the mark.

Viktor looked up, his face grim. "That's a private network," he said, his voice low. "It's not part of the major resistance groups. They're... more subtle. They work in the shadows, gathering intelligence, manipulating things from behind the scenes."

Alex frowned. "And you're sure they're not working with Eva?"

"Not sure, but highly doubtful," Viktor replied, shaking his head. "They've got their own agenda, and it's not tied to Eva's ambitions. At least not directly."

Sophia stepped forward, her eyes narrowed. "So, they might be useful?"

"They might," Viktor agreed. "But trust comes at a price, and their methods... they're not always clean."

Alex looked over at Sophia, the decision clear between them. The private network might be their only chance to gain an advantage, but dealing with them could drag them deeper into the web of intrigue and danger. Still, it was better than sitting in a room, waiting for something to happen.

"We need to meet with them," Alex said after a beat, his voice firm. "We have no other option."

---

The streets of Belgrade felt different by night. The city, which had once pulsed with energy and life, now felt like a shadow of itself, its vibrant heart stifled by the weight of war. As Alex and Sophia made their way through narrow alleys and darkened streets, the reality of their situation grew heavier. They weren't just fleeing anymore—they were taking risks, making moves that could turn the tide of their struggle.

They reached an inconspicuous building nestled between two crumbling structures, the entrance guarded by a lone figure who motioned for them to come forward.

"Names?" the guard asked, his voice flat, impersonal.

"Sophia and Alex," she replied smoothly, her eyes scanning their surroundings. "We're here to talk."

The guard studied them for a moment, then nodded, stepping aside to let them through.

Inside, the air was thick with a sense of quiet urgency. The building, which looked like little more than a dilapidated warehouse on the outside, was buzzing with activity. People moved through the shadows, speaking in hushed tones, their faces grim, focused. There was an undercurrent of tension, a feeling that this was a place on the edge, where everything could change with a single wrong move.

Alex could feel it—the weight of the choices they were about to make. It wasn't just about survival anymore. It was about the fate of something much larger than them.

They were led to a room at the back of the building, where a tall man with a sharp, calculating gaze awaited them. He didn't rise when they entered, but his eyes scanned them with a sense of quiet appraisal.

"You're the ones looking to change things," he said, his voice low, yet commanding.

Alex nodded, stepping forward. "We don't have much time. We need information. We need to know what's happening, and we need to know if you can help."

The man—whose name was Lucian—leaned back in his chair, fingers steepled. "Help?" he repeated, a slight smile tugging at his lips. "I don't offer help, not without something in return. And you're already in deeper than you realize."

Sophia's eyes narrowed. "What's that supposed to mean?"

Lucian met her gaze, his expression unreadable. "It means that the game you're playing—it's not just about running from Eva anymore. There's a larger game at play. And if you want to survive it, you'll need to understand the rules."

Alex exchanged a quick glance with Sophia. The moment had come to decide whether they would risk their lives on Lucian's terms or walk away, hoping to find another way.

"We're listening," Alex said finally, his voice steady.

Lucian smiled slightly, then motioned to a map laid out before him, much like the one Viktor had shown them earlier. "Then let's begin. There are forces at work here that none of you truly understand. And if you're to survive, you'll need to understand them quickly. Starting with this—" He tapped a marked area on the map. "The heart of Belgrade. The seat of power. But it's not just about what's inside. It's about what's hidden beneath it."

Alex felt his pulse quicken. The heart of Belgrade. Beneath it.

He had no idea what Lucian was referring to, but he could feel the weight of what was being asked of them. They were no longer just fighting for their survival. They were on the brink of something much larger. Something that could either save or destroy everything they had fought for.

Lucian's fingers hovered over the map, tracing the lines with slow deliberation. His voice dropped to a whisper, though the intensity of his words made it feel as if they were being shouted in the confined space.

"What you see on this map," he said, "is the surface. But below Belgrade, beneath the buildings, the streets, the history itself, there's another world—a world you won't find on any official record. This underground network isn't just about survival. It's about control. And those who control it pull the strings of everything above."

Sophia leaned forward, her brow furrowing. "Underground network? What are you talking about?"

Lucian looked at her, his expression hardening. "I'm talking about the things you never thought existed—the infrastructure that keeps this city running despite the chaos. The ones who control it have been here longer than any of us, manipulating events, shaping the future of this place."

Alex felt his stomach twist. "And you think they're involved in the war? In the political instability?"

Lucian's eyes met his, and for a moment, Alex thought he saw something darker behind them—something personal. "They've been involved in every major shift, every coup, every revolution.

And now, they're positioning themselves for the final blow. Eva's ambitions? They're just part of the chaos. But the real players, the ones who will determine the future of this city... they are in the shadows. They always have been."

Sophia's voice was sharp, cutting through the thick tension in the room. "So, what exactly do you want from us?"

Lucian smiled, but it was devoid of warmth. "I want you to get close to the power source—the heart of the city, where their plans are being forged. And I want you to destroy it. Burn it to the ground."

Alex felt the weight of his words settle in. Destroy the heart of the city? It sounded impossible. But something in Lucian's demeanor told him that this wasn't just a suggestion. It was an ultimatum.

"And why should we trust you?" Alex asked, his voice steady despite the gnawing sense of danger.

Lucian's smile faded, replaced by something more calculating. "Because, like you, I have something to lose. And if you don't do this, you won't have a chance to stop them from taking everything."

The room grew colder, the silence hanging between them like a heavy fog. Sophia glanced at Alex, the weight of the decision pressing on both of them. There was no easy way out. If they walked away, they risked missing a chance to uncover the truth and stop a force that could reshape the entire city. But if they accepted, they would be diving deeper into the abyss, with no guarantee of survival.

Finally, Alex spoke, his voice low but resolute. "We'll do it. But we need information—everything you know."

Lucian's eyes gleamed with a flicker of approval. "Of course. I'll give you the tools you need to succeed. But understand this—once you go down this path, there's no turning back."

The words echoed in the room, a warning, a promise, and a threat all in one.

Hours later, Alex and Sophia found themselves in the heart of Belgrade's underground world, a network of tunnels, secret chambers, and hidden rooms that had been untouched by the chaos above. It was a world older than the city itself, a relic of power and secrecy, where every step felt like it brought them closer to an unknown end.

As they navigated through the dark corridors, the air thick with dust and decay, Alex couldn't shake the feeling that they were being watched. Every shadow seemed to move, every creak of the floorboards made him tense. They had crossed into enemy territory, and there was no way of knowing who—or what—was waiting for them.

At the far end of the tunnel, a door loomed before them, its metal surface cold and unyielding. Lucian had given them the key, but even with it in hand, Alex felt a surge of doubt. This was it. Whatever lay beyond this door would determine their fate.

Sophia placed her hand on the door, her fingers brushing the handle. She turned to Alex, her expression hard but focused.

"This is it," she said, her voice low. "Once we open this door, there's no going back."

Alex nodded. "We do this together."

With a deep breath, they pushed the door open.

Beyond it was a vast, cavernous space—an enormous chamber filled with ancient machinery and strange devices that hummed with life. The walls were lined with monitors, cables snaking across the floor like veins feeding into the heart of the machine. In the center of the room stood a large, imposing device, its purpose unclear, but its presence undeniable.

"This is it," Alex whispered, feeling the weight of the room press down on him. "This is the heart of it all."

Sophia stepped forward, her eyes scanning the room, taking in every detail. "What is this? What are they using it for?"

Before Alex could respond, a voice echoed from the shadows.

"You shouldn't have come here."

The voice was familiar—and yet, it was not. It was low and cold, carrying the weight of authority.

Alex spun around, his heart racing as he saw the figure step into the light.

Eva.

Eva stood before them, her eyes gleaming with a mixture of recognition and cold calculation. Her presence was as imposing as the machinery surrounding them, and the air seemed to hum with tension as she stepped forward, her heels clicking sharply against the concrete floor.

"I knew you would come," Eva said, her voice smooth, almost mockingly. "Did you really think it would be this easy? That you could just waltz in here and destroy everything?"

Alex and Sophia exchanged a glance, the weight of the situation settling deeper into their bones. They had come prepared for anything, but Eva's appearance was a twist neither of them had expected. The silence in the room was deafening, the humming machines and flickering monitors the only sound breaking the stillness.

Alex's mind raced. "You're the one behind all of this," he said, his voice steady, though his insides churned with a mixture of anger and disbelief. "You're the one pulling the strings. But why? What's your endgame?"

Eva smiled, but it was a thin, dangerous smile that didn't reach her eyes. "You're too late to understand the full picture, Alex. By now, you should have realized that nothing in this world is as it seems. Everything you think you know is a lie, a carefully constructed illusion."

Sophia's hand tightened around her weapon, her voice low but controlled. "What is this place? What are you planning to do with all this power?"

Eva's gaze flicked to the machinery behind her, a flicker of something dark passing across her features. "This place, these machines... they're not just for surveillance or control. They're for something much bigger. For reshaping the world. We have the power to rewrite history itself, to control perception, to dictate the future. This is no longer about Belgrade, or even Serbia. This is about the world—about the new order we're creating."

Sophia stepped forward, her eyes narrowing. "A new order? You want to control everything, don't you? But what's the cost? What are you willing to sacrifice to achieve this?"

Eva's expression darkened, her smile vanishing entirely. "The cost is irrelevant. Sacrifices must be made for progress. You of all people should understand that, Sophia."

A chill ran through Alex as he remembered the conversations they'd had about sacrifice, about what they were willing to give up for the sake of survival. But this was different. What Eva was proposing wasn't survival—it was domination.

"You think you can control everything with this?" Alex asked, stepping closer, his voice rising with defiance. "You think you can just reshape reality, rewrite history? But you're forgetting one thing. People aren't machines. They won't just bend to your will. Not without a fight."

Eva's eyes glinted with amusement. "You don't understand, Alex. The fight is already over. This is the future. And you are already too deep in it to escape."

Without warning, she reached out, her fingers brushing a nearby console. The room pulsed with a strange energy, and Alex felt a surge of unease crawl up his spine. The machines began to hum louder, the monitors flickering erratically. It was as if the room itself was alive, responding to her touch.

A loud clang echoed through the chamber as a massive gate at the far end of the room began to open, revealing a dark, ominous tunnel leading further into the bowels of the underground complex. Through the widening gap, Alex could just make out the shadowy figures moving within.

Eva's smile returned, but it was cold and unfeeling. "You've walked into my domain. Now, you will see the true power of what we've built. Welcome to the future."

The words hung in the air like a death sentence.

Before Alex or Sophia could react, the figures in the tunnel began to emerge—soldiers, heavily armed and seemingly unstoppable. They were flanked by large mechanical drones, their cold, emotionless eyes scanning the room for threats.

Alex's heart pounded in his chest. They were surrounded.

"Take them," Eva commanded, her voice now devoid of the warmth she had once held. "And make sure they don't leave alive."

The soldiers began to move toward them, the heavy clank of their boots on the stone floor reverberating in the confined space. Alex's mind raced, his instincts kicking into overdrive as he realized the danger they were in.

"Run!" Alex shouted to Sophia, already making a break for the narrow door they had entered through. There was no time to fight, not with the number of armed soldiers closing in. They had to escape—had to get out before it was too late.

Sophia didn't hesitate. She was already at his side, her hand gripping his arm as they sprinted through the labyrinth of tunnels. Behind them, the soldiers were closing in fast, their footsteps echoing louder with each passing second.

But as they rounded a corner, Alex's heart sank. The tunnel ahead was blocked—a dead end.

"Shit!" he hissed, looking around desperately for an escape. There had to be a way out. There had to be!

Sophia's eyes darted around, scanning for any possible exit. "There!" she shouted, pointing to a small opening in the wall, barely big enough for them to crawl through.

Without a second thought, Alex pushed forward, shoving his body through the gap. Sophia followed closely behind, both of them scrambling to make it through the narrow space before the soldiers caught up.

They emerged on the other side into another dark corridor, their breathing ragged as they tried to process what had just happened. Eva's words echoed in Alex's mind, haunting him like a distant warning. The fight was far from over—but the road ahead was more treacherous than they had ever imagined.

Alex and Sophia stumbled down the dark corridor, their breath heavy and shallow. The sound of soldiers' footsteps was distant, but still close enough to make every step they took feel like a race against time. The flickering lights overhead cast eerie shadows on the walls, stretching and shrinking as they hurried forward, the sense of urgency thickening with each passing second.

"We can't keep running forever," Sophia muttered, her voice tinged with both exhaustion and frustration. "Eventually, they'll catch up. We need a plan."

Alex nodded, though his mind raced with a dozen different strategies. None of them felt like they would work. Not against the soldiers, not against the network Eva had built. He wasn't just up against an enemy force—he was up against a vision for the future, one that Eva was willing to destroy anyone who stood in her way to see realized.

They came to another intersection, the tunnel splitting in two directions. Alex hesitated, instinctively pulling Sophia to a stop.

"We need to think this through," he said, his voice low, even as the rush of adrenaline coursed through him. "If we go left, it leads to more tunnels, but they'll know we'll try to escape that way. If we go right, it might lead to an exit, but it's a risk."

Sophia's gaze hardened. "We've been making risky decisions since we set foot in this place. We don't have the luxury of waiting."

Alex clenched his fists, frustrated by the limited options and the growing pressure. The walls felt as though they were closing in, the weight of the moment pressing down on them both.

Sophia's eyes flickered toward the right passage. "We move fast. We don't stop until we hit the end. If it's another dead end, we fight our way out. If it's the exit, we take it."

He nodded, forcing himself to believe they had any real chance of getting out alive. With a silent agreement, they turned to the right and pressed on.

The tunnel seemed endless, each step echoing like a countdown. They barely exchanged words, knowing that speaking would only waste precious seconds. The walls, now slick with moisture, were cold to the touch as Alex's fingers brushed them, grounding him in the reality of their situation.

Suddenly, the tunnel narrowed. At first, it seemed like an obstruction, but then Alex saw the door—a large metal hatch at the far end of the corridor. It stood ajar, barely enough to slip through.

Without a word, they sprinted toward it, their footsteps almost silent on the wet floor. As they neared the hatch, the sound of the soldiers' pursuit grew louder, an unmistakable rhythm of heavy boots that made Alex's blood run cold. They had mere seconds before their enemies would be upon them.

Alex shoved the hatch open, his heart pounding in his chest. They tumbled through it and into an open, bleak space—a vast chamber of metal and concrete that stretched for miles in every direction. It was the kind of place you only saw in nightmares, abandoned but somehow still alive with the hum of hidden machinery, the air thick with decay.

Sophia caught her breath, scanning the room with sharp eyes. "Where are we?"

Alex didn't have an answer. The chamber seemed like a forgotten corner of the complex, one that wasn't meant to be found. It was empty, except for the strange, unmarked equipment lining the walls. His gaze moved to the far corner, where a dim light flickered faintly.

"Let's move," he urged. "We'll find something—anything—that can help us get out of here."

They moved cautiously, but time was running out. Every moment they lingered, the soldiers would be closing in, and Eva's plan would unfold without any chance of stopping it. The sound of their footsteps was drowned out by the constant hum of machinery, a reminder that they weren't truly alone in this dark, forgotten place.

As they reached the far corner of the chamber, Alex's eyes fell on something unexpected—a map, pinned to the wall. It looked old, frayed at the edges, but the symbols on it were clear enough. This was no ordinary facility. It was a network of interconnected underground bunkers, a labyrinth built for a purpose far beyond simple survival.

The map indicated several escape routes, but they were all marked with red crosses. They were traps, clearly designed to mislead or destroy anyone attempting to escape.

But one path remained unmarked, leading to a small, unmarked exit at the far end of the complex.

"That's our way out," Alex whispered, feeling a surge of hope. They had a chance—just one.

Sophia nodded, her expression determined. "Then let's move."

The air grew colder as they advanced, the weight of their every footstep reverberating through the hollow silence of the chamber. They reached the door, and Alex hesitated, his hand on the cold metal handle.

Before he could push it open, a loud crash echoed from behind them. The sound of boots, heavier now, reverberated through the chamber. Their time was up.

Sophia's eyes widened in panic. "They're here!"

Alex didn't wait. He threw the door open, and the two of them bolted into the unknown. The chase had begun in earnest.

The door slammed shut behind them, the heavy thud of metal reverberating through the stillness of the corridor. Alex's heart raced, but he didn't allow himself a moment to catch his breath. They had no time to waste.

They ran down the narrow hallway, the soft echo of their footsteps almost drowned by the sound of their own breathing. The air was thick and damp, and every turn seemed to lead them deeper into the unknown. Alex could hear the soldiers' pursuit in the distance, their voices cutting through the quiet like knives, but they were still a few moments away.

Sophia glanced over her shoulder, her face pale, but her expression was resolute. "Do you think we can outrun them?" she asked, her voice tight.

Alex didn't answer immediately, weighing the possibilities in his mind. "Not forever," he said grimly, "but we just need to get to the exit. We can't let them trap us in here."

Ahead, the hallway seemed to stretch on endlessly, the occasional flicker of a light above casting fleeting shadows along the walls. There was no sign of where they were headed, no indication of the exit they were desperately seeking. But they pushed on, each step taking them further away from the soldiers, and yet closer to an uncertain future.

Suddenly, the path forked again—two tunnels, one to the left, one to the right. Alex's instincts told him to go left, but Sophia reached out, grabbing his arm and pulling him toward the right.

"Wait," she said, her voice sharp. "I think I heard something down that way. Something... off."

Alex hesitated, torn between trusting his instincts and considering her words. He didn't know the layout of the facility, but Sophia's hunches had saved them more than once before. He nodded reluctantly.

"Right it is," he muttered.

They turned and rushed down the right tunnel, the sound of their footsteps now louder, more urgent. The tunnel narrowed even further, the walls pressing in on them, forcing them to move in single file. The air grew colder, and Alex could feel the chill creeping into his bones.

As they rounded another corner, they came to a stop. The hallway opened up into a large, open space—vast and dimly lit, the shadows stretching across the floor in all directions. Alex's eyes scanned the room, instinctively searching for any sign of danger.

It wasn't long before he saw it.

In the center of the room stood a large, metallic structure, covered in rust and decay. It looked like some kind of generator or control center, with a series of large, coiled wires protruding from it, some sparking with electricity. Around it, scattered debris littered the floor, evidence of hasty departures or forgotten work. The entire place seemed abandoned, yet there was a strange sense of life in the air—an ominous hum that reverberated through the metal walls.

Sophia took a step forward, her gaze fixed on the structure. "This doesn't look right. We should keep moving."

But Alex wasn't listening. Something about the generator intrigued him—it felt like the key to something bigger. Maybe it was the way the wires seemed to pulse, or how the machinery seemed... alive.

He approached it cautiously, reaching out to touch one of the wires, only to pull his hand back when a sudden shock of electricity surged through the air. The hair on the back of his neck stood up.

"Alex, get away from there!" Sophia shouted, but Alex was already moving, his mind racing.

The hum of the machine seemed to grow louder, as if responding to his presence. He could feel the heat radiating from the device, and the air seemed to grow thicker, charged with a strange energy.

A crackling sound echoed from the walls, and Alex spun around just as the lights flickered violently.

And then, the wall to their left collapsed.

Chunks of concrete and steel rained down, and from the dust and debris emerged a group of soldiers—armed, their faces masked, their eyes cold and determined. They had caught up.

Sophia's voice broke through the tension. "We have to go. Now!"

Alex didn't hesitate this time. He grabbed Sophia's arm and pulled her towards the far side of the room. But as they ran, Alex felt the ground tremble beneath his feet. The generator—whatever it was—seemed to be powering up, its hum now a steady roar. And then, a deafening explosion ripped through the chamber.

The blast sent Alex and Sophia sprawling, their bodies thrown against the hard floor. Pain shot through his side, and for a moment, the world spun around him. Dust filled his lungs, and his ears rang.

When he managed to push himself up, he found Sophia already on her feet, her face grim.

"Are you okay?" she asked, though her voice was tight with fear.

Alex nodded, though his ribs ached with every breath. "We need to get out of here, now."

The soldiers were closing in, their presence unmistakable. The explosion had only bought them a few precious seconds. Alex's mind raced—there was no time to linger. They had no other option but to run.

He grabbed Sophia's hand, and together they bolted toward the far end of the room, their feet pounding against the floor, their breath coming in sharp gasps.

The only question now was whether they could escape the labyrinth—or if the maze would finally swallow them whole.

They reached the far end of the room, where a small, narrow door stood ajar. Alex didn't stop to question why it was there or who had left it open. The only thing that mattered now was getting through it.

He pushed the door open, its rusty hinges groaning in protest. The dim light from the generator flickered behind them, casting long shadows in the narrow hallway that stretched ahead. The air was thick with the smell of damp concrete and something metallic, but there was no time to focus on the details. Every second counted.

Sophia was right behind him, her grip tightening around his hand as they moved further into the corridor. They ran in silence, the only sound their hurried footsteps and the occasional distant clang of metal from somewhere in the dark depths of the complex.

The tunnel twisted and turned, leading them deeper into the unknown. Alex couldn't remember how long they had been running. It felt like hours, though he knew it had only been minutes. The adrenaline was beginning to wear off, leaving behind a gnawing exhaustion that threatened to slow him down. But he couldn't stop. Not now.

"We're almost there," Sophia whispered, though Alex wasn't sure whether she was trying to convince him or herself.

He didn't reply. Instead, he focused on the path ahead, every sense heightened as he anticipated the next turn, the next challenge that awaited them.

And then, just as they rounded another corner, they stumbled into a dead end.

The walls were solid, the narrow passageway abruptly halting in front of them. Alex froze, his breath catching in his throat. There was no way forward.

"Dammit," he muttered under his breath, trying to calm his racing heart. He turned to look at Sophia, her face as pale as his own. They were trapped.

Behind them, the faint sound of footsteps grew louder. The soldiers were getting closer, and there was no more time to waste. The walls felt like they were closing in, the oppressive silence of the hallway pressing in on him. His mind raced, desperate for a solution, for a way out.

Then, just as hope began to slip away, a faint sound reached his ears. A soft, almost imperceptible click.

Before he could process it, the wall in front of them shifted. Slowly, it slid open, revealing a narrow, hidden passage beyond.

Alex didn't hesitate. He grabbed Sophia's hand and pulled her forward, the door closing behind them with a soft hiss. The passage was even darker than the corridor they had just fled, but it was their only chance.

They moved quickly, navigating the cramped space with barely enough room to breathe. The air was stale, and the walls felt like they were closing in on them with each step, but Alex didn't allow himself to think about it. Not now.

"Where does this lead?" Sophia asked, her voice trembling slightly.

"I don't know," Alex admitted, his voice tight. "But we don't have a choice."

They kept moving, their footsteps echoing in the narrow tunnel, each step carrying them further into the heart of the complex. They didn't know what awaited them on the other side, but they couldn't afford to look back.

Finally, after what felt like an eternity, the tunnel opened up into a larger chamber. This one, unlike the others, was completely still. There was no sound, no movement. Just the silence of an abandoned space, as though it had been untouched for years.

Alex paused, his heart still racing, his senses alert. Something felt wrong. There was a presence in the air, something that made the hairs on the back of his neck stand up. He glanced around the room, his eyes scanning for any signs of danger.

Sophia stood beside him, equally tense. "What is this place?"

Alex didn't answer. He was too focused on the strange feeling in the air, the sense that they were being watched. Something wasn't right, and he had no intention of sticking around to find out what.

"We need to move," he said, his voice low but urgent.

They started across the room, the floor beneath their feet creaking as they walked. Each step felt heavier than the last, the weight of their situation pressing down on them. They had no idea where this new path would lead, but they knew they couldn't turn back.

Then, just as they reached the far wall, a sudden movement caught Alex's eye. A shadow shifted, almost imperceptible, but enough to send a jolt of fear through his body.

Before he could react, the figure stepped into the light.

It was a man—tall, wearing a military uniform, his face obscured by a helmet. His presence was imposing, and the way he moved suggested that he knew exactly what they were doing here. There was no mistaking it—this man was no ordinary soldier.

Alex's mind raced. Who was he? Was he friend or foe?

"Stay back," the man's voice was calm, but there was an underlying menace to it that sent a chill down Alex's spine. "You're not supposed to be here."

Alex didn't hesitate. He pulled Sophia behind him, standing his ground. "What do you want from us?" he demanded, his voice sharp.

The man didn't answer right away. Instead, he took a step forward, his movements slow and deliberate.

Then, without warning, the ground shook beneath them, and a loud rumble filled the room. It was as if the entire complex was coming alive, responding to something they couldn't see.

Sophia gasped, her eyes wide with fear. "What's happening?"

The man's expression didn't change. "You've activated it," he said simply.

"Activated what?" Alex demanded, his heart pounding in his chest. "What is going on here?"

But the man didn't answer. Instead, he stepped aside, revealing a hidden door behind him.

"You'll find your answers through there," he said. "But I'm afraid it's not going to be easy."

Alex stared at the man, his pulse quickening. What did he mean by "activated it"? He didn't have time to process it; they had no choice but to move forward.

Sophia's hand tightened around his, her fingers cold with fear. "We have to go, Alex," she whispered, her voice strained.

Without another word, Alex stepped toward the hidden door. It slid open smoothly, revealing a dark, narrow corridor beyond. The faint hum of machinery vibrated through the walls, almost like a heartbeat, pulsing in time with the rapid beat of his own heart.

They moved quickly, the air growing heavier as they went deeper into the complex. The walls seemed to close in on them, the darkness growing more suffocating with every step. The silence was unnerving, broken only by their footsteps and the distant thrum of unseen engines.

They reached another door, this one much larger, made of thick steel. It seemed impenetrable, but the hum of the machines was louder here, as if the room behind it held the answers they were searching for.

Sophia's hand was shaking as she reached for the handle, but Alex stopped her. "Wait," he murmured, his mind racing. Something was off. The very air felt wrong here—charged, like it was waiting for something.

A sudden metallic clang sounded behind them, echoing down the corridor. The hairs on the back of his neck stood up. He turned quickly, instinctively, but saw nothing. The shadow of the man in the military uniform was gone.

"We're not alone," Alex said, his voice low, urgent.

Sophia nodded, her face pale. "What now?"

"Move quickly," Alex replied. "We don't know how much time we have."

With a final glance over his shoulder, Alex grabbed the door handle and pulled it open. The sight before them took his breath away.

Inside the room, a massive control center stretched out, filled with rows of computers and monitors. The faint green glow of the screens illuminated the darkened space, casting eerie shadows on the walls. At the center of the room stood a large, cylindrical device, its purpose unclear but ominous.

The room seemed alive, buzzing with energy. The air was thick with the hum of the machinery, and the distant sound of gears turning echoed through the silence. But it wasn't just the machines that caught Alex's attention—it was the screens.

The monitors flickered, displaying cryptic symbols and maps that seemed to shift and change with every passing second. Red dots appeared on various locations across the globe, lighting up like a warning system. A map of the world, fragmented and covered with blinking indicators, dominated the largest screen.

"God," Alex breathed, stepping forward. "This... this is bigger than we thought."

Sophia stood frozen, her eyes wide in horror. "What is all this?"

Alex didn't answer right away. His eyes darted from screen to screen, trying to make sense of the chaos unfolding before them. A particular map caught his attention—an image of the United States, with lines of red crossing over key cities, like a digital strike map. His stomach twisted with dread.

"Whatever this is," he said slowly, "it's not just a research project. It's a weapon."

Suddenly, the sound of heavy footsteps echoed from the hallway behind them. They turned, hearts racing, but before they could react, the door slammed shut with a deafening clang.

A voice came over the intercom, smooth and cold. "You should not have come here."

Alex's breath caught in his throat. He didn't recognize the voice, but it was authoritative, laced with a venomous calm. It sent a chill through his bones.

He glanced around the room, his mind racing. There had to be a way out.

Sophia's voice cut through the tension. "Alex, look!" She pointed to one of the monitors where a countdown timer was ticking down, its red digits flashing ominously.

"Thirty minutes," Alex muttered, watching the seconds tick by. "We need to figure out what this countdown is before it hits zero."

He moved toward the nearest console, trying to make sense of the controls. But the buttons and screens were alien to him, and the language on the monitors was unfamiliar. It was like looking at a puzzle with no pieces that fit.

Sophia stepped up beside him, her eyes scanning the screens. "We need to disable the countdown," she said, her voice tight. "Whatever this is, it's not going to end well if we don't stop it."

Alex nodded, his mind scrambling for a solution. He glanced at the cylindrical device in the center of the room, its pulsating light flashing in time with the countdown. That was the key.

They moved toward it, but as they did, a low, ominous hum filled the room, growing louder with each passing second. The walls began to tremble, the vibrations shaking the floor beneath their feet.

"Alex, we have to hurry!" Sophia cried, panic rising in her voice.

Alex reached the device, his fingers flying over the controls. A series of symbols flashed on the screen in front of him—none of which made any sense. He cursed under his breath.

Then, as if in response to his frustration, a new prompt appeared: Enter security code.

Alex froze. He had no idea what the code was.

Suddenly, the voice over the intercom spoke again, but this time it was more personal, almost mocking. "You think you can stop this, don't you? You have no idea what you're dealing with."

The room shook again, the countdown now at fifteen minutes.

"We don't have time for this!" Alex shouted, his frustration boiling over. But then, as he stared at the screen, a strange idea clicked in his mind.

The symbols on the screen weren't just random. They were patterns, repeating in a way that suggested a hidden code.

He quickly began entering the symbols in the order he remembered seeing them, his mind racing as he hoped beyond hope that this was the right approach.

Sophia was watching him closely, her hand gripping his arm as if her life depended on his next move.

Finally, after what felt like an eternity, the screen flickered—and then went dark.

For a brief, terrifying moment, Alex thought he had failed. But then, the countdown froze.

The room was silent.

They had bought themselves a little time.

But the bigger question remained: What would happen when the countdown finally reached zero?

The silence in the room was suffocating, the absence of the countdown's ticking a stark contrast to the rapid thrum of Alex's heartbeat. He stood frozen in front of the now dark screen, his breath shallow, waiting for any sign that their actions had made a difference. The seconds felt like minutes, and the seconds stretched into what seemed like an eternity.

Sophia's grip on his arm tightened. "What did you do?" she whispered, her voice trembling.

"I don't know," Alex admitted, the weight of the moment pressing down on him. "But we stopped it for now. I think we've bought ourselves some time."

Before he could speak further, the intercom crackled to life again, its harsh sound cutting through the air.

"You think you've won?" The voice was colder this time, tinged with amusement. "That countdown was only one piece of a much larger plan. You're too late."

A chill crawled down Alex's spine. The voice was mocking, its confidence unshaken, as if it knew they were just pawns in a much bigger game.

"Stay alert," Alex said, his voice steady despite the rising tide of fear. "We can't let our guard down."

Sophia nodded, but her eyes were wide, scanning the room. It felt like they were being watched, the very walls pressing in on them. The oppressive atmosphere, the hum of the machinery, and the cold, calculated voice on the intercom all pointed to the same thing: they were in deep—deeper than they had imagined.

The door they had come through remained locked, and there was no sign of any other exit. The massive cylindrical device in the center of the room stood still, almost waiting, its ominous presence casting a long shadow.

Alex turned to the console beside the device, his mind racing for any kind of clue, any way to make sense of the madness surrounding them. He could feel the weight of the minutes pressing down on him. The voice was right: they had only stopped one countdown. They didn't know what else was in motion.

A flashing symbol caught his attention—a small, almost hidden detail on the screen that hadn't been there before. It looked like a series of coordinates, but the numbers seemed scrambled, shifting before his eyes. He leaned in closer, trying to decipher the meaning.

"Alex..." Sophia's voice was strained, and when he turned to look at her, her face was pale.

"Something's wrong," she said quietly.

A loud bang echoed from the hallway. The door slammed again, the sound reverberating through the complex. They both froze, instinctively moving closer to the center of the room, where they could keep an eye on both the door and the device.

The voice on the intercom was back, but now it was tinged with impatience. "You're wasting time. The mechanism is already in motion. You can't stop it. No one can."

Alex clenched his jaw, his fists tight at his sides. They had no choice now. They had to find a way to stop whatever was coming—and fast.

Suddenly, the lights in the room flickered, and a low growl reverberated through the walls. The hum of the machinery seemed to grow louder, vibrating through the very air around them.

Sophia gasped as the ground beneath them trembled. "What's happening?"

"Get ready," Alex said, his voice tight. He had no idea what was coming next, but he knew it wouldn't be good.

As if on cue, the enormous cylindrical device began to glow brighter. Pulses of light shot from it, illuminating the room with a flickering, erratic glow. The air was thick with energy, like the calm before a storm. Alex's instincts screamed at him to move, to get out, but there was nowhere to go.

Then, the device's hum shifted, becoming deeper, more resonant. A strange, otherworldly noise filled the room, a sound that felt like it was coming from the very core of the earth.

A red light blinked on one of the monitors, followed by a strange series of coordinates and symbols flashing faster than Alex could read. The lights in the room began to flicker violently, the hum of the machinery vibrating through the air. The temperature dropped, and Alex could feel the cold creeping into his bones.

"What the hell is happening?" Sophia whispered, her voice barely audible over the growing noise.

"I think it's beginning," Alex muttered, his stomach churning. "Whatever this is, it's not just a countdown. It's something bigger... and we've just triggered it."

The ground trembled again, this time more violently. The walls shook, the very foundation of the complex groaning under the pressure of whatever was happening. The humming noise grew louder, more insistent, and the lights flickered in rapid succession.

Suddenly, the floor beneath them cracked open with a deafening roar. The ground gave way, and Alex barely had time to react before they were both falling—plummeting into the darkness below.

The last thing Alex saw before the darkness swallowed them whole was the bright, pulsing light of the device, now fully activated.

The fall felt endless. Time seemed to stretch as Alex and Sophia tumbled into the abyss, their bodies twisted and disoriented. The roar of the crash deafened them, and the chaotic screech of metal echoed through the darkness. Then, suddenly, the world seemed to stop spinning.

Alex hit the ground with a sickening thud, his breath knocked out of him. He groaned, pushing himself up, his hands scraping against the cold, rough surface beneath him. Sophia landed beside him with a sharp gasp, and he could hear her wheezing as she struggled to regain her breath.

"What... what just happened?" she asked, her voice weak but laced with fear.

Alex pushed himself to his feet, his legs shaking beneath him. His mind raced to process what had just transpired. The device—the countdown—had triggered something beyond their control. But what? What had they unleashed?

The room around them was pitch black, save for the faint, eerie glow coming from a series of strange, mechanical devices lining the walls. The air was thick with dust and a chilling, oppressive silence that seemed to suffocate them. Their surroundings were unfamiliar—an underground chamber, cold and damp, with walls lined with strange symbols and an architecture that didn't belong to any time period Alex could recognize.

"Stay close," Alex said, his voice low and cautious. He could feel the hair on the back of his neck standing on end. They were not alone. He could sense it.

Sophia nodded, her eyes wide with fear. She glanced nervously at the dark corners of the room, her hand reaching for Alex's arm. "Do you think anyone else is down here?"

Alex shook his head slowly. "I don't know, but we need to get out of here. This place... it feels wrong."

They moved cautiously through the chamber, their footsteps muffled on the cold stone floor. The strange machines hummed softly, as though alive, each one exuding an energy that sent a chill through Alex's bones. Some of the machines appeared to be dormant, while others glowed with an unsettling light, their inner workings concealed behind layers of metal and glass.

Sophia's voice broke the silence. "Alex, look at this." She pointed toward one of the machines, her finger trembling.

Alex followed her gaze, and his breath caught in his throat. The machine she was pointing to was different from the others. It had a large, central core—a dark, pulsating orb—surrounded by metallic arms that extended outward. The orb pulsed with an eerie light, and the air around it seemed to shimmer.

"What is that?" Sophia whispered.

"I don't know, but I think it's connected to what's happening," Alex replied, his eyes narrowing. He approached it cautiously, his instincts telling him not to touch anything, but he had to know. They had to understand what they were dealing with.

The orb flickered, a high-pitched noise emanating from it. It was as though the entire room responded to its pulse, the machines around them vibrating in unison. Alex took a step back, his mind racing. He felt the weight of the moment, the growing sense of urgency. If they didn't stop whatever was happening, they could be too late.

Suddenly, the orb burst with light, blinding them both. Alex instinctively shielded his eyes, and for a moment, everything went completely white. Then, as quickly as it had started, the light faded. He opened his eyes, blinking rapidly to adjust to the sudden change.

What he saw chilled him to the core.

The walls of the chamber had changed. The strange symbols were now glowing with a sickly green light, and the floor beneath them seemed to pulse, as though it were alive. The machines around them had begun to hum louder, the energy in the room building with each passing second.

"Alex," Sophia whispered, her voice trembling. "This... this is not good."

"No," Alex agreed, his voice hardening with resolve. "We have to find a way to stop this—whatever it is."

They began to move again, their steps quicker now, as they searched for any clue, any sign of what they could do to reverse what had been set in motion. But as they reached the far corner of the room, a low growl sounded from the shadows, followed by a series of mechanical whirring noises.

Alex's hand went to the gun at his side, but before he could draw it, a figure stepped out of the darkness.

It was humanoid but not human—tall and skeletal, its eyes glowing with the same eerie green light that now filled the chamber. Its movements were jerky, robotic, and its body seemed to be covered in a layer of blackened metal, a fusion of flesh and machinery.

The creature's lips peeled back into a twisted grin. "You're too late," it said, its voice guttural and cold. "The process has begun. You can't stop it now."

Alex's heart sank. The situation was worse than he had feared. They weren't just up against some rogue device; they were facing something far more insidious, a force that was far beyond their understanding.

Sophia's voice shook as she whispered, "What are you? What do you want from us?"

The creature cocked its head, its glowing eyes narrowing. "What I want is irrelevant," it replied coldly. "What you should be concerned about is what *it* wants." It gestured toward the machines, which now hummed louder, their lights flickering and dimming in time with the rhythm of the creature's voice.

Alex clenched his fists. This was no longer just about surviving. It was about stopping an apocalypse before it was too late.

The creature's words echoed in the cavernous chamber, their meaning sinking deep into Alex's chest. Whatever was unfolding before them, it was far beyond anything they could have imagined. He could feel the tension in the air, thick with anticipation, as though the room itself was holding its breath. The machines hummed in a twisted symphony, growing louder with every passing second, and the orb at the center of the room pulsed menacingly.

Alex stepped back, his instincts screaming at him to run, but he couldn't. Not yet. They needed answers.

"What *is* it?" he demanded, his voice steady despite the dread creeping up his spine. "What's happening here?"

The creature tilted its head, as though considering the question before answering with cold detachment. "It is inevitable," it said simply. "The foundation of this world is cracking, and the new order is rising. The machines will awaken, and they will reclaim the Earth."

Sophia's hand clenched around Alex's arm, her grip tight with fear. "This can't be real," she muttered, as if trying to convince herself more than anyone else.

Alex's mind raced. He had seen too much—there was no time for disbelief. If what this creature was saying was true, the world was on the brink of collapse, and they were caught in the eye of the storm.

"What do you mean by the new order?" Alex pressed, his voice sharper now. "What's your part in this?"

The creature's lips twisted into a smile that held no warmth, just a cruel, knowing mockery. "I am the harbinger of what's to come. A servant of the process." It took a slow step forward, its metallic limbs creaking like old machinery. "You think you can stop it? That you can turn back time? You can't. It's already too late. The seed has been planted."

Sophia recoiled slightly, her face pale with fear, but Alex stood firm, his mind grinding through the possibilities. There had to be a way to fight back. There had to be.

"We're not going to just stand here and let you destroy everything," he said, his voice full of defiance.

The creature chuckled, a low, unsettling sound that made the hairs on Alex's neck stand up. "You think you have control, but you don't. You never did. The machines are coming. And soon, there will be nothing left to fight for."

Sophia's voice was trembling, but she found the strength to speak. "How do we stop it? If we can stop it at all?"

The creature's grin widened, a grotesque rictus that stretched unnaturally across its face. "The process is irreversible. All that remains is to witness the end of this world and the beginning of a new one." It raised one of its long, skeletal arms, and Alex could see the faint blue light flickering beneath its skin—an unsettling reminder of the power it held. "It will not be long now. The final phase will begin soon."

A sudden, blinding light flashed from the machines, and Alex was momentarily blinded. He shielded his eyes instinctively, the world around him turning to a blur of shifting shapes and glowing lights. When his vision cleared, the creature was gone. In its place, the orb in the center of the room pulsed with a sickly green light, the machines now vibrating violently as if alive.

"Alex..." Sophia's voice broke through the chaos, fragile but urgent. "We need to get out of here. Now."

He turned to her, his pulse quickening. She was right. They had no time to waste. Whatever was happening, it was escalating—and they had no way of knowing how far it had already gone.

He grabbed her arm and pulled her toward the entrance they had come through, but as they approached the doorway, the ground beneath them trembled. The door slammed shut with a deafening crash, trapping them inside.

"No," Alex muttered, staring at the closed door with disbelief. He reached for his gun, but before he could draw it, the walls around them began to shift. The stone cracked and groaned, the symbols on the walls glowing brighter, and the very air seemed to distort.

"We're not alone," Sophia whispered, her voice barely audible.

Alex turned toward the far side of the room, where the shadows had begun to shift. From the darkness, more figures emerged—humanoid creatures, like the one they had seen before, their bodies a twisted fusion of flesh and metal. There were more of them now, each one taller, more menacing, their eyes glowing with the same eerie green light.

As one of the creatures stepped forward, its voice echoed through the room, deep and resonant. "You cannot escape what is inevitable."

Alex's heart raced. There was no way out. No way to outrun whatever was happening.

Sophia grabbed his arm, her eyes wide with panic. "What do we do?"

The answer was simple, but its weight was crushing. They had to stop the machines. Whatever this process was, it wasn't just a matter of survival—it was about saving the world, or what was left of it.

Alex took a deep breath, his resolve hardening. "We fight."

The machines hummed louder, their metallic limbs stirring to life. The creatures surrounding them shifted, their unnatural forms gliding silently across the room. Alex's grip tightened around his gun, his finger hovering over the trigger, but his mind raced with uncertainty. Every instinct told him to strike first, but he knew that this wasn't a fight that could be won with brute force alone.

Sophia's breath was shallow beside him, her body rigid with fear, but there was something else in her eyes now—a spark of determination. She wasn't about to give up, not now. And neither was he.

"We need to find the control center," Alex said, his voice steady despite the rising tide of panic in his chest. "If we can shut them down from there, we might have a chance."

Sophia nodded, her eyes scanning the room as the figures drew closer, the air thick with tension. The creatures' eyes flickered with that same unsettling green light, their movements calculated, deliberate. They were not here to negotiate. They were here to end things.

Alex and Sophia backed away toward the far side of the room, where a set of stairs spiraled downward into what appeared to be a lower level. The creatures watched them, motionless, waiting for them to make their move. Every step they took felt like an eternity, the sound of their footsteps amplified by the cavernous chamber.

The hum of the machines became deafening as they reached the stairs, the walls shaking with the weight of their power. The stairs descended into the unknown, but there was no turning back now. They had to move quickly, before the creatures descended upon them.

As they reached the bottom of the stairs, they were met by a massive chamber. The air was thick with heat and the smell of oil and metal. In the center of the room stood a massive control panel, flickering with light and pulsing with the same eerie green glow. It was the heart of the machine—the place where everything converged.

"We have to destroy it," Sophia said, her voice trembling with urgency. "This is it. This is the only way to stop them."

Alex nodded, but as he stepped forward, something shifted in the air. A low growl echoed from the shadows, and the creatures, who had been watching from the top of the stairs, suddenly moved with terrifying speed. They were closing in.

"Get to the control panel!" Alex shouted, his heart pounding as he pushed Sophia ahead of him. He fired his gun, aiming for one of the creatures, but the shot missed, ricocheting off the wall. The creature didn't flinch. Instead, it leaped forward, its metallic claws glinting in the dim light.

Sophia reached the control panel first, her fingers dancing over the buttons with a frantic urgency. The screen flickered, then went black, only to come back to life with a warning: *System failure imminent.*

The creatures were almost upon them now. Alex fired again, this time hitting one of the creatures in the shoulder. It staggered, but didn't fall. It snarled, its body shifting and contorting in a grotesque imitation of pain, before it charged again.

"Do it now!" Alex screamed.

Sophia slammed her palm against a large red button in the center of the panel. The entire room shuddered, and for a moment, everything went silent. But then the machines began to whine, their gears grinding against each other in a horrifying symphony. The lights flickered, the hum of the energy around them intensifying until it felt like the whole world was about to implode.

The creatures recoiled, their bodies twitching as if in response to a signal from the machines. They froze for a moment, and then, as if realizing what had happened, they turned and rushed back toward the stairs, their once-calculated movements now desperate.

"Alex!" Sophia's voice broke through the chaos. "It's not enough! We have to destroy the core. We need to finish it!"

But Alex was already moving, his gun raised as he fired once more at the descending creatures. He knew they couldn't let the machines reactivate. They had to end it here and now.

Without hesitation, he bolted toward the central core of the machine, his eyes locking onto the glowing heart of the system. The machines were starting to power back up, their lights flickering violently, and the creatures were closing in again.

Sophia was at his side, her breath ragged as they reached the core. She pulled a small device from her pack—a detonator. She handed it to him, and together, they attached the device to the core.

"This is it," Alex muttered, his hand trembling as he pressed the button. The explosion that followed was deafening. The world seemed to collapse around them, the shockwave sending them both crashing to the ground.

For a moment, everything was still. The machines, the creatures—they were gone. Silence filled the chamber, broken only by the soft crackle of fire and the distant sound of collapsing metal.

Alex slowly pushed himself up, his body aching from the fall. He looked around, the remnants of the machine scattered in all directions. There was no sign of the creatures. No sign of the danger that had nearly consumed them all.

Sophia was standing beside him, her expression a mixture of exhaustion and relief. She reached out, her hand finding his, and together, they stood in the midst of the ruin they had caused.

"It's over," she whispered, her voice barely audible in the stillness.

Alex didn't answer. He couldn't. There was too much left to process. They had won—for now—but at what cost? The world had been saved, but the path forward was uncertain. There were still so many questions. What was the creature? Where had it come from? And what was the true purpose of the machines?

As the dust settled, one thing was certain. The war wasn't over. It was only just beginning.

The silence was overwhelming, thick with the weight of the destruction they had wrought. The air smelled of burnt metal and ozone, the remnants of the machine core still smoldering, its once-powerful hum now replaced by the eerie stillness of a world left to contemplate its own survival. Alex and Sophia stood amidst the wreckage, their eyes scanning the room, seeking any sign of movement, any indication that their enemies had truly been vanquished.

But there was nothing. Only the distant echoes of a battle fought, and won—for now.

Sophia exhaled slowly, her shoulders slumping as the adrenaline that had fueled her throughout the ordeal began to drain from her body. She looked at Alex, her gaze filled with a mix of exhaustion and disbelief.

"We did it," she said, her voice quiet, as though the enormity of what they had just done hadn't fully settled in yet.

Alex didn't answer immediately. His mind was still racing, processing the enormity of their actions. They had destroyed the machine. They had destroyed the creatures. But was it enough? Would the threat really end here?

The nagging doubt twisted in his chest. He turned to look at the remnants of the control panel, the flickering lights and charred remains of the once-mighty system. There was something unsettling about how easily it had all come to an end. Too easy, almost.

"It's over for now," he said finally, his voice low, thoughtful. "But I don't think it's the end of the war. They'll come back. They'll find a way."

Sophia's eyes met his, a flicker of determination flashing behind her tired expression. "Then we'll be ready."

Alex nodded, his gaze sweeping the room once more. The creatures were gone, but the machines? He knew they were only a small part of a much larger, more complex network. They couldn't have been the only ones. If they had been, then why had the world been thrust into chaos in the first place?

But those questions would have to wait. For now, there was only the present—the aftermath of their struggle. And the world that had been left in the wake of the destruction.

Sophia walked over to the remains of the machine core, her fingers brushing the blackened surface, as if testing the finality of it all. She paused for a moment, then turned back to Alex, her eyes filled with a strange mixture of hope and dread.

"What do we do now?" she asked, her voice barely above a whisper.

Alex's thoughts flickered briefly to the future, to the uncertain road that lay ahead. They couldn't go back to the way things were. Too much had changed, too much had been lost. The world was fractured, its fragile peace shattered by the very machines they had just destroyed.

But there was a sliver of hope, too. They had survived. Against all odds, they had triumphed. They were no longer just survivors; they were the ones who had fought back. And maybe, just maybe, that would be enough to spark something greater—a rebellion, a resistance, a new world built from the ashes of the old.

"We rebuild," Alex said, his voice steady. "One step at a time. And we prepare. Because this isn't over. We have to make sure it never happens again."

Sophia nodded, her face hardening with resolve. "We'll fight. Whatever it takes."

The two of them stood there for a long moment, in the center of the ruin, surrounded by the wreckage of a world they had just saved. But in their hearts, they knew that this was only the beginning.

The war for humanity's future had only just begun.

The days that followed felt like a blur, each one blending into the next as Alex and Sophia navigated the wreckage of their former lives. The world around them was a shattered reflection of what it had once been, cities reduced to crumbled ruins, entire populations scattered and broken. And yet, amid the desolation, there was a stirring—a quiet, persistent movement that whispered of hope.

In the aftermath of the machine's destruction, rumors began to spread. Stories of their victory, of the resistance that had risen from the ashes of a crumbled world. Slowly, almost imperceptibly at first, others began to gather. Survivors from all corners of the Earth, drawn to the idea of rebuilding, of fighting back against the shadows that had threatened to swallow them whole.

Alex and Sophia found themselves at the center of this new movement, not as leaders, but as symbols. They were the first to have dared to challenge the system, the first to have faced the machines head-on and lived to tell the tale. And though they had no desire for power, they knew that the road ahead would demand leadership—whether they wanted it or not.

Their first task was to rally the scattered factions of survivors. Trust had been shattered, alliances broken by years of warfare and manipulation. Rebuilding that trust would be no small feat. But Alex and Sophia knew that it was the only way forward. They needed to unite the survivors under one cause: to ensure that no power, no machine, no shadow would ever again be allowed to hold the world hostage.

The journey was perilous. Each settlement they visited brought its own set of challenges—hostile groups who had their own vision for the future, individuals who had grown too distrustful of anyone, even those who claimed to be allies. Yet, through each encounter, Alex and Sophia found that their resolve only hardened. They weren't just fighting for survival anymore; they were fighting for the very soul of humanity. For a future where people could live without fear of machines controlling their every move.

As they traveled, the resistance grew, fueled by the promise of something better. They began to forge alliances with remnants of old governments, military factions, and even groups of scientists who had once been part of the system they had destroyed. These alliances were fragile, each one tested by the weight of history and the scars of the past. But with every agreement, every handshake, they moved one step closer to the kind of world they envisioned—a world free from the tyranny of machines, from the lies that had once governed every aspect of life.

But not all was peaceful. In the shadows, there were whispers of a new threat—a force that had been lurking, waiting for the right moment to strike. A group of individuals who had escaped the chaos of the machine war, who had hidden in the cracks and crevices of the old world, biding their time. They were the ones who had never truly believed the machines were defeated. The ones who still thought they could use the remnants of that power for their own ends.

Sophia's mind often returned to the chilling thought: Had they truly destroyed the machines? Or had they only scattered them, like broken pieces of a puzzle waiting to be pieced back together?

In the dead of night, when the wind howled through the ruined cities, Alex found himself thinking the same thing. They had won a battle, but the war was far from over. If anything, it had only just begun. The shadow that had loomed over humanity for so long was not one that could be easily erased.

There was a deep unease settling in his gut, one that he couldn't shake. The machines had been destroyed—or so they thought. But there were always remnants, always hidden corners of the old world where the system might still be lurking, waiting to rise again. And as long as those remnants existed, as long as there were people who had once sworn loyalty to the machine, the fight would never truly be over.

Sophia came to him one evening as he sat by the fire, the flickering light casting long shadows across her face. She knelt beside him, her expression thoughtful.

"We can't let our guard down," she said softly, her voice carrying the weight of the unspoken fears that had begun to haunt them both. "Not for a second."

Alex met her gaze, his own face etched with the same weariness. "I know. But what if it's not just about machines anymore? What if we're facing something far worse?"

Sophia's lips tightened, her jaw setting in a way that told him she understood exactly what he meant. They had already fought an enemy that was cold, methodical, and ruthless. But what if the true threat was something more insidious? Something that had taken root in the hearts and minds of people—humanity itself?

The thought chilled Alex to his core. The real war might not be with the machines. It might be with the darkness within.

And so, as they moved forward, their resolve only grew stronger. They would continue to rebuild, to fight, to unite the scattered remnants of humanity. But they would also remain vigilant, ever watchful for the shadows that might one day rise again.

In the end, it would not be the machines they had to fear.

It would be the people who had learned to live in their shadow.

As the days wore on, Alex and Sophia's fears began to materialize. Their efforts to rebuild and unite the survivors seemed to be attracting more attention than they had anticipated, both from allies and enemies alike. The fragile alliances they had forged began to show signs of strain. Old grudges resurfaced, old wounds reopened, and the distrust that had festered for so long began to bubble up to the surface.

Every step forward seemed to lead to two steps back. The shadow of the past loomed larger than ever, threatening to engulf the fragile hope that had begun to take root in the hearts of the survivors. For every town they liberated, for every city they rebuilt, there was a faction waiting in the wings to tear it all down. The struggle for power was as fierce as the one they had fought against the machines, and it became clear that this new war—one born not of technology but of human ambition and fear—would be far more dangerous than they had ever imagined.

Sophia had noticed the change in the people they encountered. They had once been eager, desperate for a new beginning, but now there was a sense of hesitation, even fear. The scars of the machine war were still fresh, but now there was something more insidious at play—an invisible enemy that was slowly poisoning the minds of the people. It was as if the darkness of the old world was creeping back in, infecting everything it touched.

One evening, as they sat by a campfire, Alex turned to Sophia with a grim expression. "We need to face the truth," he said quietly. "We can't keep going like this. We can't pretend that we've won."

Sophia looked at him, her eyes filled with understanding. "You're right. But what do we do? How do we fight an enemy that isn't visible? How do we stop the poison that's spreading in people's hearts?"

Alex shook his head, frustration creeping into his voice. "I don't know. But we have to try. If we don't, everything we've fought for will be lost."

They both knew that the world was teetering on the edge of another collapse. The machines may have been destroyed, but the battle for humanity's soul was far from over. The true test was not just survival—it was what kind of world they would rebuild in the wake of the old one's destruction.

Days turned into weeks as they moved through the ruins of civilization, trying to piece together the remnants of society. They encountered pockets of resistance, some friendly, some hostile, all shaped by the same fears and uncertainties that had plagued humanity for so long. No matter where they went, they encountered the same struggle—the desire for power, the hunger for control, the fear of the unknown.

It was in one such town that they encountered a man named Marcus. He was a survivor of the machine war, one of the few who had managed to stay hidden for years after the initial collapse. When Alex and Sophia met him, they could see the weariness in his eyes, the weight of his experiences etched into his face. Yet, there was also something else—a coldness, a hardness that set him apart from the others they had met.

Marcus didn't trust them at first. Like many others, he had grown suspicious of anyone who claimed to have a vision for the future. He had seen too many false prophets rise and fall in the aftermath of the war. But over time, Alex and Sophia earned his respect. They weren't like the others who had tried to manipulate the survivors for their own gain. They didn't seek power for themselves; they sought something more elusive—a future where humanity could live in peace, free from the shadows of the past.

But as they spent more time with Marcus, they began to notice that he wasn't quite the ally he seemed to be. There was a darkness in his eyes, a cold calculation in his words. It was subtle at first, a passing comment here or there, a hint of something more beneath the surface. But soon, the truth became clear—Marcus had his own vision for the future, one that didn't align with Alex and Sophia's.

His ambition, masked by his stoic demeanor, began to show itself in unexpected ways. He rallied others to his cause, speaking of a new world order, a world where the survivors would no longer be at the mercy of machines or outside forces. They would take control, rebuild civilization on their own terms. He spoke of strength, of domination, of a world where only the strong would survive.

Alex and Sophia were torn. They had seen the darkness that lay within the hearts of men during the war, but Marcus's vision was different—it was the same, twisted ideology that had driven the machines in the first place. The belief that only a few deserved to rule, that power was the only true currency in this new world.

"His vision is the same as the machines," Sophia said one night, her voice tinged with worry. "He doesn't want peace. He wants control. And he'll stop at nothing to get it."

Alex nodded grimly, knowing she was right. But what could they do? Marcus had already gathered a significant following, and his influence was growing by the day. It was a fight for control, a fight for the future of humanity itself.

The question was, who would win? Would it be the survivors who longed for a new world, free from the chains of the past? Or would it be those like Marcus, who sought to reshape the world in their own image, to become the new rulers of a fractured planet?

The battle lines were drawn, and once again, Alex and Sophia found themselves caught in the middle of a war that was no longer just about survival—it was about the soul of humanity itself.

As Alex and Sophia prepared for what was shaping up to be an inevitable confrontation with Marcus and his growing faction, they couldn't help but feel the weight of their past decisions. Every step they had taken in the last few months had been driven by hope—the hope that they could rebuild, that humanity could recover from the devastation of the machine war. But now, that hope seemed to be slipping through their fingers, replaced by a growing sense of dread.

The survivors they had gathered around them were beginning to question their vision of the future. Some saw the pragmatism in Marcus's words, the appeal of a world where strength was rewarded and the weak were left behind. Others, however, clung to the idea of rebuilding a society based on equality and compassion. The tension between these two factions grew palpable, and what had once been a tentative alliance of survivors was now fracturing under the weight of differing ideologies.

Sophia spent long hours with their closest allies, trying to rally support for their cause. But it was becoming clear that their message was no longer resonating with everyone. The scars of the past were too deep, and the world they now inhabited was too harsh to simply wish away. People were starting to look for something more concrete—something that promised safety, security, and power.

"We can't let him win," Sophia said one evening, her voice tight with determination. "If Marcus takes control, everything we've fought for will be destroyed. His world is one of fear and domination. It's no better than what we had before."

Alex stood by the fire, watching the flames flicker and dance in the night air. "I know," he said quietly. "But it's not just about stopping him. It's about offering something else, something better. We have to remind people of what we were fighting for, before the machines took over—freedom, unity, hope."

"But how do we convince them?" Sophia asked, her face troubled. "How do we show them that peace, real peace, is possible when the world is falling apart around us?"

Before Alex could answer, a shout echoed through the camp. The look on the face of the runner who arrived breathlessly at their tent said it all: Marcus was marching on their position.

The time for diplomacy was over.

The night that followed was filled with the sounds of distant gunfire, the low hum of engines, and the crunch of boots on the cracked earth. Alex and Sophia stood side by side, watching their people prepare for the battle they had known was coming, but never truly believed would arrive.

"We have one shot at this," Alex said, his voice steady despite the chaos unfolding around them. "We don't win this battle, and we lose everything. We don't just lose control of the land, we lose the future we've been fighting for."

Sophia nodded. "We'll give them a fight they won't forget."

The next few hours were a blur of action. The survivors rallied behind Alex and Sophia, forming a makeshift defense as Marcus's forces closed in. The battle was brutal, far more chaotic than they had expected. Marcus's men were well-armed and disciplined, driven by a sense of purpose that mirrored their leader's. But Alex and Sophia's people had something different—an unshakable belief that they could rebuild a better world.

As the sun rose the next day, the battlefield was littered with the remnants of a fierce clash. The ground was scarred with the marks of war, the air thick with smoke and the smell of blood. For a brief moment, it seemed as though the battle had ended in a draw—Marcus's forces had retreated, but not without inflicting significant damage.

Sophia surveyed the aftermath, her heart heavy with the weight of the loss. They had won this battle, but the war was far from over.

Marcus would return, of that she was certain. The battle lines were now drawn, and there would be no turning back.

"We've only just begun," Alex said, his voice low as he looked out over the ruins of the battlefield. "This is just one chapter in a much larger story."

Sophia glanced at him, her expression determined. "Then let's make sure we write it the way we want it to be told."

With the smoke of battle still hanging in the air, they gathered their people together, knowing that the real fight was just beginning. They were no longer fighting just for survival—they were fighting for the soul of humanity itself.

· · · ·

## ○ Old Enemies Resurface

THE WIND HOWLED THROUGH the ruins of the once-proud city, now nothing more than a shell of its former self. Broken glass crunched beneath boots, and the faint smell of ash lingered in the air, a constant reminder of the conflict that had torn everything apart. Alex Novak moved carefully through the shadows, his eyes scanning every corner, every building, for signs of life—or danger. The world had changed, but some things remained the same. Old enemies had a way of resurfacing when least expected.

His team had been traveling for days through the desolation, their supplies running low, morale even lower. But this was a place Alex knew well. He had once walked these streets as a diplomat, negotiating peace deals that now seemed like relics from another time. Back then, the world had been full of possibilities, a fragile hope that perhaps humanity could avoid the mistakes of the past. Now, as he stood in the heart of the ruins, he couldn't help but wonder where it had all gone wrong.

"Move up, quickly," Alex whispered, his voice barely audible over the gusts of wind. Behind him, his team obeyed without question, accustomed to his command. Emma Carter, the sharp-witted journalist who had joined their cause, scanned the area with a practiced eye. Despite the devastation around them, her determination remained unshaken. If anything, the apocalypse had only fueled her resolve to uncover the truth.

"I don't like this," Danny Reeves muttered under his breath, his hand gripping the rifle at his side. He had been a soldier, once, but his past was a dark one—one that he couldn't escape no matter how hard he tried. His eyes flickered with unease, a constant reminder of the war crimes he'd committed, the blood on his hands. The ghosts of his past never left him, no matter how far he ran.

"Keep your head on straight," Alex said, giving Danny a stern look. "We're not here for ghosts."

But even as the words left his mouth, Alex knew they were all haunted in one way or another. There was no escaping what they had been, who they had become. The world had broken them, reshaped them into something else, something harder. But this—this felt different. This place had a history. A history that Alex wasn't ready to confront just yet.

They reached the entrance of a ruined building, the walls cracked and broken, windows shattered like teeth in a mouth too long forgotten. Alex motioned for them to stop. His eyes narrowed, his instincts telling him that something was wrong. This wasn't just any ruin. This was where it had all started—his ties to the old world, the power structures he had once served. And now, as he stood on the precipice of everything that had been lost, he realized that the past wasn't done with him yet.

Suddenly, a movement caught his eye. In the distance, beyond the shattered windows of a nearby building, a figure appeared.

Alex's heart skipped a beat. He knew that gait, that silhouette. It was him—the one man Alex thought he would never see again.

"Victor Lynn," Alex muttered under his breath, the name a curse on his tongue.

The ruthless tycoon, now more of a warlord than a businessman, had been a shadow in Alex's life for years. Their paths had crossed in the old world, in boardrooms and government halls, where deals were made with a handshake and lives were collateral. But after the war, after the collapse, Victor had become a force unto himself. He had carved out his own empire, built on the bones of nations, using his wealth and influence to control the few remaining resources in the world. To Alex, Victor represented everything that had gone wrong. The greed, the manipulation, the power.

Now, it seemed, Victor was here, in the ruins, a constant reminder that some enemies never truly fade away.

"Get down," Alex ordered, lowering his voice to a whisper. He pulled Emma and Danny into cover, his eyes never leaving Victor's figure. They had to move fast, but quietly. If Victor had somehow found them—or if he had known they were coming—it wouldn't be long before more of his people arrived.

But Alex couldn't shake the feeling that this confrontation was inevitable. The past had a way of catching up, of surfacing when least expected. And this time, Alex wasn't sure if he could outrun it.

Victor's figure disappeared into the building, his movements deliberate and confident. Alex could feel the weight of old grudges pressing down on him. He couldn't let Victor win again, couldn't let him continue to tear the world apart for his own gain.

But as much as Alex wanted to go after him, to end this chapter once and for all, there was a greater concern at hand. The mission.

Sophia's work—the stabilizer—was too important to risk in a personal vendetta. He had to stay focused.

"Stay low. We move out in ten," Alex said, signaling for them to prepare to move. He needed a plan. He needed information. But above all, he needed to understand why Victor was here, what he wanted, and how far he was willing to go to get it.

As they readied themselves to leave their position, Alex's mind raced. Victor wasn't just an enemy from his past—he was a threat to the future, to everything Alex was fighting for. And now, that threat had resurfaced, ready to claim whatever was left in this broken world.

The ghost of Victor Lynn was back, and it wasn't going to be easy to shake him off this time.

Alex's thoughts were a whirlwind of strategy and fear as he glanced at his team. Every second felt like a countdown. The longer they stayed, the more likely they were to be caught in Victor's web—again. He couldn't afford that. Not when they were so close to their goal.

"Emma, Danny," Alex whispered, "we need to move fast. Stay quiet. We don't know how many of them are inside. Let's use the alley to the left, then circle around to the back. If Victor's still in there, we'll have to deal with him once we have the information."

Emma nodded without a word, her face a mask of determination. Danny, on the other hand, hesitated, his haunted gaze flicking toward the building where Victor had disappeared. Alex could see the conflict in his eyes—old memories, old regrets. They had all been scarred by the war, but for Danny, the lines between the past and the present were especially blurred.

"Focus, Danny," Alex urged, his tone firm but not unkind. "We're in this together. Whatever happened before, it doesn't matter now."

For a moment, the weight of his words seemed to settle in, and Danny's tense posture relaxed, though only slightly. He gave a curt nod and followed as they crept around the back of the building, careful to stay out of sight.

The back entrance was a metal door, rusted and bent from years of neglect. Alex's hands were steady as he checked the lock, careful not to make a sound. It clicked open with a soft groan, and they slipped inside, into the dark, silent interior of the building.

The air inside was thick with dust and the smell of decay. The remnants of an old office—cracked desks, overturned chairs, papers scattered like leaves in the wind—lined the walls. But what caught Alex's attention was the faint glow coming from deeper within the building, a soft, eerie light. Victor was here, and so was something else. Something that had drawn him to this place.

They moved through the darkened halls with precision, every footstep deliberate. Alex's senses were on high alert. He could feel the weight of history pressing down on him, the legacy of every decision he had made—and every mistake. The walls seemed to close in as they approached the source of the light. It was coming from an open door at the far end of the corridor, the shadows stretching long in the dim illumination.

Alex motioned for the others to stop. He took a deep breath, his heart pounding. He couldn't afford to let his guard down, not now. He motioned for Emma and Danny to stay close as he edged toward the door, his hand on the handle.

Inside, the scene before him was almost surreal. Victor stood in the center of a makeshift command room, surrounded by maps, blueprints, and monitors. The glow came from a large screen in front of him, displaying an array of data—coordinates, names, lists. It was a plan. But for what? Alex's stomach churned. Whatever Victor was doing here, it was bigger than he had anticipated.

"Victor," Alex called, his voice low but unmistakable.

Victor didn't turn around immediately. He let the silence stretch out, savoring the moment. When he finally spoke, his voice was cool, almost amused.

"Alex Novak," he said, turning slowly. A smirk tugged at the corners of his lips. "I didn't expect to see you here. Still playing the hero, I see."

Alex's jaw clenched. "You never were good at understanding the difference between right and wrong, Victor."

Victor's eyes narrowed. "You think you're any better than me? You've been fighting a losing battle from the start. We're all just trying to survive, in the end. Some of us just do it with more... style."

The words stung, but Alex didn't flinch. Instead, he took a step forward, his voice steady but full of intent. "You've taken everything. You've manipulated people's lives, destroyed nations, and for what? Power? Control? It's over, Victor. The world is done with people like you."

Victor's smirk faded, replaced by something more dangerous. "You think you're different? You think you've somehow managed to escape the same greed that drives us all? You're wrong. You've just been hiding behind your so-called ideals. The truth is, you're as much a part of this world as I am. We're all just trying to carve out our place in it."

Emma's voice broke through the tension, sharp and pointed. "You're not the only one with a vision for the future, Victor. But unlike you, we're not willing to sacrifice everything to achieve it."

Victor's eyes flickered toward her, and for a moment, the mask of arrogance cracked. "You should be careful who you align yourself with, Emma. This fight isn't about ideals—it's about survival."

Alex moved closer, his resolve hardening. "This isn't survival. This is destruction. And I'm here to stop you."

Victor took a step forward, his expression hardening. "You'll never stop me, Alex. You never could. The world is changing, and it's people like me who shape its future. You're just a relic of the past, holding onto a dream that's already dead."

The words hung in the air, thick with the weight of years of conflict and betrayal. But Alex was no longer the man he had been before the war. He had seen too much, lost too much. And he wasn't going to let Victor's twisted version of the future become the new reality.

"You can shape the future, Victor," Alex said, his voice low and determined. "But it won't be a future I'm a part of."

Victor chuckled darkly, his eyes never leaving Alex's. "We'll see about that."

As the tension between them grew, Emma stepped forward, her voice steady and resolute. "We'll fight you, Victor. And we won't stop until the world is free of people like you."

Victor didn't respond immediately. He simply watched them, his gaze calculating, as if weighing his options. And then, with a curt nod, he turned his back on them, walking toward the glowing screen once again.

"This isn't over," he said, his voice cold. "But it will be soon enough."

As Alex, Emma, and Danny exchanged a look, they knew that Victor's words weren't an empty threat. The game was only beginning.

• • • •

## ○ Danny's Redemption Begins

THE AIR WAS THICK WITH the acrid scent of burning rubble as Danny moved through the wreckage of the city. It had been years since the bombs fell, but the scars of the war lingered in the crumbling buildings, the shattered streets, and the haunted eyes of those who survived. For him, the war had never ended. It lived in the dark corners of his mind, in the faces of the men and women he had failed, in the bloodstains he could never wash away. The ghosts of his past were everywhere, lurking just beneath the surface, and every step he took felt like a penance he could never finish.

The group had settled in a temporary camp just outside the ruins of the old city, a place that had once been a thriving hub of commerce and life. Now, it was nothing more than a carcass, picked clean by scavengers and warlords. The survivors huddled in makeshift shelters, their faces hollow from hunger and fear. Danny was no different, except he carried a weight the others couldn't see—a weight that pressed down on his chest and stole the breath from his lungs.

He was a soldier. A killer. He had been trained to fight, to destroy. But what had he really fought for? The war had ended, but the consequences of his actions, the things he had done in the name of survival, still haunted him. The orders he had followed without question, the people he had killed, the friends he had betrayed—all of it hung around him like a suffocating fog. Now, with the world in ruins and everything he had known turned to dust, he was left to pick up the pieces of a broken man.

His comrades saw him differently. To them, he was just another soldier, another survivor doing what needed to be done. But Danny knew the truth. He wasn't just trying to stay alive. He was trying to atone. He had spent the last few years running, hiding from the past, but now there was no more hiding. There were no more excuses. It was time to face the things he had buried deep inside, to confront the demons that had followed him across battlefields and through the darkest corners of his soul.

It was a quiet night when the first real shift began. They had just finished a mission, a dangerous foray into a nearby stronghold controlled by one of the warlords who had emerged in the wake of the global collapse. The operation had gone as planned, but as usual, Danny felt nothing but emptiness after the job was done. The adrenaline had faded, leaving only the hollow ache of guilt.

Sitting by the fire, Danny watched the others. Alex was speaking to Sophia, their faces illuminated by the flickering flames, their voices low and steady. Emma, as always, had her nose buried in a journal, her mind seemingly far away. The camp was quiet, save for the occasional crackle of the fire and the distant howl of the wind. But for Danny, the silence was deafening. It was in the quiet moments that the memories came rushing back—the faces of the people he had killed, the screams of his comrades as they fell, the blood that stained his hands.

But tonight, something was different. For the first time in years, he felt a flicker of something more than guilt—a tiny spark of something that might be redemption. He had spent so long running from the past, but here, surrounded by people who had their own wounds to heal, something inside him began to shift. Maybe, just maybe, there was a way to make things right. Maybe he could find a path forward, not just for himself, but for the others as well.

The thought was fleeting, barely more than a whisper in the back of his mind, but it was enough to make him sit up straighter. He wasn't sure what the road to redemption looked like, or if it even existed, but for the first time, he was willing to try.

As the night deepened, Danny found himself standing up, his boots crunching softly against the dry earth. He moved toward the edge of the camp, where the remnants of an old city wall stood, a skeletal reminder of what had once been. There, in the stillness, he let the silence wash over him. The wind tugged at his jacket, and for the first time in a long time, he felt something resembling peace.

The weight that had pressed so heavily on his chest seemed to lift, just a little.

He knew that redemption wouldn't come easily. It wasn't something that could be earned overnight, or even over a lifetime. But it was a start. And for the first time, that was enough.

## ○ Sophia's Resolve

SOPHIA SAT IN THE DIMLY lit laboratory, the soft hum of the machinery the only sound in the room. Outside, the world burned. The distant rumble of explosions echoed faintly through the shattered windows, a constant reminder of the chaos beyond these walls. Yet in this small corner of the devastated city, the promise of salvation lay on a table in front of her—a device, sleek and deceptively simple, capable of reversing the environmental collapse that had ravaged the planet.

Her hands hovered over the stabilizer, her fingers twitching with the weight of what it represented. The world needed it, but so did those who had driven the planet to the brink of destruction. Victor Lynn, the ruthless tycoon who controlled the remnants of society's most vital resources, had already shown his interest. He had made it clear—his empire would stop at nothing to claim her work.

Sophia knew what he was capable of. She had seen the devastation firsthand—the burning cities, the starving masses, the wars fought over water and food. Victor had built his wealth on the suffering of others, and now, he wanted to use her invention to secure his grip on the future. But that was something she couldn't allow. The stabilizer was meant to save lives, not extend the reign of a tyrant.

She had always known that science could be both a blessing and a curse. Her resolve had been tested many times in her life, but nothing had prepared her for this moment. She had sacrificed so much to bring this technology to fruition—years of research, countless sleepless nights, and the loss of friends who had believed in her cause. And now, it all came down to a single choice: keep her invention hidden, or risk it falling into the wrong hands.

Sophia's gaze shifted to the blueprints pinned to the wall. There, in the intricate designs of her stabilizer, was a path to healing—restoring ecosystems, revitalizing the planet's dying resources, and offering a glimmer of hope for future generations. It was her legacy, and she couldn't allow it to be tarnished by greed. But the weight of that decision pressed heavily on her chest. She was not just a scientist now. She was a potential savior—or a destroyer.

The door to the lab creaked open, and Alex stepped inside, his presence steady and unwavering. He had become more than just an ally in these dark times. He was a leader, someone she trusted with the impossible task of bringing order to the shattered remnants of civilization. But even he could not know the full extent of the danger they faced.

"How much longer, Sophia?" Alex's voice was soft, tinged with the exhaustion that had settled over them all. "We can't afford to wait much longer. Victor's men are closing in, and every minute counts."

Sophia didn't answer immediately. Her eyes lingered on the stabilizer. In that moment, she felt the crushing weight of the world's expectations on her shoulders. She had dedicated her life to science, to finding solutions, but this—this was different. The consequences of failure were too great. The planet was already dying. And yet, to hand over the key to its salvation to someone like Victor Lynn... she couldn't bring herself to do it.

"I'm not ready," she finally said, her voice low, almost a whisper. "I can't just give this away. It's too important."

Alex stepped closer, his face etched with concern but also understanding. "I know," he said quietly. "But we don't have much time. If we wait too long, we might lose everything."

Sophia turned to face him, the weight of her decision pressing heavily on her. She had known this moment would come, but that didn't make it any easier. Her resolve wavered for a fraction of a second, the possibility of giving in, of handing the device over to Victor, tempting her. But she quickly shut down the thought. She could not—would not—let it happen.

"I have to finish it," she said firmly, her voice gaining strength. "If we don't act now, we lose everything. But if I hand this over to him, it's over for all of us."

She turned back to the stabilizer, her hands shaking slightly as she adjusted the settings. The machine would work. She knew it would. But first, they needed to survive the coming storm.

"Get ready," Sophia said, her voice steady now. "We're not just fighting for survival anymore. We're fighting for the future."

And with that, her resolve hardened, like steel forged in fire. There was no turning back now.

## ○ Splintering Loyalties

THE CAMP WAS QUIET, too quiet. The usual murmur of conversation and rustling of makeshift tents was replaced by a tense stillness that hung heavily in the air. Alex stood near the perimeter, his eyes scanning the horizon, but his thoughts were elsewhere. His mind was occupied with the growing rift among the group. The unity that had brought them this far was fraying, and it was becoming harder to ignore the signs.

Danny leaned against the charred remains of a building, his arms crossed, his gaze fixed on the ground. The memories of the war still clung to him like a second skin, but now, it was the memories of the group's early days together that haunted him. He had fought alongside Alex, fought to keep the hope alive, but the cracks were starting to show. They were all changing, some more than others.

Sophia was among them, her face etched with the exhaustion of the last few days, but her eyes were still sharp. She was the key to everything—her invention, the stabilizer, was the only hope for restoring the earth's dying ecosystems. Yet, it wasn't just the weaponization of her technology that worried Alex. It was her quiet determination to see it through, no matter the cost. He knew the stakes, but did she?

Emma's arrival had stirred things up further. Her investigative reports on Victor Lynn had opened a window to the empire that had profited from the chaos, but her methodical approach and her relentless pursuit of truth sometimes felt at odds with the desperate need for action. She had uncovered the darkest corners of the world's corruption, but now, in this fragmented world, was the truth enough to save them?

"Alex," Danny's voice broke through his reverie. "We need to talk."

Alex turned to face him, his jaw tightening. "About what?"

"I've been thinking about this," Danny said, his voice low but firm. "About what we're doing. About Sophia's plan. We've trusted her with too much, and I'm starting to wonder if we're making a mistake."

Alex's heart sank. He had expected this conversation, but hearing the words out loud made it feel real. "What do you mean?"

"We're relying on something that might not even work. We're putting everything into this one device, this one hope," Danny continued, his eyes darkening. "But what if it's all just a last-ditch effort? What if she's just trying to redeem herself for what happened?"

The words hung in the air like a fog. Alex had seen Danny struggle with his past, with the guilt that still gnawed at him, but he had never expected this kind of doubt. "You think Sophia's lying to us?"

"I think she's as lost as we are," Danny said quietly. "We're all searching for something to hold on to. But maybe we're not meant to fix this. Maybe we're just meant to survive."

Alex looked at him, feeling the weight of the decision pressing down on him. "And what do you want me to do with that? Just abandon everything we've fought for?"

"I don't know," Danny admitted, shaking his head. "But I do know we can't keep pretending like everything's fine. We're splintering, Alex. The group is falling apart."

The truth of his words settled heavily in the pit of Alex's stomach. He had seen the cracks before, the subtle disagreements and the quiet whispers, but hearing Danny's confession brought it all into focus. They were losing their way, and he didn't know how to fix it.

Sophia approached them then, her face a mask of determination. "We can't afford any more doubts. We need to act now. The longer we wait, the harder it'll be."

Alex looked at her, his mind racing. He didn't want to let go of hope, didn't want to believe that they had reached the point of no return. But the seeds of doubt were planted, and he could see it in the eyes of his people. They were fractured, their loyalty splintering into pieces, just like the world they were trying to save.

"We're running out of time," Alex said, his voice barely above a whisper. The words felt like a promise, but in his heart, he knew it was a warning. Time had never been on their side, and now, it seemed as though it was slipping away faster than they could keep up.

As the sun dipped below the horizon, casting long shadows over the wasteland, Alex realized that the real battle wasn't just against the forces outside their camp. It was against the fracture within their own ranks. The splintering loyalties had begun, and how they responded would decide the fate of their mission—and perhaps the future of the world itself.

The evening air grew colder as the shadows stretched across the broken landscape. Alex remained silent, lost in thought, staring at the horizon where the remnants of a world that once thrived now lay in ruins. He could hear the faint murmurs of his comrades, but it was as though a wall had gone up between them, separating them into different factions—each pulling in a different direction. And in the midst of it all, there was Sophia, the unwavering force behind their mission.

Alex had once believed in the cause, in the idea that they could change things, that they could fix what had been broken. But now, each passing day seemed to pull him further away from that belief. Danny's words echoed in his mind, replaying over and over again. *What if we're just meant to survive?*

Sophia approached him again, her steps measured, her eyes searching his face for any sign of weakness. "You've been quiet," she remarked, her tone sharp, almost accusing. "We need your focus, Alex. We need you to lead."

Alex didn't meet her gaze. He couldn't. There was too much uncertainty, too much doubt festering inside him. The stakes were too high, and the path they were on was more treacherous than he'd ever imagined.

"I'm leading," he said, the words coming out flat. "But I'm not sure it's the right path anymore."

Sophia's expression hardened. "What are you saying? This isn't the time for doubt."

"There's always time for doubt," Alex shot back, his voice rising in frustration. "Especially when everything we've been doing feels like it's falling apart. People are questioning their loyalty, their trust. Danny... he's not the only one."

Sophia's gaze faltered for a moment, just enough to betray her. She had been so focused on the mission, on the stabilizer, that she hadn't seen how much the strain was affecting the group. She opened her mouth to argue, but Alex cut her off.

"We're not a unified front anymore. People are breaking off. I can see it in their eyes."

She stepped closer, her voice low and fierce. "This isn't a time for divisions. There's too much at stake. You know that as well as I do."

Alex closed his eyes, breathing in deeply. He wanted to believe in her, wanted to believe that they were on the verge of something monumental. But the weight of her words—of her unshakable confidence—felt like a burden now, not a source of inspiration. It was a constant reminder of how much they were risking. And how little they had to show for it.

"I know," he said finally. "But at what cost, Sophia? How far are we willing to go? How many lives are we willing to sacrifice for this cause?"

Sophia's expression softened, her determination not waning but tempered with something else. "I'm not asking for sacrifices. I'm asking for hope. We all agreed on this, Alex. We knew what we were up against."

"Did we?" Alex's voice wavered. "Because I'm not sure anymore."

There was a long pause, and for a moment, the only sound was the wind, carrying with it the distant cries of the broken world they were trying to save. It was a haunting sound, a reminder of what they had lost. What they might never regain.

"I know you're struggling," Sophia said, her voice gentler now. "But you can't give up. Not now. We need to stick together."

"You think we're together?" Alex laughed bitterly. "We're fractured, Sophia. Every decision we make pulls us further apart. I don't know how to fix that."

She stepped closer, her hand reaching out, almost as if to steady him, but Alex stepped back, his eyes now filled with something darker—desperation, anger, fear. "I don't know how to keep leading when I can't even keep us united."

Sophia studied him for a long moment, her gaze unreadable. Finally, she spoke, her voice firm. "Then you need to find a way, Alex. Because if we fall apart now, if we lose our unity, it's over for all of us."

Her words cut through him, sharp and direct, but they didn't offer the clarity he had hoped for. Instead, they only deepened the confusion swirling in his mind. He had always believed that leadership meant guiding people, showing them the way. But what if he had been wrong? What if, in trying to lead them, he had only pushed them further into chaos?

He looked past Sophia, his gaze drifting over the camp, watching the others as they carried out their tasks. There was a weariness in their eyes now, a tiredness that went beyond the physical strain. It was a weariness of the soul, a fear that perhaps, they were all chasing a dream that was destined to slip through their fingers.

As the night settled in, and the stars above remained silent witnesses to their struggles, Alex felt a chill deeper than the cold air surrounding them. They were splintering. And despite everything they had fought for, the cracks were only growing wider.

## ○ The Cost of a Secret

THE COST OF A SECRET is never fully understood until it's too late. Alex had learned that the hard way, long before the world had crumbled into a shadow of its former self. But now, in this barren world, secrets were more dangerous than ever. They had a way of twisting and turning, growing until they consumed everything in their path, devouring even the last vestiges of trust.

Sophia's discovery was a secret that could change the course of humanity, and Alex knew it. The stabilizer she had developed, the technology that could reverse the environmental damage caused by decades of greed and negligence, was powerful beyond comprehension. But it was also deadly in the wrong hands.

When Sophia had first shared the prototype with Alex, she had insisted it was a solution, not a weapon. But Alex knew better than to take her words at face value. Everything had a price in this world—especially hope. And that price was a secret that could tear apart everything they were fighting for.

Victor Lynn's men were already on their tail. Alex could feel the weight of their eyes upon him even when they weren't around, like ghosts lurking just beyond the edge of his vision. The word had spread. There was no going back now. The decision had been made, and it was a decision that would haunt him for the rest of his life.

He looked over at Sophia, who was hunched over her equipment, eyes focused intently on the device. The glow from the machine reflected in her glasses, casting a soft, almost ethereal light across her face. But there was no serenity in her expression. There was only the weight of responsibility, the burden of a choice she hadn't asked for.

"How much longer?" Alex asked, his voice low.

Sophia didn't look up from her work. "Just a few more adjustments. But Alex... are you sure this is the right thing to do?"

Her voice was steady, but there was a tremor in it, one that betrayed her true feelings.

He didn't answer immediately. How could he? There was no right answer anymore, not in a world that had turned its back on everything that once mattered. The past was a distant memory, and the future felt more like an illusion than a possibility.

Sophia was right to question. She had no idea how deep the secret ran, how much danger it carried. But he did. And the truth, no matter how much it hurt, was that sometimes, a secret had to be kept, no matter the cost.

The wind howled outside, a chilling reminder of how fragile their existence had become. The world was broken, and there was no one left to fix it. But they could still try. They had to.

"Do you trust me?" Alex finally asked.

Sophia looked up, meeting his gaze. Her eyes, once full of hope and determination, were now clouded with doubt. "I trust you with my life, Alex. But I don't know if I trust what this... thing will do to us."

He nodded, swallowing the bitterness rising in his throat. He understood. They were on the edge of a precipice, and the only way forward was through the darkness. But the darkness had a way of consuming the light, of devouring everything in its path.

And Sophia's invention—her secret—was both their salvation and their doom.

Alex took a step forward, placing a hand on her shoulder. "We'll face it together. We don't have a choice."

She nodded, but it was clear that the burden of the secret weighed heavily on her. It wasn't just the device that was at risk—it was their souls. What they were about to do could change everything, and in doing so, it could tear apart everything they had fought to rebuild.

A distant rumble echoed through the night, signaling the arrival of another storm. Alex turned his gaze toward the horizon, where the faint outline of the enemy's camp loomed in the distance. Time was running out. They had to make their move, and they had to make it now.

The cost of the secret was high, but the cost of inaction was even higher.

And Alex knew that no matter what happened, there would be no going back.

# 6. Fortress of Fear

## ○ Victor's Domain

The imposing silhouette of Victor Lynn's compound loomed over the desolate landscape like a fortress from a forgotten age. The tall iron gates, once adorned with the insignia of power, were now rusted and worn, but still formidable. Beyond them, the sprawling estate stretched endlessly, a mockery of the devastation that had consumed the world outside. Behind high walls and razor wire, the air was thick with the scent of cold metal and dust. It was a place of isolation, where the war had never quite reached, where Victor ruled with an iron fist, undisturbed by the chaos beyond his gates.

Inside the compound, life carried on as if the world hadn't crumbled. The marble floors, once polished to perfection, now seemed to reflect a chilling emptiness, a testament to the artificial luxury that had become his kingdom. Victor had built his empire in the aftermath of the war, taking advantage of the resources that were left to carve out a safe haven for himself and his followers. But it was a haven born of exploitation and violence, and its foundation was a thin veneer of order over chaos.

Alex stood at the edge of the compound's perimeter, his eyes scanning the high walls. He had been here before, long before the world had descended into ruin. Back then, it had been a symbol of wealth and influence, a beacon for those who sought to align themselves with power. Now, it was nothing more than a cage for the man who had turned the war into his own personal fortune.

"Are you sure about this?" Danny's voice broke through the silence, his tone filled with uncertainty. He had never liked this place, had always felt the weight of its oppressive presence. It wasn't just the high walls or the menacing guards who patrolled the grounds; it was something deeper, something intangible. Victor's domain was a place where humanity had been abandoned in favor of control, where survival came at the cost of everything else.

"We don't have a choice," Alex replied, his gaze never wavering from the gates. "Sophia's work is the key to everything. If we don't act now, the world will be left to rot while men like him consolidate their power."

Emma, standing to the side, studied the compound with a mixture of disgust and intrigue. She had infiltrated places like this before, but Victor's stronghold was different. It wasn't just about resources; it was about control, about bending others to his will. She knew that his influence extended far beyond these walls, that his reach could destroy whatever remained of the fragile alliances they had forged. But there was also something about Sophia's technology that intrigued her—something that could tip the scales in their favor, if they could just get to it.

"We'll need a plan," she said, her voice steady but sharp. "Victor won't just hand over Sophia's work. He'll fight for it, and so will the people who work for him."

Alex nodded, the weight of his decision settling heavily on his shoulders. "We don't have time to waste. If we don't get to Sophia first, someone else will. And I don't think Victor plans to save anyone but himself."

Inside the compound, Victor was watching them—though they didn't know it yet. His presence was felt even without his physical form, a shadow that loomed over everything. He knew who they were, and he knew what they wanted. For years, he'd kept his power safe, manipulating the remnants of the world for his own benefit. But now, with the discovery of Sophia's stabilizer, everything was at risk. The technology could either save the world—or destroy it completely. And Victor wasn't about to let anyone take that choice away from him.

The guards, dressed in dark uniforms, stood like statues, their eyes scanning for any sign of trouble. They had seen many attempts at infiltration over the years, but none had ever succeeded. Victor's grip on his domain was absolute, and no one would breach it without consequences. They were loyal, yes—but they were also afraid. The consequences of failure here were never just physical; they were psychological. People didn't leave Victor's compound unless he allowed it, and not everyone who entered left with their sanity intact.

Alex took a deep breath, feeling the tension in the air. There was no turning back now. They had to go in, had to confront Victor and secure Sophia's invention. The future of the world depended on it, and yet, there was a gnawing doubt in the pit of his stomach. Could they truly succeed in this place of absolute control? Would they be able to stand against the man who had mastered the art of survival in the most ruthless of times?

As they moved closer to the gates, Alex couldn't shake the feeling that they were walking into the lion's den, unaware of the traps that lay in wait. The stakes were higher than ever, and with every step, the tension only deepened. The walls around Victor's domain weren't just physical—they were a metaphor for everything that had gone wrong in the world. A symbol of greed, power, and the lengths people would go to preserve their vision of the future, no matter the cost.

But Alex couldn't afford to doubt. Not now, not when the lives of so many were at stake. He glanced back at Danny and Emma, both of them looking just as determined, just as willing to face the unknown. They were in this together, and together, they would have to navigate the maze of betrayal and deceit that awaited them inside.

## ○ Behind the Walls

THE WALLS OF VICTOR Lynn's fortress rose like a monolithic symbol of oppression and control, a silent reminder of the empire he had built from the ashes of the old world. The fortified compound stood on the edge of a desolate city, its perimeter guarded by armed sentries, surveillance drones cutting through the barren skies. It was a place where power and fear were measured in equal parts, a sanctuary for those who thrived on scarcity and conflict.

Alex felt the weight of the walls before he saw them, a suffocating sense of isolation that seemed to seep into his very bones. The journey had been long, the landscape nothing but dust and decay. The earth itself seemed to be holding its breath, as if waiting for something, anything, to break the silence. But here, within this compound, the world was alive with the hum of machinery, the bustle of men and women who existed solely to serve the will of Victor Lynn.

His group had made their way through the gates under the guise of seeking sanctuary, but the truth was far less innocent. They were here to infiltrate, to learn the secrets Victor had buried behind these impenetrable walls. The group had heard rumors of a device—Sophia's device—that could change everything. The stabilizer, as she called it, could reverse the environmental collapse, could stabilize what was left of the planet's dying ecosystems. But Victor, a man who had built his empire on the destruction of the old order, would stop at nothing to control such a weapon.

Inside, the walls were lined with cold, sterile corridors, and the scent of metal and concrete hung heavily in the air. Alex walked ahead, his mind racing with the weight of their mission. Each step felt like it might be their last. His eyes flicked to Danny, who walked silently behind him, his hand resting lightly on the grip of his weapon. There was a quiet tension between them, an unspoken understanding of the dangers they faced. They had survived so much already, but this... this was different. This wasn't just a battle for resources or power—it was a fight for humanity's future.

They passed guards who didn't so much as glance their way. Their faces were blank, their eyes empty. They had all been molded by the regime, shaped into tools of control. Alex couldn't help but wonder how many of them had once been ordinary people, caught in the same trap of survival that had claimed so many others. The line between the oppressor and the oppressed had blurred here, behind these walls.

They reached the central hall, where the walls stretched even higher, as if to emphasize the power that lay within. In the distance, Alex could see a set of reinforced doors—Victor's personal chambers, no doubt. Beyond those doors lay answers, lies, and possibly the key to saving everything that was left of the world. But getting there would not be easy. The fortress was a maze of secrets and traps, each step forward bringing them closer to the heart of darkness.

Sophia's presence loomed over them, her mind racing with the possibilities of what the stabilizer could do. She had warned them—Victor would never let it go without a fight. He had his own plans for the device, plans that involved consolidating his power, not saving the world. And if Alex was being honest with himself, he knew the odds were stacked against them. They were outnumbered, outgunned, and outclassed in almost every way. But the stabilizer was humanity's last hope, and they had come too far to turn back now.

As they neared the doors, Alex motioned for the others to halt. His heart raced in his chest, each beat loud in his ears. Behind these walls, in the very heart of Victor's empire, everything would either fall into place—or collapse entirely. There would be no middle ground.

A faint sound broke the silence—a door opening, a set of footsteps approaching. Alex's grip tightened on the handle of his weapon, his body tensing in response. This was it. The walls had ears, and they were about to be heard.

But as the figure emerged from the shadows, Alex froze, his breath catching in his throat. It wasn't a guard, but someone he had not expected to see here—someone who could change everything. Emma. Her face was pale, but there was a fire in her eyes, a determination that mirrored his own. She motioned for them to follow.

"We need to hurry," she whispered, urgency in her voice. "Victor knows you're here. The clock's ticking, and it won't be long before all of this goes to hell."

Alex nodded. They had no choice now. They were already too deep inside, too close to turning back. The walls might have ears, but within them, they would find the truth that could either save or doom them all.

He turned to his team, the weight of the world on his shoulders, and nodded once more. This was the point of no return. Behind these walls, they would either break or become the catalyst for a new beginning.

## ○ The Weight of Power

THE ROOM FELT HEAVY, as if the air itself was burdened by the unspoken weight of their collective decisions. Alex stood at the window, staring out over the ruins of the city. Beyond the broken skyline, fires still burned in the distance, remnants of a civilization that had crumbled under its own greed. The world outside was a wasteland, and within the walls of this makeshift headquarters, the people who remained were no better than scavengers fighting over the scraps.

He could hear the faint hum of a generator powering the base, a constant reminder of how precarious their existence had become. Everything was temporary now. Power, shelter, food—all of it hung by a thread, controlled by those with enough resources to keep it all spinning. He'd never imagined he'd find himself in this position, leading a group of survivors, struggling not just to stay alive, but to cling to some semblance of morality in a world that had lost its bearings.

Sophia's voice broke his thoughts. "We can't keep running like this, Alex. We need to decide, once and for all, what we're going to do with the stabilizer."

Her words cut through the tension in the room, each one carrying an edge of urgency. She stood near the table, a map of the remaining habitable zones spread out before her, her fingers tracing the lines that marked safe passageways. The stabilizer—her breakthrough technology—was the only hope for reversing the damage done to the environment. It was the key to survival, but it was also a deadly weapon in the wrong hands. And those hands, Alex knew, were never far away.

Victor Lynn had made it clear from the start that he would stop at nothing to take control of the device. His empire was built on exploiting the very resources that had triggered the conflict. Power, for him, wasn't just about survival—it was about dominance. And Sophia's stabilizer could give him that dominance in ways that no army ever could.

"I know," Alex replied, his voice low. He turned away from the window, walking over to the table. The flickering light above cast long shadows across his face, deepening the lines that had appeared in just a few short months of leadership. "But we can't just hand it over to him. We need to use it. We need to make sure it gets to the right people."

Sophia's gaze hardened, a familiar resolve settling over her features. "The right people? And who exactly are they, Alex? The last remnants of civilization are either holed up in their fortified cities or fighting each other for control. There is no 'right' anymore. There are only the ones with the power to make the world bend to their will."

Her words echoed in the silence of the room. Alex clenched his fists, trying to push back the frustration that rose in his chest. He wanted to believe there was still good in the world, that some way out of the nightmare still existed. But every day, that belief slipped further from his grasp. The weight of the power in this room, in their hands, was crushing.

"Are you willing to let Victor have it?" Danny's voice broke in from the doorway. He had been standing there for a while, silent, waiting for the right moment to speak. His worn-out uniform and battle-scarred face showed the toll that war had taken on him, but there was still something in his eyes—something that hadn't yet been broken.

"I'm not willing to let him have it," Alex said. "But I also can't make this decision alone."

Sophia gave him a sharp look. "And that's exactly why we're in this mess. Leadership isn't about consensus, Alex. It's about making the hard calls."

Alex met her gaze, feeling the weight of her words sink in. She was right. But how could he make those calls when every decision seemed like a step toward further destruction? The world was in ruins, and whatever choice they made next could be the one that sealed their fate.

He ran a hand through his hair, feeling the exhaustion creeping into his bones. They needed to act fast. Victor was already consolidating power, securing alliances with the strongest factions.

If they didn't move quickly, the stabilizer wouldn't be the key to saving anyone—it would be the key to their own extinction.

"Then we fight," he said, his voice firm. "We make sure the stabilizer gets to the people who need it. We don't let it fall into Victor's hands. No matter the cost."

Danny stepped forward, his eyes narrowing. "Are you ready to make that kind of sacrifice? To put everything on the line?"

Alex's heart thudded in his chest. He didn't have the luxury of time to weigh every option. The world outside was crumbling faster than they could keep up with, and if they hesitated, they would lose. But the cost of winning, of taking this step, was something Alex had to confront head-on. It wasn't just the stabilizer at stake—it was the future of humanity itself.

He looked around at his team, at the people who had stood by him when it would have been easier to turn away. They were all waiting for him to make the next move, to take the burden of power and decide what kind of world they would rebuild. But the weight of that power felt unbearable.

"We fight," Alex said again, his voice steady despite the storm raging inside. "But we fight for the future, not for power. That's the only way we'll win."

Sophia nodded, her expression softening, though the hard edge remained in her eyes. "Then we need a plan. And fast."

Alex glanced at the map in front of her, his mind already racing ahead, plotting their next move. It wouldn't be easy. The path ahead was fraught with danger, and they were all walking a razor's edge between survival and annihilation. But for the first time in a long while, Alex felt a flicker of hope. There was a chance—just a chance—that they could turn the tide.

The weight of power, heavy and suffocating, settled on his shoulders. But this time, he was ready to carry it.

## ○ Emma's Discovery

EMMA CROUCHED LOW BEHIND the crumbling remains of a building, her breath shallow as she peered through the jagged window. The world outside was a desolate wasteland, a place that had once been teeming with life, now reduced to a graveyard of steel and stone. But there, in the midst of it all, was something she hadn't expected to find—a trail of information, a thread that might just unravel the mystery of what had really happened to the world.

She hadn't meant to dig this deep. At first, it was just a few passing inquiries, questions no one else dared ask, not with the threat of Victor Lynn's forces watching every corner. But Emma wasn't like the others. She wasn't afraid of the dark secrets that lingered in the shadows. She was the kind of person who had always searched for the truth, no matter the cost. And the truth, she suspected, was far more dangerous than any of them had realized.

Her fingers moved quickly over the battered laptop in front of her. The glow from the screen illuminated her face, casting long, sharp shadows that seemed to echo her anxiety. A single document appeared, hidden within the labyrinth of corporate files she had hacked into over the past few days. It was buried deep, encrypted beyond any measure she'd seen before. But she had cracked it, piece by piece.

Victor Lynn's name appeared, unmistakable. His influence, his power—his dirty dealings, all carefully documented. But this wasn't just about money. No, this was about something far darker, something that had been orchestrated long before the war had begun. Emma's heart raced as she read further, her eyes widening in disbelief. Lynn had known about the impending resource collapse. He had known about the wars, the famine, the environmental destruction—before it all happened. And he had planned for it, not only to profit but to control the very forces of nature itself.

Her mind raced as she pieced it all together. Sophia's work, the stabilizer, was more than just a last-ditch effort to save the world—it was a tool, a weapon that Lynn could use to consolidate even more power. He could control who lived and who died, all with the flick of a switch. The technology was dangerous, but in the hands of someone like him, it could be catastrophic.

Emma's fingers hovered over the keyboard. Should she send the information to the others? Should she confront Alex, tell him what she had found? The decision was heavier than any she'd ever made. Her instincts told her that this knowledge could change everything, that it could be the key to toppling Victor's empire, to saving whatever was left of humanity. But it could also destroy them all.

The sound of distant footsteps made her freeze. She quickly closed the laptop, pushing it under a pile of debris just as the door to the building creaked open. Her pulse thudded in her ears as she tried to steady her breath. They were getting closer.

"Emma?" a voice called softly, just on the other side of the room.

It was Alex. She could hear the concern in his voice, but also the weariness that had taken over him in recent days. They had all been on edge, ever since Sophia's discovery became public knowledge. The last few days had been a blur of danger, uncertainty, and betrayal, and Emma had spent most of it trying to stay one step ahead.

She stood quickly, brushing off her clothes and trying to force a calm expression onto her face. There was no way she could tell him now. Not here, not with the enemy so close.

"I'm fine," she called back, her voice steady despite the storm raging inside her. "Just a little... tired. I'll be out in a minute."

The footsteps retreated, and Emma allowed herself a moment of relief. But it was fleeting. The discovery she had made was too important to be buried, too dangerous to be ignored. She needed to get the information to Alex, to Sophia, to the others. But at what cost?

She took a deep breath, steadying herself for what was to come. The truth was out there, but getting it into the right hands would be far more difficult than she had ever imagined.

## ○ The Price of Defiance

THE WIND HOWLED THROUGH the cracked windows of the crumbling building, a constant reminder of the world that had fallen apart. The city was a graveyard of what once was, the remains of human ambition scattered like forgotten relics in the ruins. Inside, Alex stood at the window, his gaze fixed on the distant horizon, where the fires from the last skirmish still smoldered.

He could feel the weight of the decision he had just made pressing down on him. The group had gathered in the dimly lit room, their faces worn and tired, their eyes reflecting the same exhaustion that had settled deep in his bones. The rebellion was no longer just a matter of survival—it had become a war of ideals, a battle between what was left of humanity's soul and the brutal forces that sought to crush it.

"Are you sure about this?" Emma's voice broke through his thoughts. She stood behind him, her arms crossed, her brow furrowed in concern.

He turned to face her, meeting her gaze. "If we don't act now, we risk losing everything. We've seen what Victor and his people are capable of. If we don't stop them, we'll never have a chance to rebuild anything."

Emma exhaled sharply, her breath clouding in the cold air. "But you know what this means. The consequences won't be something we can undo."

"I know," Alex replied quietly. "But sometimes, defiance is the only option left."

The tension in the room was palpable as the rest of the group shifted uncomfortably, each of them weighing the decision in their own way. Sophia, who had been silent up until now, finally spoke.

"If we move forward with this, we're committing ourselves to a fight we may not be able to win," she said, her voice calm but firm. "Victor will stop at nothing to maintain control. And we're not just fighting for survival anymore; we're fighting for something bigger. For a future."

Alex's eyes met hers, a silent understanding passing between them. Sophia was right. This wasn't just about taking down Victor—it was about sending a message to anyone who still believed in something better, something worth fighting for.

"We don't have the luxury of waiting," he said, his voice steady despite the chaos swirling inside him. "We've seen what's out there, and I'm not going to sit back and watch it all burn."

Danny, who had been leaning against the wall, arms crossed, finally spoke up. "You're asking us to take a risk. A big one. And if we fail, there's no turning back."

Alex nodded. "I'm asking you to believe in something—something that goes beyond us. We don't fight for the sake of fighting. We fight because we have to. We fight because there's still a chance, however small, that we can make things right."

The room fell silent, each person lost in their own thoughts. Alex could feel the weight of their eyes on him, the burden of leadership pressing harder with each passing moment. He knew that the decision they were about to make would change everything. There would be no going back, no retreat into the safety of apathy.

"Alright," Emma said finally, breaking the silence. "I'm in."

One by one, the others nodded. Danny, Sophia, even the quiet members of the group—each of them stood, a unified front in the face of the impossible. It was a moment of fragile hope, a spark in the darkness that could either ignite a revolution or extinguish them all.

Alex let out a breath he hadn't realized he'd been holding. They were with him. They were willing to take the risk, to defy the very forces that had brought the world to its knees. And though he knew the road ahead would be fraught with peril, in that moment, he believed that they could succeed.

"We move at dawn," Alex said, his voice firm. "Get ready."

As the others began to prepare, Alex lingered at the window, watching the dying light of the day fade into darkness. The wind howled once more, carrying with it the promise of a storm to come. But it also carried something else—a sense of purpose, a defiance that would echo through the ruins of their world.

It was the price they would pay for freedom. And it was a price they were all willing to make.

The cold night enveloped the city as the rebels moved in the shadows, each one of them slipping through the wreckage of what had once been a thriving metropolis. The streets, now littered with debris and the remnants of war, felt like a maze of forgotten memories. The quiet was almost oppressive, broken only by the occasional distant rumble of what remained of the fighting.

Alex moved with purpose, his mind sharp despite the weariness that clung to him. He could feel the weight of the plan settling around him, each step taking him further into dangerous territory. The path they had chosen was uncertain, and the risk of failure loomed over them all like a dark cloud. But there was no turning back now.

Sophia was close behind, her footsteps light but determined. She had always been the voice of reason, the one who measured the cost of every decision. Yet tonight, there was a fire in her eyes, a fierceness that matched Alex's own. She knew what was at stake, and she was ready to pay the price.

Emma and Danny followed, moving swiftly but silently, their faces grim with the knowledge that this was no longer just a skirmish—it was a turning point. A battle that could tip the scales of power and reshape the future of their world.

They reached the outskirts of Victor's stronghold just as the first light of dawn began to break. The once-gleaming tower now stood as a hulking monument to corruption, a reminder of how far their enemies were willing to go to maintain control. The fortress was heavily guarded, its walls lined with armed sentries who patrolled the perimeter with precision.

Alex surveyed the scene, his mind racing. They couldn't afford to be seen, not even for a moment. The risk of detection was too great. Their only chance was to infiltrate the base under the cover of darkness, using the blind spots in the surveillance system to their advantage.

"Remember," Alex whispered, his voice barely audible. "Once we're in, there's no turning back. Stay together, stay silent, and above all—trust each other."

Sophia nodded, her jaw set with determination. "We'll get through this."

The plan was simple: get inside, plant the explosives, and get out. But in a world like theirs, nothing was ever as simple as it seemed. The risk of failure was high, and the consequences of being caught would be catastrophic.

They moved forward, sticking to the shadows as they made their way toward the base. Their hearts pounded in their chests, but they kept their focus. This was their moment. The culmination of everything they had fought for.

As they neared the walls, Emma stopped and pointed to a gap in the security—an unguarded section that would allow them to slip inside unnoticed. They crouched low, slipping past the perimeter fence, each step bringing them closer to their target.

Inside, the atmosphere was thick with tension. The halls of the stronghold were silent, save for the occasional echo of footsteps in the distance. They had to move fast. The explosives were planted with precision, each device set to detonate at the exact moment they were safely out of the blast radius. They worked in a synchronized rhythm, their movements practiced and swift, but the pressure weighed heavily on them. One mistake, and everything would unravel.

As they finished, Danny placed a hand on Alex's shoulder. "It's done," he said, his voice low but filled with certainty.

Alex gave a curt nod. "Now we get out."

But just as they were about to retreat, the sound of footsteps echoed down the hallway. Someone was coming.

Their hearts skipped a beat. They had no time to lose. The exit was too far, and their cover was compromised. Alex cursed under his breath, but his mind raced for a solution.

"We have to go now," he whispered urgently. "Stay close and follow me. Don't stop."

The group sprinted toward the nearest exit, their footsteps louder now as the tension reached its peak. Alex could hear the guards getting closer, their voices just out of reach, but drawing nearer with every passing second. The world outside seemed a lifetime away.

They reached a door, only to find it locked. Sophia quickly retrieved a small device from her bag, her fingers working in a blur as she disabled the lock. The door clicked open just as the sound of boots reached their ears.

"Go!" Alex shouted, shoving the door open. They poured into the alleyway just as the first of the guards rounded the corner.

The explosion came seconds later. The earth trembled beneath their feet as the shockwave from the blast tore through the stronghold. A plume of smoke and fire erupted from the building, rising high into the sky like a signal to the world.

For a moment, everything was silent. Then, the sounds of chaos erupted as alarms blared and voices screamed in panic.

They didn't stop. They couldn't afford to. They ran, the world around them spinning with the sounds of destruction. The plan had worked, but the price they would pay for this defiance was only just beginning.

The city was already starting to stir as the first rays of sunlight touched the horizon. But for Alex and his team, the world felt as though it had been plunged into an abyss. They moved quickly through the narrow alleyways, each step taking them farther away from the explosion that had shattered Victor's stronghold. Yet the growing tension in the air seemed to pulse with a kind of malevolent energy. They were no longer just rebels; they were fugitives, marked by the act they had just committed.

The streets were chaotic, filled with the sounds of sirens and the hurried footsteps of those trying to comprehend the destruction. People were shouting, running for cover, unsure of who had struck the blow. But the explosion was a statement—a declaration that their defiance had not been in vain.

Alex glanced over at Sophia, her face drawn, yet there was a spark of fierce resolve in her eyes. She was processing the danger they were in, but also the enormity of what they had just done. The enemy would be coming for them soon—if they hadn't already.

"We need to split up," Alex said, his voice firm but filled with a quiet urgency. "Meet back at the safe house in three hours. Don't let anyone follow you."

Danny shook his head, his eyes narrowed. "They'll be looking for us. The city's crawling with their men."

"I know," Alex replied. "But the longer we stay together, the easier it will be for them to catch us. We'll be safer alone, at least for now. The distraction will buy us time. Use it wisely."

There was no time to argue. They all knew the risks. The consequences of getting caught would be dire. They shared one last look—one of understanding—and then, without another word, they dispersed into the labyrinth of streets that led in every direction.

Alex's heart raced as he darted into the shadows, his mind constantly scanning his surroundings. He could feel the weight of the decision bearing down on him. The explosion was only the beginning. They had made their move, but what came next would be even more dangerous. Victor's empire was vast, and the consequences of defying it would come down on them like a storm.

As he turned a corner, he nearly collided with a group of civilians fleeing the scene. They didn't recognize him, but the fear in their eyes mirrored the anxiety that gnawed at his own chest. The rebellion had just escalated into something much bigger. The repercussions of what they had done would ripple through the city, through the entire region.

Alex's pace quickened as he continued to weave through the crowds. He had to get to the safe house—he couldn't afford to be caught now. The city, once familiar, now felt like a maze designed to trap him. The familiar streets seemed alien, transformed by the chaos that was unfolding.

Every corner he turned, every alleyway he slipped through, was another step toward his uncertain future. He had done what he believed was necessary, but he couldn't shake the feeling that the worst was yet to come.

Back at the safe house, Emma was already waiting. Her face was pale, her hands trembling slightly as she adjusted her gear. The explosion had rocked her to her core, but she was ready. She had always been the one to keep a level head, to push through the panic. But this time, the weight of their actions seemed to hover over her like an impending storm.

"You made it," Alex said, his voice steady but carrying the exhaustion of their escape.

She gave him a curt nod. "Barely. But we can't afford to rest just yet. They'll be looking for us, and if they know where we are... we'll be sitting ducks."

"Any word from Danny and Sophia?" Alex asked, his eyes scanning the door, waiting for the others to arrive.

"Not yet," Emma replied. "But they'll be here. They're tough. If anyone can slip through, it's them."

The room was dimly lit, the smell of old wood and dust filling the air. It was the perfect place to lay low, at least for a while. But Alex knew they couldn't stay hidden for long. As the hours ticked by, the feeling of impending danger only grew stronger. They had defied a system built on fear and control, and that had made them targets in a game where the rules were unforgiving.

Hours later, the sound of a door creaking open broke the stillness. It was Sophia. Her clothes were torn, her face smudged with dirt, but there was a determined look in her eyes. She moved quickly, shutting the door behind her with a soft click.

"They're already looking for us," she said, her voice tight. "I barely made it out."

"Same here," Danny said, entering just behind her. He was out of breath, his hair disheveled, but his eyes were sharp. "We're not out of the woods yet."

They all sat down, each of them lost in their own thoughts for a moment. The weight of what they had just done seemed to settle in like a heavy cloak. The city was on the brink of a new kind of war, one where every rebel, every defector, every dissenter would be hunted with ruthless efficiency.

Alex glanced at the others. They had made it this far, but the road ahead would be more perilous than ever. Their rebellion had been a spark, but sparks, as they knew too well, could either ignite a fire or burn out before they had a chance to spread.

"We've made our mark," Alex said, his voice low but resolute. "But the cost is only just beginning."

The night dragged on in silence, each of them lost in their own thoughts. The atmosphere in the safe house felt heavier with every passing minute. Alex couldn't shake the sense that the walls were closing in. Their defiance had set something in motion, and now they were just waiting for the storm to hit.

"What's the plan?" Sophia asked, breaking the silence as she wiped the grime from her face. "How do we survive this? They'll come for us, we know that. But where do we go from here?"

Alex looked around at the faces of the people who had chosen to stand beside him. They weren't just allies anymore—they were family, bound by a shared purpose, by a shared sacrifice. But the questions hanging in the air were impossible to ignore.

"We move forward," he said, his voice tinged with resolve. "There's no turning back. The only way out now is to keep going. We've made our stand, but the fight isn't over."

Danny let out a low, frustrated sigh. "That's all well and good, Alex, but how do we fight an enemy like this? We've got nothing. No resources, no backup. Just our wits and a handful of weapons. And they've got the entire city at their disposal."

Alex's eyes hardened. "You think I don't know that? We've been outmatched from the start. But they've underestimated us. The people are starting to notice. The explosion—people will start talking. It will spread. And we can use that. We need to build alliances, find support wherever we can. This isn't just about us anymore. It's about waking up the rest of them, the ones who've been living in fear for too long."

Sophia nodded. "But where do we even begin? How do we make them listen?"

"We start with what we have," Alex replied, his voice steady despite the storm raging in his mind. "We use the chaos. The world is already shifting. We just need to make sure we're in the right place when it all collapses."

Danny crossed his arms, looking unconvinced. "And if they catch us before we can get anything going?"

"We won't let them," Alex said, the words slipping out with more conviction than he felt. "We've got one advantage: They don't know exactly where we are yet. We need to keep moving, stay unpredictable. And when the time is right... we strike again."

The others nodded, though doubt lingered in their eyes. It was clear they weren't sure how long they could keep up the pace, how many more risks they could take. But they had no choice. They had stepped into the arena, and now they were in it for the long haul.

The following days blurred together in a haze of uncertainty. Alex and his team slipped in and out of the shadows, doing everything they could to stay under the radar. But no matter how careful they were, it was impossible to escape the weight of the price they had paid.

Every move they made felt like a gamble. Every moment was filled with the awareness that the enemy was closing in. Victor's forces were relentless, using every resource at their disposal to hunt down the rebels responsible for the explosion. Rumors were spreading—talk of insurgents, of a resistance that was suddenly awakening. The people were beginning to talk, but in the streets, fear still reigned.

Alex knew they couldn't afford to remain silent for long. There was too much to lose. The first wave of resistance had begun, and if they didn't build on it now, it would dissipate like a forgotten whisper in the wind.

Weeks later, the tension had reached a boiling point. They had made contact with a small underground faction, one that had been working in secret to gather intel and resources. But trust was a fragile thing, and Alex knew that forging an alliance would be a delicate task.

He met with the faction leader in a darkened alley, a place where shadows concealed more than just the night. The leader was a woman named Elena, her face weathered by years of hiding, her eyes filled with a fire that reminded Alex of the early days of their rebellion.

"You're late," Elena said, her voice sharp as she stepped forward, her eyes scanning the street for any sign of danger.

"I wasn't sure I could trust the contact," Alex replied, his tone even. "But we've been doing this long enough to know that patience is as important as anything else."

Elena's lips twitched into something that could have been a smile, though it didn't quite reach her eyes. "You're the ones who set off the explosion, aren't you?"

Alex nodded. "We did."

"And you're still alive?" she asked, raising an eyebrow. "That's a feat in itself."

"We're not here to talk about survival," Alex said, his voice hardening. "We're here because we need help. We're out of time."

Elena studied him for a long moment, as if weighing the decision. "And why should I help you? You're nothing but a bunch of rebels with a few bullets and a bad plan."

"Because it's not just about us anymore," Alex said, meeting her gaze. "We're all fighting for something bigger now. If you want to keep living in fear, that's your choice. But we're not backing down."

Elena's gaze hardened, and for a moment, it felt like the air between them had turned to ice. But then, without a word, she turned and gestured for him to follow her.

The alliance with Elena's faction marked a turning point for Alex and his team. They had finally found a group that was willing to take the fight to Victor's empire, to challenge the system from within. But as they prepared for what would be their next move, Alex couldn't shake the nagging feeling that the true cost of their defiance was yet to be fully revealed.

The storm was coming, and it would take everything they had to survive it.

• • • •

## ○ Escape and Sacrifice

THE AIR IN THE COMPOUND was thick with the scent of smoke and the distant echo of gunfire. Alex could hear the faint crackle of the comms system in his ear, the only indication that the outside world still existed. The world that once was. Now, it was nothing more than fractured remnants, desperately clinging to whatever shred of hope they could find. They were deep inside the heart of Victor Lynn's stronghold, a fortress designed to withstand not just the forces of nature, but the insatiable thirst for power that had corrupted every corner of society.

Sophia moved quickly, her hands trembling as she adjusted the settings on the small device she'd been working on for months. The stabilizer, her dream and her curse, was their only chance. If they could just get it into the right hands, it might reverse the environmental collapse that had ravaged the planet. But it wasn't just the device they needed to escape with—it was their lives. Victor's men were closing in, and every step they took brought them closer to the precipice of failure.

"Move," Alex whispered, his voice low but urgent. "We have to go now."

They'd planned for this. Or so they thought. Escape routes had been mapped out, alternate paths secured. But there was no way to predict the chaos that would erupt once the alarm had sounded, once Victor realized his prized possession was slipping away. The whole compound was alive with movement, the threat of an ambush hanging in the air like a storm waiting to break.

Danny was at the rear, keeping watch as Alex ushered Sophia ahead. His hands were steady on the rifle, but his eyes were distant, haunted by the weight of his past. The war, the atrocities, they were never far from his mind. Every mission, every firefight, felt like another step deeper into the abyss. He hadn't asked for redemption, but somehow, in this moment, it was all that mattered.

"You're sure about this?" he asked, his voice betraying a rare crack of uncertainty. "This thing—Sophia's invention—it could really work?"

Sophia glanced over her shoulder, her face pale but determined. "It's not a guarantee. But it's our best shot. If we don't try... we're done."

Her words hung heavy in the air, the reality of their situation pressing down on them all. There was no going back now. The stakes had always been high, but now they were fighting for something more than just survival. They were fighting for the future, for a chance at redemption not just for themselves, but for everyone who had been forgotten in the wake of the war.

As they neared the exit, Alex's mind raced. Victor's forces were closing in on all sides, the once-secure perimeter now a maze of shadows and hidden dangers. He'd underestimated the man's reach, underestimated how far he would go to keep his empire intact. He should have known better.

"Get to the transport, now!" Alex barked, his hand gripping Sophia's arm as he pulled her along. They broke into a sprint, the sound of footsteps thundering in the hallway behind them. The metallic door to the outside world was within sight, just ahead—freedom, or what little was left of it. But as they reached it, a burst of gunfire shattered the silence, the deafening crack sending a jolt of panic through their ranks.

Danny spun, his rifle up in an instant, eyes scanning the hallway. The trap had been sprung. They were surrounded.

"Damn it!" Alex cursed under his breath, drawing his own weapon. There was no time to think, no time for hesitation. "Move, move, move!"

They bolted toward the door, the weight of their lives—and the future of the planet—pushing them forward. The sounds of pursuit grew louder, closer, but they were nearly there. The transport vehicle sat just beyond the gate, its engine idling in the gloom, ready to carry them away from the chaos.

But as Alex reached for the door, a shadow lunged from the side, knocking him off balance. He hit the ground hard, the wind knocked from his lungs, his gun slipping from his grasp. Instinctively, his hand shot out, grabbing the nearest object—an old metal pipe—and swung it at his attacker. The figure recoiled but didn't fall, a grim smile twisting on their face.

Victor's men were relentless. But so were they.

Sophia reached the door first, pushing it open, her breath ragged as she yelled, "Alex, get up!"

Alex's world spun as he struggled to regain his bearings. Every muscle screamed for rest, for respite, but there was no time. He shoved the attacker away, scrambling to his feet, just as another wave of gunfire ripped through the air. He darted toward the door, his legs burning, his heart racing. They were so close, yet it felt like the end.

Danny, ever the protector, covered their retreat, firing on instinct, forcing the enemy back just long enough for Alex to reach the transport. With a final, desperate lunge, Alex dove into the back of the vehicle, pulling Sophia in behind him. Danny was next, his breath heavy with exertion, his face a mask of determination. The engine roared to life, and in an instant, they were tearing through the gate, away from the compound, away from the only place that had once offered them hope.

But escape came at a price.

As they sped into the night, Alex's gaze fixed on the horizon, knowing that they had only just begun the fight. The road ahead was fraught with peril, and Victor would not stop until he had what he wanted. But as the compound faded into the distance, he felt something stirring within him—a flicker of defiance, of hope, that maybe, just maybe, they could change the course of history.

But that would come later.

For now, they were alive. And that was all that mattered.

# 7. Chains of the Past

## ○ Danny's Confrontation

Danny's fists clenched at his sides as he stood before the ruined building, the memory of what had happened here still fresh in his mind. The wind howled through the broken windows, carrying with it the scent of ash and decay. His breath came in shallow bursts, his heart thumping in his chest. This was it—the place where everything had changed. The place where his past had caught up with him.

It wasn't supposed to be like this. The war had promised clarity, a purpose that made sense in the chaos of battle. But now, in the aftermath, all he could see was destruction. The faces of the people he had fought for and against haunted him—victims, soldiers, innocents. There had been no winners in that war, only survivors, and some of them weren't even that.

"Danny," a voice called from behind him, low and steady, a tone of authority that still made him bristle despite the years that had passed. Alex stood a few steps away, his face unreadable, but his eyes searching, as if trying to read Danny's soul. The two men had been through hell together, yet this moment felt different. The lines between them had blurred, and in the silence of this ruin, they seemed impossibly far apart.

Danny didn't turn. He didn't need to. "I know what you're going to say," he muttered, his voice rough, as though it had been scraped raw by the wind. "I've heard it before."

Alex took a step closer, his boots crunching on the broken glass scattered across the ground. "You're not alone in this," he said, his voice softer now. "But you have to face it, Danny. You have to confront what you've done."

The words hit harder than any bullet had. Danny's hands trembled, but he forced them into fists again, willing himself to keep it together. "Face it?" He laughed, the sound bitter and hollow. "What do you want me to do, Alex? Apologize to the ghosts? To the families of the people I killed?"

Alex shook his head slowly, his expression tight. "That's not what this is about. This isn't about finding redemption. It's about understanding that you can't escape your past. We all have one. But it's what we do next that matters."

Danny turned finally, his eyes locking with Alex's, the weight of their shared history pressing down on him like a physical force. "What if I'm not the man you think I am? What if I'm nothing more than a killer? A machine?"

Alex's gaze didn't falter. "Then that's what you'll have to prove, Danny. Not to me. To yourself."

The silence between them was suffocating, as if the air itself was holding its breath. Danny's mind raced, his thoughts tangled in a web of doubt, guilt, and anger. Could he really prove anything to himself? Was it even possible to forgive the man he had become?

Suddenly, a distant noise pierced the quiet—the sound of footsteps, too heavy to be ignored. Alex stiffened, his hand instinctively reaching for the weapon at his side. Danny's eyes snapped to the source of the sound. He had learned to recognize the subtle shift in the air that meant danger was close.

"I didn't come here to talk about that," Danny muttered, his voice low and dangerous now. "But it looks like we're about to have another fight."

Alex nodded, his hand still gripping his weapon. "We don't have time for regrets, Danny. Not yet."

They moved toward the edge of the ruined building, where shadows shifted and the unknown crept closer with every passing second. Danny's heart pounded in his chest, but it wasn't the weight of his past that drove him forward now. It was survival. And the brutal truth was, survival came first. Always.

As the shadows closed in, he could almost feel the ghosts of his past watching him, waiting for him to make his move. But for now, they would have to wait. He had a fight to finish.

## ○ Unfinished Business

THE SOUND OF THE WIND was deafening, a constant howl that reverberated through the hollowed-out remnants of the once-bustling city. Alex stood by the ruins of a collapsed skyscraper, his gaze lost in the distance, where the grey horizon seemed to merge with the ashen skies above. The world had been reduced to this—desolate, broken, and cold. Yet, despite the endless destruction, there was something that still gnawed at him, a sense of unfinished business that refused to be ignored.

His group had come so far, endured so much. But there was one thing he couldn't shake: the war. The war that had torn everything apart, and the role they had all played in it, whether directly or indirectly. It was impossible to escape the shadows of the past, and every day, it haunted him. The faces of the fallen, the promises made, the decisions that couldn't be undone. He had thought he could bury it, that the survival of the group would be enough to wash it away, but it wasn't.

He could feel Danny's presence behind him before the man even spoke. The heavy footsteps, the familiar weight of guilt that seemed to follow him like a dark cloud. Danny had never truly found peace. The horrors they had witnessed, the blood they had spilled—it was a part of him now, inextricable, like a scar that could never heal.

Alex turned to face him. "You're not just here for the supplies, are you?"

Danny's eyes didn't meet his at first. Instead, he stared at the ground, his face a mask of inner turmoil. "I didn't come here to talk about the past, Alex," he muttered, his voice thick with unspoken emotion. "But it's not over. You know it's not."

Alex felt a pang of frustration twist in his chest. "You don't think I know that? Every time I close my eyes, I see it—the war, the decisions, the people we've lost. I'm haunted by it, just like you."

"I didn't come to argue," Danny said, his voice softer now. "I came to make it right. At least... try to."

There was a long pause. Alex could feel the weight of the silence between them, heavy and oppressive. He had always respected Danny, but the burden of the past had driven a wedge between them, one that neither of them could bridge easily. But there was a shared understanding now, an unspoken agreement that they had to face what was left undone, no matter the cost.

"How?" Alex asked, his voice barely above a whisper.

Danny stepped forward, a determined look in his eyes. "I know where Victor's holding his next shipment. And I know what he's planning to do with it. If we stop him, it might just be enough to give us a chance—a real chance to rebuild. But we have to act fast."

Alex's mind raced. Victor Lynn. The name alone stirred a deep sense of anger in him, a reminder of everything that had gone wrong. Lynn had played the war to his advantage, exploiting the chaos for profit while manipulating the world's fragile system to his benefit. The same man who had been behind the collapse of governments, the destruction of entire nations. Stopping him could be the key to reversing some of the damage, but it wouldn't be easy.

"You know this isn't going to be simple, right?" Alex said, his voice heavy with the weight of reality.

Danny gave him a look, as if to say, *What else is new?*

"I'm not asking for easy," Danny replied. "But we can't keep running from the past. We can't keep pretending that we didn't play a part in all this." He gestured toward the ruins around them. "This is on all of us. If we want any kind of future, we have to confront it—head-on."

Alex closed his eyes for a moment, taking a deep breath. He had seen too many people like Danny—people who had been consumed by the consequences of their actions, struggling to find redemption in a world that seemed to offer none. But maybe, just maybe, there was a way out. Not for everyone, but for some.

"We'll need the others," Alex said finally, his voice resolute. "This isn't a fight we can win alone."

Danny nodded. "I'll talk to them."

As they began to walk back to the camp, Alex felt a weight lift off his shoulders, just a little. The path ahead was uncertain, the future unclear. But for the first time in a long while, he had a sense of purpose. They weren't just fighting to survive anymore. They were fighting for something greater. And maybe, just maybe, they could make things right.

The past had left its scars, but Alex knew that if they were going to build anything from the ashes of their former lives, they had to confront the unfinished business that had haunted them all. No more running. It was time to face what they had done—and make sure that whatever came next would be a future worth fighting for.

## ○ Ghosts of the War

THE RUINS OF THE ONCE-thriving city stretched endlessly in every direction, a shattered skeleton of its former self. Broken glass crunched beneath Alex's boots as he walked cautiously through the wreckage, the air thick with the scent of dust and decay. There were no more sounds of life here—no children's laughter, no hurried footsteps of workers trying to get home before curfew, no distant hum of vehicles. Only the oppressive silence remained, like the city itself had been swallowed whole by the past.

Alex stopped at what used to be a corner shop. Now, it was little more than a crumbled facade, its shelves long emptied, the windows shattered by the shockwaves of a battle that had left no one untouched. He ran his hand across the remains of a metal sign, now twisted and rusted. The faded logo of a once-popular café lingered there, an echo of a time before the war, before everything changed.

"Do you think they ever knew how it would end?" Danny's voice broke the silence, low and gruff. He had appeared behind Alex, his presence as silent as the graveyard they were walking through. "Before the bombs dropped, I mean."

Alex didn't answer immediately. He turned, his gaze catching the far-off horizon where the last hints of sunlight were dying, suffocated by a smoke-choked sky. The question haunted him more than he cared to admit. Had anyone truly understood the cost of their actions? The war hadn't just torn cities apart—it had shattered people, families, nations. In the end, everyone lost.

"I doubt it," Alex said finally. "But I guess that's the problem. No one ever thinks it's going to be this bad, until it's too late."

Danny nodded slowly, his eyes distant, as if he were seeing something far beyond the ruins around them. "The ghosts... they don't leave. They stay with you, even after the dust settles." He rubbed a hand across his face, the weariness of his words seeping into the air like a heavy fog.

For a moment, Alex didn't speak. He knew what Danny was referring to. The war had not only taken lives, it had taken parts of souls. They were both haunted, walking reminders of what they had done, what they had survived. Memories, blood-soaked and fragile, clung to them like a second skin. And no matter how far they walked or how many miles they put between themselves and the battlefield, those ghosts were always waiting, lurking at the edges of their minds.

Alex exhaled sharply, fighting to keep his composure. "We can't keep running, Danny. We have to face them... face what we've done. If we're going to fix any of this, we need to confront the ghosts. Not just the ones in our heads, but the ones in the world, too."

Danny's laugh was bitter, and there was a coldness in it that didn't belong to the world they used to know. "You think we can fix any of this? The war's over, Alex. The world's done. It's just a matter of time before the last of us are gone."

Alex shook his head, refusing to accept the defeat in Danny's voice. "No. It's not over. Not yet." He turned and began walking again, his footsteps firm, determined. "We still have a chance."

The city seemed to recoil as they moved through it, as if the buildings themselves knew they were the last remnants of something that would never return. The ghosts of the past were everywhere, lingering in the abandoned streets, in the twisted remains of homes and businesses. They were the people who had lived and loved here, the ones who had died too soon. The war had taken everything from them—everything except their memories.

As Alex walked deeper into the heart of the city, the weight of those memories pressed against him. He couldn't shake the faces of the people who had once stood here, who had once had lives to live. They had been torn apart by the same conflict that had torn apart the world itself. The lines between the living and the dead were becoming harder to see.

But Alex was determined to find a way out of the darkness. There had to be a way to rebuild, to move forward from this. Even if it meant facing the ghosts head-on.

Alex paused at the edge of a collapsed building, his mind still processing Danny's words. The ghosts were everywhere now, and he could almost hear their whispers, carried by the wind that swept through the skeletal remains of the city. The past was alive in these ruins, in the remnants of lives that once had purpose, now reduced to ash and memory.

"What about you?" Alex finally asked, his voice low, carrying an edge of challenge. "How are you going to face them?"

Danny didn't respond right away. He glanced at the crumbling structure they were standing near, a place that once served as a hospital. The large windows were shattered, and the walls, now scarred with time and war, seemed to exhale the collective suffering of those who had once passed through. Danny's eyes narrowed slightly, and for the first time, Alex saw a flicker of something—regret, maybe, or perhaps guilt. It was quickly buried, replaced by the cold, detached mask Danny usually wore.

"I'm not sure," Danny finally said, his voice tight. "Maybe I'll never face them... Maybe I'll just keep moving. Just like everyone else. Keep surviving."

Alex clenched his fists, the frustration bubbling up again. He could feel the pull of the ghosts in his own mind, those fragments of the war that never fully let go. The faces of fallen comrades, the victims they had failed to save, the people they had lost. They all whispered to him, demanding answers he didn't have. But Danny's defeatist attitude... it struck a nerve.

"You can't keep running forever, Danny," Alex said sharply, turning to face him. "We have to confront this. We owe it to them, to everyone we left behind. You're not the only one carrying this burden. We all are."

Danny's gaze met his, and for a moment, the weight of their shared trauma hung between them like a heavy fog. Alex could see the cracks in his facade, the vulnerability that Danny fought so hard to hide. But Danny didn't speak. He simply turned away, taking a few slow steps in the direction of the distant horizon.

Alex followed, knowing there was nothing more to say. They walked in silence for a while, each lost in their thoughts. The ghosts weren't just memories—they were alive in every corner of this war-torn world. The faces of the fallen had become a part of the earth itself, embedded in the rubble and twisted metal that had once been a home, a place of peace.

The sound of distant gunfire echoed faintly in the background, an ominous reminder that even though the official fighting might have stopped, the war was far from over. In the ashes of empires, the survivors were left to pick up the pieces, but there was no map to guide them. The future felt as fractured as the cities they had once fought to protect.

"Look around you, Danny," Alex said, his voice steady. "This is our mess. And it's not going to fix itself. The ghosts might never leave, but we can't let them control us."

Danny's lips pressed into a thin line, but he didn't respond. Instead, he looked out over the devastated cityscape, his eyes distant again. The ghosts of the war were settling deeper into the earth, feeding on the sorrow, the regret, the anger that people like Danny carried. But Alex refused to let them consume him. He couldn't.

He had made a promise—to himself, to those who had died, to the people who were still fighting for something. There was still a chance, and he wasn't going to let it slip away, not without a fight.

"Whatever happens next, Danny," Alex said with resolve, "we're going to make sure it counts. We can't let this be the end of us."

Danny glanced at him once more, the faintest trace of something—hope, perhaps—flashing in his eyes. Then he turned away again, a silent agreement passing between them. They didn't have the answers, not yet. But they had each other. And maybe, just maybe, that would be enough to face the ghosts of the war.

As they trudged further into the desolation, the day began to fade, casting long shadows over the ruins. The faint orange hue of sunset touched the broken walls like a final, tender caress, almost as if the world itself was mourning. Yet, there was no peace in the air, only the heavy weight of loss, the undeniable imprint of years spent in conflict.

Alex glanced at the horizon again, the memories of battles past still haunting him. The war had taken everything—homes, families, futures—but it had also given something back, something darker and more insidious. The truth: survival was no longer a simple matter of staying alive. It was a war of the mind, of the soul.

Danny, a few steps ahead, paused at the edge of a ravaged square. He kicked a piece of debris away from his path and looked up. A faint smile crept across his face, but it wasn't one of joy. It was the kind of smile someone wore when they were trying to hide something they didn't want others to see.

"We keep moving forward, don't we?" Danny's voice was quieter now, the edge of his earlier cynicism gone, replaced by something else—perhaps resignation, or the flicker of understanding.

Alex nodded but didn't answer right away. They had been walking for hours, and his legs ached, the weight of their journey pressing down on him. But it wasn't just the physical strain that weighed him down; it was the realization that, no matter how far they traveled, the ghosts of the war would follow.

"The world's broken, Danny," Alex said, his voice low but steady. "But if we don't try to fix it... if we just let it stay like this... then it really will be the end. Not just for us, but for everyone."

Danny's gaze flicked to him, searching his face for any sign of weakness, any crack in his resolve. But Alex held his ground. The ghosts of the past weren't just memories—they were warnings, reminders of what could happen again if they failed to learn from their mistakes.

"Is it even possible to fix it?" Danny asked, his voice almost lost in the wind. "I mean... look around us, Alex. The war ended, but nothing's really over. There's no rebuilding without the pieces to put back together."

Alex didn't have an answer for him. How could he? The world they had known was gone, replaced by a fractured reality where the boundaries of right and wrong were no longer clear. Trust was a luxury they couldn't afford. Everyone they met could either be a friend or a threat, and it was getting harder to tell the difference. The only thing that remained certain was the conflict inside each of them—the battle between hope and despair, between redemption and damnation.

"We still have each other," Alex said, almost as a mantra. "And we have the people who need us. We can't just walk away."

Danny didn't respond immediately. His eyes dropped to the ground, his brow furrowed as if he were searching for something, anything, to grasp onto. Finally, he nodded, slowly.

"Maybe you're right," he said. "But I can't promise I'll be able to shake off the ghosts. Not all of them."

Alex's heart sank, but he didn't show it. He couldn't afford to. If they were going to get through this, they had to keep moving forward, no matter the cost. They didn't have the luxury of being haunted by their past forever. The ghosts would always be there, but they had to learn to live with them. To carry them, instead of letting them drag them down.

As night fell, the darkness enveloped the city, hiding the scars of war, but also providing a temporary reprieve from the harsh reality they were living. The faint hum of distant machinery, the occasional burst of gunfire—it was all part of the new world order.

A world where survival had become a game of endurance, and the rules were written in blood.

They set up camp in the shadow of a collapsed tower, its once-proud silhouette now nothing more than a twisted monument to the devastation. The fire flickered between them, its warmth a small comfort against the biting cold of the night.

"We'll make it, Alex," Danny said suddenly, breaking the silence that had settled over them. His voice was quieter now, less cynical, as if a part of him had finally found a sliver of hope in the bleakness around them.

Alex looked at him, the faintest trace of a smile tugging at the corners of his lips. He didn't know if it was true, but it was enough to hear it.

"We'll make it," Alex echoed. And in that moment, they both believed it, if only for a heartbeat.

The night passed slowly, the crackling fire the only sound in the otherwise oppressive silence. They took turns keeping watch, but neither of them could shake the feeling that they weren't alone. The remnants of the war had created an unsettling stillness, as if the world itself was holding its breath, waiting for the next inevitable disaster.

Alex stared into the fire, his thoughts spinning. The weight of the past was like a heavy cloak draped over his shoulders. It wasn't just the ghosts of the war he had to confront—it was the question of what came after. What did it mean to survive when everything that made the world worth living for had been reduced to rubble?

In the distance, the faint rumble of an engine reached his ears. He sat up, instantly alert, his hand resting on the hilt of his weapon. The sound grew louder, closer, until the silhouette of a vehicle appeared against the moonlit horizon.

"Someone's coming," Alex said in a low voice, nudging Danny awake.

Danny groaned, blinking against the fading remnants of sleep. He straightened up slowly, his eyes squinting toward the approaching vehicle. "Could be trouble," he muttered.

Alex nodded, his fingers twitching at the thought of another confrontation. He knew that trust was a currency few could afford in this broken world, and even fewer people remained untouched by the chaos of the war. The unknown was always a threat, a reminder that every encounter could either be a lifeline or a deadly trap.

The vehicle came to a halt not far from their camp. It was a battered old truck, caked with dirt, its tires worn thin from endless miles of rough terrain. The headlights flickered before shutting off, and the engine died with a soft sputter.

Alex and Danny exchanged a glance, both of them wary. They couldn't afford to be complacent.

A figure stepped out of the truck, silhouetted by the moonlight. A tall man, his face obscured by a hood. He moved with a slow, deliberate gait, the sound of his boots crunching on the gravel almost too loud in the silence.

"Who are you?" Alex called out, his voice firm, demanding an answer.

The man paused, then lifted his head, revealing a scarred face. His eyes, sharp and calculating, locked onto Alex and Danny.

"Name's Viktor," the man said in a gravelly voice. "I don't want trouble. Just need some help."

Danny stood slowly, eyeing the newcomer with suspicion. "Help? What kind of help?"

Viktor looked around, his gaze flicking toward the ruins surrounding them. "I've been following your trail for days. I know you're not the type to hide in the shadows like the others. You fight, you survive. And right now, I need someone who knows how to do both."

Alex didn't lower his guard. "And why should we trust you?"

Viktor stepped closer, his hands held up in a gesture of peace. "Because I'm not asking for a favor. I've got information—information that could help you find what you're looking for. And I'm offering it to you."

Danny took a step forward, narrowing his eyes. "What kind of information?"

Viktor's lips curled into a tight, knowing smile. "The kind that might just lead you to the heart of what's left of this war. To the people behind it. The ones who still pull the strings from the shadows."

Alex's heart skipped a beat. The war was supposed to be over, but the remnants of its power still lingered, crawling beneath the surface, unseen but ever-present. If Viktor's words were true, it meant that the fight wasn't over—not by a long shot.

"What's in it for you?" Alex asked, his voice guarded but curious.

Viktor's expression darkened, his eyes narrowing with a mix of regret and resolve. "Survival. Revenge. And the hope that maybe... just maybe... there's still something worth fighting for."

There was something about Viktor that unsettled Alex, a hunger that was buried deep in his eyes. But there was also a certain urgency in his voice that felt genuine.

Alex exchanged another glance with Danny, who looked like he was weighing the same questions.

"Alright," Alex said, after a long pause. "We'll listen. But don't think for a second that we'll just follow you blindly."

Viktor nodded, a grim look crossing his face. "Fair enough. Just hear me out. The rest will come after."

As Viktor began to speak, outlining the delicate web of information he had gathered, Alex's mind raced. Could this be the opportunity they had been waiting for? Or was it another trap, another ghost to haunt them?

The future felt as uncertain as ever, but one thing was clear: the ghosts of the war had not finished their work. And neither had the survivors. They still had a long road ahead.

Viktor's voice faded into the crackling of the fire as he began to outline what he knew. His words were calculated, careful—almost as if he'd rehearsed them for a long time.

"There's a network of people," Viktor continued, "those who helped orchestrate this war from the very beginning. They're still out there, hiding in plain sight. They control what's left of the economy, the power structures. But more importantly, they control the narrative. The public's perception of what happened, who the real enemies are... it's all been twisted. I've seen it firsthand."

Alex's brow furrowed. "What do you mean by 'the narrative'? People are still fighting, still dying. The truth's in the bloodshed, Viktor. Not in some story they're trying to sell."

Viktor's face hardened. "That's exactly what they want you to believe. The war didn't just happen. It was planned. Every bomb, every assassination—it was part of a larger design. You think it's chaos, but it's been controlled from the start."

Danny shifted, uneasy. "So you're saying it's all some big lie? That the people who are suffering don't matter?"

"No," Viktor replied quickly, shaking his head. "Not exactly. The people—the soldiers, the civilians—they matter. But their suffering is the price of something much bigger. And those who control the war, who pull the strings behind the scenes—they've already moved on. They've got their sights set on something even greater."

Alex stood up suddenly, his hand gripping the edge of a nearby boulder as he processed Viktor's words. "So why come to us? What could two people like us do against that kind of power?"

Viktor's eyes bore into him, full of quiet intensity. "Because you're not just two people. You're survivors. You've made it this far while others fell. You understand what it means to fight—not just for victory, but for survival. That's why you matter."

The words hit harder than Alex expected. There was truth in them. They had fought for so long, not because they had any grand vision of changing the world, but because they had no choice. Surviving was the only thing that kept them going.

"So what do you want us to do?" Alex asked, his voice low.

Viktor paused, taking a breath, his face softening for a brief moment. "I need you to help me track them. To bring the truth to light, if it's still possible. But there's a catch. They'll do anything to stop us. They'll kill anyone who gets in the way."

"We've faced worse than that," Danny said, his tone defiant, though Alex could see the uncertainty in his eyes. "You're asking us to hunt ghosts, Viktor. People who think they're untouchable."

"I'm asking you to fight," Viktor replied. "Not ghosts, not shadows. These are people. Real people. They just happen to be hiding behind layers of power, wealth, and influence. But they're still human."

Alex stared into the fire, the flames dancing and crackling, the embers glowing red. He could hear the faint whistle of the wind outside their small camp, a constant reminder of how fragile their existence had become. They weren't just surviving. They were trying to hold onto something—something that felt increasingly out of reach.

"I don't know," Alex said after a long silence, his voice more to himself than anyone else. "We've fought long enough. Do we really want to keep fighting? Do we even know what we're fighting for anymore?"

Viktor's eyes softened, and for the first time, Alex saw something other than calculation. There was a weariness in them, something that echoed Alex's own thoughts. "I don't have all the answers. But I do know one thing. If we don't fight, if we just walk away... the war, everything that's been done, it'll be for nothing. The people who died, the things we've lost—it'll all have been a waste."

Danny exchanged a glance with Alex, his eyes searching, weighing the words, the uncertainty, the cost. Finally, after a long moment, he spoke.

"We're in this already. It's just a matter of how far we go."

Alex nodded, his mind made up. He didn't have all the answers, but he knew one thing: as long as the war's ghosts still haunted the world, there would be no peace. And as long as there were people willing to fight, they still had a chance to make a difference.

"I'm with you," Alex said to Viktor, his voice steady now. "But we need to move quickly. We don't know how much time we have before they come for us."

Viktor's face darkened, his mouth tightening into a thin line. "I was hoping you'd say that. We need to find the heart of the operation. If we can disrupt it, we might just have a shot at stopping them."

The fire crackled as the wind picked up, carrying with it the distant rumble of thunder. The storm that had been building, both in the sky and on the ground, was about to break.

And this time, Alex wasn't sure if they'd be ready for it.

• • • •

## ○ Sophia's Vision at Risk

SOPHIA SAT IN THE DIMLY lit lab, her eyes fixated on the monitor in front of her. The data, once so promising, now seemed to spiral out of control. The stabilizer—a device capable of regenerating ecosystems, of reversing the environmental collapse that had gripped the planet for decades—was slipping from her grasp. The codes she had worked tirelessly on were no longer aligning. Something was wrong, and she couldn't afford to waste any more time.

She ran a trembling hand through her hair, glancing at the scattered papers around her. Her invention had been the beacon of hope in a dying world, and now it was on the verge of failure. The weight of the task at hand pressed down on her like a thousand tons of stone. The future, it seemed, hung on the fragile edge of her success—or her failure.

The door creaked open behind her. She didn't need to turn around to know who it was. Alex had a way of entering without a sound, his presence filling the room before he even spoke.

"Still at it?" he asked, his voice tinged with both concern and admiration.

Sophia didn't answer immediately. Her fingers hovered over the keyboard, typing in commands with mechanical precision. There was no time for pleasantries, no time for small talk. The world wasn't waiting for her to fix it.

"Nothing works," she muttered, almost to herself. "The stabilizer is destabilizing the ecosystem instead of fixing it. I don't know why."

Alex stepped closer, watching the numbers flicker on the screen. He could see the frustration in her eyes, the desperation that only someone who had staked everything on this one invention could understand.

"You're close," he said quietly, more to reassure himself than her. "I know you are."

Sophia shook her head, frustration seeping through every pore. "Close? I was close a year ago, Alex. Now it's too late. If we don't fix this, we'll be nothing more than the last remnants of a dying world."

He placed a hand on her shoulder, an anchor in the storm that threatened to swallow them both. "You've given everything for this, Sophia. We can't give up now."

Her breath caught in her throat as she looked up at him. "You don't understand. It's not just the stabilizer anymore. It's everything. This device was supposed to save us. Now, if it fails, it will end us faster than any bomb could."

She turned back to the monitor, her fingers hovering over the keyboard once more. A faint whirring noise filled the silence, the sound of the machine processing data—data that she no longer trusted.

Alex stayed silent, sensing the tension in the air. He had seen her determination before, that unwavering resolve that had carried her through years of setbacks. But now, something had shifted. He could see the cracks in her armor, the doubt that had crept in like a slow poison.

"There's always another way," Alex said finally, his voice low. "We just need to find it."

Sophia's hand fell away from the keyboard, her body slumping in defeat. "What if there isn't? What if we've already run out of time?"

Her words hung in the air, a stark reminder of just how fragile their situation had become. She had put all her faith in this device, in the idea that she could turn the tide of a dying world. Now, the dream of salvation seemed like a distant memory, a fading echo of a time when hope was still something to reach for.

Alex stepped away, pacing slowly around the lab, his mind racing. He had always trusted Sophia—trusted her intellect, her vision for a better future. But now, for the first time, he wasn't sure if that vision could survive the weight of their reality.

"We need to get you some help," Alex said suddenly, his voice cutting through the silence.

Sophia looked up, startled. "Help?"

"Not just any help. We need someone who can see the things you're missing—someone who can help you push the boundaries even further. There's no shame in needing assistance, Sophia."

She frowned, the thought of bringing someone else into her project unsettling her. She had spent years building this, and the idea of involving someone else felt like admitting failure. But deep down, she knew Alex was right. She was too close to the problem to see it clearly anymore.

"You think it's that simple?" she asked, her voice tinged with skepticism. "That we can just find someone who has the answers we don't?"

"I'm not saying it's simple," Alex replied. "But I am saying we can't do this alone anymore. You can't."

Sophia sat back in her chair, the weight of his words sinking in. She had always believed she could solve this on her own. The stabilizer had been her dream, her salvation for a world on the brink of extinction. But now, with the clock ticking and the world slipping through her fingers, she had to consider the impossible.

Could she really allow someone else to take part in this? Could she trust them with her vision, with the very future of the planet?

Her fingers hovered over the keyboard again, but this time, it wasn't to type commands. Instead, she found herself searching for something else—something she hadn't known she needed until now.

"Alright," she said finally, her voice quieter than before. "We'll find help. But if they mess this up, Alex..." She trailed off, her gaze hardening. "There won't be a second chance."

Alex nodded, understanding the weight of her words. "I know. But we can't afford to fail."

The future, it seemed, was slipping through their fingers, but maybe—just maybe—there was a chance left.

## ○ Alex's Breaking Point

ALEX STOOD AT THE EDGE of the crumbling building, looking out over the city that had once been full of life and hope. Now, all that remained were the remnants of civilization, piles of rubble, and distant echoes of what had been lost. His fingers gripped the cold metal railing, the only thing separating him from the drop below. The weight of the world had settled on his shoulders in a way that no training, no strategy, had ever prepared him for. Every decision he made seemed to lead to a new complication, a new betrayal.

He had always considered himself a man of reason, someone who could think through the chaos and find a solution. But now, every path forward felt like a dead end. The group that had followed him this far, the survivors who looked to him for leadership, were becoming less certain of his ability to lead them through the storm. The doubt was creeping in. The moral compromises he had made, the sacrifices he had encouraged—what had they led to? Was it all for nothing? His eyes scanned the horizon, but nothing seemed to offer any answer.

The radio in his hand crackled with static, and then Emma's voice broke through. "Alex, we need to talk. Now."

The urgency in her tone pulled him from his thoughts, and he straightened, turning towards the makeshift command center they had set up in an old warehouse. He moved with purpose, though his legs felt heavy, as though every step was a reminder of how far he had strayed from the man he had once been.

Inside, Emma was pacing, her brow furrowed in frustration. "It's falling apart, Alex," she said, her voice barely above a whisper. "We can't keep pretending we're in control."

"I know," Alex replied, his voice tight. "But what else can we do? We can't just give up."

"We've been surviving, Alex. That's all we've been doing. Survival isn't enough anymore."

Alex ran a hand through his hair, his mind racing. He had always prided himself on being able to think several steps ahead, but now every choice seemed to lead him into deeper waters. "What do you suggest, then? What do we do when we have nothing left but scraps of a world that doesn't even remember how to function?"

Emma stopped pacing and looked him in the eyes, her expression softening. "We fight, Alex. We fight for more than just survival. We fight for the future."

The words hit him like a punch to the gut. It wasn't the first time he'd heard them, but now, in this moment, they felt like a challenge. She was right. But how? How could they fight when the enemy wasn't a single force, but the very collapse of everything they had once known?

"I can't keep doing this," he muttered, his voice breaking for the first time in weeks. "I don't know how to fix it anymore."

Emma stepped closer, her presence grounding him in a way that only she could. "You don't have to fix everything, Alex. But you can fix this. One choice at a time."

For the first time in days, Alex felt something stir within him. A flicker of the man he used to be. But it was faint, and he was still unsure if it was enough to overcome the weight of his doubts.

"We'll have to make some impossible choices," he said, the words coming out slower than he intended. "Some choices that might cost us everything."

Emma nodded, her face hardening with resolve. "We're already paying the price for the choices we haven't made."

For a moment, the room was silent, and Alex was left to wrestle with the weight of what he knew needed to happen next. The stakes had never been higher. Their survival—no, the survival of everything they cared about—depended on the decisions they would make in the coming days.

The enemy wasn't just Victor Lynn or any of the factions they had fought against. The true enemy was the fear that had taken root in his own heart, the doubt that had clouded his judgment. And that fear, Alex realized, had to be confronted head-on.

"I'm in," he finally said, his voice steadier now. "We fight. We fight for the future."

Emma's expression softened, but there was no smile. Not yet. But in her eyes, Alex saw something that reminded him of what they were still fighting for: hope. Even in the darkest of times, it could still be found, even if it seemed like only a flicker.

They didn't have all the answers, but for the first time in a long while, Alex felt like they had a chance.

The road ahead would be long, fraught with dangers, and he knew the choices would only get harder. But as he stepped back from the window, his resolve hardened. This was his breaking point, the moment where he either gave in or found the strength to push forward. And he would push forward.

For the future.

For the fight.

And for the chance to rebuild what had been lost.

## ○ The Shattered Bond

THE WIND HOWLED THROUGH the desolate city streets, carrying with it the scent of decay. Buildings that once stood proud now lay in ruins, their skeletal frames jutting into the gray sky like the bones of a forgotten civilization. The world outside had crumbled, but inside the small, makeshift shelter, the flickering light of a single lamp cast long shadows on the faces of the survivors. Alex sat across from Danny, the silence between them thick and suffocating, heavy with unspoken words and shared history.

It had been days since the ambush, days since everything had started to unravel. The tension was palpable, the fractures within the group widening, like cracks in a dam waiting to burst. But nothing seemed more fragile than the bond between Alex and Danny. Once, they had been brothers-in-arms, two soldiers fighting side by side in a war that had torn the world apart. Now, they were strangers caught in a web of guilt, distrust, and unresolved anger.

Danny's eyes avoided Alex's gaze, his jaw tight, the weight of his past too much to bear. Every movement he made seemed to carry the burden of the decisions he had been forced to make. The war had done this to them—broken them, twisted them into something unrecognizable. But it wasn't just the war. It was what had happened after. The betrayal. The choices that had driven them apart.

"Danny..." Alex's voice cracked the silence, low and steady, but tinged with frustration. "We can't keep doing this. We need to trust each other again."

Danny clenched his fists, his knuckles white, the muscles in his arms tensing. "Trust? After everything? After what I did? I don't deserve your trust. Not after the things I've done. Not after the things we've all done."

Alex exhaled sharply, his fingers tapping nervously on the edge of the table. He knew Danny was right. There was no going back. The past had shaped them, molded them into something different, something scarred. But in this broken world, trust was all they had left. Without it, they were doomed to fall apart completely.

"We're still here, Danny. We're still alive, and that means something. It means we have a chance to fix this—fix ourselves."

Danny's eyes flicked to Alex's for the briefest of moments, but it was enough. The old connection was there, hidden beneath the layers of anger and regret. It had always been there, like a faint echo in the background, a reminder of who they once were. But the question lingered in the air: Was it enough?

A sudden noise from outside the shelter broke the fragile moment between them. Both men stood at once, their instincts kicking in. Alex moved toward the door, his hand resting on the hilt of his knife. Danny followed, his gaze flickering back to Alex before he too prepared for whatever was coming.

It was a reminder, in the worst possible way, that the world outside offered no second chances, no redemption. And it was this unforgiving world that had shattered their bond. But there was still time, still a chance to rebuild, if only they could face the demons of the past together.

As the door creaked open, they stepped out into the unknown, side by side once more. The bond between them was fragile, but it wasn't entirely broken. Not yet. And that, in this world of ruin, was enough. For now.

# 8. A World in Flames

## ○ The Rebels' Last Hope

The night was thick with smoke, the sky above a choking blanket of ash and flame. In the ruins of what had once been a bustling city, the last remnants of a once-proud rebellion huddled in the shadows, waiting for dawn that might never come.

Alex stood among them, his face etched with the lines of exhaustion and doubt. His eyes, once filled with the fire of defiance, now carried the weight of too many failures. The rebellion was crumbling, its leaders either dead or scattered, and with each passing hour, the hope of a brighter future seemed more and more like a fading memory.

He glanced over at Sophia, who was hunched over a makeshift table, her fingers moving feverishly across a tattered map. Her brow was furrowed, her expression tense. The weight of her invention—the stabilizer—hung heavy in the air. It was supposed to be their salvation, the one thing that could turn the tide in their favor. But in the wrong hands, it could be the final nail in humanity's coffin.

"How much longer?" Alex asked, his voice low, barely audible over the distant crackling of fires and the occasional muffled explosion.

Sophia didn't look up. "We're close. We need one more supply drop, and then we can begin the process."

Alex's heart sank. They had been close for days now, but every time they thought they had what they needed, something went wrong. It was as though the world itself was conspiring against them, refusing to let them succeed.

"The enemy's closing in," Danny said, his voice cutting through the silence. "We don't have much time."

Alex turned to face his second-in-command, the one person he trusted more than anyone else. Danny's worn, battle-hardened features were grim, but there was something else in his eyes—a flicker of resolve that Alex had seen before, in the darkest of times.

"We fight or die," Alex replied. "There's no other choice."

"We can't do this alone," Danny said, his tone firm but urgent. "We need the other factions to join us. But they're scattered, leaderless... They won't come unless they know we have a chance."

Alex knew he was right. The alliance with the other factions had been fragile from the beginning, built on mistrust and desperation. And now, with everything hanging by a thread, they couldn't afford any more doubts, any more delays.

"I'll reach out," Alex said. "But we need to be quick. Once the enemy realizes we're on the move, they'll come for us with everything they have."

Sophia's eyes flicked up from the map, locking onto Alex's. There was a strange intensity in her gaze, a mixture of hope and fear. "The stabilizer," she said, her voice tight with urgency. "It's the only thing that can make this work. We need to get it to the right place, or all of this—" She gestured to the map, to the scattered remnants of their forces. "—will be for nothing."

Alex nodded, feeling the weight of her words settle heavily on his chest. They had come too far, sacrificed too much, to let it all slip away now.

"We'll get it done," he said, his voice harder now. "We fight until the end."

The rebel camp stirred as the word spread. They would make their final stand. The wind howled as the flames from distant battles lit the horizon, casting long shadows over the earth. For the first time in days, Alex felt the flicker of something deep within him—a spark of defiance, a glimmer of the hope that had driven him to this point.

They would either rise from the ashes or be consumed by them.

And so, the rebels prepared for their last stand. Weapons were checked, plans were drawn, and every last ounce of strength was summoned. There was no turning back. The final chapter of their story was about to be written.

The night dragged on, thick with the weight of unspoken words and preparations. Each moment seemed to stretch into eternity as the rebels gathered their remaining strength, eyes scanning the horizon for any sign of the enemy. The silence between them was heavy, each person locked in their thoughts, aware that the coming battle might be their last.

Sophia remained at the center of their makeshift command post, her mind racing over the final steps of her plan. The stabilizer was ready, but they were still missing a crucial component—something that had eluded them for weeks. Without it, the device would be nothing more than a shiny piece of scrap metal. And if they couldn't get it to work, their last hope would be extinguished before it had even begun.

"We need the codes," she said, breaking the silence. Her voice was barely above a whisper, but the urgency in it was unmistakable.

Danny stepped forward. "The codes are with Victor. We know this. But how do you plan to get them?"

Alex's eyes narrowed. They had been trying to crack Victor's secure network for weeks, but it was like trying to pick a lock that had no key. The man was brilliant and paranoid, and he had placed more obstacles in their path than Alex cared to count. Every failed attempt had cost them dearly.

"We don't have a choice," Alex said, his voice hardening. "We go after him. Now."

Sophia hesitated, her fingers tracing the lines on the map. "If we make a move on Victor's base, they'll know we're coming. It'll be over before it begins."

"We can't keep hiding," Danny said, his voice grim but determined. "If we don't act now, we'll be too late. The enemy's already massing forces. We need to strike first."

Alex understood the stakes. Their survival depended on getting the stabilizer operational, and for that, they needed those codes. There was no room for second chances, no more time to wait. The enemy would be on them soon, and they would have to act with everything they had.

"We go in, we get the codes, and we leave. Fast. No mistakes." Alex's words were sharp, the weight of the decision hanging in the air. This was their final chance to turn the tide.

Sophia nodded, but the doubt in her eyes was clear. "If Victor catches wind of this... it could be worse than just losing the stabilizer. He'll hunt us down. One by one."

"I know the risks," Alex said. "But we've lost too many already. We fight for those who are still standing."

The rebels gathered their gear, each movement deliberate, the weight of their choices pressing on their shoulders. They weren't just fighting for themselves anymore—they were fighting for a future that seemed ever more out of reach.

Alex looked to Sophia, who was securing the stabilizer to her pack, her face set in grim determination. "We can still win this, right?" he asked quietly, though part of him wasn't sure if he believed it anymore.

Sophia's eyes met his, and for the briefest moment, her resolve wavered. "We have to," she said, though the doubt in her voice was undeniable. "If we fail... everything is lost."

The rebels moved out under the cover of night, the city around them silent and eerie in its desolation. The air was thick with tension, every step they took echoing in their ears. The path to Victor's base was treacherous, a labyrinth of crumbling buildings and abandoned streets. They moved like shadows, each of them knowing that any misstep could be their last.

As they neared the outskirts of Victor's territory, the tension escalated. The faintest sound—an unusual rustle in the air, a distant footstep—felt like a thunderclap in the silence. Alex held up his hand, signaling for them to stop.

"They're out there," Danny muttered, his eyes scanning the area. "I can feel them."

Alex's pulse quickened. The enemy was close, but so was their goal. They could see the flickering lights of Victor's fortress in the distance, a sprawling complex that seemed to pulse with power. This was it—their final chance.

Sophia stepped forward, her voice steady despite the tension. "Once we're in, there's no turning back. We do what we came for, then we get out. Fast."

The group nodded, the gravity of the mission weighing on them. They had no illusions about what lay ahead. The enemy was formidable, and Victor's forces were ruthless. But they had no choice. There was no more time to waste.

With a deep breath, Alex gave the signal. The rebels advanced, moving in tight formation, the weight of their last hope pressing down on them. It would either be their salvation or their doom.

## ○ Betrayal in the Ranks

THE TENSION HAD BEEN building for weeks, but nothing could prepare them for the blow that came with the morning light. The air, once filled with the hopeful murmurs of a rebellion on the rise, now felt suffocating, thick with the scent of betrayal. Alex stood by the makeshift window, looking out over the desolate landscape, trying to steady his breath. The sun barely broke through the clouds, casting long shadows across the ruined city. This was supposed to be their moment—their chance to strike back. Yet, the revelation shattered everything.

"How could he?" Danny's voice cut through the silence, raw with disbelief. He stood in the doorway, his frame stiff, his eyes burning with a mixture of anger and sorrow.

Alex turned, his face pale. "I don't know," he muttered, rubbing his temples as if the pressure could help clear the fog of confusion. "But we can't ignore it. It's too dangerous."

The letter, torn and bloodstained, had been left on the table in the center of their camp, an act too deliberate to be anything other than a message. The traitor was one of them. Someone in their midst had turned, feeding information to Victor Lynn. Alex had spent years negotiating in a world of secrets, but this? This was different. This wasn't a negotiation—it was a dagger to the heart.

Danny's fists clenched, and his breath quickened. "We need to act now. Find out who did this before it's too late."

The others had already gathered around the table, their faces grim. Sophia, who had once been the quietest of them all, now stood with her jaw set tight, her gaze unwavering. The destruction of her research, the only hope left for a chance at saving what little remained of the Earth's ecosystems, was no longer a theoretical threat. Now, it was a reality.

Alex knew what they were all thinking. The fight for survival had always been hard, but now it seemed that their greatest challenge wasn't the enemy outside the gates—it was the enemy within their walls.

"Everyone's a suspect," Emma spoke up, her voice steady despite the storm raging inside her. "We have to trust no one. Not even ourselves."

The weight of her words hung in the air, settling heavily in the room. Trust—something so vital in this fractured world—had always been their strongest weapon. But now, that weapon was shattered, and without it, they were vulnerable.

"I'll check the records," Danny said, his voice sharp. "If someone has been leaking information, there will be a trail. We find it, we find the traitor."

Alex nodded, though his heart was heavy. He had fought for every inch of ground they'd gained, every person who had stood by them. But now, as he stared at the faces around him, he realized just how fragile their unity was. Each of them had their own pasts, their own motives—and somewhere among them, someone had decided their fight for survival wasn't worth the cost of loyalty.

Hours passed in tense silence as Danny sifted through the records, the rest of the group kept watch. Time seemed to stretch, every second more unbearable than the last. Finally, Danny emerged from the back room, his expression unreadable.

"I've got something," he said. "A name."

Alex's blood ran cold. He knew what this moment was. It wasn't just the uncovering of a traitor—it was the unraveling of everything they'd worked for. The future of their world, the lives of their people, and the tenuous alliances they had built over the past months were now in jeopardy.

The name Danny held in his hand was one Alex hadn't expected.

"James," Alex whispered. "James Turner."

James. The man who had been with them from the start, the one who had fought beside them, bled beside them. The one who had shown the most promise, who had carried the weight of their hopes as much as anyone. And now, he was the one who had sold them out.

"We need to confront him," Danny said, his voice low, almost cold. "Now."

Alex shook his head. "No. We can't act impulsively. This isn't just about him anymore. It's about the survival of everyone here. We need to do this carefully."

The group was silent, their eyes flicking nervously between one another. Alex could see the fear in their expressions. Fear not just of James, but of what his betrayal meant for them all. How could they trust anyone now?

But there was no time to dwell on that. Victor Lynn wasn't the only threat they had to face. The world outside was crumbling, and they were running out of time. The rebellion they had worked so hard to ignite could not falter—not now.

"We'll confront him," Alex said finally, his voice hardening. "But we do it together. No one moves without the others. We'll make him tell us everything—about Victor, about who else might be involved. And we'll make sure he doesn't live to cause more damage."

With a final glance at the group, Alex turned, his mind already racing through the next steps. The future of their cause—and their survival—depended on how they handled this betrayal. They could either tear each other apart or unite in the face of it.

There was no middle ground.

## ○ The Fall of the Fortress

THE BITTER WIND HOWLED through the cracked, charred walls of what was once a formidable fortress. The sprawling complex, now reduced to rubble and shadow, stood as a silent testament to the violence and greed that had shaped this world. The once imposing structure, a symbol of power and security, was now a crumbling relic of a time long past. Its tall, iron gates—once unyielding—now hung crooked and broken, unable to withstand the relentless tide of chaos.

Alex stood at the edge of the ruins, his breath shallow, his mind racing. The battle had been brutal, more so than he'd ever anticipated. The survivors, those few who remained loyal to their cause, had fought tooth and nail to tear down the fortress walls. The weight of leadership pressed heavily on his shoulders as he surveyed the wreckage—each fallen comrade a reminder of the stakes they had all gambled with.

The sound of distant gunfire echoed in the stillness, a cruel reminder that the war was far from over. The rebels had been victorious, but at what cost? Victory meant nothing if they couldn't hold onto it. The fortress had been their last bastion, their final chance at resistance against the ruthless tyranny of Victor Lynn. But now, with the structure lying in ruins, the fate of their movement rested on fragile hopes.

Danny was the first to approach, his face smeared with dirt and blood. His eyes were hollow, yet there was something in them—an unspoken understanding, a deep resignation. "It's over," he muttered, more to himself than to Alex. His voice, though low, carried the weight of years spent in a war that had torn both body and soul.

Alex didn't answer right away. His gaze was fixed on the remnants of the fortress, his mind running through the possibilities. There was no turning back now. The walls were down, the gate shattered. They were vulnerable. And yet, the flicker of something else stirred in him—a small ember of hope that had refused to die, no matter how many times it had been smothered by despair.

"Is it really?" Alex asked quietly, as if testing the words. "We still have Sophia's invention. We still have a chance to make this right."

Danny shook his head, wiping the sweat and grime from his forehead. "And what if we don't?" he asked, his voice rough with a mixture of frustration and exhaustion. "What if this is the last stand? What if we're just one more name on a list of failed revolutions?"

Alex clenched his fists, the familiar fire of determination igniting deep inside him. He couldn't let go. Not now. Not when they had come so far. The dream of restoring some semblance of balance, some chance of rebuilding what was lost, was still alive within him.

"We fight," Alex said, his tone steady, unwavering. "We fight because we have to. Because if we don't, then Victor wins. He wins, and everything we've fought for... everything they've died for... will have been in vain."

Emma emerged from the smoke-filled haze, her expression grim. She had seen too much, felt the weight of too many lost lives. Yet her resolve was unbroken. "The world is watching us," she said, her voice laced with a quiet urgency. "We can't fail now."

There was a pause as the weight of her words settled in, each of them understanding the gravity of what was ahead. The fortress was fallen, but the real battle was only just beginning. It was no longer about reclaiming the past; it was about shaping a future from the ashes of destruction.

Sophia arrived at the scene, her steps slow but determined. She held in her hands the device that could change everything—the stabilizer that might just give the earth a fighting chance. She had worked for this moment her entire life, but now, in the midst of this chaos, the weight of her invention seemed almost unbearable.

"We're not done," she said, her voice strong, though it trembled slightly. "This is only the beginning. We have to move quickly. There's no telling how much time we have left."

Alex nodded, understanding the urgency. But in his heart, a nagging doubt began to creep in. What if it was already too late? What if Victor's influence had already spread too far, his grip on the world too strong to break? They had destroyed his fortress, but that was only one battle. The war for the future was far from over.

A sudden explosion rocked the ground beneath them, pulling Alex from his thoughts. The sound was deafening, followed by a plume of smoke rising into the air. His heart skipped a beat—Victor's forces were closing in. The real fight was about to begin.

"Get to the safe zone," Alex shouted, his voice cutting through the chaos. "Now! Everyone, move!"

The survivors scattered, moving with a sense of urgency that matched the gravity of the situation. Alex caught a glimpse of Danny, Emma, and Sophia as they made their way to the extraction point, each of them weighed down by their own burdens, but each of them still willing to fight for a future that seemed more uncertain with every passing second.

As Alex turned to follow, his gaze lingered on the shattered remnants of the fortress. It was gone. But in its place, something else was rising—a spark of defiance, a flicker of resistance. The fall of the fortress wasn't the end. It was the beginning of a new chapter. And Alex, for all his doubts and fears, was ready to face whatever came next.

The escape route was narrow, winding through the once-pristine halls that now lay in tatters. The air smelled of smoke and burning debris, an acrid mix that stung Alex's lungs with every breath. His heart pounded in his chest as he moved swiftly through the wreckage, the sound of boots pounding on cracked stone echoing off the walls. They had to get out—fast.

Behind him, he could hear Danny's voice, low and tense, barking orders to the others. Emma's sharp commands followed, directing everyone with military precision. But Alex's thoughts were far from the immediate danger; they were on what lay ahead.

The stabilizer was their last hope, but even that was a fragile thread in a world teetering on the edge of destruction.

They reached the underground tunnel, the faint light from their flashlights casting long shadows on the walls. Alex glanced over his shoulder to see Sophia, her face set in grim determination, still clutching the device that might just save them all. But she looked exhausted, her pale skin drawn tight over her features. The weight of the world rested on her shoulders, and Alex knew that if she faltered, so would they all.

"We're almost there," Emma's voice cut through his thoughts. "Keep moving."

But before they could take another step, the ground trembled beneath their feet. A deafening roar echoed from above, followed by the sound of crumbling stone. The tunnel entrance was shaking, the ceiling threatening to collapse.

"We don't have much time!" Danny shouted.

Alex gritted his teeth. The walls of the fortress were coming down, and Victor's forces were relentless. But there was no turning back now.

"We push through," he said, his voice steady despite the chaos. "Get to the extraction point. We don't stop until we're out."

They moved faster, their pace quickening as the rumble of explosions grew louder, nearer. The tunnel seemed to stretch endlessly before them, the light flickering and sputtering as the walls continued to tremble. But they had to hold on, had to believe that they could survive this.

Finally, they emerged from the tunnel, the cold night air hitting them with a rush of relief. They weren't free yet, but the surface felt like a small victory in itself.

Alex scanned the horizon, searching for any sign of their extraction team. In the distance, the dim glow of a vehicle's headlights shone through the haze. The safe zone was within reach.

But before they could move toward it, a dark silhouette appeared against the backdrop of the ruined fortress. Victor's men.

They were already here.

Alex's instincts kicked in. "Everyone, take cover!" he yelled.

Gunfire erupted, cutting through the air with a brutal crack. Bullets whizzed past, narrowly missing. Alex dove behind a crumbling wall, his hand instinctively reaching for his weapon. He heard the sharp reports of Danny and Emma's guns as they returned fire, but the odds were not in their favor. Victor's forces were too many, too well-armed.

"We need to push through!" Alex shouted. "We can't let them get us now!"

Sophia was crouched beside him, her hands trembling as she fiddled with the stabilizer's settings. Her face was pale with fear, but her resolve never wavered. "I can't promise it'll work," she said breathlessly. "But if I can just get it calibrated—"

The air was thick with tension, and the fight for survival felt endless. The rebels fired back, creating a temporary barricade, but it wouldn't last. Alex knew this would be their last stand, and they had to make it count.

Suddenly, Emma's voice rang out, urgent and commanding. "Move! Now!"

The extraction team had arrived. The vehicle screeched to a halt, and a cloud of dust filled the air as its doors flung open. The rebels ran, darting through the hail of gunfire. Alex, Danny, and Sophia sprinted forward, adrenaline coursing through their veins. Each step felt like an eternity, the world around them a blur of chaos and violence.

As Alex neared the vehicle, a sharp pain exploded in his side. He stumbled but managed to stay on his feet, ignoring the searing agony as he dove into the safety of the vehicle's open door.

"Go! Go!" he yelled to the driver, his voice strained. The vehicle lurched forward, throwing them all against the seats as they sped away from the battleground.

The sounds of battle faded into the distance, but the weight of what they had just survived hung heavy in the air. They were alive, yes. But the war was far from over.

The vehicle sped through the night, the streets of the ruined city nothing but shadows in the distance. The wind whipped through the open windows, a harsh reminder that their fight wasn't over. Alex could still hear the distant echoes of gunfire, the remnants of a war that had claimed everything they once held dear.

As they reached their temporary safehouse, Alex exhaled sharply, feeling the tension leave his body for a moment. But it wouldn't last long. He knew that they had bought themselves only a little time, and in this world, time was a luxury they couldn't afford.

Sophia, still clutching the stabilizer, sat in silence. Her face was pale, her eyes haunted by the magnitude of what had just transpired. But there was a fire in her gaze—an unwavering determination.

"We'll rebuild," Alex said, his voice low, but resolute. "We have to."

Sophia nodded slowly, looking down at the device in her hands. "We rebuild, or we die trying."

For a long moment, the room was silent. The rebellion had suffered a tremendous blow. The fortress was gone. But there was still a chance, however small. And as long as they had breath in their bodies, they would continue to fight.

The fight was far from over, and the true test was just beginning.

The safehouse was stark, its walls bare except for the occasional piece of equipment or map. The only source of light came from the flickering glow of a single lamp, casting long shadows across the room. As they settled in, the exhaustion of the escape weighed on each of them, but they knew rest would be a fleeting luxury.

Alex paced the room, his mind working at a fever pitch. Every plan they had laid out was now in tatters. The fall of the fortress wasn't just a physical loss—it was a blow to their morale, a symbol of the fragility of their resistance. The rebellion had been built on the foundation of that stronghold, and now, it was nothing more than rubble.

"What now?" Danny's voice broke the silence, the question hanging heavily in the air. The young man's face was smeared with dirt and blood, his usual cocky demeanor replaced by an uncertain edge. It wasn't often that Danny showed vulnerability, but the events of the last few hours had shaken him, as they had shaken them all.

"We regroup," Alex replied, his voice firm but not without an undercurrent of weariness. "We adapt. We rebuild."

Emma, sitting at the table, cleaning her weapon, looked up. Her face was unreadable, but her eyes betrayed a quiet sorrow. She had lost many friends in the chaos of the last few days. But she too was a survivor, and she knew that survival meant action, not grief. "We can't keep running forever," she said, her voice low. "Victor's forces will come for us again. They're relentless."

"I know," Alex said, his gaze shifting to Sophia, who was still hunched over the stabilizer, her fingers deftly working on the device. Her focus was intense, but Alex could see the strain in her posture, the burden of responsibility that seemed to weigh her down more with every passing moment.

"We need time," Sophia muttered, not looking up. "I need more time to calibrate this. If I can just get it right..."

"Time's something we don't have," Danny interjected, his voice sharp. "We need a plan. And we need it now."

Alex took a deep breath, trying to quell the sense of urgency rising within him. "We'll use the stabilizer as soon as it's ready. But we need more than just that. We need to strike back."

"How?" Emma asked, her voice skeptical. "Victor has the upper hand now. We've lost too much."

Alex met her gaze, his expression resolute. "We've lost, yes. But we're still breathing. And we're still capable of striking at his weaknesses."

The room fell into a heavy silence as Alex's words hung in the air. The gravity of their situation was undeniable. But as the seconds ticked by, an idea began to form in his mind, one that felt like a long shot but the only one they had.

"We strike at the heart of his operation," Alex said slowly, his voice firm with conviction. "We disrupt his supply lines. We hit his tech centers. If we can take down his ability to track us, to control his forces, we might have a chance."

Sophia looked up from the stabilizer, her eyes meeting Alex's. "That's going to be risky. But it's the only thing that might work."

"I'm in," Emma said, her voice steady. "If it gives us even a slight chance to take him down, I'll do it."

Danny, after a long pause, nodded. "Same here. We don't have much left to lose."

The plan wasn't perfect. It wasn't even certain. But it was their only shot.

---

Hours passed as they prepared for their next move. The tension in the safehouse was palpable, each member of the team focused on their tasks with grim determination. Sophia's hands never stopped moving, adjusting the stabilizer as she worked through the device's complex mechanics. It was the one piece of technology that could potentially turn the tide of the war, but only if it was calibrated perfectly.

"Almost there," she said, a note of exhaustion in her voice. "Just a few more adjustments."

Alex watched her for a moment before turning his attention to the others. "When we go in, it'll be all or nothing. We'll need to work together, or this whole thing falls apart."

"We'll hold it together," Emma said, her tone resolute. "We've been through worse."

"We have," Alex agreed. "But this time, we're not just fighting for survival. We're fighting for our future."

The room grew quiet again as the team continued their preparations. The weight of their task was heavy, but there was a shared understanding that this was the only path forward. They would either succeed, or they would die trying.

When Sophia finally stepped away from the stabilizer, her eyes were filled with a quiet resolve. "It's ready," she said, her voice steady.

Alex nodded, and for a moment, he allowed himself to feel a fleeting sense of hope. They weren't done yet. They still had a chance.

"Let's move out," Alex ordered.

The team gathered their gear, checking weapons and supplies, preparing for the mission ahead. Their movements were swift, practiced, as they made their way out of the safehouse and into the unknown.

As they stepped into the night, the shadows of the ruined city stretched before them. But for the first time in days, Alex felt the smallest spark of hope.

They would take the fight to Victor. And this time, they would be ready.

## ○ Sophia's Final Prototype

SOPHIA STOOD IN FRONT of the machine, her hands trembling as they hovered over the console. The air in the lab was thick with the hum of machinery, the walls lined with failed experiments and discarded hopes. This final prototype was more than just another attempt; it was the culmination of years of sacrifice, sleepless nights, and relentless pursuit. Yet, as she gazed at the intricate mechanisms in front of her, doubt crept into her mind.

The stabilizer. The device that could change everything.

For months, Sophia had worked tirelessly, refining the technology she had once believed was impossible. The world outside had crumbled, driven to its knees by conflict, greed, and the depletion of resources. But this device—this final prototype—was her answer. It could heal the ravaged ecosystems, replenish the oceans, restore the soil. It could restore hope, even in the darkest of times.

But at what cost?

Her thoughts were interrupted by the sound of footsteps behind her. She didn't need to turn around to know who it was. Alex, ever the pragmatist, always with a sense of urgency in his voice, stepped into the room.

"Is it ready?" he asked, his voice laced with a mix of hope and hesitation.

Sophia didn't answer immediately. Her fingers brushed against the cold surface of the console, the final wires and connections that would activate the stabilizer. She knew that this moment would define everything—the fate of the world, the future of those who remained, and the legacy of her work. It was a moment she had imagined countless times, yet now that it was upon her, it felt different, heavier.

"I've done everything I can," she said, her voice barely above a whisper. "It's not perfect, but it's our only chance."

Alex stepped closer, placing a hand on her shoulder, a silent gesture of support. He had been with her through the darkest days, when her work seemed futile, when others had given up on her vision. He had never doubted her, and for that, she was grateful. But even his presence couldn't chase away the gnawing fear in her chest.

"Do you think it'll work?" he asked softly.

Sophia hesitated. "I don't know. I've tested it on smaller scales, on controlled environments. But this... this is different. This could either save us... or destroy us completely."

The weight of her words hung in the air, thick and suffocating. She had always known that the stabilizer carried immense risk. The technology was untested on a global scale. The resources needed to power it were scarce, and the political landscape was unpredictable. If it fell into the wrong hands, the consequences would be catastrophic. Victor Lynn, the tycoon who had manipulated the world into war, had made it clear that he would stop at nothing to seize control of Sophia's invention. She couldn't afford to fail now.

"I trust you," Alex said, his voice steady. "We all do."

Sophia finally turned to face him, her eyes locking with his. She saw the unspoken words in his gaze—faith, hope, and a shared resolve. But there was also something else: the understanding that this might be their last chance.

She took a deep breath, her fingers pressing against the control panel. The machine powered up with a low, steady hum, its systems coming online one by one. The lights above flickered, casting long shadows across the lab, as if the very world was holding its breath.

In the silence that followed, Sophia's mind raced. This was it. The moment she had worked for, the moment that would either save the planet or condemn it to further ruin. The stabilizer could reverse the environmental collapse, restore ecosystems, and bring balance to a world teetering on the edge of oblivion. Or, it could trigger an irreversible chain reaction, devastating everything in its wake.

There was no turning back now.

She pressed a final button, and the room filled with a blinding light. The machine hummed louder, its systems coming to life in a symphony of sound and motion. For a moment, it felt as though the very fabric of reality was bending around them, the world outside the lab forgotten, swallowed by the intensity of the moment.

And then, just as quickly as it had started, the light faded. The hum died down. The room was silent.

Sophia stood frozen, her heart pounding in her chest as she waited for the machine to either collapse or succeed. Every fiber of her being was focused on that single moment, the fragile hope that she had poured everything into.

Slowly, she exhaled, her breath shaky. The screen in front of her flickered, showing signs of life. The readings were stable. The machine was holding.

Her heart skipped a beat as she realized what it meant: The stabilizer was working. It was actually working.

But then, a new sound filled the room. A distant rumble, faint at first but growing louder by the second. It wasn't from the machine. It wasn't from the lab.

It was coming from the outside.

Sophia's eyes widened. The ground trembled beneath her feet as if the earth itself was awakening. The stabilizer was working—but was it enough? Was it too late?

"Alex," she whispered, her voice tight with fear, "we might have just made a terrible mistake."

## ○ Alex's Resolve Tested

THE WIND HOWLED THROUGH the skeletal remains of the once-vibrant city, the ruins now a barren testament to humanity's failed ambitions. Alex stood at the edge of what had been a bustling marketplace, now reduced to piles of rubble and the echo of footsteps long silenced. His gaze lingered on the broken buildings, the remnants of a world that had been, and still was, slipping through his fingers.

They had come so far. The map in his hand had once been a guide to something hopeful, something that promised a new beginning, but now it felt like a relic of a past life. Sophia's invention, the stabilizer, was their last chance—a thread of salvation in a world that had nearly forgotten how to dream. Yet, Alex could not shake the feeling that it was slipping away, just like everything else.

The air smelled of decay, of desperation, but also of something darker—betrayal. He felt it, creeping in from every corner, from every whisper in the wind. The group was fractured, each person carrying their own fears, their own doubts, and the uncertainty of their mission weighed heavily on their shoulders. The hope that had driven them here was faltering, and Alex couldn't ignore it any longer. They had already lost too much.

"We're running out of time," Emma's voice cut through the silence, sharp and insistent. She stood beside him, her eyes scanning the horizon. "Victor's not going to wait forever. And neither are the rest of them."

Alex turned to her, his jaw tightening. He could see the exhaustion in her eyes, the weariness that had slowly crept in over the weeks of their journey. But there was something else there too—something that spoke of resolve, of an unyielding belief that they could still make a difference. Her words were true, but they didn't make the decision any easier.

"I know," he replied, his voice barely above a whisper. The weight of their mission was suffocating, pressing in from all sides. "But we're not just up against Victor anymore. We're fighting against the world itself."

The realization was as cold as the wind that whipped around them. They weren't just trying to save the planet. They were trying to save humanity from itself—from the greed, the corruption, and the countless mistakes that had led them here. It wasn't just a fight for survival anymore. It was a fight for the soul of what remained.

Alex's mind raced, his thoughts swirling in a chaotic dance. He knew what needed to be done, but that didn't make it any easier to commit to. Every step forward felt like a gamble, a bet against the impossible. But he couldn't stop now. He had promised them a future, a chance at something better. If he faltered, if he turned away, they would all be lost. And worse—he would be lost too.

"You don't have to do this alone," Danny's voice came from behind, gruff and steady, a familiar presence that steadied Alex's wavering resolve. "We're in this together. We've come this far for a reason."

Alex glanced over at Danny, seeing the same haunted look in his eyes—the weight of the past pressing down on him. Danny had been a soldier once, a man who had fought in wars that Alex couldn't even imagine. Now, that same soldier stood before him, offering his support in a fight that seemed even more impossible than the battles he had fought before. Alex wasn't sure if that made him stronger or more fragile.

"I know," Alex said again, his voice thick with the emotions he couldn't quite voice. "But this... this is bigger than all of us. If we don't stop Victor now, if we don't take the stabilizer from him, nothing will change. It will just be more of the same."

Sophia had trusted him. She had put everything on the line for the chance to bring her invention to life. The stabilizer wasn't just a piece of technology—it was a symbol of the last remnants of hope. But Victor wanted it for himself, to control, to manipulate, to cement his rule over the broken remnants of civilization. Alex couldn't let that happen. Not after everything they had been through.

The decision, though, had never been so clear. It wasn't just about the mission anymore. It was about his own belief in what he was fighting for. There was no turning back. There could be no hesitation.

"Let's finish this," he said, turning back toward the path ahead. His voice was calm now, steady, as though he had come to terms with what lay before them. There would be no more second-guessing, no more wondering if they were doing the right thing. They had come too far to stop now.

Emma and Danny nodded, their expressions hardening with the same resolve. They had all made their peace in their own ways. The time for doubt had passed.

As they moved forward, Alex could feel the weight of the world pressing down on him, but he also felt something else—something lighter, something that had been missing for so long: clarity. The path was set. The fight was on. And there would be no turning back.

It was a hard truth, but it was the truth nonetheless.

## ○ A Spark in the Ashes

THE WIND HOWLED THROUGH the skeletal remains of the city, carrying with it the scent of burnt wood and the bitter taste of ash. Buildings, once towering symbols of human achievement, now lay in ruins, hollow shells consumed by the insatiable hunger of war. Among the wreckage, Alex and his group moved like ghosts, their footsteps silent against the cracked pavement. Each of them carried their own burden, a weight they couldn't escape, no matter how far they walked or how deep they buried their secrets.

Alex's eyes scanned the horizon, his mind constantly calculating the risk of every step they took. In this world, trust was a fragile thing, a commodity more precious than food or water. But as much as he hated to admit it, he had no choice but to rely on his team. They were all he had left.

Sophia walked beside him, her head down, fingers tightly clutching the small device she had managed to keep hidden from Victor's men. The stabilizer, a creation that could save what remained of the Earth's decaying ecosystems, had become the focal point of their struggle. If they succeeded, they might just have a chance at rebuilding. But if Victor found out what she had done, it would be the end of them all.

"Alex," she whispered, breaking the silence. Her voice was soft, but there was an edge of urgency in it. "We're running out of time. I don't know how much longer this thing will hold up."

Alex glanced at her, his face hard, but his eyes filled with something softer—guilt, maybe, or the weight of responsibility. "We'll make it work. We have to."

The group reached the edge of the old city square, where they stopped to take a brief rest. The ruins around them were eerily silent, the remnants of a once-thriving place now reduced to rubble. Only the distant rumble of thunder, an ominous reminder of nature's fury, interrupted the stillness.

Danny was the first to speak. "We're not the only ones out here," he said, scanning the area with a trained eye. His posture was tense, alert—always on edge, as if the next threat could be right around the corner.

"Keep your guard up," Alex muttered. "Victor's men are still looking for us. We can't afford to be careless."

Sophia's gaze wandered over the wreckage, her thoughts distant. She was lost in the enormity of it all—the scope of the devastation, the weight of her actions. The stabilizer was more than just a device; it was a promise. A promise that they could still fix things, that there was still a chance. But with each passing day, the world seemed to slip further from their grasp. The longer they stayed hidden, the more desperate they became. And soon, desperation would turn to recklessness.

"There's nothing left to fix," Danny said, his voice heavy with cynicism. "The world's gone to hell, and no matter what we do, it's not coming back. Maybe we're just fooling ourselves."

His words hung in the air, a challenge to everything they'd been fighting for. For a moment, the group fell silent, the weight of his statement sinking in. But then Alex shook his head, his resolve hardening.

"No," Alex said, his voice low but steady. "We're not fools. We're survivors. And as long as we're still breathing, we have a chance. If we can get to the coast, to the safe zone..."

He didn't finish the sentence. They all knew the stakes. The coast was their last hope—a place rumored to be free of Victor's reach, a place where they could finally catch their breath and regroup. But getting there wouldn't be easy. They'd have to cross territory controlled by warlords, factions, and mercenaries—people who had no interest in peace, only power.

"We're not alone in this," Emma spoke up, her voice cutting through the tension. "There are others out there, people who want change. People who are waiting for someone to lead. They need to know what we have."

Her words seemed to ignite something in the group. A spark. A flicker of hope amidst the ash. It was small, fragile, but it was there. The fire of resistance, of rebellion, was still burning in their hearts.

"We're the spark," Alex said, his tone fierce, his eyes alight with determination. "We're the ones who light the way."

Sophia nodded, her lips pressed into a tight line. The stabilizer in her hands felt heavier now, but she knew that it was more than just a machine. It was the hope of a broken world, the thing that could turn the tide. They had no choice but to fight for it.

"We move out at dawn," Alex ordered, his voice commanding. "Get some rest. We need to be ready."

As the group settled into the ruins for the night, each of them lost in their own thoughts, the world around them seemed to hold its breath. The battle was far from over, but they had something that could change everything: a spark in the ashes. And with that spark, maybe, just maybe, they could ignite a fire strong enough to bring the world back from the brink.

The night dragged on, stretching its dark fingers across the broken landscape, as if reluctant to let go of the remnants of the day. But the stars, faint and distant, glimmered above them like small promises, reminders of the world that once was. It felt like an eternity since they had seen the stars without the haze of smoke or the glare of fire. They had forgotten what it was like to see the sky untouched.

Alex lay awake, his eyes wide open, staring into the void above. He could hear the wind howling through the ruins, but his mind was far from the sounds around him. His thoughts were consumed by the journey ahead, by the fragile hope that still clung to them despite the odds. It was the only thing that kept him moving forward—this desperate belief that there was still something worth fighting for.

Beside him, Emma shifted uneasily in her sleep, her face contorted with the strain of the past few weeks. They had all been through too much. Each one of them carried scars, both visible and hidden. And yet, there they were—still breathing, still fighting.

But how long could they keep going? How long before the spark that burned within them was snuffed out by the weight of their circumstances?

Sophia's soft breathing broke the silence, and Alex turned his head slightly to see her, curled in a tight ball, her hand clutching the stabilizer. He knew she was restless too. She was the most hopeful of them all, the one who believed the world could still be healed. But even she was beginning to crack under the pressure. The device in her hands was both their salvation and their curse—something Victor would do anything to destroy. The knowledge that it was within their reach should have been comforting, but instead, it only added another layer of tension to their already fragile existence.

They had to keep moving. They had to keep going.

As the first light of dawn began to creep over the horizon, Alex rose to his feet, silently waking the others. Their faces were weary, their eyes hollow with exhaustion, but there was a certain determination in each of them—a resolve that wouldn't be broken by the darkness, by the fear that gnawed at them from within.

"We move out now," Alex said quietly. "We need to cover as much ground as we can before the sun's too high. Victor's men won't rest long, and neither can we."

Danny was already up, his rifle slung over his shoulder, his expression unreadable. He had the look of someone who had given up everything, someone who was no longer afraid of what might come. But that wasn't true. Deep down, they all feared what was to come. The world had taken everything from them, and they knew they had nothing left to lose.

Sophia nodded, her grip on the stabilizer tightening as she stood. "Let's go," she said, her voice steady despite the turmoil within her. She wasn't just carrying a device—she was carrying the hope of everything they had left. It was a heavy burden, but it was one she couldn't put down.

The group moved in silence, their footsteps muted by the dust and rubble. The ruins of the old world stretched endlessly before them, a wasteland that once thrived with life, now a monument to their failure. The roads they walked had long since been abandoned, and the city that had once been the heart of civilization was now just another nameless ruin. But somewhere, hidden among the wreckage, there was a glimmer of possibility.

They would find it. They had to.

As they moved through the desolate streets, the sound of distant gunfire reached their ears, sharp and unnerving. Alex's hand instinctively went to his sidearm, his senses heightened. It wasn't close, but the sound was a reminder that danger was never far. He glanced at Danny, who nodded without saying a word. They were ready for whatever came their way.

They pushed forward, their resolve hardening with each step. The sky above, once a vast expanse of promise, now seemed to close in on them, heavy with the weight of uncertainty. But for the first time in a long while, Alex felt something stirring within him—a spark, flickering but undeniable. It was a spark of defiance, of resistance, of the unwillingness to simply fade into the shadows of the past.

They would fight for the future. They would fight for what was left.

And with that thought in his mind, Alex led his team toward the unknown, where the last hope for salvation—and perhaps the last hope for the world itself—waited to be ignited.

# Act 3: The Reckoning

# 9. The Last Stand

## ○ A Desperate Mission

The sun hung low in the sky, casting long shadows over the shattered remnants of the city. The streets, once teeming with life, were now silent, save for the distant echo of footsteps on cracked concrete. Alex stood at the edge of a decimated building, his eyes scanning the horizon. The mission ahead was dangerous, perhaps suicidal, but there was no turning back.

The group had gathered in what used to be a small, makeshift hideout—an old theater that had once been a haven for laughter and dreams. Now, it was a bunker for survivors, its walls lined with maps, weapons, and supplies. The air inside was thick with tension, the weight of what lay ahead pressing down on everyone.

"We don't have much time," Alex said, his voice steady, though the unease lingered just below the surface. "We strike tonight. If we wait any longer, the entire mission will fall apart. The stabilizer is our only chance. Sophia's invention... it's the key to turning everything around. We can't let Victor get his hands on it."

Sophia, who had been quietly inspecting her work, glanced up from the table where she had spread out her notes. Her face, always calm, betrayed a flicker of fear. "You're asking us to walk into the lion's den," she said, her voice quiet but firm. "Victor has an army at his disposal. And we have nothing but a handful of weapons and hope."

Danny stepped forward, his expression hardening as he looked at Sophia. "Hope's all we've got left," he said. "And if we don't act, everything we've fought for, everything we've lost, will be for nothing."

Emma, who had been silent until now, finally spoke up. "And what about the others? The ones we've left behind in the wasteland? We can't fight a war on every front."

"We fight the war that matters," Alex said, his voice growing more resolute. "This isn't just about us anymore. It's about all the people out there who still believe that something can be salvaged. We have to give them that hope. Even if we don't make it out."

There was a long pause, the gravity of his words hanging in the air. The others exchanged glances, each of them grappling with their own fears and doubts. But beneath it all, there was a shared understanding—a bond forged in the fires of this new world. They had no choice but to push forward.

"Okay," Sophia said, after a moment, her decision made. "We do this together, or not at all."

Alex nodded, and with that, the plan was set. They would move under the cover of darkness, infiltrating Victor's compound from the west side, where the security was weakest. The entrance was heavily guarded, but there was a back way in—a maintenance tunnel that led directly to the heart of the compound. From there, they would split up. Danny and Alex would disable the perimeter defenses, while Emma and Sophia would make their way to the lab, where the stabilizer was being kept.

The night air was cold as they moved through the ruins of the city. Every corner was a potential threat, every shadow a possible enemy. Alex's heart pounded in his chest, the weight of the mission bearing down on him. There was no room for mistakes. They couldn't afford another failure.

The streets were eerily empty, the occasional distant sound of gunfire reminding them of the dangers lurking just beyond the horizon. As they approached the outskirts of Victor's compound, Alex signaled for them to halt. The compound loomed ahead, a fortress of steel and stone, its towering walls casting a dark shadow over the city.

"Stay sharp," Alex whispered, his voice barely audible. "We move fast. We move quiet."

They crept forward, the shadows providing some semblance of cover, but the closer they got, the more exposed they felt. Every creak of a broken door, every snap of a twig underfoot, seemed like an alarm in the silence. The tension was palpable, each step drawing them closer to the most dangerous moment of their lives.

At the entrance to the compound, they encountered their first obstacle—two guards standing near the gate, their weapons slung lazily over their shoulders, unaware of the approaching danger. Danny moved swiftly, his training kicking in as he silently took down the guards, his hands never leaving his sidearm. Within seconds, the guards were incapacitated, their bodies hidden in the shadows. The team moved on, undetected, but the danger was far from over.

Inside the compound, the air was thick with the smell of oil and rust. The walls seemed to pulse with the hum of machinery, and the faint sound of voices drifted through the corridors. Alex motioned for the team to follow him as they navigated the labyrinth of hallways, each turn bringing them closer to their goal—and closer to Victor's wrath.

They reached the maintenance tunnel entrance, hidden behind a rusted metal door. It was barely large enough for them to squeeze through, but it was their only way in. One by one, they crawled through the narrow passage, the sound of their breaths the only thing breaking the oppressive silence.

As they emerged on the other side, the compound lay before them—dark, silent, and waiting.

The mission had begun, and there was no turning back now.

## ○ Crossing Enemy Lines

THE AIR WAS THICK WITH the scent of burning wood and metal, remnants of the war that had ravaged the city. Alex moved silently, his boots crunching softly on the rubble, barely making a sound. The once-vibrant streets were now twisted ruins, the skeletal remains of buildings looming over him like silent witnesses to the destruction. Every step felt like a journey through a forgotten world, where survival was the only currency that mattered.

His breath was shallow, the weight of their mission pressing on his chest like a vice. He glanced at his team, each one lost in their own thoughts, the burden of what they were about to do weighing heavily on them all. Danny, his eyes sharp and calculating, kept to the shadows, his rifle slung across his back, fingers twitching as if they were already on the trigger. Emma was at the rear, her camera hidden beneath her jacket, eyes scanning every movement, ever aware of the dangers lurking in every corner. And Sophia, always the quietest, was close to him, her face pale but resolute. They all knew what was at stake.

The plan was simple, in theory. Break into Victor Lynn's compound, infiltrate his inner circle, and gather the evidence they needed to bring him down. But nothing was ever simple in this new world. Trust was a luxury they could no longer afford, and the lines between friend and foe had long since blurred. Every corner could hide an enemy, every whisper could be a trap. And time was running out.

"We need to move," Alex muttered, his voice barely audible, even to those closest to him. "The longer we stay here, the more chances we give them to find us."

Sophia nodded without speaking, her eyes scanning the horizon. She had been quiet ever since they had made the decision to come here, to risk everything. Her invention—something that could change the course of the planet's recovery—was at the heart of Victor Lynn's plans. If they failed here, there would be no hope left. It was as simple and brutal as that.

Danny gave a short nod and gestured toward the alleyway ahead. It was their best route to the compound, a narrow gap between two collapsed buildings, barely wide enough for them to squeeze through. But it was their only option. Any other path would lead them straight into the heart of Victor's surveillance network.

With a signal from Alex, they moved as one, slipping through the shadows like ghosts. The city was eerily quiet, save for the occasional distant gunshot or the soft murmur of movement in the wreckage. It was hard to believe this had once been a thriving metropolis, a center of power and commerce. Now, it was nothing more than a graveyard.

As they reached the entrance to the alley, Alex's hand went to the small device at his belt, checking their coordinates one last time. The map was out of date, like everything else in this world. But it was all they had. They had no choice but to trust it.

"Ready?" he asked, his voice low.

Danny's response was a grunt, his eyes scanning the darkened passageway. Emma adjusted the strap on her camera, her fingers brushing the lens. Sophia didn't say anything. She never did before a mission. But Alex could feel the tension radiating from her, as if she were carrying the weight of the world on her shoulders.

They moved forward.

The alley was narrow and twisted, a maze of discarded debris and fallen bricks. Alex kept his hand on his weapon, every sense alert to the slightest sound. They couldn't afford any mistakes now. Not with so much on the line.

Ahead, the walls of Victor Lynn's compound loomed like a fortress, its high gates secured by layers of metal and barbed wire. This wasn't going to be easy. The compound was heavily guarded, and the moment they stepped onto Victor's territory, every move would be monitored. The only hope was to blend in, to disappear into the shadows and wait for the right moment to strike.

They reached the compound's outer wall without incident, but the hard part was just beginning. Alex signaled for Danny to take the lead, and the soldier moved toward the chain-link fence, his movements smooth and calculated. They couldn't risk triggering any alarms. Danny had trained for this, and it showed. His hands worked quickly, cutting through the wire with a precision born of years of experience.

A few moments later, the gap was wide enough for them to slip through. The inside of the compound was a far cry from the ruins of the city. It was a well-organized fortress, with guards patrolling every corner and high-tech security systems watching their every move. Victor had built an empire, and now, it was time for Alex to tear it down.

They moved quickly, slipping past the guards and blending into the shadows. Every step was a calculated risk. The tension in the air was palpable, and Alex couldn't shake the feeling that they were being watched. But there was no turning back now. They were already inside.

"Keep close," Alex whispered, his voice barely audible. "No heroics. We move as a unit."

The team nodded in agreement, their movements synchronized. They were close now. The heart of the compound was within reach.

But even as they approached their goal, Alex could feel the weight of the decision pressing down on him. The stakes had never been higher. The world's future rested on what they did next.

Would they succeed in their mission, or would they become just another casualty in the endless cycle of war and ruin? Only time would tell.

As they approached the heart of the compound, the silence seemed to deepen, wrapping around them like a heavy cloak. The walls of the fortress were lined with cameras, their lenses glinting in the dim light. The closer they got to Victor's inner sanctum, the more guarded the path became. Alex's instincts screamed that they were getting too close, too exposed, but there was no turning back. They had no choice but to press forward.

They reached the building that housed Victor's command center, a sleek, modern structure in stark contrast to the crumbling remnants of the city around them. It was surrounded by guards, all heavily armed, their eyes scanning the area with methodical precision. Alex's heart pounded in his chest as he crouched beside a rusted fuel tank, his breath shallow. He could feel the weight of the mission closing in on him, but he kept his focus, knowing that one wrong move could end everything.

"Danny, take the left flank," Alex murmured, his voice barely more than a breath. "Emma, you're with me. Sophia, stay low and keep watch."

Without a word, they dispersed, each person moving into position. The plan was risky, but they had no other option. The security around the building was too tight to try a frontal assault. They had to get in unnoticed, or they would never get the chance to expose Victor's plans.

Alex and Emma moved in synchrony, sliding between shadows, their movements almost fluid. The guards didn't seem to notice them, too focused on their patrols to sense the encroaching threat. Emma, ever the observer, kept her camera hidden, but her eyes were sharp, scanning every inch of the surroundings, ready to capture anything that could give them an advantage.

They reached the door, a sleek metal structure guarded by a retinal scanner and a keypad. Alex had expected this. He didn't have the expertise to bypass such security, but Danny did. The soldier was a master of hacking, a skill honed from years of experience in the field.

A few seconds passed before Danny's voice crackled over the comms, his tone steady despite the tension.

"Door's clear. Move."

With a swift push, Alex nudged the door open, the sound barely audible against the hum of the compound. They slipped inside, their eyes adjusting to the dim interior. The air was cold, sterile, as though the building itself was devoid of life. But they knew better. The true danger was always lurking in the most unexpected places.

The interior of the command center was a maze of blinking monitors, each one showing a different part of the compound, tracking every movement. It was the heart of Victor's operation, where all decisions were made, where lives were traded for power. They had to reach the central server room, where the critical information was stored—the evidence they needed to destroy him. But getting there would not be easy.

Alex signaled for Emma to take the lead as they crept forward, their footsteps muted on the cold tile floor. They passed several offices, their occupants oblivious to the intrusion. It was eerie—like a world within a world, where everything seemed normal, even though the entire place was built on lies and deceit.

Sophia, trailing behind them, kept a vigilant eye on the security feeds. She had always been the most cautious, but that caution had saved them more than once. Her mind worked quickly, analyzing the feeds for potential threats.

They reached the server room door. It was thick, reinforced, and had another layer of security—this time, a biometric scanner. The time was running out, but Danny was already at work, his fingers flying over a small device that interfaced with the scanner. There was a moment of tension, and then the door clicked open.

Inside, rows upon rows of servers hummed softly, their blinking lights casting an ominous glow in the otherwise dark room. Alex's heart raced. They had made it. But the danger wasn't over yet.

Sophia moved to the central terminal, typing in the commands they had scrounged together from their limited intel. The room was still too quiet, too perfect—like a trap waiting to spring.

"Just a few more seconds," Sophia whispered, her voice tight.

Suddenly, an alarm blared, cutting through the silence with a deafening shriek. Red lights flashed across the room, and the doors to the server room slammed shut, locking them inside.

"Dammit," Alex cursed under his breath. "We've been compromised."

"Move!" Danny shouted, his voice filled with urgency. "We have to get out now!"

Sophia slammed her hand on the console, her eyes wide with panic. "I almost—just—wait!"

But there was no time. The security forces would be here any second, and they couldn't afford to be caught. Alex grabbed Sophia's arm, pulling her toward the exit as Emma and Danny covered their retreat. The adrenaline coursed through his veins as he heard the sound of boots pounding down the corridor behind them. They were being hunted, but they couldn't stop now.

They burst through the door, into the hallway, just as the first wave of guards rounded the corner. Alex didn't hesitate. He fired, taking down two of them before they had a chance to react. The others ducked for cover, returning fire. It was a deadly dance, a battle of life and death with no room for error.

"Go!" Danny yelled. "I'll cover you!"

They sprinted down the hallway, dodging bullets and debris, the sound of the firefight echoing in their ears. The compound had become a battlefield, and they were the prey.

As they reached the outer wall, Alex knew that the hardest part was still ahead. They had to escape, and escape quickly. But the reality of what they had just discovered gnawed at him. They had the evidence. They had everything they needed to bring Victor down. But at what cost?

Would they make it out alive, or had they just signed their own death warrants?

The escape route was nothing more than a narrow alley between two crumbling buildings, a pathway that offered little cover and even less hope. But it was the only chance they had left. The compound was alive with chaos now, sirens blaring, the rush of footsteps growing louder as guards poured into the area. Alex's thoughts raced. They had to make it to the extraction point, but the danger was far from over.

"Keep moving!" Alex barked, his voice low but firm, his eyes scanning the darkened streets ahead. "We're not safe yet."

Emma and Sophia were right behind him, their faces tense with the same grim determination. Danny, ever the strategist, was keeping an eye on the rear, ensuring they weren't followed.

The streets outside the compound were eerily empty, a stark contrast to the frantic activity inside. The city had been abandoned for years, the ruins of once-bustling neighborhoods now filled with the remnants of the old world. A faint breeze carried the scent of dust and decay, a reminder of what had been lost in this global conflict.

They moved quickly, but with caution. The path to their extraction point was longer than expected. Alex's mind kept replaying the images from the server room—the data they had uncovered about Victor's plans, the key to bringing down his empire. But as they pushed forward, the weight of the mission began to settle heavily on his shoulders. There was still much to do, and no guarantee they would make it out of this alive.

As they rounded a corner, a sudden burst of gunfire shattered the silence. Alex instinctively dropped to the ground, pulling Emma and Sophia with him. Danny returned fire, his shots precise and calculated, but the enemy had them pinned down. They were surrounded.

"They know we're here," Danny muttered, his voice tight as he reloaded. "We need to get to that extraction point—now."

Alex's mind raced, trying to figure out their next move. They couldn't fight their way through the whole compound, not with their numbers thinning. Their best chance was to make a break for it. The extraction point wasn't far, but they had to move quickly—and quietly.

"On three," Alex whispered, his voice low but steady. "We run. Stay close. Stick to the shadows. We make it, or we die trying."

There was no hesitation in their eyes. This was it. No second chances.

"One... two... three!"

They sprang to their feet, sprinting toward the nearest alleyway. The sound of footsteps chasing them was deafening, but they didn't look back. They couldn't. Every moment counted.

As they raced through the desolate streets, the wind howled in their ears, whipping up dust and debris in their wake. The extraction point was in sight—a small building on the outskirts of the city, their only hope for escape. But as they neared the building, a black SUV skidded to a halt in front of them, blocking their path.

Alex's heart skipped a beat. They were trapped.

The doors of the SUV opened, and men in dark uniforms emerged, their faces hidden behind helmets. The leader of the group stepped forward, a smirk playing at the corners of his lips.

"I'm afraid this is where your little mission ends," he said, his voice cold and menacing.

Alex's mind raced. There was no time to fight. They had to act, and fast.

Without thinking, he pulled the small device from his pocket—the one Sophia had worked tirelessly to hack into the compound's security systems. In one swift motion, he activated it, sending a surge of electricity through the nearby power grid. The lights flickered, and the SUV's engines sputtered.

"Move!" Alex shouted.

In the confusion, Danny dove toward the vehicle, throwing a grenade under it. The explosion rocked the street, sending the men in dark uniforms scattering. They had mere seconds to make their move.

"Go, go, go!" Danny shouted as the smoke from the blast began to fill the street.

They ran, not looking back. They were almost there, just a few more steps. But as they reached the entrance to the extraction building, a sharp pain shot through Alex's side. He stumbled, falling to his knees as blood began to soak through his shirt.

"Alex!" Emma cried, her voice filled with panic.

Alex gritted his teeth, refusing to give in. He couldn't stop now. Not when they were so close.

"We're not done yet," he gasped, pushing himself back to his feet. "Keep moving."

With one final burst of energy, they made it inside the building. The extraction team, a group of highly trained operatives, was waiting for them. They ushered them in quickly, locking the door behind them.

As the building's doors slammed shut, Alex collapsed against the wall, his breathing ragged. His body ached, every movement a reminder of the hell they had just survived. But despite the pain, despite the uncertainty of what was to come, he felt a sense of victory.

They had the evidence. They had exposed Victor's operation. The fight wasn't over, but they had dealt a powerful blow.

"Get him to the medics," Emma ordered, kneeling beside Alex.

"I'll be fine," Alex muttered, though his voice was weak. "We have bigger problems now."

Outside, the world was changing. The data they had gathered would ripple across the globe, exposing the corruption, the manipulation, and the lies that had held the world in its grip for so long. Victor's empire was crumbling, but there was still much to be done. They had only just begun.

As the extraction team set to work, Alex's mind was already turning toward the next step. There would be no rest until the world knew the truth. But for now, he allowed himself a moment to breathe, knowing that they had crossed enemy lines and survived. It wasn't over. But they had won today.

• • • •

## ○ Sophia's Sacrifice

THE WIND HOWLED THROUGH the cracked windows, carrying with it the scent of smoke and decay. Sophia stood before the console, her hands trembling as she adjusted the final settings on her device. Her invention, the Stabilizer, had been her life's work, and now it was the world's last hope. The device could rejuvenate the environment, reverse the damage done to the planet over the years, and restore a sense of balance. But at what cost?

She glanced over her shoulder, catching the eyes of Alex and Danny. They were waiting, their expressions a mixture of hope and fear. They had been through so much together, had survived the war and the collapse of society. Yet now, in this final moment, it was Sophia's turn to make the hardest choice of all.

Her mind raced back to the early days of her research. She had been driven by a desire to save humanity, to reverse the damage inflicted by greed and environmental destruction. But somewhere along the way, the lines between right and wrong had blurred. She had built something powerful, something that could change everything. And now, that very power was about to be misused.

The device could do more than just heal the earth—it could control it. In the wrong hands, it could bring about the rise of a new world order, one shaped by power-hungry men like Victor Lynn. She had seen what he was capable of, how he manipulated resources and people to build his empire. If the Stabilizer fell into his grasp, all would be lost.

"I can't let him have it," Sophia whispered, mostly to herself. She didn't need to look at Alex to know that he understood. He had always believed in her, in the potential of her work. But now, with the stakes so high, even he had begun to question the cost.

"You know what you're asking, Sophia," Danny said quietly, stepping closer. His voice was filled with a hardness that hadn't been there before, the weight of their survival weighing heavily on him. "If you destroy it, we lose our chance to fix everything. The planet... humanity... It's all riding on this."

"I know," she replied, her voice shaking. "But if I don't, we risk giving the world to men like him. And I won't be responsible for that. I can't—"

Alex stepped forward, placing a hand on her shoulder. His touch was warm, grounding, but it didn't make the decision any easier. "Sophia, the world needs you. The Stabilizer—your work—could heal everything. It could save us. There has to be another way."

She met his gaze, her eyes filled with a deep sadness. "I can't let it fall into the wrong hands. You know I've always tried to be the one to make things right. But this time... this time, I have to be the one to make the sacrifice. For all of us."

The room seemed to close in on her, the weight of the moment pressing against her chest. She could feel the tears welling up in her eyes, but she refused to let them fall. She had made her decision, and there was no turning back.

Sophia turned back to the console, her fingers hovering over the button that would initiate the device's destruction. The decision was final. There was no going back. She had spent years of her life perfecting this invention, and now she would tear it all down, all to prevent the world from falling into chaos once again.

She closed her eyes, taking one last breath. And with a steady hand, she pressed the button.

The Stabilizer began to hum, the lights flickering as the machine powered down. A low, resonant sound filled the room, and for a moment, it seemed as though the very earth itself was holding its breath. Then, with a final, earth-shaking noise, the device shut off. The screen went dark.

Sophia exhaled sharply, her body shaking with the weight of her decision. She had done it. She had made the ultimate sacrifice, the one that would ensure the future of humanity wasn't manipulated by the greed of those who saw only power in a broken world. The machine was gone, but in its place was a fragile hope—a hope that they could rebuild without the crutch of technology, without the hand of a tyrant controlling their fate.

"Is it done?" Alex asked, his voice low.

Sophia nodded, her chest heavy with emotion. "It's done."

But in that moment, as they all stood together in the wreckage of the world they had tried to save, Sophia realized something else. The sacrifice wasn't just about the device—it was about everything they had lost, everything they had fought for, and everything they were willing to endure for the sake of a future that was still uncertain.

But they had hope. And that, for now, was enough.

## ○ The Rise of a Leader

UNDER THE SHATTERED sky, Alex stood at the edge of what was once a thriving city, now reduced to crumbling ruins. The wind swept through the skeletal remains of buildings, carrying with it the faint scent of decay. It was a far cry from the world he had once known—a world of diplomacy, negotiations, and power plays. Now, all that remained was the will to survive, and the harsh reality that survival often meant becoming something more than just a man. It meant becoming a symbol.

The survivors had gathered around him, their faces worn and weary, eyes haunted by the ghosts of the past. They were a ragtag group—farmers, soldiers, doctors, and scavengers—each with their own story of loss and survival. But in their eyes, Alex saw something he hadn't seen in so long: hope. A fragile, flickering flame that needed to be stoked before it was extinguished by the weight of despair.

He wasn't the leader they had chosen. He hadn't been the one to step forward when the world fell apart. But fate, or perhaps necessity, had thrust him into the role. In the days that followed the collapse of their society, Alex had found himself speaking to groups of survivors, offering what little guidance he could muster. He had watched them rally to his side, not because of his skill or charisma, but because, like them, he was trying to make sense of a world turned upside down. And in that shared struggle, he had unknowingly become their beacon.

Now, as the wind howled through the broken streets, Alex was faced with a choice. They had survived so far, but surviving was no longer enough. The stabilizer—the device that Sophia had worked tirelessly to perfect—was their last hope, but it wasn't without its dangers. It could heal the land, restore the balance, but it could also be weaponized, turned into something even more destructive than the war that had already ravaged the world.

The group was divided. Some saw the stabilizer as their salvation, the means to rebuild what had been lost. Others feared that in the wrong hands, it could become the weapon of a new, more insidious form of tyranny. Alex could feel the weight of their eyes on him, the silent expectation that he would decide which path they would take. The pressure was suffocating, but in that moment, Alex realized something fundamental: his role wasn't just to lead them through survival. It was to guide them toward something greater. He wasn't just the survivor; he was the one who had to decide what they would become.

With a deep breath, Alex turned back to face the group. They were waiting for him to speak, for him to give them the words that would carry them through the next phase of their journey. He had never been good with speeches, never comfortable in the spotlight. But this wasn't about him. This was about them, and what they were willing to fight for.

"We've made it this far because we've worked together," he said, his voice carrying over the wind. "We've faced the worst that this world could throw at us, and we've survived. But survival isn't enough anymore. We need to decide what we're going to do with the rest of this world. We can either let it crumble and fade, or we can fight to rebuild it. Not just for us, but for those who come after us."

His words were simple, but they struck a chord. There was a long pause, and Alex could see the shift in their faces. The fear, the uncertainty, began to fade, replaced by something else. A spark. A desire to rise above the ruins of their old world and build something new.

He could feel it now—this was the moment where his leadership would either be solidified or shattered. The rise of a leader wasn't just about taking charge. It was about making people believe in something bigger than themselves. It was about showing them that, even in the darkest moments, they could find a way to move forward.

And Alex was ready to lead them—not as a savior, but as one of them. A man who understood their pain, their fears, and their dreams. Together, they would rise from the ashes of the old world and create something worth fighting for.

But the road ahead wouldn't be easy. Victor Lynn's empire, fueled by greed and corruption, still loomed on the horizon, ready to swallow whatever remained of hope. And Alex knew that their battle was just beginning. But for the first time since the collapse, he felt something that had been missing: purpose.

The survivors weren't just fighting for survival anymore. They were fighting for the future. And under Alex's leadership, they would give everything to see it through.

## ○ The Tides Turn

THE COLD WIND HOWLED across the barren landscape, carrying with it the scent of burnt metal and charred earth. In the distance, the broken remains of a city stood like a monument to human ambition—half-destroyed buildings twisted in unnatural angles, their skeletal frames reaching for the sky. The once-bustling metropolis, now nothing more than a husk of its former glory, was a symbol of the world's rapid descent into chaos.

Alex stood at the edge of the ruin, his breath visible in the frigid air, as he surveyed the wreckage below. His eyes, dark with exhaustion, scanned the horizon for any sign of movement. The ground beneath him was cracked and scarred, the remnants of a world that had once been full of life now silent and desolate.

Beside him, Sophia's voice broke through the heavy silence, her tone sharp with urgency. "We don't have much time."

He turned to her, noting the tension in her face, the way her fingers tightened around the device she held—a small, unassuming piece of technology that had the potential to change everything. It could restore what had been lost, or it could lead them all to ruin. The choice was theirs, but the weight of that decision felt almost unbearable.

"We can't waste another minute," Alex said, his voice low but firm. "Victor won't wait forever. He's already making his move."

Sophia nodded, her gaze flickering toward the horizon. "I know. But we're not ready. Not yet."

A deep sense of foreboding settled over him. He had known that the battle ahead would be hard, but the closer they came to confronting Victor, the more it felt like they were walking into the heart of a storm. And storms, as Alex had learned over the years, had a way of changing everything.

"We're as ready as we'll ever be," he said, the weight of their journey pressing down on him. "We don't have the luxury of time. If we don't act now, everything we've fought for will be lost."

Sophia's lips tightened into a thin line, her eyes hard with resolve. She knew the stakes, knew what this meant for the world they'd once known, and the world they hoped to rebuild. "You're right," she said softly. "But we need to be smart. We can't just charge in blind. Victor's too powerful. He's not the same man we thought we were dealing with."

Alex looked at her, taking in the way she carried herself—the weight of responsibility etched into every line of her face. She had been their guiding light, the one who had brought them together and given them a cause to fight for. But now, even she seemed unsure, the uncertainty of their situation making her falter for the first time since they had joined forces.

"I know," he said quietly. "But we don't have a choice. We either stop him now, or we risk the future of everything we're trying to rebuild."

There was a pause, the air thick with the unspoken weight of their decision. Then, without another word, they turned and began to make their way down into the heart of the ruin, the sound of their footsteps the only thing that broke the silence.

---

As they moved deeper into the abandoned city, the ruins seemed to close in on them, towering structures looming like silent sentinels, watching their every move. The air felt thick with the memories of what had been lost—people, cultures, civilizations—each echoing through the empty streets.

Danny was the first to speak, his voice carrying a quiet edge. "You really think this is going to work? Taking him down?"

Alex glanced at him, his face unreadable. "It has to. We're not just fighting for survival anymore. We're fighting for something bigger than that."

Danny didn't respond immediately, his gaze lingering on the shattered remnants of the city around them. "I hope you're right."

They pressed on in silence, the weight of their task hanging over them. Every step they took brought them closer to Victor's stronghold, closer to the final confrontation that would decide the fate of what little remained of the world. The group moved with purpose now, their faces set in grim determination, each of them knowing the risks, knowing the sacrifices that lay ahead.

The world had changed, and with it, so had they. Each of them had been broken by the chaos, reshaped by the horrors of war and the loss of everything they had once known. But in the midst of the devastation, something had been forged—a new sense of purpose, a new resolve to do what had to be done, no matter the cost.

And as they neared the edge of the city, Alex felt it—an undeniable shift in the air. The tides were turning, and for the first time in a long while, he felt a spark of hope, however small. It wasn't much, but it was enough to carry them forward.

At that moment, a distant rumble echoed through the streets, a deep, resonant sound that seemed to vibrate through the very earth beneath their feet. The ground trembled slightly, and the hairs on the back of Alex's neck stood on end. He stopped, raising a hand to signal the others.

"What the hell was that?" Danny asked, his voice tense.

Alex's eyes narrowed as he scanned the horizon, his instincts screaming that something was wrong. "It's not natural. Stay alert."

Sophia looked at him, her face pale. "We're too late. He's already moved."

The realization hit him like a punch to the gut. Victor had anticipated their every move, and now they were walking straight into a trap. They had underestimated him, and now they would pay the price.

But Alex wasn't one to back down. Not now, not after everything they had endured. He could hear the sound of the storm in the distance—the rising tide of violence and betrayal that would soon engulf them all.

"We move now," he said, his voice steady despite the growing sense of danger. "No turning back."

And with that, they began to run, the winds of fate pushing them forward, toward the reckoning that awaited them in the heart of the ruins.

# ○ A New Threat Emerges

The desert stretched endlessly before them, its parched earth cracked under the heat of the midday sun. Alex squinted, trying to focus on the horizon where the sand seemed to blur into the sky. There were no more cities here, no green spaces, only ruins and the remnants of civilization's hubris. The world they had known was gone—replaced by a harsh new reality.

He wiped the sweat from his brow, but it quickly returned, his skin sticking to his clothes in the sweltering heat. The small group had been walking for days, running low on supplies, the weight of their mission pressing down on them like a constant, suffocating presence. Sophia's invention was their last hope, but with every step, the stakes grew higher, the risks more pronounced.

"We're getting close," Danny muttered, his voice hoarse from the dry air. His eyes scanned the empty landscape, ever watchful, the trained instincts of a soldier still sharp despite the weight of everything they had endured.

Emma, always the one to keep a steady pulse on the world's pulse, had been quiet for too long. Her usual fire had dimmed in the face of this new threat, the one they hadn't anticipated. "This feels wrong, Alex," she finally said, breaking the silence. "I don't think we're alone out here."

Alex's hand instinctively went to the gun at his side, his fingers brushing the cold metal. "What do you mean?" he asked, narrowing his eyes.

"Just a feeling," Emma said, her lips pursed in a tight line. "I can't explain it. But something is out there. Watching us."

Alex looked back at the others. Danny was already scanning the horizon, his posture rigid, like a man ready to fight or flee. Sophia was focused, her eyes distant, lost in thought, but her hand was never far from the device she carried—her stabilizer, their ticket to what little future the planet had left.

A low hum filled the air, almost imperceptible at first, but growing louder with each passing second. Alex's heart skipped a beat. It was the sound of engines. Not just any engines. These were the engines of a machine designed for destruction.

He had been wrong. They weren't alone out here.

The ground vibrated beneath their feet as a convoy of vehicles appeared on the horizon, a string of armored trucks cutting through the desert like dark shadows against the blinding sunlight. They were heading straight for them.

"Get ready," Alex ordered, his voice steady but tinged with urgency. "We don't know who they are, but we can't take any chances."

The convoy drew closer, and now there was no doubt in Alex's mind. This wasn't a random group of survivors. This was something organized, something purposeful.

"We need to move. Now," Emma urged, her eyes wide with apprehension.

Sophia looked at Alex, fear flashing in her eyes. "If they know what we have, we're dead. They'll stop at nothing to take it from us."

Danny gritted his teeth, stepping forward to shield Sophia. "We fight. We fight, and we survive."

But Alex knew that the fight they were about to face wasn't just about survival. It wasn't just about getting Sophia's technology into the right hands or stopping a war that had already begun. This was a fight against something far worse—a force that sought to control what little was left of the world, to claim power in the chaos. And from the look of things, they had just become its next target.

As the convoy neared, the low hum of their engines grew deafening, and Alex knew with chilling certainty that this was only the beginning. What lay ahead wasn't just a battle for resources—it was a battle for the future itself. The stabilizer, the last hope for healing the planet, had attracted more than just attention. It had attracted the worst kind of predator.

And the worst part? They didn't even know who their enemies were.

# 10. The Price of Innovation

## ○ Victor's Final Move

Victor Lynn stood at the window of his private study, gazing out over the sprawling compound below. The air was thick with the smoke of distant fires, remnants of yet another battle between the remnants of the old world and the new order he had carefully built. His empire was crumbling, but only in the most inconvenient ways—small fractures that he could still control, manipulate, and mend.

He exhaled slowly, his fingers tapping the edge of the glass. The war had changed everything, but Victor had learned that in times of chaos, true power wasn't held by those who wielded the weapons, but by those who controlled the flow of information, the resources that kept the world turning, even in the midst of ruin.

Sophia Alvarez had made a mistake. A brilliant one, but a mistake nonetheless. Her invention—the Stabilizer—was the key to controlling the future of the planet, and Victor had no intention of allowing it to fall into the hands of anyone who didn't understand its full potential. There was a simple equation in the world now: he either controlled the Stabilizer, or the Stabilizer would control him.

The door behind him creaked open, and a figure entered, silhouetted against the dim light. He didn't need to turn to know who it was. Emma Carter, the journalist, the thorn in his side, had managed to worm her way through his defenses once again. She was too clever for her own good, always finding cracks in the stories he told the world.

"You look troubled," she said, her voice laced with the kind of confidence that only a person who had survived the apocalypse could afford. "Is it the war or the new world order you're losing sleep over, Victor?"

Victor didn't smile, but he could feel the familiar tug of amusement at the edge of his mouth. "You should be careful, Emma. People like you, they get too comfortable thinking they're untouchable. And in the end, that's what kills them."

Emma took a step closer, the faint rustle of her boots on the floor the only sound in the otherwise silent room. "Is that a threat, or a warning?" she asked, her eyes narrowing.

"Neither," Victor replied, his voice cold, measured. "It's the truth. And the truth is, you're about to lose. Again."

She didn't flinch, but the tension in her shoulders betrayed her. She knew exactly what he meant. He was right. She had been digging too deep, pulling at threads that were never meant to be unraveled. She had uncovered his plans, his deals, his vast network of influence, but she hadn't realized just how much more dangerous his final move would be.

Victor turned away from the window, his eyes now cold, calculating. "You see, I don't need to hold the world's resources to control it," he continued, his tone turning darker. "I just need to make everyone believe I do."

Emma stiffened, but she remained silent, waiting for him to reveal his next move.

"In the coming days, Sophia's work will be taken from her. Her technology will be altered, repurposed, and rebranded. And the world will believe that only I hold the key to survival. They'll have no choice but to follow me, to submit to the new world I'm building. And once I've consolidated power, I'll unleash the real weapon—the one that no one, not even the rebels, can fight."

Victor leaned in closer, his breath a whisper in Emma's ear. "The mind. The human mind. I've already begun work on the next phase, Emma. The Stabilizer is only the beginning. With it, I can control their thoughts, their desires. I'll shape reality itself, and they'll never even know it."

She backed away, her face draining of color. She had suspected it, but hearing him speak of it so openly, so coldly, sent a chill through her spine. The technology Sophia had created could be used for healing, for restoration. But in Victor's hands, it would be twisted into something far more dangerous—something that could control every single person on the planet.

"And you think you can stop me?" Victor asked, his voice almost mocking, his eyes glittering with a dangerous amusement. "You think that by exposing me, by rallying the remnants of the world's old order, you can change the course of history? No, Emma. This is bigger than you. Bigger than anyone else."

She held his gaze, her jaw tight with defiance, but doubt flickered in her eyes. She had fought so hard, but Victor was always one step ahead. How could she defeat a man who was willing to sacrifice everything, including his humanity, for control?

"People like you never understand, do you?" she said, her voice low. "You think you're invincible, that no one can touch you. But all empires fall, Victor. Yours will be no different."

Victor chuckled softly, almost affectionately. "I've learned to survive, Emma. And that's what I'll do. In the end, you'll see. You'll see that the world I'm building will stand long after you and your little rebellion have faded into nothingness."

His words lingered in the room, the weight of them heavy, suffocating. Emma knew that this was it—the final move. If she couldn't stop him now, everything they had fought for, everything they had struggled to rebuild, would be lost.

But there was still one card she could play. She turned sharply, the decision made in an instant. She had no more time to waste on words.

Victor's empire might have been built on lies, but it would be torn apart by truth.

The game was far from over.

## ○ The Power of the Stabilizer

THE SUN HAD BARELY risen, casting a faint golden glow across the barren landscape. The remnants of what once had been a bustling metropolis were now nothing more than twisted steel and crumbling stone. It was a place where hope had long since fled, leaving behind only survivors — hardened, desperate, and numb to the world that had once been. In the heart of this wasteland, Sophia Alvarez stood, her face hidden behind a veil of dust and sweat, her hands trembling as she adjusted the delicate machinery that could either save or destroy everything they had fought for.

She had always known that the device, the stabilizer, would be more than just a technological marvel. It was a weapon, a key to a future that could be rebuilt — or a tool for absolute domination. The thought of it falling into the wrong hands gnawed at her, the weight of her invention pulling her deeper into a moral quagmire. If Victor Lynn got control of it, the world as they knew it would end not with a bang, but with a suffocating silence, as he crushed the last remnants of resistance under his heel.

Sophia knew the stakes. She had spent years perfecting the stabilizer, a revolutionary piece of technology capable of rejuvenating the Earth's ecosystems, purifying the air, and cleansing the oceans that had been poisoned beyond recognition. It was a solution to the global crisis — a chance at redemption for a planet on the brink of total collapse. But the very thing that could heal the world was also the ultimate leverage in the hands of the powerful.

She adjusted the control panel once more, the faint hum of the machine resonating in her chest. The stabilizer, a series of interconnected devices powered by a rare energy source, was designed to absorb the pollutants choking the planet and convert them into life-giving elements. It could undo the damage of decades, reverse the death spiral of ecosystems, and bring about a new era of balance between humanity and nature. But there were risks. If misused, it could destabilize entire regions, creating chaos on a scale unimaginable. The wrong hands could twist it into a force of unimaginable destruction, much like the war machines that had torn the world apart in the first place.

Sophia turned her gaze to the horizon, where the distant smoke of smoldering cities lingered in the air. She knew time was running out. Alex and the others were counting on her, but every passing second brought them closer to a decision she wasn't ready to make. Would she let the stabilizer fall into the hands of those who would use it for personal gain, or would she destroy it before they could seize it? The choice was a heavy one, one that no amount of intellect or logic could answer.

As if on cue, Alex appeared from the shadows, his silhouette framed by the crumbling ruins of a once-great city. His eyes were tired, but resolute, the weight of leadership etched into his features. He knew what she was facing, had seen the toll this mission had taken on her. But he also knew that there was no going back now. The group had come too far, risked too much, and lost too many. If the stabilizer was to be their salvation, it had to be used, no matter the cost.

"Is it ready?" Alex's voice was rough, carrying the burden of the world in each word. He stepped closer, his boots crunching against the dry earth.

Sophia didn't answer immediately. She had spent so long working on this, so many sleepless nights, that the question now felt almost irrelevant. Ready or not, the world was waiting.

"I don't know," she said finally, her voice a whisper of doubt. "It could save us, or it could destroy everything we've fought for." She looked up at him, the anguish in her eyes impossible to mask. "I don't know if I can trust anyone with this power."

Alex placed a hand on her shoulder, his grip firm, offering the reassurance he wasn't sure he could provide. "We don't have a choice anymore. We either use it, or we let it fall into the wrong hands. And we both know what that means."

Sophia closed her eyes, taking a deep breath. The choice was never simple, but it had to be made. There was no room for hesitation. They had to push forward.

With a final glance at the stabilizer, she activated the machine, the room buzzing with energy as the power surged through the cables, lights flickering on the console. The air seemed to thicken, heavy with the promise of change. And yet, the weight of uncertainty still hung in the air, as thick as the dust that covered the ruins of the world.

Sophia looked at Alex, and for a brief moment, the two of them shared a wordless understanding. The world was about to change, for better or for worse. There was no turning back now.

## ○ Emma's Broadcast

THE SUN WAS BEGINNING to set, casting long shadows over the ruins of what had once been a bustling city. Emma stood on the rooftop of an abandoned building, her eyes scanning the horizon, the weight of the world pressing down on her shoulders. The air was thick with the stench of decay and the distant sounds of conflict—muffled gunfire, the occasional explosion, and the low hum of helicopters circling overhead. There was no safety here, only the constant struggle to survive.

She had come to this place, this broken city, to find the truth. But the truth, as it always did, came at a price. The information she had uncovered about Victor Lynn and his insidious plans to control the world's remaining resources had sent a shiver through her. This wasn't just about power; it was about shaping the very future of humanity, molding it into something unrecognizable. His plans were too dangerous, too vast, to be ignored.

Emma's fingers trembled slightly as she adjusted the makeshift transmitter in front of her, the only connection she had left to the outside world. She had spent days scavenging for parts, cobbling together a device that might be able to broadcast her message, to tell the world what was happening, to expose the man who had turned the remnants of civilization into his personal empire. Her heart raced. This broadcast could be her only chance. If she failed, there would be no one left to tell the truth.

She took a deep breath, her gaze hardening. The world needed to know. The survivors in the wasteland, the people still clinging to hope amidst the ashes, deserved to know the reality they were up against. The fact that they were being manipulated, controlled, and pushed into a new era of despair by the likes of Victor Lynn—it was something that could not, would not, be allowed to stand.

She hit the button, and the static crackled, filling the empty space around her. The transmission had begun.

"To anyone who can hear this, this is Emma Carter," her voice was steady, though her pulse hammered in her ears. "I'm here to tell you a story. A story that no one else has the courage to tell. What you've been led to believe, what you've been told about the collapse, about the war—it's all a lie. There is a shadow over this world, and it's not the war itself. It's the people who profited from it, the ones who orchestrated the chaos, who turned nations into battlegrounds and lives into commodities."

She paused for a moment, her eyes scanning the horizon again, but there was no turning back now. The words were out, and there was no taking them back.

"Victor Lynn. The man you've been told is a savior. The one you've been told is bringing order to the world. He's not. He is the architect of this destruction, the one pulling the strings from behind the curtain. He controls the resources we need to survive, and he's using them as leverage to rebuild this world in his image, a world where those who fall in line survive, and those who resist are left to die."

Emma's fingers gripped the edge of the transmitter, her knuckles white. She knew the risks. Lynn's men were everywhere, and if they found out what she was doing... The thought sent a chill through her.

"But there is hope," she continued, her voice gaining strength. "A way to fight back. There are people—good people—who are willing to stand against him. People who won't bend to his will. And we have something he can't control: the truth. We can expose him for who he really is. If enough of us stand together, we can stop him. We can take back control."

The transmission flickered, the static crackling louder for a moment before settling. She adjusted the dial, making sure her signal was still broadcasting, still reaching out to any survivors who might be listening. There was no going back now.

"You're not alone," Emma said, her voice softer now, but no less determined. "We're all in this together. And together, we can rebuild. Together, we can reclaim what was lost. The fight isn't over, not by a long shot. The ashes of our past are all we have left, but they're also all we need. Together, we will rise from them."

She cut the transmission. The silence that followed was deafening, filled with the weight of what she had just done. She had sent the message, but now, more than ever, she had to live with the consequences.

As the last rays of sunlight faded from the sky, Emma looked out over the ruins once more, her heart heavy with the knowledge that her broadcast was only the beginning. It was a spark, small and fragile, but a spark nonetheless. And in this world of darkness, a spark was all they needed to ignite the flames of rebellion.

## ○ Danny's Redemption Fulfilled

DANNY STOOD AT THE edge of the ruins, his eyes scanning the desolate landscape that stretched before him. The once vibrant city had been reduced to rubble, a grim reminder of the cost of survival. The air was thick with the stench of burning debris, and the distant sound of gunfire echoed in the background—a constant reminder that, even in the wake of destruction, the fight for control was far from over.

His hands trembled as he clutched the worn photograph, the edges frayed from years of wear. It was a picture of a man who no longer existed, a soldier who had once fought without question, driven by orders, by loyalty to a country that had long since vanished. That man had committed unspeakable acts in the name of survival. And now, here he was, a ghost of that past, struggling to atone for the blood on his hands.

"Danny," a voice called, pulling him from his thoughts.

He turned to find Alex approaching, his face weary, eyes hollow from the weight of leadership. The world had torn them all apart, but Danny could still see the flicker of hope in Alex's gaze, a hope that seemed more fragile with each passing day.

"You ready?" Alex asked, his voice low.

Danny nodded, though doubt lingered in the pit of his stomach. Could redemption ever truly be achieved? Could the things he had done, the lives he had taken, be forgiven? Or was he destined to live with the consequences forever?

He took a deep breath and straightened his back. "Ready," he said, though the word felt foreign on his lips.

The road ahead was uncertain. Sophia's invention, the stabilizer that held the promise of a future for the world, was within reach.

But the forces aligned against them were powerful, and Danny knew that the price of their victory would be steep. They were not just fighting for survival now—they were fighting for a chance to rebuild, to offer something resembling hope to the generations that would follow. But would they be willing to pay the ultimate price?

He could feel the weight of every decision he had ever made pressing down on him. Every life he had taken in the name of duty, every betrayal he had committed—it all felt like a heavy chain, pulling him back into the darkness he had tried so desperately to escape.

As they walked, the wind picked up, sending ash swirling around them, blurring the line between past and present. Danny's mind raced, replaying the moments that had led him here, the moments that had shaped him into the man he was now. There was no undoing the past. But perhaps, just perhaps, there was a way forward.

"You're not alone in this," Alex said, his words cutting through Danny's thoughts.

For the first time in a long while, Danny allowed himself to believe it. He wasn't alone. And maybe that was the first step toward redemption—the realization that, despite everything, there were still people who cared, people who believed in him. Maybe that was enough to start the healing process, to forgive himself.

They reached the camp where the others were waiting, the flickering light of a campfire casting long shadows on the ground. Emma was already there, her eyes scanning the horizon, ever watchful. Sophia stood by her side, her hands wrapped around a worn notebook, the blueprint for the stabilizer clutched tightly in her grip.

Danny knew what needed to be done. He had fought battles before, but this one was different. This time, the stakes were higher, and the enemy was not just a force of nature or a political regime—it was the human soul itself, grappling with the consequences of its own choices.

As they gathered around the fire, Danny's resolve hardened. This wasn't just about the invention anymore. It was about their survival, yes, but it was also about something greater. It was about reclaiming a part of themselves that had been lost—something that had slipped away in the chaos of war, in the madness of the world they had once known.

And maybe, just maybe, redemption wasn't about erasing the past. Maybe it was about learning to live with it, to use it to fuel the fight for a better future.

"You ready to make it right?" Alex asked, his voice steady now.

Danny looked around at the faces of the people who had come to trust him, who had fought beside him when it seemed like the world had already fallen apart. He wasn't sure what the future held, but in that moment, he knew one thing for certain: he was ready to fight for it.

"Yeah," he said, his voice filled with a quiet determination. "Let's do this."

And with that, they set off into the night, ready to face whatever came next, knowing that whatever the cost, they would fight to make the world, and themselves, whole again.

The night was eerily silent as they moved through the ruins, the only sound the soft crunch of gravel underfoot. The streets that had once been bustling with life now lay barren, littered with the remnants of a world that had been consumed by chaos. Streetlights flickered weakly in the distance, casting pale, sickly shadows over the cracked pavement. The sky above was a blanket of stars, but there was no peace in their beauty. The starlight felt distant, unattainable, as if the heavens themselves had abandoned this place.

Danny's mind wandered again, back to the war—back to the decisions he had made. He couldn't escape the ghosts of the past, no matter how far he ran. Each life he had taken, each mission he had carried out without question, haunted him. The faces of the innocent, the faces of those he had once sworn to protect, now appeared in his mind's eye, their eyes wide with fear and confusion.

But he had no choice. He had done what he had to do to survive. At least, that's what he had told himself at the time. Now, though, those justifications felt hollow. The weight of his actions had become unbearable.

He glanced over at Alex, who walked beside him, the line of his jaw set in quiet determination. Alex had his own demons, his own scars. But he had found a way to move forward, to channel his pain into something meaningful. Danny envied that. He wanted to find that same strength, to be more than the man he had been. He wanted to believe in something again.

The campfire ahead grew brighter as they neared, and Emma looked up from her vigil. Her face was etched with exhaustion, but her eyes still held a spark of fire, a fierce will to survive. She smiled faintly when she saw them approach.

"You're late," she said, but her tone lacked the usual bite. There was an unspoken understanding between them all now—none of them needed to say much. Their shared experiences had forged a bond stronger than words.

Danny nodded, but his gaze lingered on the fire. He wasn't sure what he expected to find in the flickering light. Hope, perhaps. Or maybe just the comfort of warmth, a reminder that they were still alive, still fighting.

Sophia, standing at the edge of the camp, raised her head as they approached. Her expression was calm, almost distant, but there was a strength in her quiet demeanor that Danny admired. She was the heart of their cause, the one who had given them something to fight for—the stabilizer. Her invention, the key to a future that seemed almost too distant to believe in.

"We've got the last piece," Sophia said, her voice low but steady. She held up a small, intricately crafted device—part of the stabilizer's core. "It's time to finish this."

Danny nodded, but his chest tightened. The stakes had never been higher. This was it—the moment they had been waiting for. Victory or defeat. Life or death. He could feel the weight of the decision pressing down on him, and he knew that whatever happened next, there would be no turning back.

"Are you sure about this?" Alex asked, his voice laced with concern.

Sophia met his gaze, unflinching. "I'm sure. This is the only chance we've got to save what's left of the world. We don't have the luxury of hesitation."

Danny stepped forward, his heart pounding in his chest. The uncertainty that had plagued him for so long was replaced by something else—something harder, more resolute. This was his chance. His chance to make things right.

"I'm with you," he said, his voice strong. He was no longer the man who had wandered aimlessly through the wreckage of the world. He was someone else now—someone who had a purpose. He had come this far, and he wouldn't stop now.

Sophia gave him a nod of acknowledgment, then turned back to the device. "We've all sacrificed too much to let this fail. This is our future. Let's make sure it's worth it."

As they gathered around the campfire, the final pieces of the stabilizer began to come together. The device, a fusion of technology and hope, was their last hope for a world that had been shattered by greed and war. It would be a fragile thing, but it was all they had left.

Danny couldn't help but wonder what would happen after this. If they succeeded, if the stabilizer worked, would it be enough to heal the wounds that ran so deep in the world? Would it be enough to heal him?

He didn't know. But he was ready to find out.

As the final components of the stabilizer were carefully assembled, the group worked in silence, each person lost in their own thoughts, the gravity of the moment weighing heavily on their shoulders. There was no room for error now; they were too close. This was their last shot, and they could not afford to fail.

Sophia connected the last wire, and the device hummed to life, casting a faint blue glow across the darkened camp. She stepped back, her expression unreadable.

"It's done," she said, her voice barely above a whisper.

Danny felt a strange mixture of awe and dread. It was as if the device itself held the power to reshape the world—or destroy it altogether. He could sense the quiet hum of energy emanating from it, like a heartbeat, steady and strong, yet fragile.

"We're not out of the woods yet," Alex said, breaking the silence. "We need to get this to the central node. The network has to be restored. If it's not—"

"We know the stakes," Danny interrupted, his voice firmer than he felt. The air seemed to crackle with tension as everyone processed what needed to come next. They had one chance to put the stabilizer in place, to initiate the sequence that would hopefully restore balance to the world. If they were successful, the cycle of violence, the endless wars, and the devastation that had swept across nations could begin to reverse. But if they failed—if the stabilizer didn't work—everything they had fought for would be in vain.

"Let's get moving," Danny said. He didn't have time for fear now. Fear had no place in this world. Only action could shape the future.

The group gathered their gear, the air thick with unspoken thoughts. Sophia, as always, led the way, moving with quiet purpose. Her confidence was contagious, even though Danny knew she was just as anxious as the rest of them. None of them could predict the outcome, but they all knew that this was a mission of no return. It was the end of the beginning, and the beginning of whatever came next.

The journey to the central node took them across the fractured remnants of once-thriving cities, now reduced to rubble. The remnants of shattered buildings stood as silent witnesses to the horrors of the war that had ravaged the planet. The sky above was a dull gray, an endless expanse of smoke and ash, as though the heavens themselves had been tainted by the violence below.

As they neared the final stretch, Danny's thoughts wandered again to the world they had left behind. To the lives lost, to the families torn apart, to the countless dreams extinguished in the flames of conflict. He knew the stabilizer would not erase the past—it couldn't. But it could offer a chance to rebuild, to create something new from the ashes. It was a spark, a flicker of hope in a world that had long forgotten what hope felt like.

The central node was hidden deep within the remains of an old government complex, a symbol of a world that had collapsed under its own weight. The building had once been a beacon of power, but now it was just another ruin, a monument to the corruption and greed that had destroyed everything.

Sophia moved quickly, her eyes scanning the horizon as she led them toward the entrance. "We're almost there," she said, her voice tight. "Just a little further."

They reached the entrance, a massive steel door that had once stood as a fortress against the world. It was now bent and twisted, its locks long broken. Sophia stepped forward and began to work on the security system, her fingers dancing across the interface. The machine responded with a low, metallic hum as it powered up, the door creaking open just enough to allow them to pass through.

Inside, the air was stale and thick with the smell of decay. The dim light from their flashlights illuminated the dusty remnants of a bygone era. The walls were lined with faded murals, images of a time when the world had believed it could endure forever. Now, those images seemed like lies, remnants of a past that had crumbled into nothingness.

They made their way down a long corridor, the sound of their footsteps echoing in the silence. Danny could feel the weight of history pressing down on them, as if the very walls were watching their every move. At the end of the corridor, a large chamber awaited them. It was empty, save for a few broken consoles and the remains of shattered equipment.

"This is it," Sophia said, her voice a whisper. "The heart of the network."

Danny's heart raced as they moved into the chamber. The central node was located at the far end, a massive machine that seemed both alien and familiar. It was the lifeblood of the network, the key to everything. Sophia approached it cautiously, her hands shaking as she connected the stabilizer to the core.

For a moment, nothing happened. The room was still, the air heavy with anticipation. And then, the machine hummed to life, its lights flickering as the stabilizer integrated into the system.

A rush of energy surged through the room, and Danny felt a strange sensation, as though the very fabric of reality was shifting. The air crackled with power, and for the first time in a long while,

Danny felt a glimmer of something—something that resembled hope.

The stabilizer was working.

But as the machine began to stabilize the system, a deep, rumbling sound echoed from somewhere far below. The ground trembled beneath their feet. The ceiling cracked, dust falling from above.

"No," Sophia whispered. "No, it's too soon. We—"

A deafening explosion interrupted her words, the walls of the chamber buckling under the pressure. In that instant, Danny understood—this wasn't just a fight for survival. It was a final test. A test of whether humanity could rise from its own ashes or whether it would be consumed by the fire of its own destruction.

As the dust swirled around them, Danny's mind raced. The stabilizer had begun the process of restoring balance, but the forces that had brought the world to the brink of ruin were not easily defeated. Would the stabilizer hold? Or had they triggered the final collapse of a broken world?

His heart pounded as the chamber shook once more. This was the moment of truth. And whatever came next—Danny was ready to face it.

The chamber trembled with another violent quake, the walls groaning as if the very foundations of the world were about to give way. Danny's pulse quickened. The stabilizer hummed louder now, its energy surging through the network like a beacon of hope amidst the chaos. He could feel it—the weight of the moment, the uncertainty of what was to come.

Sophia's hands were steady, even though her face was taut with strain. "It's working," she murmured, though her voice held no certainty. "But we need to act fast. The collapse isn't over yet."

Danny didn't need to ask what she meant. The vibrations in the air were growing more intense by the second, and the structure around them was beginning to disintegrate. They were running out of time.

"Everyone, get ready," he said, his voice sharp. "We need to get out of here now."

The group moved quickly, pushing past the fallen debris, each step a reminder of the world they were fighting to save. The pathway back to the entrance was narrow, choked with dust and rubble. Each time they moved forward, the ground beneath their feet threatened to crack open further, but they didn't stop. They couldn't.

Sophia led the way, her eyes scanning the walls for signs of structural weakness. Her usual calm demeanor had been replaced by a hard, determined edge. Danny could see the toll this mission had taken on her—on all of them—but there was no room for hesitation now.

As they neared the entrance, the first waves of destruction began to settle. The building around them was collapsing in slow motion, and the ceiling above them was buckling. They pushed forward, adrenaline driving them, but Danny could see the doubt in their eyes—none of them knew if the stabilizer had truly worked. None of them knew what kind of world they were returning to.

Then, just as they reached the door, another explosion rocked the building. The walls seemed to buckle in on themselves, and for a brief, terrifying moment, Danny thought they were done. But the force of the blast sent them hurtling forward, and the door finally gave way. They stumbled into the open air, the world outside still dark and shrouded in smoke, but alive with the hum of change.

They had made it.

But even as they stood there, gasping for breath, the first signs of the new world began to take shape. The stabilizer, though imperfect, had set in motion something irreversible. A ripple effect began to spread across the planet. The machines of war began to grind to a halt, and distant, broken cities began to show faint signs of revival.

It was far from over, but there was a chance now—a real chance for humanity to rebuild. The old world was gone, destroyed by its own excess, but in its place, something new and fragile was emerging. The air, once thick with the acrid stench of smoke, now felt cleaner, as if the Earth was drawing in its first deep breath after a long and suffocating nightmare.

Sophia was the first to break the silence. Her voice was hoarse, but there was a light in her eyes that hadn't been there before. "We did it."

Danny looked around, taking in the wreckage, the remnants of the old world scattered like forgotten memories. "We did," he said softly. But the victory felt hollow, like something they could barely hold on to.

Alex was the next to speak, his tone more cautious. "It's just the beginning. The hard part starts now. We don't know what's coming."

Danny nodded. He knew that this wasn't a clear-cut win. The world was still broken, still fragile, but the stabilizer had created the opportunity for change. It had opened a door—whether they would walk through it or fall into the same patterns of destruction that had plagued humanity for centuries remained to be seen.

"We'll figure it out," Danny said, more to himself than anyone else. "We have to. For everyone we lost."

They stood in silence for a long moment, watching the first hints of dawn break through the smoke-filled sky. It was a slow, painful process, but the world was waking up. And for the first time in a long while, Danny allowed himself to believe that something better could rise from the ashes.

In the distance, faint flashes of light began to appear on the horizon. Signs of life, signs of hope.

The journey was far from over, but for the first time in what felt like forever, there was a future worth fighting for.

## ○ A World on the Brink

THE AIR WAS THICK WITH the tension of impending disaster. In the shattered remnants of a city that had once been a thriving metropolis, the sound of distant gunfire echoed through the ruins, mingling with the unnatural silence that followed each blast. The streets, once bustling with life, now lay abandoned, their cracked asphalt overtaken by wild plants and the forgotten remnants of a civilization that had crumbled under the weight of its own excesses.

Alex stood at the edge of a crumbling skyscraper, his gaze fixed on the horizon where smoke billowed into the sky, obscuring the sun. The world he had once known had been torn apart by a war that seemed endless, and now the fragile peace they had fought for was teetering on the edge of collapse. He could feel the weight of the decision pressing on him, each breath he took a reminder of the delicate balance that held their group together.

Behind him, the sound of footsteps interrupted his thoughts. Emma, her face grim, approached, her eyes scanning the horizon. Her presence was a comfort, but even her unshakable resolve seemed to falter in the face of what was to come.

"We're running out of time," she said, her voice low, almost drowned by the distant explosions. "Victor's forces are gathering. If we don't act now, we'll lose everything."

Alex nodded without turning to face her. His mind raced, the strategy he had been formulating for weeks now seeming inadequate against the scale of the threat they faced. He had hoped that Sophia's stabilizer, the technology that could save what was left of the planet's fragile ecosystems, would be enough to turn the tide. But in the hands of Victor Lynn, the brutal tycoon who had profited from the war and exploited every corner of the earth, it was just another weapon to control and dominate.

"We need a plan," Alex muttered, more to himself than to Emma. "And we need it now."

Sophia, who had remained silent for the past hour, stepped forward, her face shadowed with uncertainty. The scientist's once-optimistic idealism had been battered by the harsh reality of the world they now inhabited. The device she had developed—the stabilizer—was their last hope, but it was also a ticking time bomb. In the wrong hands, it could cause far more destruction than anything they had already seen.

"We don't have a choice," Sophia said softly, her voice filled with the weariness of someone who had spent too many nights weighing the cost of what was to come. "The stabilizer can't wait. It's our only shot at stopping Victor. But we need to move quickly—before he gets to it first."

Alex turned to her, his face etched with the same exhaustion that weighed down on all of them. He had never been one to rush into anything without careful consideration, but time was something they no longer had.

"We'll take it to the heart of his operation," Alex said, his voice firm. "It's the only way to ensure it's used for good."

Emma shook her head. "You're not thinking clearly, Alex. If we march in there like we're going to take him down in one shot, we'll be walking into a massacre. We need more than a desperate assault—we need leverage."

The words hit Alex like a blow to the chest. She was right, of course. They couldn't just charge in blindly. Victor was too powerful, his forces too vast. They had to be smart—strategic.

"We'll find a way," Alex said, though doubt lingered in his eyes. The road ahead seemed more treacherous than ever. They had already lost so much. What more would they have to sacrifice to stop Victor?

Sophia's hand shook as she clutched the stabilizer's prototype, the device that could either heal or destroy. Her fingers, once so steady and confident, trembled as she adjusted the settings, testing its functions. She was no longer just a scientist; she had become the reluctant savior of a dying world.

"I'll give you what I can," she said quietly, not looking at either of them. "But we can't afford mistakes."

The silence that followed was suffocating. Each of them knew the stakes were higher than ever. As much as they wanted to believe that this mission could save them all, there was a bitter truth they couldn't escape: success would mean the rebirth of a world in chaos. Failure, however, would seal their fate.

The world was on the brink.

And so were they.

---

The tension in the air thickened as the hours passed. The team gathered their supplies, each person aware that the next few days could determine not just their future, but the future of humanity itself. Their mission was a calculated risk, but it was the only one left.

Victor Lynn's forces were on the move. They had been preparing for this moment for years, amassing power and resources while the world around them crumbled. And now, with Sophia's stabilizer within his grasp, Victor stood poised to finalize his grip on the remnants of civilization.

But Alex, Emma, Danny, and Sophia weren't willing to let that happen. The road ahead was uncertain, but they had come too far to turn back now. Every step was a gamble, but for the first time in what felt like forever, they felt the faintest stirrings of hope.

Hope that they could stop Victor. Hope that they could reclaim what had been lost. And hope that, in the end, they would survive.

The night stretched on, suffocating in its quiet, a prelude to the chaos that awaited them. Beneath the starless sky, the team gathered in their makeshift base, a hollowed-out building that once had been a bustling hub of activity. Now, it served as their last bastion against a world that was falling apart around them.

Alex sat at a dusty table, the map of the city sprawled before him. He ran his fingers over the routes they had plotted, the veins of the city like scars, marking the path to Victor Lynn's stronghold. It was a maze of rubble, barricades, and checkpoints, a place where the once-strong walls of power had been replaced by fortresses of greed and control. Every step they took in this city could be their last.

"We have to move fast," Alex muttered, his eyes scanning the map for any hint of a weakness in Victor's defenses. "If we waste time, we'll never get close enough."

Sophia was busy with the stabilizer, making final adjustments, her brow furrowed with concentration. She knew the weight of the device she held in her hands. It was the key to everything, the only hope they had of stopping Victor from cementing his rule over what was left of the world. But the pressure was taking its toll. Every moment she spent with the device felt like a countdown to something irreversible.

Emma leaned against the wall, arms crossed, watching the room with sharp eyes. Her role in the coming mission was clear: they needed someone who could navigate the terrain, find a way through Victor's defenses, and survive the inevitable confrontation that would follow. She was the tactician, the one who would find the angles they hadn't seen, who would lead them to the heart of the enemy's stronghold.

"Alex," she said, her voice breaking the silence. "I know you're thinking of rushing in. But we can't just charge in blindly. We need to disrupt Victor's control before we even get close. Without that, the stabilizer won't matter."

Alex met her gaze, frustration flickering in his eyes. "I know. But every minute we waste, we risk giving him more power. He's already too strong. We have to move fast, or we'll lose everything."

Sophia spoke up, her voice softer but no less firm. "We don't have to destroy everything to win, Alex. We need to be smart. Take down his infrastructure, his supply lines. If we disrupt his network, we can cripple his forces without putting everyone at risk."

It was a hard pill to swallow, but Alex knew she was right. They couldn't just focus on a head-on confrontation with Victor. They needed to take out his support system, weaken his hold on the city before they could even think about taking him down.

Emma nodded, her mind already working through the possibilities. "I can get us close to the communications hub. If we disable it, Victor won't be able to coordinate his forces. But it's risky. He'll have guards everywhere."

"We're not asking for easy," Alex said, his voice tight with resolve. "We're asking for the chance to stop him."

The plan took shape over the next few hours, each member of the team contributing their expertise, their skills, their very survival instinct. It was a plan born of necessity, one that combined stealth, speed, and precision. But it was also fragile. One wrong move, one miscalculation, and it would all fall apart.

As they gathered their gear, preparing for the night's mission, there was a palpable sense of urgency in the air. The silence outside the building was broken only by the occasional thud of distant explosions, reminders that the war wasn't just happening in their minds—it was real, it was everywhere. The world they had known was a world in ruin, and their mission was to change that.

But as they made their final preparations, a nagging doubt lingered in the back of Alex's mind. Was it possible? Could they truly stop Victor and save what was left of the world? Or were they simply too late, too small against the storm of power and destruction that was bearing down on them?

He shoved the doubt aside, focusing instead on the plan, on the team, on the task ahead. They had no other choice but to move forward. The world was on the brink, and this was their chance to turn the tide.

The streets were eerily quiet as they moved out under the cover of darkness, shadows slipping through the broken remnants of the city. The air was thick with the scent of burning rubber and decay, a constant reminder of the violence that had swept through the city. Every corner, every abandoned building, felt like it held a secret—a trap waiting to spring, a snare waiting to catch them.

They moved swiftly, keeping to the shadows, their steps as silent as possible. Emma led the way, her eyes scanning the surroundings for any signs of movement. She was the first to spot the guard checkpoint up ahead, a line of armed men stationed at a crumbling intersection. They were vigilant, scanning the streets for any sign of intrusion. But they hadn't yet noticed the small team slipping through the darkness.

"We take them out quietly," Emma whispered, her voice barely audible. "No noise. We don't have time for a full-blown firefight."

Sophia nodded, clutching the stabilizer tightly to her chest. She was the most vulnerable of them all—her focus on the device, her scientific mind unable to fully prepare for the raw violence they were about to face. But she had no choice but to trust them. To trust Alex, Emma, and the plan they had crafted.

The confrontation was swift and silent. Emma and Alex moved like shadows, disarming the guards with practiced ease. Their training and experience paid off, and within minutes, the checkpoint was neutralized. They moved forward, one step closer to their goal.

The closer they got to Victor's stronghold, the more tense the atmosphere became. The streets were lined with traps, with hidden cameras, and with forces loyal to Victor, ready to protect their leader at all costs. But with each obstacle they overcame, they grew more confident. They had made it this far, and they couldn't afford to stop now.

The moon hung low in the sky, casting long shadows across the crumbling ruins of the city. It was a cruel reminder of the beauty that had once been, now drowned in the devastation of war. Each step they took felt like a defiance against the silence, against the finality of the collapse. Yet, for all their preparation, they were not free from the looming sense of dread that clung to them like a second skin.

As they neared the communications hub, the intensity of the mission grew. The streets were becoming less familiar, more hostile, as if the city itself was rejecting their presence. The walls seemed to close in around them, the echoes of distant gunfire serving as a grim soundtrack to their every move.

"We're getting close," Emma said, her voice tense but steady. She had become the de facto leader of the group during the journey, her ability to stay calm under pressure a stabilizing force for the others. "Keep your eyes open. This is where it gets dangerous."

Sophia's hands trembled slightly as she adjusted the stabilizer, her mind racing through every calculation, every possibility. "I know. But we have to succeed. If we don't disrupt his communication system, all of this will have been for nothing."

Alex's jaw tightened. "We'll do it. We just need to stay sharp."

The complex loomed ahead, a fortress of concrete and steel, its once-pristine exterior now scarred with the marks of battle. It was a symbol of Victor's power, an imposing structure that controlled everything from military movements to propaganda broadcasts. If they could neutralize it, the ripple effect would be enough to cripple Victor's entire operation.

The team took their positions, slipping into the shadows as they surveyed the area. The communications hub was heavily guarded, a collection of armed men standing watch outside, their eyes constantly scanning for threats. The building was fortified, but it wasn't invincible. They had studied the plans for weeks, finding every weak point, every blind spot.

Emma motioned for the others to follow. With practiced precision, they moved into position, each step measured, every movement deliberate. They had to remain unseen—one wrong move, and the entire operation would be compromised.

"On my mark," Emma whispered, her breath steady despite the weight of the task. She knew that this was the moment that would decide everything.

A soft wind stirred the debris around them, a fleeting reminder of the world that had once been. The faint sound of footsteps echoed in the distance, but they were too far to pose an immediate threat. Emma's eyes flicked to Alex and Sophia, her signal to move forward.

With a quick, fluid motion, Alex and Emma took down the first guard, their hands swift and lethal, the silence of their actions a testament to their training. Sophia followed closely behind, her eyes never leaving the stabilizer. They had to keep it safe, keep it functional. The device was too valuable, too fragile.

The rest of the guards were dispatched just as quickly, their bodies falling silently to the ground. In mere moments, the outer perimeter was clear. But the real challenge lay inside.

The door to the communications hub stood before them like a final barrier between them and their goal. Emma moved toward it, her fingers brushing the keypad, her mind calculating the exact sequence needed to bypass the lock. It was a simple code, one they had anticipated, but it would only take one mistake to seal their fate.

"Almost there," Emma said, her voice barely above a whisper.

The door clicked open, and they slipped inside, their movements like shadows in the dark. The interior was cold and sterile, a stark contrast to the chaos outside. Rows of servers hummed in the background, their blinking lights offering a false sense of normalcy in the heart of a world falling apart.

Sophia stepped forward, her hands shaking slightly as she began to work on the stabilizer's connection. She had never felt this kind of pressure before—this was not just a scientific task. This was the future of the world hanging in the balance. She had to succeed.

Alex and Emma kept watch, their eyes scanning the room for any signs of movement. The seconds dragged on, each one a lifetime. They knew the risks—if Victor discovered their presence, it wouldn't matter how far they'd come. They would be hunted, destroyed before they could even activate the device.

"Done," Sophia said, her voice tight with relief. "It's connected. We can initiate the disruption sequence."

The room seemed to hold its breath as they waited. Every second felt like an eternity, the tension thick in the air. Sophia's fingers hovered over the device, and Alex couldn't help but feel the weight of their mission pressing down on them.

Emma's eyes were on the door. "We need to move. Now."

Sophia hit the button.

The room lit up with a bright flash of blue as the device powered up. For a moment, nothing happened. Then, the servers began to sputter, their lights flickering erratically. The hum of the machines grew louder, more chaotic, until the entire room seemed to pulse with an electric energy.

Outside, the first sign of trouble came in the form of alarms. The faint sound of sirens echoed from the far side of the building, growing louder with every passing second. It was only a matter of time before Victor's forces realized something was wrong.

"We've done it," Sophia breathed, but there was no time to celebrate. The countdown had begun.

Emma was already moving, signaling for them to fall back. They had no choice but to flee—the disruption was only the first step. They had to survive long enough to ensure that Victor couldn't stop them, long enough to see their mission through.

As they raced through the building, the sounds of footsteps grew louder, a harsh reminder of the danger closing in on them. They had to make it out alive, or all of this would have been for nothing.

The building was a maze, its corridors twisting and turning in every direction. Emma led the way, her instincts guiding her as she moved with urgency, the weight of their mission still fresh in her mind. Sophia followed closely behind, her face pale with tension, while Alex kept watch, scanning every corner for any sign of pursuit.

The alarms blared louder now, and the sound of footsteps echoed down the hallways, growing nearer. The guards would be coming, and they needed to move faster. The disruption they had triggered would not go unnoticed for long.

"We can't stop. Keep moving," Emma ordered, her voice steady despite the adrenaline coursing through her veins. She had led countless missions before, but this one felt different. This one carried the weight of an entire world on their shoulders.

They reached the elevator shaft, and Emma immediately began working on the control panel. Sophia pressed her hand to the stabilizer, ensuring it was still intact. They couldn't afford any mistakes now.

The elevator doors slid open, but instead of finding safety, they were met with the sight of a squad of guards rushing toward them. There was no time for hesitation. Emma shoved Sophia and Alex into the elevator and quickly slammed the door shut, trapping the guards on the other side.

"We'll have to take the stairs," Emma muttered. "The elevator is compromised."

They sprinted toward the stairwell, their footsteps thundering against the concrete as they ascended higher into the building. With each step, the weight of their situation grew heavier. The disruption had worked—Victor's network was faltering, but that meant they were now on the clock. The countdown was ticking, and they had no choice but to make it out alive.

The tension in the air was palpable, thick with the fear of being caught, of failing. They reached the top floor, and Emma didn't hesitate—she burst through the door, signaling for the others to follow. They were almost there.

But then, the unexpected happened.

A figure appeared from the shadows, stepping into their path. Tall, with sharp eyes that seemed to pierce through the darkness, he was the last person they expected to see. Victor's right-hand man, Marcus.

Emma froze for a split second, but it was long enough. Marcus smiled, a cruel twist of his lips. "I'm afraid your little mission is over."

He moved quickly, pulling a weapon from his side. The situation had just taken a dangerous turn.

"Get back!" Emma shouted, pushing Sophia and Alex behind her as she instinctively reached for her own weapon. The tension in the air seemed to thicken, the weight of their choices crashing down on them.

Marcus took a step closer, his eyes gleaming with a dangerous confidence. "You think you can just waltz in and take down everything I've built? You have no idea who you're dealing with."

"We're not afraid of you," Alex spat, his voice steady despite the fear rising in his chest.

Marcus's smile only widened. "You should be. You're in my world now, and I don't take kindly to intruders."

The silence that followed was deafening, broken only by the sound of their labored breathing. Emma's mind raced, calculating their options. She knew they had no choice but to fight—they couldn't allow Marcus to stop them now.

"Move!" Emma shouted, signaling for Alex and Sophia to take cover as she took aim. Her fingers were steady, the pressure of the moment sharpening her focus. She couldn't afford to miss.

The world seemed to slow as the first shot rang out. The blast echoed through the hallway, the sound of the gunshot sharp and final. Marcus's eyes widened in surprise, but he was quick to react, ducking behind the nearest pillar. The confrontation had just begun, and the stakes had never been higher.

But Emma wasn't about to let him win. Not now, not when they were so close to ending this nightmare.

The battle raged on in the narrow hallway, a deadly game of cat and mouse. Emma's heart pounded in her chest as she moved with purpose, every muscle in her body screaming for action. She could hear the rapid fire of gunshots, the cries of battle echoing through the concrete walls. They had no time to lose.

Sophia was the first to make her move, darting toward Marcus's position. She was quick, her movements fluid, her mind focused on the task at hand. She didn't hesitate, not even for a second. It was clear that she understood the stakes, understood the danger they were in.

"Stay focused!" Emma shouted as she took another shot, narrowly missing Marcus as he ducked out of sight.

The sound of footsteps approaching from behind caused Emma's blood to run cold. More guards were coming, and they were trapped. There was no way out.

"This is it," Emma whispered, her voice barely audible above the chaos. "We're going to have to fight our way out."

Sophia, still moving with precision, nodded. "I'm ready."

And with that, the battle escalated, and the future of their mission hung in the balance.

The walls of the building felt as though they were closing in on them, each moment more suffocating than the last. Emma's heart raced, her senses sharp, every instinct honed for survival. The odds were stacked against them, but surrender was never an option. They couldn't afford to lose now. Not when they were so close.

Marcus's figure moved behind the pillar, and Emma's eyes narrowed. She knew he was calculating, always a step ahead. But so was she. She had spent years learning how to predict her enemies' moves, and now it was time to use that knowledge.

"Alex, move to the left," Emma called, her voice low but urgent. "Sophia, take the right. I'll keep him distracted."

Without waiting for a response, Emma dashed toward the center of the hallway, drawing Marcus's attention. He took the bait, firing in her direction, but she was already diving behind the corner of the nearest doorway. The blast from his weapon ricocheted off the walls, deafening in its intensity.

Alex and Sophia didn't hesitate. They moved quickly, their training kicking in. Sophia was the first to make it around the corner, taking a shot at Marcus's exposed flank. The bullet grazed his shoulder, but it was enough to make him retreat further behind cover.

The tension crackled in the air, thick and suffocating. Emma's mind raced as she repositioned herself, calculating their next move. She could feel the weight of the situation, the pressure of knowing that one misstep could cost them everything.

"Now!" Emma shouted, her voice a sharp command that cut through the chaos. She dove forward, rolling to the side, and took a shot at Marcus's hiding spot. The bullet struck the pillar, sending debris flying. Marcus grunted, his frustration mounting.

Sophia and Alex were right behind her, moving in sync, a well-oiled machine. They pressed forward, inching closer to Marcus's position, the sound of their footsteps barely audible over the gunfire.

Marcus wasn't going down easily. He was relentless, his movements quick and calculated. He fired again, but this time Emma was ready. She dodged the shot and rolled to the side, narrowly avoiding the spray of bullets. She could feel the heat of the weapon's blast as it passed just inches from her, but she didn't falter.

"Keep him suppressed!" she shouted. "We need him distracted."

Sophia and Alex responded immediately, their guns firing in tandem. The shots rang out, forcing Marcus to duck back behind cover. Emma took a deep breath and steadied her aim. This was it. They had to finish this now.

She stepped out from her hiding place, her gun raised and ready. Her fingers tightened around the trigger, and for a split second, everything seemed to slow down. She could hear the rapid pounding of her own heart, the buzz of adrenaline in her veins.

The moment was fleeting, but it was enough. She fired.

The shot hit its mark, striking Marcus in the chest with a sickening thud. He staggered back, his eyes wide in disbelief, before he crumpled to the ground.

For a brief moment, there was silence. The sound of gunfire ceased, and the world seemed to pause. Emma stood motionless, her breathing heavy, the adrenaline slowly fading as the reality of what had just happened sank in.

"He's down," Alex said quietly, his voice a mix of relief and caution. He was still on alert, scanning the hallway for any signs of movement.

Emma didn't answer right away. She was still processing the outcome. They had won this round, but the battle was far from over. They had killed Marcus, but there would be others. Victor would send more men, and they still had to escape the building. The mission was far from complete.

"Get to the rooftop," Emma said, her voice steady despite the chaos. "We need to get out of here before reinforcements arrive."

Sophia nodded, moving quickly to Emma's side. Alex followed close behind, his gun still drawn, his eyes sharp as they navigated the narrow hallway. They reached the stairwell and began their ascent, the sounds of the building's alarms growing louder in their ears.

They were running out of time.

As they reached the rooftop, Emma's eyes darted over the landscape. The city sprawled before them, an expanse of steel and concrete that had once symbolized power and control. Now, it was a battleground, a symbol of everything that was slipping away.

She knew that they couldn't stay here for long. The rooftops would offer some cover, but it wouldn't be enough to escape undetected for long. They needed to find a way to leave the city before the full force of Victor's network descended upon them.

Sophia was the first to spot the helicopter hovering in the distance, its blades slicing through the air. It was their escape route—their lifeline. But the closer it came, the more Emma realized they weren't alone.

A black SUV roared into view, screeching to a halt at the entrance of the building's parking lot. Several armed men spilled out, their faces set with grim determination. The hunt was on.

"We've got company," Alex said, his voice tense.

Emma didn't hesitate. She grabbed Sophia's arm and pulled her closer. "Get to the chopper. I'll hold them off."

Sophia opened her mouth to protest, but Emma shook her head. "We don't have time. Go. Now."

With a final, reluctant glance at Emma, Sophia nodded. She turned and sprinted toward the helicopter, her legs pumping as fast as they could carry her. Alex followed, keeping close behind.

Emma turned to face the oncoming threat. She could hear the sound of boots pounding the rooftop, and she knew that time was running out.

But she wasn't about to let them take her down without a fight.

• • • •

## ○ The Collapse

THE WIND HOWLED THROUGH the ruins of what had once been a thriving metropolis. Now, it stood as a hollow skeleton of glass and steel, a monument to humanity's hubris and its downfall. The Collapse had come suddenly, as such things often do in history: a sharp, decisive rupture in the fabric of a world already stretched thin by years of conflict and greed. There was no final warning, no ominous prelude. One moment, the world was as it had always been — a machine, albeit sputtering, moving forward in its never-ending cycle of destruction and creation. The next, everything was dust.

Alex Novak stood at the edge of the old city center, his eyes scanning the horizon, where the remnants of buildings and twisted metal framed the pale sky. He had seen much worse in his life, and yet, something about the sheer scale of the destruction here felt different. The silence was oppressive, as if the land itself had surrendered, too tired to fight against the tide of decay.

"Is this it?" Danny's voice cut through the stillness, his tone a mixture of disbelief and resignation. He stood next to Alex, his face worn with the same exhaustion that had been etched into every survivor in these final days.

"It's close," Alex replied, his gaze never wavering. "We're running out of time."

For years, they had fought for scraps of survival, scavenging what they could from a crumbling world. But this—this was no longer about survival. This was about the very essence of what it meant to live in a world that had forgotten its own future. And it was slipping away faster than Alex could grasp it.

The Collapse had begun not with a single catastrophe, but with a thousand small fractures that had grown into insurmountable chasms. Nations crumbled under the weight of their own corruption, their leaders either lost in the chaos or holed up in their fortified bunkers, leaving the rest to rot. In the end, the fight for resources had taken its toll. Water had run out in the places it mattered most, food had become a rare commodity, and the very air had turned toxic in some regions, unbreathable even for the strongest among them.

Alex's fingers tightened around the map he held, the edges frayed and torn. It had been handed to him years ago by someone who no longer existed. It marked the last known location of Sophia Alvarez, the scientist who had developed the technology that could reverse the damage done. The stabilizer. A device capable of saving the planet, if it was still possible to save anything at all.

But Victor Lynn, the man who had seized power in the chaos of the Collapse, would stop at nothing to control it for himself. To him, it wasn't just a tool to heal the world—it was a weapon to hold dominion over what remained of the human race. His empire, built on the backs of the suffering, was growing by the day. The stabilizer was the key to his vision of a new world order, one in which he would be the undisputed ruler.

"She's out there somewhere," Alex muttered to himself, more as a reminder than a statement. "We find her, and we have a chance. We fail, and everything ends."

Danny shook his head. "You know it's not that simple."

"No," Alex said, his voice hardening. "But we don't have the luxury of simple anymore. The world is crumbling, Danny. We're running on borrowed time. If we don't do something now, all of this—" he gestured to the wasteland around them, "—will be for nothing."

His words hung in the air between them, heavy with the weight of truth. No one had imagined it would come to this. Even in the darkest times, there had been hope—a belief that humanity could rebuild, that civilization would rise again. But as the years dragged on, that hope had eroded like the very structures that once stood tall and proud. What was left now? A fragmented world where only the ruthless thrived, where survival meant sacrifice, and where the very concept of rebuilding seemed more like a distant fairy tale than a tangible reality.

A sharp noise interrupted his thoughts—a distant, echoing crash that reverberated through the remains of the city.

"Get down!" Danny barked, instinctively pulling Alex to the ground.

They pressed themselves into the rubble as gunfire rang out, sharp and rapid. The sound of a firefight. There was no telling who was out there, who was left to fight, or for what cause. It was all the same now. The fight for survival. The fight for control. In the chaos, no one was innocent.

The shots faded, but the tension remained, thick and suffocating.

"We need to keep moving," Alex said, his voice steady despite the danger. "We're not safe here."

Danny nodded, his expression hardening. The Collapse had brought with it a brutal, primal world, where allies were few, and the enemies were endless. But Alex had a goal. He had to keep moving forward. For the sake of the future—if such a thing still existed.

As they moved through the shattered streets, Alex couldn't shake the feeling that the Collapse wasn't just a series of events. It was a statement—a verdict. Humanity had failed to learn from its past, and now, it was paying the price. And if they didn't succeed, the collapse wouldn't just be the end of a city or a nation—it would be the end of everything.

They moved quickly through the empty streets, the sounds of distant gunfire still echoing in the background, reminders of the chaos that consumed the land. Alex's mind raced, though his steps remained steady. Every corner, every building, every shadow could conceal danger. The war had made everyone a potential threat, survival a matter of distrust.

As they neared the edge of the city, the landscape began to shift. The ruins gave way to barren fields, the earth scarred by craters and the skeletal remains of trees stripped of life. The environment had become its own enemy, as unforgiving as the human forces that fought over its remaining resources.

"Do you think she's still alive?" Danny asked, his voice almost lost in the wind. The question had been asked more times than Alex cared to admit.

"I don't know," Alex answered honestly, his eyes scanning the horizon. "But if there's even a chance, we take it. We don't get many of those anymore."

Danny didn't reply. There was no need. They both knew that in a world like this, hope was a luxury, and trust a rare commodity. Still, Alex couldn't bring himself to abandon the possibility that Sophia was out there, that the stabilizer could still be their salvation. It was a faint flicker, but it was enough to keep them going.

As they passed the outskirts of the city, the silence deepened. There was no sign of life, no other survivors, no soldiers. It was as though the world itself had retreated into the shadow of its own destruction.

But the silence was deceptive.

Out of nowhere, a figure appeared in the distance, moving swiftly across the desolate landscape. Alex's hand instinctively went to his weapon. They had learned the hard way not to trust anyone. The figure stopped at the edge of a broken fence, and after a tense moment, waved.

"Stay low," Alex whispered, pulling Danny behind the ruins of a collapsed building. The figure, clearly aware of their presence, didn't move any closer, but continued to signal, a beckoning motion.

"Could be a trap," Danny murmured, his grip tightening on his rifle.

"I'm not taking any chances," Alex replied, his voice low but firm. "Stay ready."

They crouched, moving in a wide arc around the figure, careful to remain out of sight. As they drew closer, Alex could make out more details—a woman, roughly their age, her face grimy but determined. She wore the ragged remnants of a military uniform, its insignia faded and barely visible.

When she noticed them, she didn't raise an alarm. Instead, she pointed to the horizon, where a faint plume of smoke rose into the sky.

"They're coming," she said, her voice sharp with urgency. "You need to move fast, if you're headed that way. Victor's men are closing in."

Alex's heart raced. This was it—this was the sign they had been waiting for. Sophia was close. The woman, noticing his intent, added quickly, "I can help, but we need to leave now. I know where she is, but they'll be on us soon."

Without hesitation, Alex nodded. They had no time to waste. The woman's words were like a lifeline, but he couldn't afford to get caught up in the past or the details. Survival meant moving quickly.

They followed her, ducking into the cover of the ruins once more. As they moved, the air thickened with tension. Every rustle of leaves, every distant sound seemed like the approach of an enemy. There was no room for error. One wrong move, and it could be the end.

Finally, they reached a small, fortified compound hidden behind a thick veil of overgrown foliage. The woman gestured for them to stay quiet as they slipped through a narrow gap in the outer wall.

Inside, the atmosphere was charged with nervous energy. There were people here—survivors, most of them dressed in improvised armor, their faces etched with weariness. It was clear they had been living on the edge for a long time.

"Where is she?" Alex asked, his eyes scanning the compound for any sign of the woman he had been searching for.

"She's here," the woman replied, nodding toward a small, dimly lit hut at the far end of the compound. "But it's not safe. Not for long."

The urgency in her voice hit Alex like a punch. Every second counted. As they moved toward the hut, the sounds of distant vehicles rumbled faintly, the telltale signs of an approaching force.

They reached the hut, and the door opened before Alex could even knock. A thin, pale woman stepped out, her eyes sharp and focused. Sophia Alvarez.

"You're too late," she said, her voice carrying a tone of grim acceptance, as if she had already known they would come but had given up hope of changing anything. Her face was drawn, and her hands trembled slightly as she held something wrapped in cloth. The stabilizer.

Alex's breath caught in his chest. They had found it. But Sophia's expression, though determined, was strained. It was clear she didn't believe in a happy ending.

"Victor knows," she said softly. "He always knew. I was never meant to survive this."

"Then we'll make sure you do," Alex said, his resolve hardening. "We're not leaving without you."

Sophia glanced at him, the faintest hint of a smile tugging at the corners of her lips. But it was a sad smile, full of resignation.

"You'll have to outrun hell to do it," she said, "but I'm willing to try."

As she spoke, the distant rumble grew louder, and Alex knew their time was running out. The Collapse had not just destroyed cities. It had shattered the world's moral compass. And if they were to have any hope of rebuilding, they would have to face the full wrath of Victor's empire, which was closing in faster than they could imagine.

The final confrontation had begun.

The ground shook as distant engines grew louder, the sound of military vehicles drawing closer. Alex's pulse quickened, and he could feel the weight of the moment pressing down on him. They were so close now—closer than he had ever imagined. The stabilizer, the key to everything, was in their hands. But Victor's men were closing in fast.

"We don't have time to waste," Alex said, his voice low but urgent. He turned to Sophia. "You need to get ready. We move now, or we're dead."

Sophia nodded, her expression hardening. Despite the exhaustion that had clearly worn her down, there was a spark of determination in her eyes. "I've been ready for this moment since the day Victor's men came to my door."

They quickly moved into action, gathering their few belongings and securing the stabilizer. Alex scanned the compound one last time, making sure no one else was around. The survivors in the camp had already disappeared into the hidden paths, leaving only the few most determined to fight alongside them.

"We head for the mountains," the woman who had led them here said, her voice steady. "It's the only way out. They'll never expect us to go there."

Alex nodded, but his instincts told him there were other dangers in the mountains. Still, it was the only route that made sense. There, in the wild, they would have a better chance of slipping past Victor's forces.

"Stay close," Alex warned as they slipped out of the compound. "Keep your heads down. We move quietly."

They worked quickly, using the undergrowth to cover their movements, slipping through the broken landscape as if they were shadows. But even as they moved, Alex couldn't shake the feeling that they were being watched. It wasn't paranoia; it was survival instinct. The world had turned into a never-ending game of cat and mouse, and no one could afford to relax.

After what felt like hours of careful travel, they reached the base of the mountains. The sun was beginning to dip below the horizon, casting long shadows across the terrain. The mountains loomed in front of them, a jagged silhouette against the blood-red sky.

"We'll make camp here," Sophia said, her voice calm, but Alex could hear the tension beneath it. "At first light, we move up."

Alex nodded, but his mind was elsewhere. In the silence that had settled over them, he could almost hear the rumbling engines of Victor's men. They were getting closer. The mountains might be their only hope, but they weren't the safe haven they appeared to be. The deeper they went, the more the terrain would change—more dangerous, less predictable.

As they settled in for the night, Alex couldn't help but feel the weight of responsibility that had been placed on him. It had been one thing to hope for survival. It was another to have a purpose, a mission, to hold the lives of others in his hands. He glanced at Sophia, the woman who had once held the answers to so many questions—and now, in their moment of desperation, was their only hope for a future.

"We'll get through this," Alex said quietly, more to himself than anyone else.

Sophia didn't answer immediately, her eyes staring into the darkening landscape. Then she spoke, her voice barely above a whisper. "It's not about surviving, Alex. It's about rebuilding. If we can't change this—if we can't stop Victor—then everything we've lost, everything we've fought for, it means nothing."

She was right. The collapse wasn't just about cities falling or armies marching. It was about the destruction of a world order that had been fragile even before the war. And if they didn't stop Victor, there would be nothing left to rebuild. The future would be lost before it even had a chance to take root.

Alex's thoughts were interrupted by a sudden sound—sharp, brief, like the crack of a twig underfoot. He froze, his heart pounding in his chest.

"Did you hear that?" he whispered to Danny.

Danny, who had been on watch, nodded, his face pale in the dimming light. "We're not alone."

Alex's hand instinctively went to his weapon, his senses on high alert. He signaled for the others to stay low, and they huddled in the shadows, waiting.

Moments stretched into what felt like an eternity. Every breath seemed too loud. The only sounds were the wind in the trees and the distant thrum of Victor's vehicles.

Then, a figure emerged from the darkness.

It was a man, moving swiftly but quietly, dressed in the torn remains of military gear. His face was obscured by a scarf, but his eyes were unmistakable—hard, calculating, and dangerous. He raised a hand in the universal sign of peace, his voice coming out as a harsh whisper.

"I'm not here to fight you. I'm here to warn you."

Alex's heart skipped a beat. He couldn't tell if this was an ally or another threat. But he couldn't afford to make any mistakes.

"Who are you?" Alex demanded, keeping his voice low.

"My name is Andrei," the man replied. "I know you're heading up into the mountains. But you need to know—it's not just Victor's men that you'll be facing up there. There are others. The warlords. They've carved out their own territories."

Alex exchanged a glance with Sophia. Warlords—merciless, opportunistic, and unpredictable. They had no allegiance except to power. If they had staked a claim in the mountains, things were going to get much more complicated.

Andrei continued, his voice tense. "There's a path, hidden, but it's the only safe way. If you want to survive, you'll need to follow it. It's your only chance."

Sophia stepped forward, her eyes narrowing. "And what do you want in return?"

Andrei's lips curled into a thin smile. "Survival. A place in your fight against Victor. I know the mountains better than anyone, and I have a stake in this war too."

Alex considered the man carefully. Could they trust him? In this world, trust was a luxury that few could afford. But the mountains were dangerous, and Andrei was offering them a lifeline.

"We take the path," Alex said, his decision made. "But you stay in the back. No tricks."

Andrei nodded, his eyes never leaving Alex's. "Agreed. Lead the way."

They didn't have much time. The sun was almost gone, and the night would bring its own set of challenges. With a final glance at each other, they set off into the darkness, their future uncertain, but their will to survive stronger than ever.

The path Andrei led them on was narrow, winding through dense thickets that seemed to close in around them. The faint light of the moon barely pierced through the trees, casting long, distorted shadows across the ground. Every step felt heavier than the last, as if the weight of the world itself was pressing down on them.

Alex kept his senses alert, his hand gripping the rifle with a tightness that reflected his growing unease. Every snap of a twig, every rustle in the underbrush, made his muscles tense, ready for danger. But the mountains, with their jagged cliffs and treacherous terrain, were both an advantage and a curse. They could hide here, but they could also be trapped.

Andrei led them uphill, the ground steep and uneven. They moved slowly, carefully, knowing that the slightest mistake could lead to disaster. Despite the urgency of their situation, Alex couldn't shake the nagging thought that Andrei wasn't entirely honest with them. There was something in the way the man carried himself—too calm, too controlled for someone who claimed to be a survivor like them.

Finally, after what seemed like hours, they reached a narrow ridge that overlooked a dark valley below. Andrei stopped and turned to face them.

"This is it," he said quietly, his voice tinged with something that felt like caution. "The path splits here. You'll need to go left. It's the safest route."

Sophia frowned, stepping forward. "And you?"

"I'll wait here," Andrei said, his hand rising to stop her. "I can't go further with you. They'll be watching. If they see me with you, I'll be dead before I can explain. But this path—" He gestured to the left, his eyes hardening. "It's your only chance."

Alex didn't like it. The mountains weren't kind, and the idea of splitting their group when they were already vulnerable seemed like a bad decision. But he had no choice. They needed to trust Andrei, at least for now.

"Are you sure you can't come with us?" Alex asked, his voice tight with the pressure of the situation.

Andrei met his gaze, his eyes unwavering. "I'm sure. You don't need me to fight your war. You need to survive the night."

Sophia's sharp eyes studied him for a long moment before she nodded. "Fine. But remember—if you betray us, we won't hesitate."

The words were blunt, but there was a truth in them that Andrei couldn't ignore. He gave them a single nod before turning on his heel and disappearing into the shadows.

The group waited for a moment, letting the stillness settle in. Then, without another word, Alex motioned for them to move. They followed the path, feeling the tension in the air thicken with every step.

The valley below stretched out before them like an abyss, and the further they went, the more it felt like they were being swallowed by the landscape. The trees grew thinner, and the wind picked up, whipping around them in harsh gusts. As they reached the edge of the ridge, Alex stopped, peering into the distance.

There was something there. Something moving.

"Get down," he whispered, his voice barely audible.

They all dropped to the ground instinctively, pressing themselves into the earth as low as they could go. Alex's heart thudded in his chest, and his mind raced to make sense of what he was seeing. At first, he thought it might be Victor's men. But no, it wasn't the familiar uniforms of the military. These figures were different—more like ghosts, shadows that seemed to blend with the darkness.

Alex's grip tightened on his weapon. His instincts screamed at him to run, to get away before whatever it was saw them, but his body remained still, frozen.

Sophia, who had been staring at the figures through the thick brush, glanced at him, her face pale. "Who are they?"

Alex shook his head, his mind struggling to make sense of the situation. "I don't know. But we need to move—quietly."

They didn't wait for another moment. They moved swiftly, slipping between trees and rocks, trying to stay out of sight. But no matter how careful they were, they couldn't shake the feeling that they were being hunted.

The figures in the valley didn't approach them directly, but their presence was undeniable. It was like they were always just beyond the edges of their vision, waiting. Watching. Every now and then, a figure would appear, its silhouette only visible for the briefest of moments, before vanishing again into the shadows.

Alex's mind was racing, but he couldn't focus on the figures for too long. They had to keep moving—keep putting distance between themselves and whoever—or whatever—was out there.

Hours passed, or maybe it was days—time seemed to lose its meaning in the darkness. The mountains were endless, each ridge looking like the last, each valley hiding even more danger. But finally, when Alex thought they couldn't go any further, they came upon a small clearing.

It was barely large enough to set up camp, but it was the first place they'd found that felt at least somewhat safe. They gathered around the fire, keeping their voices low and their movements minimal.

Sophia let out a long breath, her shoulders slumping. "We made it. For now."

But Alex wasn't sure if "for now" was enough.

The night had fallen completely, and the only sounds were the crackling of the fire and the occasional distant rumble of thunder. But deep down, Alex could feel the weight of what lay ahead. They had no allies left, no real safety, and no idea what would be waiting for them at the end of the road.

But as long as they had each other, they had a chance. And that was enough to keep fighting for.

As the fire flickered and the shadows stretched across the clearing, Alex's thoughts began to drift. He could hear the soft crackling of the burning wood, but his mind was far away. The figures in the valley haunted him, their eerie, silent movements unsettling him in ways he couldn't explain. Who were they? Why had they been watching them? And why did it feel as if they were no longer in control of their own destiny?

Sophia stirred beside him, her face tense as she stared into the fire. Her fingers twisted nervously around the strap of her pack. She had been quiet for a long time, but her silence only added to Alex's unease. He wanted to ask her what was going through her mind, but the words stuck in his throat. The atmosphere had shifted between them, and no matter how close they'd once been, they were all different now. Changed by what they'd seen, by what they had to do to survive.

"Alex," Sophia's voice broke through his thoughts, soft but urgent. "We need to talk."

He turned to face her, his brow furrowed. "About what?"

She hesitated, glancing over her shoulder as if checking for anyone who might be listening. Then she leaned closer. "About what's happening. Everything. The collapse, the figures in the valley, the way things are unraveling. You feel it too, don't you? The world's slipping away from us."

Alex exhaled slowly. "I know. But what can we do about it? We're stuck out here in the wilderness, and we're not the only ones fighting for survival."

Sophia shook her head, her expression darkening. "It's not just about survival. It's about what we're surviving *for*. We can't just keep running, Alex. Eventually, it'll catch up to us."

His eyes met hers, and in that moment, he saw the desperation behind her words. She wasn't just scared for herself; she was scared for all of them. And perhaps, for a world that had already begun to crumble beyond repair.

Alex opened his mouth to respond but was interrupted by the sound of movement from across the clearing. He instantly tensed, instinctively reaching for his rifle, but it was just Ivan, making his way cautiously toward the fire. His face was drawn, eyes wide with exhaustion, but there was a steely determination in his step.

"We need to keep moving," Ivan said, his voice low and clipped. "The longer we stay here, the more dangerous it gets. We've already been spotted."

Alex stood up, his muscles stiff from the long hours of sitting. He didn't argue—Ivan's words were as close to an order as anything they'd had in days. The atmosphere had changed; the air felt heavier, charged with a palpable tension. And the truth was, he didn't feel safe anymore. Not here. Not anywhere.

"We're not leaving yet," Sophia said, her voice sharp. "We need to plan. We need a strategy. Running around like headless chickens won't get us anywhere."

Ivan glanced at her, but the anger that flashed in his eyes was gone as quickly as it appeared. He wasn't in the mood for another argument. "The longer we stay, the more likely it is that we'll be surrounded. I'm not waiting around for that to happen."

Alex glanced at Sophia, her eyes hardening in resistance. They were both exhausted, their nerves worn thin by the constant fear, the uncertainty. But deep down, Alex knew Ivan was right. Their time in the clearing had expired.

"Ivan's right," Alex said quietly, his voice carrying the weight of his decision. "We leave at dawn. We keep moving."

Sophia's lips pressed into a thin line, but she didn't argue. Instead, she stood up, her posture tight with resolve. There was no choice but to follow the path laid out for them, no matter how fraught with danger it seemed.

The night passed in uneasy silence, each of them trying to find rest in the sporadic moments of sleep. The wind howled through the trees, a constant reminder that the world beyond their small circle was falling apart. Alex lay awake for hours, staring up at the stars. He thought about the long road ahead, about the uncertain future that awaited them. And he wondered if they would ever find peace again.

When dawn finally broke, the world seemed no different than it had been the night before—bleak, cold, and endless. The morning light cast long shadows across the landscape, and Alex felt the weight of it all pressing down on him once again.

Ivan had already packed his things by the time Alex emerged from the tent. "We go now," he said, his tone final. "We can't afford to waste any more time."

They gathered their belongings in silence, moving with mechanical efficiency, the urgency of their situation overriding any lingering doubts or fears. The valley below was still, but Alex knew it wouldn't stay that way for long. The figures they had seen the night before were out there somewhere, and though they didn't know exactly who or what they were, Alex felt an undeniable certainty that their paths would cross again.

As they set out once more into the mountains, Alex tried to shake off the sense of doom that seemed to follow them. They could keep moving, keep running, but would it be enough? Would they ever be able to outrun the collapse of everything they had known?

He didn't have the answers. All he knew was that they had to keep going—one foot in front of the other. And hope that somewhere, out there in the vast, crumbling world, they would find a way to survive.

The journey stretched on for days, with little more than the occasional stop to replenish supplies or rest before continuing their trek through the harsh wilderness. The weight of the world's collapse pressed heavily on their shoulders, and every step they took felt like it brought them closer to an unseen precipice. The world around them was bleak and unforgiving, but the uncertainty of their future was what gnawed at their hearts the most. Each night, as they set camp, the shadow of their circumstances loomed over them—how much longer could they keep this up? How long before the road they were on would end in some unspeakable disaster?

Sophia, though she had initially been resistant to Ivan's urgency, was the first to speak up as they trekked through the dense forest. Her steps were slower than usual, her shoulders weighed down by a weariness that went beyond physical exhaustion.

"We can't keep running forever," she said quietly, her voice almost lost in the rustling of the trees. "There has to be something we can do. Some place we can go... somewhere safer."

Ivan, leading the group, didn't look back. His pace remained steady, relentless. "We're safer on the move. The more we linger, the more vulnerable we become."

Alex had been thinking the same thing. But there was something in Sophia's tone, something in the way she said it, that made him pause. It wasn't just fear talking. There was an underlying question—what were they running from, exactly? What had happened to make survival their only concern?

"She's right," Alex said, his voice barely louder than Sophia's. "We've been running for days, but we're getting nowhere. We need a plan. A place to settle, even if just for a little while."

Sophia glanced at him, a spark of hope in her eyes. Ivan, on the other hand, shot them both a sharp look but didn't argue. He knew they had to rest at some point, but he wasn't ready to let go of the momentum they'd built. Not yet.

"Fine," Ivan muttered after a long pause. "We'll take a break. But it's not going to be for long."

They found a small clearing at the edge of a fast-moving stream, where they could rest and refill their water bottles. The sound of the rushing water was soothing, but it did little to ease the weight of the air around them. The tension between the three of them had grown palpable, especially since Sophia had voiced her doubts about their endless journey. Alex could feel the underlying strain, the cracks in their fragile alliance.

As they sat around the fire that night, a cold wind began to blow, carrying with it a faint, unsettling smell—something foreign, something dangerous. Alex stood up abruptly, his senses on high alert.

"Sophia," he called, his voice tight. "Do you smell that?"

She paused, then nodded slowly, a frown knitting her brow. "Yeah, it's strange. Almost metallic."

Ivan's eyes narrowed, and he scanned the darkened trees surrounding them. "Stay alert. We're not alone."

Alex didn't need to be told twice. His hand moved to the knife at his side, his eyes darting from shadow to shadow. The chill in the air had nothing to do with the temperature—it was something far worse, something creeping closer, something they couldn't see.

A branch snapped in the distance. Then another. And another.

Alex's heart began to race. The sound of movement grew louder, closer. Something was out there. Watching.

"Get your gear, now," Ivan ordered, his voice low and steady. "We're leaving."

But before they could even gather their things, the first of the figures appeared from the trees. Tall, thin, their faces obscured by dark hoods. They moved with eerie precision, their footsteps silent, their eyes fixed on the small camp. Alex's blood ran cold. The figures they had seen in the valley—the ones who had haunted their thoughts—were now here, in the flesh. The realization hit him like a punch to the gut. They weren't just watching. They were hunting.

Ivan wasted no time. He gestured for Alex and Sophia to move, and they sprinted into the woods, fear propelling them faster than they ever thought possible. The figures followed, their long strides unhurried but certain, as if they were more patient than their prey.

"Stay close!" Ivan shouted, his voice sharp as he led them through the trees. "Don't fall behind!"

Alex could hear the rustle of branches behind them, the sound of their pursuers closing in. The figures were getting closer, and though they moved silently, there was an unnatural force to their presence. A kind of weight, as if they were not just chasing them, but controlling the very environment around them.

They broke into a clearing, and for a moment, Alex thought they might be safe. But the figures were still there, just beyond the tree line, watching, waiting.

"They know," Sophia gasped, her voice trembling. "They always know."

Ivan didn't respond. His focus was entirely on the figures, his mind racing for any possible way out.

"This isn't just about survival anymore," he muttered, more to himself than to anyone else. "They're not just hunters. They're something worse. Something we can't escape."

Alex's mind raced, too. What were these figures? Who were they, and why were they so relentless? The questions spun around in his mind, but there were no answers. Not yet.

The wind picked up again, this time carrying a sound that sent a chill down Alex's spine—a low, guttural growl, almost like an animal, but not quite.

They weren't alone in the clearing anymore.

The growl echoed through the clearing, deep and guttural, vibrating in Alex's chest. It was the kind of sound that made his skin crawl, sending a shiver of primal fear down his spine. His grip tightened on the knife at his side as he turned slowly, his eyes scanning the trees and underbrush for any sign of movement.

Sophia, her breath shallow with panic, stood frozen next to him, her eyes wide in terror. Ivan, however, had already moved into action, pulling her towards the thick trees at the edge of the clearing.

"Move!" Ivan's voice was a whip-crack in the tense silence, and the urgency in his command cut through the panic that was beginning to set in.

Alex hesitated for a moment, his heart pounding in his ears. The growl had come from behind them, but now the air was still. Too still. It was like everything had frozen, waiting. Alex forced himself to turn back, but the figures were closing in on them, silent but swift, their dark cloaks billowing around them as they moved with unnerving precision.

"They know we're here," Alex muttered, his throat dry, and his fingers shook as they gripped the hilt of the knife.

"No time for that!" Ivan barked, dragging Sophia forward as he dashed toward the trees, clearly not wanting to waste any more time in the open. "Run. Don't stop!"

The air seemed to thicken as they sprinted through the woods. The figures in the clearing moved forward with a disturbing grace, not chasing, but guiding their path, leading them further into the unknown.

The growl came again, closer this time. Alex could feel its vibrations through the earth beneath his feet, and the forest itself seemed to pulse with a sinister rhythm. They were being driven deeper, further away from any semblance of safety.

Alex's thoughts scrambled. Who were these beings? What was it they wanted? Were they human at all, or were they something more—a manifestation of the collapse, perhaps, something born from the very destruction that had brought the world to ruin?

The ground underfoot grew rougher, the trees closing in, their roots twisting out like fingers reaching for their ankles. Sophia stumbled, her foot catching on a hidden rock. Alex reached out instinctively to grab her arm, pulling her back to her feet, but in that split second, they were separated from Ivan.

"Go!" Ivan's voice came from the distance, his silhouette cutting through the darkness ahead of them. "Stay with me, Sophia. Alex, keep up!"

Alex didn't wait for her to reply. He pushed forward, his legs burning with the effort to keep pace. The shadows seemed to shift in the trees, their dark shapes almost alive. The air grew colder, and with each step they took, the forest felt more oppressive.

They were getting closer to something. Alex could feel it. A presence—no, more than that. The sensation of being watched intensified, and it wasn't just the cloaked figures that haunted him anymore. There was something else, something much older, much darker, moving just beyond his peripheral vision.

And then, as they reached the edge of the clearing, Alex stopped dead in his tracks. Ahead, through the trees, there was a figure standing in the shadows, cloaked in darkness, its face hidden beneath a hood. But it wasn't like the others. There was something unnatural about its presence, something that made the air feel like it was bending around it.

It wasn't a person.

It was a thing—an entity, an impossibility.

The ground seemed to tremble beneath Alex's feet, as though the very earth was reacting to its presence. The creature did not move, but Alex could feel its eyes on him, a cold, malevolent gaze that bore into his soul.

Sophia stopped beside him, her breathing ragged. She stared at the figure, her body frozen in fear. "What is that? What is it?" she whispered, her voice barely audible.

Ivan had caught up with them, but he, too, stopped when he saw the figure. He didn't speak, his jaw clenched, and his eyes hard as he surveyed the scene.

The entity remained still, its features indistinct, but Alex knew one thing for certain: it wasn't something they could run from. It was something they would have to face.

The growl came again, louder now, and Alex felt the familiar pressure of the other figures closing in on them. They were trapped.

"Get ready," Ivan said quietly, his voice low but steady. He drew a weapon from his side—a sleek, metallic object that gleamed under the dim light filtering through the trees. It was a weapon of some sort, but Alex had never seen anything like it before.

The creature, the thing in the shadows, seemed to sense their movement. Its head turned slightly, its presence pressing down on them like an invisible weight. The figures behind them advanced, their movements silent but purposeful, like a wave gathering force.

Alex's heart hammered in his chest, but his mind was strangely calm, focused. This wasn't about surviving anymore. It was about confronting whatever this was. There was no going back.

Ivan stepped forward, his weapon aimed at the creature. "You've made a mistake," he muttered under his breath. But it wasn't just a threat. It was a warning. A last, desperate attempt at control.

The creature's hood shifted slightly, revealing nothing but shadows, as if its very face was a void, consuming everything around it.

Without warning, it lunged forward, faster than anything Alex had ever seen. The air seemed to crackle with its energy as it moved toward them, an inescapable force.

And in that moment, Alex knew they were no longer just fleeing the collapse of the world—they were facing it head-on.

The creature's movement was an explosion of motion, an unstoppable force that blurred the line between reality and nightmare. Alex barely had time to react as it surged toward them, its form now a twisting shadow that seemed to devour the space around it. The world around them seemed to slow, stretching time into a taut wire ready to snap.

Ivan reacted first, his weapon flashing in the dim light as he fired. The shot rang out, a sharp crack that split the tension hanging in the air. The projectile hit the creature, but it passed right through, like a wisp of smoke swirling around the darkness. The impact didn't even cause it to falter. Instead, the entity twisted, its form elongating as if mocking their attempts to fight back.

Alex's heart raced. There was no time for hesitation. They had no weapons that could touch it, no tools that could fight this thing. They were unarmed against an unstoppable force.

"Move!" Ivan shouted, his voice breaking the air like a whip. He turned, grabbing Sophia and yanking her towards the trees, his face set in grim determination. But even as they retreated, Alex could feel the weight of the creature's presence pressing down on them, pushing them back.

Alex hesitated for a split second, the knife in his hand feeling almost laughable against the terror they were facing. But it wasn't the knife that could save them. It was their minds, their ability to outwit and outlast.

"We have to get to the clearing!" he yelled, turning to run, his legs pumping as adrenaline surged through him. The clearing was their only chance—at least there, they might be able to see their attackers coming, or even use the terrain to their advantage.

Sophia stumbled beside him, struggling to keep up. Her face was pale, streaked with dirt, and her eyes were wide with fear. "Alex, what is that thing?" she gasped, her voice ragged as she tried to keep pace.

"I don't know, but we're not fighting it with force," Alex replied, his breath coming in ragged bursts. "We have to outsmart it."

The woods were a blur around them, trees and roots twisting like the fingers of some great beast, trying to drag them into the earth. Behind them, the creature moved with terrifying ease, its form flowing through the shadows as though it was the darkness itself. Its growls were closer now, vibrating through the ground and filling their minds with dread.

Ivan's voice crackled through the silence ahead. "The clearing is too exposed! We need to make it to the ridge. We can't stay in the open."

Alex nodded, understanding instantly. The ridge would give them some cover, at least, a higher ground to fight from. He turned, pushing forward with renewed urgency. But Sophia stumbled again, her legs giving out beneath her.

"Help me!" she cried, her voice breaking. "Please, I can't—"

Alex reached out without thinking, catching her by the arm and hauling her upright. "Come on, we're almost there. Just a little more."

Ivan had already reached the ridge, his form a dark silhouette against the sky. He was turning back to them, shouting something, but the words were lost in the howling wind. The sound of the creature's growl was deafening now, the very earth trembling beneath them.

Suddenly, there was a sharp, crackling noise. The air shifted, and before Alex could process what was happening, he saw the creature—its form materializing in the air before him. It had crossed the distance in an instant, faster than any human could comprehend.

It was no longer just a shadow. It had taken shape, revealing an eerie, contorted form that seemed part-human, part-beast. Its eyes gleamed with a malevolent intelligence, its face an unrecognizable mask of terror and rage.

Alex's heart skipped a beat. They weren't going to escape.

In that moment, time seemed to freeze. The creature towered before them, its very presence distorting the air around it. Alex could feel its gaze on him, burning through him like a fire.

Ivan was still yelling, pulling Sophia behind him as he readied his weapon, but Alex knew it wouldn't help. They were dealing with something beyond their comprehension, something that had no place in the world they had known.

Suddenly, the creature moved again, its body a blur as it struck. Ivan fired once more, but this time, the creature dodged with inhuman agility. The world seemed to slow as the impact of the blow hit Ivan, sending him crashing to the ground.

Alex's stomach lurched as Ivan's body lay motionless on the ground, his weapon falling from his hand. The creature loomed over him, its form shifting as if it was feeding off their fear.

Sophia screamed, but the sound was drowned out by the howling wind, by the creature's growl, which now seemed to come from every direction. Alex knew they were out of time. They couldn't survive here. They had to run, even if they were running from something that couldn't be outrun.

But his legs wouldn't move.

The creature's eyes locked onto his. In that moment, it was as if everything—the forest, the clearing, the ridge—disappeared. There was only the creature, and there was only fear.

A voice cut through the air, sharp and clear, breaking the spell. "Alex, we have to go now!"

It was Sophia. Her voice, filled with panic, was enough to jolt him back to reality. He didn't think, didn't question. He grabbed her arm and pulled her toward the ridge. The creature was close, too close. But they had no choice.

The ridge was their only chance.

Alex's pulse hammered in his ears as they stumbled up the ridge. His mind was a blur of fear and instinct. Behind them, the creature's presence felt like a crushing weight, pressing down on them, the air growing heavier with every step. The darkness of the forest seemed to close in, swallowing the path ahead. He could hear its growl, now a low rumble that vibrated through his bones, and the sound of it moving—relentless, unstoppable.

Sophia was breathing heavily, struggling to keep up. Her hand was slick with sweat as she gripped Alex's arm. "We're not going to make it," she gasped, her voice quivering with fear.

Alex didn't answer. He couldn't. The words wouldn't come. He pushed forward, each step feeling like it could be their last.

But the ridge was close now. They were almost there. They could make it to higher ground, where at least they could see their enemy before it reached them.

A deafening roar split the night, and Alex spun around just in time to see the creature leap toward them. Its massive form blurred in the moonlight, impossibly fast, impossibly strong. The ground seemed to shake as it landed in front of them, blocking their way.

Sophia screamed, her voice echoing through the night as she backed away. Alex's heart raced. There was no escape now. The creature was between them and safety.

It was an animalistic nightmare, its eyes gleaming with an intelligence far beyond anything human. The air around it was thick, warping like a heat haze, as if the creature itself bent reality to its will. Its limbs stretched unnaturally, extending like dark tendrils that snaked toward them.

"Get back!" Alex shouted, pulling Sophia behind him. His hand went to the knife at his belt, though he knew it was useless. But he had to do something.

The creature tilted its head, its gaze fixed on him, as though it was considering his challenge. It wasn't a mindless predator—it understood the fear in their eyes, the desperation in their movements. And it relished it.

Alex tightened his grip on the knife. He had no plan, no strategy, just raw instinct. He darted forward, swinging the blade in an arc aimed at the creature's chest. But it was too fast. The creature effortlessly dodged, its form shifting with unnatural fluidity. Alex barely had time to register the movement before the creature was upon him, its shadow swallowing him whole.

It moved so quickly that Alex couldn't react. One of its limbs shot out, striking him with terrifying force. The world tilted, and he was thrown backwards, his body slamming into the ground with bone-crushing impact. Pain exploded through him as he struggled to breathe, his vision swimming with dark spots.

Sophia's scream pierced through the haze, but it felt distant, muffled. He tried to move, to get up, but his limbs felt like lead. Blood dripped from his mouth, and he tasted the metallic sting of it as he forced himself to rise.

The creature was looming over him now, its form impossibly tall, its presence consuming every ounce of the space around them. It didn't speak, didn't need to. Its mere existence was a command, an overwhelming force of nature that could not be resisted.

"Alex!" Sophia's voice was frantic now. She was still there, still alive, still fighting.

Through the fog of his pain, Alex saw her move—saw her lunging toward the creature, her hands outstretched. In a final, desperate act, she grabbed at the creature's leg, her fingers digging into its skin as though she could claw through the darkness itself.

"Run!" Alex shouted, his voice hoarse. He couldn't protect her. He could barely protect himself.

But Sophia didn't listen. She gritted her teeth, her face a mask of determination. The creature jerked back in a swift motion, its limbs contorting, but Sophia clung on. Her hands were a vice, refusing to let go.

The creature growled in frustration, its monstrous form writhing with anger, but then, something changed. The ground beneath them shifted, and Alex felt the air grow colder. A strange energy filled the space, a force that radiated from the creature itself.

It was no longer simply a predator—it was something far darker, something ancient.

Suddenly, the creature twisted, a tendril of darkness shooting out to wrap around Sophia's neck. She gasped, her hands releasing their grip as the creature lifted her effortlessly off the ground. Alex's blood ran cold.

"No!" he screamed, the sound tearing from his throat.

But there was nothing he could do. His body was too slow, too weak to intervene. The creature's grip tightened, and for a moment, all Alex could hear was the sound of Sophia choking, her breath strangled by the creature's power.

Then, just as quickly as it had lifted her, the creature flung her aside, her body crashing against the ground with a sickening thud. She lay still, motionless, her body crumpled like a ragdoll.

Alex felt his stomach lurch, bile rising in his throat as he scrambled toward her, his legs uncooperative. He reached her side, his hands trembling as he checked for a pulse. Her skin was cold, her face pale and lifeless.

"No... no, no..." Alex whispered, his voice breaking.

The creature loomed over them, watching, waiting. It knew what had just happened. It knew the moment it had struck. Alex could feel the weight of its gaze, the suffocating presence that threatened to crush his mind.

Sophia was gone.

Tears burned in Alex's eyes, but there was no time for them. The creature wasn't finished. It wasn't done with them yet.

The ridge was their last hope, but now it felt like a tomb. The wind howled around them, and the creature's growl filled the air, its presence a constant, gnawing reminder of the terror they had unleashed.

There was no way out. No way to fight back.

Alex stood, his hands bloodied and trembling, his heart racing in his chest. There was only one thing left to do now.

Survive.

Alex's thoughts were a chaotic whirlwind as he stood over Sophia's lifeless body. Grief threatened to swallow him whole, but he couldn't afford to fall apart—not yet. The creature was still there, its dark presence growing stronger, a suffocating force pressing against his chest.

He took a deep breath, forcing himself to focus. The cold air bit at his skin, but it wasn't enough to freeze his resolve. He had to move. He had to fight. There was no time to mourn, no time for weakness.

The creature, watching from the shadows, seemed to sense his shift in determination. It let out a low, guttural growl, almost as though it were challenging him. The ground beneath Alex's feet vibrated with its power, an unsettling reminder of how outmatched he was.

But Alex was done running. He wasn't going to let it win.

His eyes darted around the ridge, searching for something—anything—that could give him an advantage. There was a jagged rock nearby, sharp and jagged like a broken tooth. It was a long shot, but it was the only weapon he had.

Without hesitation, he grabbed the rock and stood, holding it out in front of him like a spear. His pulse hammered in his ears, and his breath was shallow, but he couldn't stop now. He could still save himself—he had to.

The creature shifted in the shadows, its form rippling like smoke, as though it were made of the very darkness itself. Alex's grip tightened around the rock, and he forced himself to stay focused. He couldn't let fear take over, not again.

With a primal roar, the creature lunged forward, its tendrils reaching for him. Alex swung the rock in a desperate arc, connecting with one of its limbs. The impact sent a shockwave through his arm, but it didn't slow the creature down. It was like striking a wall of solid darkness.

The creature retaliated with a vicious swipe. Alex barely managed to duck in time, the air around him buzzing with the force of its strike. His heart raced as he felt the wind of its limbs brushing against his skin. He was close—so close to being taken.

But then, something shifted. The creature hesitated. Its form flickered, as if a glitch had occurred in its existence. Alex took the opportunity, charging forward, throwing all his weight into a desperate attack. The rock slammed into the creature's side, and for the first time, it recoiled.

For a moment, Alex thought it might be over. But then the creature's form reassembled, its shadow stretching unnaturally, twisting, reforming. It wasn't just a monster—it was something far older, something beyond human comprehension.

Alex stepped back, his chest heaving with exhaustion. His body felt like it was made of lead, each movement sluggish, like dragging himself through mud. But his mind was clear, sharper than ever. He had only one chance left.

The creature was stronger than anything he had ever faced, but he knew this land. He knew its secrets. And if he could use them against the creature, he might survive.

In the distance, a flicker of light caught his eye. A cluster of trees stood on the far side of the ridge, their branches thick with something unnatural. A spark of hope flickered in his chest. It was the only way.

But the creature wasn't done yet. Its form surged forward again, its growl a deep, terrifying echo that resonated in Alex's bones. He barely had time to react before the creature was upon him, tendrils reaching, slithering toward him like serpents.

With every ounce of strength he had left, Alex sprinted toward the trees. The creature was close—too close. He could hear its heavy breathing, feel its presence closing in around him. His legs screamed with the effort, but he couldn't stop.

He reached the trees, and as he did, the ground beneath him trembled. He looked down, just in time to see the earth crack, splitting open as though the land itself was rebelling against the creature. The trees began to glow, their branches twisting in the air like ancient symbols.

The creature hesitated. For the first time, it seemed unsure, as if it recognized something in the land that it couldn't touch.

Alex's heart raced. He reached out, touching one of the glowing trees. The energy that coursed through him was overwhelming—ancient, powerful. It was as though the trees were alive, their energy flowing through him, offering him strength. He wasn't alone anymore.

The creature screeched, its form flickering again, more violently this time. It recoiled from the trees, as if the very light was burning it. Alex didn't understand what was happening, but he didn't care. He had a chance.

With a shout, Alex pushed forward, using the power coursing through him to shove the creature back. It screeched in pain, its form distorting further. The shadow recoiled, as if it were afraid of the light, the ancient power surrounding him.

For a moment, Alex felt invincible, as if he had tapped into something far greater than himself. He fought back, pushing the creature farther away, until it howled in defeat. Then, with a final, terrifying screech, it retreated into the darkness, its presence fading like a nightmare at dawn.

Alex collapsed to his knees, gasping for breath, his body trembling with exhaustion. The forest was silent now, the eerie growls of the creature gone, replaced by the soft rustling of the trees.

But the battle wasn't over. It couldn't be. Something had changed. The creature wasn't just hunting him—it was hunting something greater. And Alex was sure that he hadn't seen the last of it.

The ridge was quiet now, but the war had only just begun.

Alex remained kneeling in the eerie stillness of the forest, the weight of the moment settling heavily on his chest. His mind buzzed with questions, his thoughts scattered like leaves in the wind. What had he just faced? What was the creature? And what was this power in the trees that had saved him?

His breath came in shallow bursts, his limbs aching from the strain of the fight. The exhaustion was overwhelming, but the adrenaline had yet to wear off, keeping his senses sharp. Slowly, he stood, wiping the dirt from his hands and looking around.

The trees glowed faintly, their light casting an ethereal sheen over the landscape. It was a strange sight, almost as though he had crossed into another world. The shadows no longer seemed threatening, but there was a deep, underlying sense of mystery that made him wary.

He stepped closer to one of the glowing trees, his fingers brushing against its bark. It felt warm—alive in a way that no tree should. The energy he had felt earlier surged once more, like a ripple of electricity running through his body. He jerked his hand away, the sensation fading as quickly as it had come.

Alex took a deep breath and forced himself to focus. He needed answers. He needed to understand what was going on, and he had no time to waste. He looked back at the ridge, the path he had taken to reach this strange grove. There was no sign of the creature, but he knew it hadn't been defeated for good. It would return. They always did.

His mind drifted to Sophia. The image of her lifeless body haunted him, but there was no time to mourn. If he didn't find a way to stop the creature, if he didn't find a way to fight back, her death would be meaningless.

He turned toward the dark horizon, where the first hints of dawn were creeping over the mountains. A new day, but the battle was far from over. The world was crumbling around him, and the creature was just one of many threats that lurked in the shadows.

He needed to move, to keep searching, to find something—someone—that could help him. The answers were out there, hidden in the ruins of the old world. The trees, the creatures, the power—it was all connected, and he would find out how.

With a heavy sigh, Alex turned away from the grove and began walking into the unknown, the faint glow of the trees fading behind him. His mind was set. There was no turning back now. He would survive. He would fight. And he would uncover the truth of what had caused the collapse of the world.

As the light of dawn began to break over the horizon, Alex felt a glimmer of hope. It was small—almost imperceptible—but it was there. The light at the end of the tunnel was still a distant dream, but it was there.

And he would reach it, no matter the cost.

Alex's footsteps crunched through the underbrush as he made his way deeper into the wilderness. His mind was racing, but his body was weary. He had been running on fumes for what felt like an eternity. The strain of the battle with the creature had left him drained, and the long trek through the dense forest wasn't helping. Yet, he couldn't afford to stop. Every fiber of his being screamed that he was being hunted—that whatever had attacked him would return, and it would be stronger this time.

His thoughts kept drifting back to Sophia. The image of her lifeless form, her blood staining the ground, burned into his mind like an indelible mark. He hadn't been able to save her. There had been no time to act. And now, she was gone.

But the feeling of guilt gnawed at him. He had to keep moving forward. For her. For everyone. The collapse of the world, the creatures, the strange, pulsing power that he had felt in the forest—it all connected somehow. There had to be answers, and he had to find them.

Hours passed, and the landscape around him began to change. The dense forest began to thin out, and soon, he found himself standing at the edge of a cliff. Below, the remnants of what had once been a thriving city lay in ruin, the skeletal remains of buildings jutting out of the ground like broken teeth. Smoke still rose from the wreckage, and the distant sounds of screams and chaos carried on the wind.

Alex felt a pang of dread. The city had been a focal point before the collapse, and it seemed to be teeming with life again—though it was far from the life he remembered. These weren't survivors; they were something else. And whatever they were, they had been drawn to this place by the same power that had once caused the world's downfall.

He turned away from the edge of the cliff and descended into the valley below, moving cautiously. The terrain was treacherous, and the occasional creak of a distant tree or the rustle of leaves made him jump. The forest no longer felt like the haven it had once been. Now, it felt like a trap.

As he walked, his thoughts shifted again to the power he had felt earlier, the pulse that had flowed through the trees and into him. It wasn't just energy—it was something ancient. A force that had been hidden, lying dormant until now. Had it always been there, or had the collapse of civilization somehow awakened it? And what was its true purpose?

He wasn't sure, but he couldn't afford to wait around to find out. Whatever it was, it was dangerous. He had to find out how to harness it—use it to survive. The stakes were too high now.

Suddenly, a rustling sound came from behind him, and Alex spun around, heart racing. His hand instinctively reached for his weapon, but before he could pull it free, a voice rang out from the shadows.

"You've come a long way, haven't you?"

Alex froze. The voice was cold, detached, yet familiar in some strange way. From the darkness, a figure emerged—a tall, thin man cloaked in tattered garments. His face was obscured by the shadows of his hood, but his eyes gleamed with a sharp intensity.

Alex's instincts told him to fight, but something in the stranger's demeanor made him hesitate. There was a quiet confidence in his movements, an almost unnatural calmness that unnerved him.

"Who are you?" Alex demanded, keeping his hand on the hilt of his blade.

The figure tilted his head, studying Alex with a curious expression. "A traveler. Like you, perhaps. Searching for answers. For something to hold onto in this broken world."

Alex didn't trust him. Not for a second. But there was something compelling about the man's words, something that made him wonder if this was the help he had been seeking.

"I don't need help," Alex replied, his voice harsh.

The stranger's lips curled into a faint smile. "Perhaps not. But everyone needs something. Even you."

Before Alex could respond, the man turned and gestured for him to follow. "The city holds many secrets, you know. Not all of them are lost."

Reluctantly, Alex followed him. His thoughts were a whirlwind, but one thing was clear: this man knew something. And maybe—just maybe—he could help Alex make sense of it all.

As they moved closer to the ruins of the city, the air grew thick with the smell of decay and fire. The buildings loomed like giants, their fractured walls casting long shadows in the dying light. And somewhere, deep within the heart of the city, the answer to the world's collapse awaited.

Alex didn't know what he would find, but he knew he couldn't stop now. Not when the stakes were so high.

The city sprawled before them like a haunted labyrinth, its once-proud architecture now little more than skeletal remnants of a forgotten civilization. Alex's boots scraped against the cracked pavement, the sound echoing through the empty streets. The air was thick with dust, and the stillness of the place was unsettling. It was as if the city had been frozen in time, caught in a moment of inevitable destruction.

The stranger moved with a fluidity that seemed unnatural, gliding through the rubble as if he were one with the decay. Alex kept his distance, though his curiosity was piqued. Who was this man? What did he know about the collapse, about the power that had twisted the world?

They walked in silence for what felt like hours, weaving through the ruins. The remnants of old shops, homes, and factories stood like broken statues, their windows shattered, their walls covered in graffiti. The world had moved on, but the past refused to let go. The faint sound of distant voices, indistinct but urgent, drifted to Alex's ears, sending a shiver down his spine.

Finally, they reached what appeared to be an old cathedral. Its towering spires had crumbled, and the large iron doors were warped and half-rusted, but it still held an air of grandeur. The stranger stopped in front of the doors and turned to Alex.

"This is where it all began," he said, his voice low and almost reverent. "The power you're searching for, the answers you need, are inside."

Alex hesitated. There was something about the man's words that felt too... easy. As though he were being led into a trap. But the pull of his desire for answers was too strong. He stepped forward, his heart pounding as he reached for the handle.

The door creaked open with a groan, revealing the dim interior of the cathedral. The air inside was stale, heavy with the scent of mildew and dust. Faint beams of moonlight filtered through the broken stained-glass windows, casting colorful patterns on the floor. The atmosphere was oppressive, as though the walls themselves were suffocating beneath the weight of forgotten prayers.

"Come," the stranger urged, stepping into the shadows. "We don't have much time."

Alex followed, his senses heightened, every step echoing in the vast emptiness. The silence in here was deafening, broken only by the sound of their footsteps. As they moved deeper into the cathedral, Alex noticed strange markings on the walls—ancient symbols, their meanings long lost to time. They seemed to pulse faintly, as if alive, reacting to his presence.

At the altar, the stranger finally spoke again. "This place was built to harness the power that destroyed everything. It was never meant to be understood by men. But there are those who still seek it, those who believe that the answers lie in the past."

Alex's stomach twisted. "What power are you talking about?"

The man turned to face him, his expression serious, almost grim. "The collapse. The things that have been unleashed. They were never meant to happen. But those who controlled the world before the fall—they knew. They knew this was coming."

Alex felt a cold chill wash over him. "And you want me to what? Help you fix it? What are you, some kind of cultist?"

The stranger shook his head. "No. I'm not here to fix it. I'm here to make sure it doesn't happen again. To stop those who want to use this power for their own gain."

"Who are they?" Alex demanded, stepping closer.

"They are the ones who survived," the man replied. "The ones who saw the collapse coming and learned how to manipulate the forces that tore the world apart. They're the ones who have been pulling the strings ever since, hiding in the shadows. But they can't control it forever."

Alex's mind reeled. The collapse, the creatures, the power in the trees—it was all part of a much larger, more terrifying plan. The world was not as it seemed. There were forces at play that were far beyond his understanding.

The stranger's gaze was intense. "You've seen it. The power that flows through the trees, through the ruins. It's not just nature; it's something far older, something that was always meant to be hidden. But it's out now. And if it's not contained, it will consume everything."

Alex's pulse quickened. "And you want me to help you stop it?"

"I want you to help me find the source," the man said. "We can't stop it until we understand where it's coming from. The collapse wasn't an accident—it was a warning. The world is on the brink of something far worse. And only by confronting it, by confronting the truth, can we hope to prevent it."

Alex felt his throat tighten. He had no choice. He didn't fully understand what was at stake, but he couldn't ignore the urgency in the stranger's voice. He had to do something.

"I'll help you," Alex said, his voice steady despite the storm of questions swirling in his mind. "But where do we start?"

The man nodded, a faint smile crossing his lips. "Follow me. The answers are closer than you think."

As they made their way deeper into the cathedral, Alex couldn't shake the feeling that they were being watched—that the walls themselves were closing in. The truth was out there, hidden in the darkness, and he was about to uncover it.

The deeper they ventured into the cathedral, the more the air thickened, as if something was awakening. Alex could feel it in the pit of his stomach—an almost palpable presence that seemed to draw him closer to the heart of this place. The walls, once silent, now whispered faintly, their secrets swirling in the spaces between the broken stones. The stranger moved with purpose, his shadow melding with the darkness as they crossed the ancient stone floor.

Suddenly, the man stopped before a grand archway, its edges worn and faded. A sense of finality hung in the air. "This is where it ends," he said, his voice barely a murmur.

Alex hesitated, a wave of dread washing over him. This wasn't just a cathedral—it was something else. He stepped forward, compelled by a force he couldn't explain. The archway seemed to beckon him, promising answers, or perhaps a deeper mystery.

As they entered, the cathedral's interior changed. The once-barren space was now filled with intricate carvings, symbols that seemed to pulse with an energy of their own. Some appeared to shift when Alex's gaze lingered too long, twisting into patterns that made his head spin. The air was electric with an eerie hum.

The stranger spoke, his voice heavy with the weight of history. "This is the Nexus. The center of it all. The place where the energy converges. The power of the collapse, the force that destroyed the old world, was born here. But it wasn't just an accident—it was a reckoning. A reset."

Alex looked around, his pulse quickening. "A reset? What do you mean?"

The stranger motioned for him to follow as he stepped toward a large, circular altar at the center of the room. Upon it lay an object—a relic, partially obscured by a thick veil of dust. "This," he said, "is the key to everything. It was designed to harness the power, to control it. But those who created it—those who tried to wield this force—they underestimated what they were dealing with."

Alex's heart pounded as he approached the altar. He could sense the power radiating from the object, though he couldn't explain how or why. It was as if the air itself had changed, thickening with the weight of the past. "So, this is the cause of everything? The power that brought the world to its knees?"

"Not just the cause," the man replied, his voice grim. "It's the solution. But it's also a danger. In the wrong hands, it could mean the end of all things. The collapse wasn't a natural disaster. It was a reckoning. A punishment for what we had become."

Alex stepped closer, his fingers grazing the surface of the relic. The symbols etched into it were ancient, and yet they seemed familiar, as if he had seen them in his dreams. A low hum vibrated through the air, and for a moment, he could almost hear the echo of voices in the distance, faint whispers that made his skin prickle.

"What does it do?" Alex asked, unable to tear his gaze away from the object.

The stranger's eyes darkened. "It doesn't *do* anything, not on its own. It's not just a tool. It's a conduit. A bridge between the old world and the new one. It connects us to forces we were never meant to understand."

Alex felt a surge of anxiety. The weight of his decision loomed over him. "And you want me to help you use it?"

"No," the stranger said sharply. "I want you to help me stop it from falling into the wrong hands. The same forces that caused the collapse—they're still out there. They'll stop at nothing to claim this power, to use it to bring about something far worse than the world we left behind. If they succeed, there will be no escape. There will be no future."

The room seemed to grow colder, the walls pressing in on him. Alex's mind raced. The collapse, the creatures, the strange energy—it was all connected to this ancient power. But who were these forces the stranger spoke of? And why was he the one to stop them?

"I don't understand," Alex admitted, his voice shaking slightly. "Who are they? What do they want with this power?"

The stranger's expression grew even darker. "They are the remnants of the old world. Those who believed they could control everything, shape reality itself. They are the ones who manipulated the collapse, using it to reshape the world in their image. But they failed, and now they're hiding in the shadows, waiting for the right moment to strike again."

Alex felt the weight of the stranger's words settle over him. This was bigger than anything he had ever imagined. The collapse wasn't just a tragedy—it was part of a plan, a calculated move by those who sought ultimate control. And now, he was being asked to stop them.

"Where do we go from here?" Alex asked, his voice firm despite the uncertainty swirling in his chest.

The stranger stepped away from the altar, his eyes scanning the room. "We find the others. There are people who understand this power, who can help us stop the ones who would use it for their own gain. But we have to move quickly. The longer we wait, the more dangerous it becomes. We don't have much time."

Alex nodded, his resolve hardening. He didn't know what awaited them, but he knew one thing for certain—he couldn't turn back now. The fate of the world, it seemed, was in his hands.

As Alex and the stranger turned to leave the altar, the air around them seemed to shift, thickening with an ominous weight.

The cathedral, with its ancient walls and forgotten whispers, felt like a place out of time. It had once been a sanctuary, but now it was a tomb, the final resting place of a world that had tried and failed to wield forces beyond its understanding.

"We need to move fast," the stranger said, his voice low, as if even the cathedral walls could hear them. "The longer we stay here, the more attention we draw."

Alex nodded, his eyes still fixed on the relic. He had come to this place seeking answers, but what he had found was far beyond anything he had expected. The collapse, the creatures, the remnants of the old world—it was all connected to this object, this conduit of unimaginable power.

As they made their way toward the exit, Alex's mind raced. He couldn't shake the feeling that something was watching them. The whispers, though faint, grew louder in his ears. It was as if the very air was alive, aware of their presence. The stranger moved quickly, his steps echoing in the silence, but Alex couldn't help but glance over his shoulder, certain that they were not alone.

They emerged into the cold night air, the cathedral's silhouette looming behind them like a shadow in the distance. The streets were eerily quiet, the usual bustle of the city absent, as if the world itself had stilled in anticipation.

"Where do we go now?" Alex asked, his breath forming mist in the chilly air.

The stranger paused, his eyes scanning the empty streets. "There's a safe house. A place where we can lay low and gather information. But we can't take the direct route. We need to be careful."

The journey ahead was uncertain, filled with danger and unknowns. But Alex had no choice but to follow the stranger. There were too many unanswered questions, too many risks to ignore. He had been thrust into a world he barely understood, and yet it felt like the only path forward was to keep moving.

They slipped through the narrow alleys, avoiding the main roads. Alex's senses were heightened, every sound amplified in the stillness of the night. The city, once familiar, now felt alien, as though it had transformed overnight into a labyrinth of danger and secrets.

As they neared the safe house, the stranger stopped suddenly, motioning for Alex to crouch down. He followed the man's lead, his heart pounding in his chest. From the shadows, a group of figures appeared, moving with deliberate purpose. They were cloaked, their faces obscured by hoods, but Alex could feel the danger emanating from them.

The stranger tensed, his hand on the hilt of a blade hidden beneath his cloak. "Stay down," he whispered, his voice urgent. "They're not here for us, but they're close enough to be a problem. We can't afford to be seen."

Alex held his breath, his mind racing. These were the shadows the stranger had spoken of—the remnants of the old world, those who sought the power of the relic. He could feel the tension building, a sense of impending violence hanging in the air. The cloaked figures moved past them, unaware of their presence, their footsteps echoing in the silence of the streets.

As they waited in the shadows, Alex's thoughts swirled. The stranger had warned him that time was running out, that the forces after the relic were relentless. But what did that mean for him? What role did he play in all of this? He had no answers, only the gnawing feeling that whatever was happening, it was much bigger than him.

When the figures had passed, the stranger gave a signal, and they continued on their way, slipping into the hidden safe house. It was a small, nondescript building tucked away in a forgotten corner of the city, its entrance concealed by a heavy, weathered door.

Inside, the atmosphere was thick with the scent of old books and the faint hum of machinery. The stranger motioned for Alex to follow him down a narrow corridor, leading to a small room at the back of the house. It was sparsely furnished, with only a table and a few chairs, but there was a warmth to the place, a sense of safety that Alex hadn't felt since the collapse.

"Sit," the stranger said, gesturing to one of the chairs. "We need to talk."

Alex sank into the chair, his mind still reeling from everything that had happened. The cathedral, the relic, the shadowy figures—it was all too much to process. But he had no choice but to listen, to learn what he could, because he knew one thing for sure: the world he had known was gone, and the only way forward was through the uncertainty that lay ahead.

The stranger leaned against the wall, his eyes fixed on Alex. "The relic is just one part of a much larger story. The collapse wasn't an accident, it wasn't some natural disaster—it was engineered. There are people out there, those who tried to control the power, to use it to remake the world. But they failed. And now they're trying to finish what they started."

Alex swallowed hard, trying to make sense of it all. "And we're supposed to stop them?"

The stranger nodded. "Yes. But it's not going to be easy. There are forces at work that we can't fully comprehend. And there are people, like you, who hold the key to stopping them."

The words hung heavy in the air, the weight of the stranger's meaning sinking into Alex's chest. He had no idea how he fit into this story, but one thing was clear—his life was no longer his own. The collapse had taken everything from him, and now it seemed that the future of the world rested in his hands.

The silence in the room was oppressive as Alex tried to process the weight of the stranger's words. He stared at the floor, his mind racing, trying to grasp the enormity of what had just been revealed. The collapse, the relic, the mysterious figures—they were all part of something much bigger, something that threatened the very fabric of reality itself.

"How do you know all of this?" Alex finally asked, his voice hoarse with uncertainty. "Why are you helping me?"

The stranger's expression softened for a moment, but there was still an air of mystery about him. "I was once part of the system that tried to control the power. But I saw what it could do, what it was capable of. I defected—left them before it was too late. Now, I'm one of the few who understands the true threat."

Alex's pulse quickened. "You're saying there are more people like you? People who know what's really going on?"

The stranger shook his head slowly. "Not many. Most have either been silenced or consumed by their own ambitions. The collapse destroyed everything, but it also revealed the hidden structures—the shadow organizations, the elites who still hold power in this broken world. The relic, the one you found, is the key to unlocking it all. And that's why they want it."

Alex's thoughts were a whirlwind. He had never asked for any of this. All he had wanted was to survive, to find some semblance of normalcy after the world had torn itself apart. But now, as he sat in this dimly lit room with a stranger who seemed to know more about the collapse than he did, it was clear that normalcy was a luxury he could no longer afford.

"Why me?" he asked quietly. "Why did the relic choose me? I'm just... ordinary. I don't have any special skills. I'm not a soldier or a scientist or anything."

The stranger's gaze was intense as he studied Alex. "It's not about what you can do, Alex. It's about what you can endure. The relic chose you because you have something others don't—a resilience, a resistance to the forces at work. You survived the collapse, and that's not something everyone can say. But there's more to it than that. You're connected to this in ways you don't understand yet. And that's why we need to keep moving."

Alex felt a chill run down his spine. "What do you mean 'connected'?"

The stranger straightened up, his voice dropping to a whisper. "The relic, the power it holds—it's not just a physical object. It's a conduit. It's a link between worlds, between the past and the future, between the living and the dead. The ones who want it are not just after its power—they're after the control it offers over reality itself. And you, Alex, have become part of that equation."

Alex felt his breath catch in his throat. "Are you telling me that I'm the key to... all of this?"

The stranger nodded gravely. "Yes. You and the relic are bound together now. Whether you like it or not, your fate is tied to the future of the world. And right now, that future is uncertain. If the wrong people get their hands on the relic, it will mean the end of everything. But if we can keep it safe, if we can uncover its secrets, we might be able to stop them."

Alex stood up abruptly, his mind spinning. He didn't know what to think. It felt like everything he knew about the world was a lie. He had been living in a broken, shattered version of reality, but now it seemed like the very fabric of that reality was unraveling, and he was right at the center of it.

"What's the plan then?" Alex asked, his voice tinged with disbelief. "How do we stop them?"

The stranger's eyes darkened. "We find the others who are still fighting. We gather information, we form alliances, and we make sure the relic stays out of their hands. The road ahead won't be easy.

There are dangers we can't even begin to predict. But we can't wait any longer. Time is running out."

For a moment, there was silence between them, heavy with the weight of the situation. Alex didn't know if he was ready for what lay ahead. He had never asked for this responsibility, never asked to be the one to bear the weight of the world on his shoulders. But as he looked into the stranger's eyes, he realized that there was no turning back. The collapse had already changed everything, and now he had to change with it.

He nodded slowly, his resolve hardening. "Alright. Let's do it."

The stranger offered a small, approving nod. "Good. We start tomorrow. Rest up tonight. We'll need all the strength we can get."

Alex didn't feel tired, not really. His mind was too busy, too filled with questions and doubts. But the stranger was right—he would need to be sharp, ready for whatever came next. And for the first time since the collapse, he felt a flicker of something he hadn't felt in a long time: hope.

The next day arrived with an eerie stillness hanging in the air. Alex woke early, the remnants of his uneasy sleep still clinging to him like a second skin. His mind was a storm of thoughts, but now, more than ever, he needed clarity.

The stranger—whose name Alex still didn't know—had warned him that time was against them. The collapse had sent everything into chaos, but now there was something worse: a hidden war fought in the shadows, between those who sought to reshape the world and those who just wanted to survive it. The relic was a powerful weapon in this struggle, but its true purpose was still a mystery.

Alex found the stranger waiting for him outside, his figure silhouetted against the morning light. The man looked even more enigmatic in daylight, his features sharp and his posture tense. He wasn't a soldier, Alex thought, but there was something in the way he carried himself—a quiet intensity—that spoke of battles fought and lost.

"We don't have much time," the stranger said, as if sensing Alex's need for answers. "The people after the relic won't wait for us to figure out what to do with it. They have resources, intelligence, and people who've been hunting this thing for years. You're not just carrying the relic—you're carrying a target on your back. So, let's get moving."

Alex nodded, though the weight of the words didn't quite sink in yet. He had spent most of his life running from the fallout of the world's collapse—surviving, adapting—but now he had no choice but to fight. But for what? And how?

They traveled in silence for a while, the sounds of the crumbling world around them a constant reminder of everything that had been lost. The city had once been alive with activity, with people going about their daily lives as if the world would never end. Now, it was a skeleton of its former self, abandoned and decaying. The streets were empty, save for a few wandering scavengers, picking through the wreckage. There was a quiet sadness in the air, a sense that something irreversible had happened.

The stranger led Alex to an old, fortified building at the edge of the city. It looked like it had once been a government facility—a place of power and order. Now, it was a shadow of what it had been, guarded by a few weary souls who had clearly seen better days.

Inside, the atmosphere was tense. The people here were a mix of rebels, survivors, and former operatives who had all seen the collapse in their own way. Some of them greeted the stranger with nods, others with wary glances. There was a palpable distrust in the air, as if everyone had learned the hard way that trust could be a dangerous thing.

"Alex," the stranger said, turning to him as they entered the building, "meet the others. These people are the only ones left who can help us stop what's coming."

Alex hesitated at the threshold, his heart racing. He didn't know any of these people. They were strangers to him, and in this world, trust was a fragile commodity. But as he looked around, he could see the determination in their eyes—the same look that had driven him this far, and now, it seemed, was going to take him even further.

A tall woman with dark, tightly pulled hair approached them. She was wearing a tattered military jacket, her face hardened by years of survival. Her eyes flicked over to Alex, sizing him up before she spoke.

"You're the one," she said, her voice low and guarded. "The one with the relic. I hope you know what you've gotten yourself into."

Alex swallowed, feeling the weight of her gaze. "I'm not sure I do," he admitted. "But I'm here now, and I'm willing to fight. If that means stopping whatever's coming... then that's what I'll do."

The woman studied him for a moment longer, then nodded. "Good. We need all the help we can get. You'll learn what you need to know, but time is short. We don't have the luxury of slow moves. The people who want that relic will stop at nothing to get it."

Another figure stepped forward, this one a man with a grizzled beard and a scar running across his face. He looked like a man who had lived through too many battles to count. His eyes were tired but sharp.

"We've all been through hell," the man said. "But this... this is different. We're not just fighting for survival anymore. We're fighting to stop the end of everything."

Alex nodded, feeling the weight of his role in all this pressing down on him. He had never wanted to be a hero, never wanted to carry the burden of the world's fate on his shoulders. But here he was, standing in a room full of people who had all seen too much and lost too much. They had no choice but to fight, just as he did.

"What's the plan?" Alex asked, trying to shake off his doubts and focus on the task at hand.

The woman with the military jacket stepped forward again. "We're going to gather intelligence, make contact with other factions who might be willing to join our cause, and keep the relic safe. But we need to move quickly. The longer we stay here, the more chance the enemy has to track us down."

Alex glanced at the relic, still tucked away in his bag. It felt heavier now than it ever had before. The burden of what it meant, of what was at stake, was real—and it was only just beginning to sink in.

"Let's get to work," he said, the weight of the moment finally grounding him.

The next phase of their mission was about to begin, and Alex knew that there was no turning back. He had to fight, not just for himself, but for the world that was teetering on the edge of destruction. And with every step, the stakes were getting higher.

As the days stretched on, Alex found himself adapting to the harsh rhythm of this new world. The constant tension, the unspoken fear that hung in the air, and the weight of the relic in his bag—everything was a reminder that they were racing against time. Every decision, every move felt like it could tip the balance one way or the other.

They made contact with several factions over the following weeks, but none seemed to fully understand the gravity of the situation. Some were wary of joining a cause that felt too unstable, others were consumed by their own survival, unwilling to risk their lives for something they couldn't see. Alex had learned, through harsh experience, that trust was a luxury no one could afford.

The stranger—whose name Alex now knew to be Kalen—remained a constant presence at his side. Kalen had seen the collapse from a different angle, as a former operative of the very government that had once tried to keep control. But now, he had turned his back on it, fully aware that the systems that had once governed their world were beyond saving. Still, there was a coldness to Kalen, a detachment that made Alex uneasy. He knew the man had a past, but Kalen rarely spoke of it. He led without emotion, without hesitation, as if he had already lost everything he cared about.

Alex wasn't so sure. He could sense the cracks in Kalen's tough exterior—the rare moments of vulnerability that slipped through when he thought no one was watching. But Alex wasn't the type to press. They needed each other, and that was enough for now.

The rest of the group was equally diverse, a mix of former military, scavengers, and tech experts, all of them hardened by years of survival. There was Elara, the quiet woman with the haunted eyes, who seemed to know things—things about the collapse, about the factions who had risen in its wake. She had a way of seeing the bigger picture, even when everything around them seemed to be falling apart. Then there was Mark, a tech specialist who had become the group's eyes and ears, hacking into enemy systems, gathering information, and decrypting files that could help them in their fight. His humor was dry, his personality sharper than his gadgets, but when the chips were down, he was someone you could rely on.

One evening, as the team gathered around a small campfire, Kalen looked over at Alex, his expression unreadable. The flames flickered, casting eerie shadows across his face.

"It's coming," Kalen said, his voice low but firm. "They know we have the relic. And they're getting closer."

Alex tensed, his hand instinctively reaching for the relic in his bag. The weight of it seemed to grow heavier with each passing day. They had tried to hide it, to keep it safe, but it was becoming increasingly clear that the people hunting them weren't going to stop.

"Who are they?" Alex asked, his voice steady despite the fear gnawing at him. "What do they want with it?"

Kalen stared into the fire, his face flickering with the light. "There are different factions," he said slowly. "But the one you need to worry about is The Syndicate. They're ruthless, organized, and they don't care who they have to crush to get what they want. They've been searching for the relic for years, but it's not just a weapon. It's a symbol. A key to something much bigger."

"Something bigger?" Alex repeated, his brow furrowing. "Like what?"

Kalen paused, his eyes narrowing as if he were weighing whether or not to say more. Finally, he spoke, his voice a mere whisper.

"A way to control the collapse. To turn the world into their own image. The relic—whatever it is—holds the power to reshape the new world order. And they will stop at nothing to get it."

The words hung in the air, heavy with meaning. Alex's mind raced, trying to process what Kalen had said. A way to control the collapse? Was that even possible?

"How do you know all this?" Alex asked, his voice a mix of curiosity and suspicion.

Kalen's gaze darkened. "I used to work for them. The Syndicate, I mean. Before everything fell apart. I was part of their operations—doing what I had to do to survive. But I didn't sign up for this. This... power grab. And now, they'll use whatever means necessary to get their hands on the relic."

Alex swallowed hard, the realization sinking in. Kalen's past was far more complicated than he had led on, and now, it was clear that the stakes were much higher than they had originally thought.

"What happens when they get it?" Alex asked, his voice barely above a whisper.

Kalen looked up at him, his eyes hardening. "That's what we need to stop. The Syndicate has already begun to consolidate power. They've infiltrated governments, corporations, and even smaller resistance groups. Once they have the relic, they'll be able to control the remaining resources, manipulate the survival factions, and force the world into a new hierarchy—one where they rule everything."

Alex felt a cold shiver run down his spine. The world he had known—before the collapse—seemed so distant now, but the thought of it being remade in the image of The Syndicate was enough to make his stomach turn.

"Then we need to stop them," Alex said, his voice hardening with resolve. "We can't let them have it."

Kalen nodded, his eyes locking with Alex's. "We will. But it won't be easy. We're up against an enemy that has resources, manpower, and no qualms about destroying anyone who gets in their way. But we have something they don't. We have the element of surprise. And we have each other."

Alex looked around at the group—Elara, Mark, and the others. They were all in this together, bound by a common cause, a common goal. The odds were against them, but for the first time since the collapse, Alex felt a spark of hope. They might have a chance after all.

The fire crackled as the wind howled outside, and in that moment, Alex realized that the journey ahead was going to be long, difficult, and filled with uncertainty. But they had no choice but to keep moving forward.

The night seemed endless, the cold biting at their skin as they sat huddled around the fire, each person lost in their thoughts. The future was uncertain, but the weight of the relic—of what it symbolized—pressed down on Alex like a storm cloud. He felt the urge to move, to act, to find some way to tip the scales in their favor before The Syndicate closed in.

The following morning, the group packed up their camp in silence, the air thick with unspoken tension. Kalen had given them their next move: they would head east, toward the ruins of an old military base, a place that was rumored to hold valuable supplies and, more importantly, intelligence. If they were to survive the coming storm, they needed information—anything that could help them understand The Syndicate's next move and how they could stop it.

As they moved through the desolate landscape, Alex couldn't help but notice the changes in the world around them. The collapse hadn't just shattered governments and economies; it had shattered the very fabric of society. Buildings, once grand, now stood as hollow shells of their former selves. Nature had begun to reclaim the earth, but even that felt different—darker, more twisted. The forests were thicker, the winds colder, as if the land itself had become an unwilling participant in the downfall.

They passed through ghost towns, their streets empty but for the occasional scavenger, and Alex couldn't shake the feeling that they were being watched. The remnants of the world's old conflicts had left scars—both visible and invisible. War had not just ravaged the landscape, but the people, leaving them broken, desperate, and mistrustful. And in this broken world, no one could be trusted, not even those who fought alongside you.

By the time they reached the ruins of the military base, night had fallen again, and the air was thick with a sense of foreboding. The base was eerily quiet, the buildings half-collapsed, their skeletal remains casting long shadows in the moonlight. Mark led the way, his eyes scanning the perimeter, fingers poised over his portable scanner.

"Nothing's showing up on the radar," he muttered, eyes narrowing. "We should be good for now, but keep your heads down."

Kalen nodded, his expression grim. "We'll move fast. The longer we stay, the more likely it is someone will catch wind of us. We can't afford that."

As they entered the base, Alex's senses heightened, every sound amplified in the oppressive silence. The place felt haunted, like a tomb where the echoes of its past still lingered. The walls were covered in faded murals, reminders of a time before the collapse—of the ideals that had once held the world together. Now, all that was left were remnants of a world gone wrong.

Inside, the group split up, searching for anything useful. Elara moved to the communications tower, while Mark started digging through old computer systems, trying to find anything that might help them. Alex's attention was drawn to a room in the far corner of the base, a storage area filled with crates and rusted metal shelves. He hesitated for a moment, then moved toward it, feeling a strange pull toward the darkness within.

Inside, he found nothing of particular value—just more supplies, more remnants of a world that had long since crumbled. But then, tucked away behind a pile of old military equipment, he noticed something that made his blood run cold: a set of blueprints, faded but still legible. They depicted a structure, something massive, hidden beneath the earth. The words at the top of the page read: "Project Haven."

Alex's heart skipped a beat. He had heard rumors of Project Haven, but no one had ever confirmed its existence. It was said to be a secret facility, one that could change the course of the collapse, one that might hold the key to rebuilding—or destroying—what was left of the world.

He carefully folded the blueprints and stuffed them into his bag, his mind racing. This was it—this was the lead they needed. If they could find Project Haven, they could find a way to stop The Syndicate before it was too late. But the more Alex thought about it, the more he realized that Project Haven might not be the salvation they were hoping for. What if it was a weapon? What if it was something worse?

Suddenly, a loud crash echoed through the base, followed by the sound of heavy boots marching. Alex's heart pounded in his chest as he exchanged a look with Kalen, who immediately signaled for the group to retreat.

"It's them," Kalen whispered. "The Syndicate's found us."

In that moment, everything seemed to slow down. Alex felt his breath catch in his throat. The relic, the blueprints, the race against time—it was all coming to a head.

"Move!" Kalen ordered, his voice sharp as the group sprang into action.

They ran, adrenaline pumping through their veins as the sound of pursuing footsteps grew louder. The base, once a symbol of power and authority, had now become a deadly trap. Every corner felt like a potential ambush, every shadow hiding an enemy. But they couldn't afford to stop. Not now.

As they made their way back toward the entrance, Mark stumbled, a cry escaping his lips as he fell to the ground. Elara reached out, pulling him up by the arm, but the damage was done—he had been hit, the wound already beginning to bleed. There was no time to stop, no time to think.

"Get him out of here!" Kalen barked. "We'll cover you!"

Alex turned, drawing his weapon as the first wave of Syndicate soldiers appeared from the shadows. He fired, the sound of gunfire ringing out in the empty halls. The group scattered, fighting for their lives, knowing that this could be the end.

But even as they fought, Alex couldn't shake the thought that the relic—the key to everything—was still out there, still in their hands, and that the Syndicate would stop at nothing to get it. It was a race against time, a fight for survival. And as the battle raged on, Alex knew one thing for certain: they had no choice but to keep moving forward.

The sound of gunfire echoed through the base, a grim reminder of the world they now inhabited. Alex's heart raced as he sprinted through the corridors, Mark limping behind him, supported by Elara. The cold steel of the walls seemed to close in on them as they ran, their footsteps the only sound in the otherwise silent, decaying complex.

Kalen's voice crackled through their earpieces, urgent and sharp. "There's a way out through the south exit. Get to the control room and we'll meet you there."

"On our way," Alex replied, his voice tight. They needed to move fast; the Syndicate's soldiers were closing in, and their only hope was to escape and regroup before they could be surrounded.

As they rounded a corner, a loud explosion rocked the building, throwing them off balance. Alex stumbled, barely managing to keep his footing. The walls groaned and cracked as debris fell from the ceiling. They had to keep moving, but now the base was falling apart around them, the structure itself collapsing under the pressure of the chaos. The Syndicate was throwing everything they had at them.

"Elara!" Alex called out, his voice laced with panic. She had fallen behind when the explosion struck, and he couldn't see her in the haze of smoke and dust.

"I'm here," her voice answered, sharp but steady, cutting through the turmoil. "Keep going, we'll catch up."

Alex didn't hesitate, pushing forward with the others, but his mind was racing. How long could they keep outrunning the Syndicate? How long before the base became their tomb?

Finally, they reached the control room, the door heavy and reinforced. Kalen was already there, a determined look on his face. His hand was on a panel, fingers flying over the buttons in rapid succession. "Hurry up," he barked as the sound of distant footsteps reverberated down the hall. "We don't have much time."

Alex slammed into the wall next to him, breathing heavily as Mark and Elara caught up. Sweat beaded on his forehead, his thoughts spinning. The blueprints, the relic—what had they uncovered? What if Project Haven wasn't just a secret base but a weapon, something more devastating than they could imagine?

Kalen's eyes darted over to Alex, reading the turmoil on his face. "We're not out of this yet. We get to Project Haven, and we figure this all out. But for now, we've got to survive."

The door to the control room slid open, revealing the chaos outside. A dozen Syndicate soldiers appeared, their guns raised, their eyes scanning for any sign of movement.

Kalen didn't flinch. Instead, he stepped forward, his voice calm but dangerous. "We're not surrendering," he said coldly, his hand hovering near his sidearm. "You're going to have to kill us to get to that relic."

Alex stood beside Kalen, his breath steadying, his grip tightening around his own weapon. The past months had tested him in ways he never imagined, but the fear of failure, of letting the Syndicate win, was something he couldn't live with. Not now.

The soldiers hesitated, their eyes narrowing as they assessed the situation. Alex felt the tension in the air, each moment stretched thin with anticipation. But the silence was broken by a single voice, deep and calculated.

"I don't think that will be necessary," a man said, stepping into the dim light of the corridor. His dark suit, pristine even in the midst of all this chaos, stood in stark contrast to the wreckage surrounding them. He was older, his hair graying, but his eyes were sharp, calculating. He was someone who had seen countless battles, someone who commanded respect.

"Who are you?" Kalen demanded, his hand still on his weapon, though his posture had shifted, as if he recognized the man as someone important.

The man smiled coldly. "I'm someone who's going to make sure you're on the right side of history. You don't want to be my enemy, Kalen. Not today."

The Syndicate soldiers relaxed their grip on their guns, but the tension didn't subside. Alex could feel it in his bones—a game of cat and mouse, where their lives were the stakes.

"Your relic," the man continued, his voice almost too calm. "It's not the answer you think it is. You believe Project Haven will help you win, but what if I told you it's only part of the puzzle? What if I told you that you're playing right into our hands?"

Kalen's jaw tightened. "You think we're fools? We know what's at stake here. We're not going to let you control the future."

The man chuckled, as if amused by Kalen's defiance. "You misunderstand. I'm not here to control the future. I'm here to guide it. The collapse of the world? That's just the beginning. The real game starts now."

Alex's mind spun. He had no idea what this man was playing at, but one thing was certain: the Syndicate wasn't just after power—it was after something much more dangerous.

He looked at Kalen, who seemed to be processing the same thoughts. It was clear now that the battle they were fighting wasn't just about survival—it was about control over what came next. But the questions lingered in Alex's mind: What was Project Haven?

What role did the relic play in all of this? And who could they trust?

"You'll never control us," Alex said, his voice steady, his resolve hardening.

The man's expression didn't change. "We shall see," he said softly, before turning away. "The game is just beginning."

With that, the doors to the control room slammed shut, and the world outside seemed to fade away. Alex stood, the weight of their situation pressing down on him more than ever. Whatever they thought they knew, whatever plan they had been following—it was all about to change.

They had no choice but to move forward. But now, Alex wasn't sure where the path would lead.

Alex's mind raced as the doors shut behind them, plunging them into a tense silence. The weight of the man's words hung in the air, thick with ominous uncertainty. "The game is just beginning." What did that even mean? And what part did the Syndicate have to play in all of this? Was Project Haven truly just a stepping stone to something far worse?

Kalen broke the silence, his voice low and grim. "We can't trust him. Whatever he's saying, it's all part of the plan. He's just playing his part."

Alex nodded, though the nagging feeling in his gut wouldn't go away. "But what's his part? And why does he know so much about Project Haven?"

"We need to get to the bottom of this," Mark spoke up from behind, his voice hoarse but filled with determination. He was still struggling to keep up, his leg still injured from the explosion earlier, but his resolve was clear. "We need answers. And we need to get out of here before this place becomes our grave."

Alex glanced over at Elara, who had been eerily quiet since they'd entered the control room. She was staring at the data terminal in front of her, her fingers tapping furiously across the keys. The room had been designed for speed, the screens flashing with a myriad of information that Alex couldn't fully process.

"Elara?" he asked, his voice unsure.

She looked up, her face tight with concentration. "I'm trying to access the base's archives. If I can pull up any files on Project Haven—on whatever the Syndicate is really after—I might be able to make sense of it."

Alex walked over, trying to block out the sound of distant explosions and the shifting weight of the base collapsing around them. The entire structure felt as though it were teetering on the edge of oblivion, but they had no choice. The answers lay within the chaos.

"Any luck?" he asked, leaning over her shoulder.

"Not much yet," Elara muttered, her eyes scanning the data on the screen. "But... wait... there's something here." She paused, her fingers slowing as she read the information on the terminal. "Project Haven isn't just a weapons program. It's... a network. A control system. It's designed to manipulate global events on a massive scale."

Kalen's expression darkened as he moved closer. "Manipulate how? The entire world's geopolitical situation?"

"Exactly," Elara said, turning to face him. "From food supply chains to military conflicts, from economic crises to climate manipulation—it can control the flow of almost every major event on a global scale. The Syndicate isn't just controlling nations. They're controlling the very fabric of reality."

Alex felt the floor beneath him shift as if the world itself had just tilted sideways. "This... this is madness. You're telling me Project Haven is controlling everything? People's lives, economies, wars?"

"That's what the documents say," Elara confirmed, her voice barely above a whisper. "This isn't just about power. This is about complete control. The Syndicate wants to bring the world to its knees, and Project Haven is the tool to do it."

Mark shook his head, disbelief written across his face. "How could something like this exist? How could we not know about it?"

"Because they've been working on it for decades," Kalen said, his voice low. "The Syndicate has been infiltrating governments, corporations, military forces... making sure they have the right people in place. Everyone thinks this is about money, but it's about much more than that."

Alex ran a hand through his hair, the enormity of their situation dawning on him. "So we're not just fighting for survival. We're fighting to stop a global takeover."

Elara's fingers flew over the terminal again. "I'm pulling up more data now. If we can get access to the mainframe... we can shut this down. It's risky, but it's our best shot."

Kalen nodded, a steely glint in his eyes. "Then let's move. We can't waste time. Every second we stay here, they're closing in on us. We need to get to the mainframe and destroy whatever's left of Project Haven."

Alex felt the weight of the world on his shoulders. But there was no turning back now. This wasn't just about escaping the Syndicate—it was about saving what little remained of freedom. Whatever the Syndicate had planned, they had to stop it. The collapse of the world wasn't inevitable. Not yet.

He turned to face the team, his voice firm. "Let's go."

With a final glance at the flickering screens, they moved swiftly, cutting through the corridors with a sense of urgency. The sounds of the crumbling base behind them, the echoes of the explosions and gunfire, only added to the madness of the moment. But they couldn't afford to be distracted. The fate of the world was hanging by a thread.

As they reached the mainframe room, the door was locked, a heavy security system barring their way. Kalen stepped forward, his expression calm. "Elara, you're up."

Elara approached the panel with confidence, her hands flying over the interface. The countdown on the screen was ticking away, each second that passed bringing them closer to disaster. Finally, with a soft beep, the door clicked open.

Inside, the mainframe room was a sprawling, high-tech fortress, a web of interconnected systems and data nodes. But there was no time to admire the complexity. The clock was ticking, and the Syndicate was getting closer.

"Let's get to work," Alex said, his voice steady. "Elara, you know what to do."

Elara nodded, her face focused. "I'll need a few minutes to disable the network, but I can't guarantee it'll work. They've built in fail-safes."

"Then we'll make sure they don't have a chance to activate them," Kalen said, pulling out his weapon and checking it for readiness. "We protect the system while she works."

Alex stood at the entrance, watching the door as his heart pounded. The tension in the air was palpable, thick with the fear of what might come next. But this was their chance—their only chance—to stop the Syndicate from rewriting the future.

"Let's finish this," Alex said, his voice resolute.

And so, they waited, knowing that whatever happened next would decide the future of the world.

The seconds stretched like hours as Elara worked. Her fingers moved with practiced precision, but even she couldn't mask the tension that filled the room. The dim glow from the data panels bathed their faces in a ghostly light as they stood guard, their weapons ready, eyes scanning the shadows for any sign of movement.

Outside, the base groaned under the strain of its imminent collapse. The explosions had become more frequent, the sound of crumbling concrete and twisted metal reverberating through the walls. It was clear that the Syndicate wasn't going to let them escape easily. They knew what was at stake. And they had everything to lose.

Elara's brow furrowed as she worked, sweat beading on her forehead. "I'm getting closer," she muttered, her voice taut with concentration. "But there's something strange here. The systems are more complex than I thought. It's like they've anticipated this."

Mark, who had been pacing anxiously, stopped and turned toward her. "How much longer?"

"I don't know," Elara replied, her voice tinged with frustration. "Maybe a few more minutes. But if we don't get it right, they'll know we're here. The entire facility is wired to detect unauthorized access. Once that happens, we're finished."

Alex's eyes darted to the entrance, then back to the terminal where Elara was working. Time was slipping away, and every passing second felt like a countdown to their death.

Kalen shifted, his hand tightening around his weapon. "We need to be ready. We can't afford any mistakes."

Elara didn't respond, her focus absolute as she typed in a series of commands. The data streams on the screen flickered, then froze. For a moment, the room was completely silent.

"Got it," Elara breathed out, her shoulders sagging with relief. "The system is down."

But before anyone could react, the loud *clank* of metal echoed through the room. Alex's heart skipped a beat. "That wasn't us."

The door to the mainframe room exploded inward, a blinding flash of light preceding the arrival of armed Syndicate operatives.

They poured in like a tidal wave, their weapons raised, their faces masked in cold determination. They were ready for a fight.

Alex didn't hesitate. His training kicked in, and in an instant, he drew his weapon, firing a burst that took down the nearest operative before diving behind a row of data consoles. Mark was close behind, returning fire, while Kalen sprinted to Elara's side, pushing her out of harm's way.

"Move!" Kalen shouted, as he took down two more Syndicate agents in rapid succession.

Alex barely registered the chaos around him as his focus zeroed in on the enemy forces. The Syndicate was closing in, and they needed to move—fast. His mind raced, calculating their options.

"We can't stay here!" he yelled over the gunfire, ducking as a bullet whizzed past his ear. "Get to the back exit!"

Mark fired another round, felling a third operative. "The back exit's blocked!" he shouted. "We'll be trapped!"

Elara was at the terminal again, her fingers flying across the keys. "Wait! I can't disable the whole system, but I can reroute the facility's defenses. It'll give us a window to escape."

Alex didn't hesitate. "Do it!"

With a few more rapid keystrokes, the flashing screens turned red, and the sound of metal gears shifting echoed throughout the base. A moment later, the walls seemed to tremble as heavy security doors slammed shut, blocking the Syndicate operatives' advance.

But the reprieve was only temporary.

"Let's move!" Alex commanded, as he led the team through a side corridor. They ran, adrenaline coursing through their veins, the sound of enemy pursuit growing louder behind them.

They pushed their bodies harder, knowing that the clock was ticking, and they couldn't afford to waste any more time. The base was crumbling, and it wouldn't be long before it came down completely.

As they rounded a corner, they encountered more Syndicate agents. This time, however, the team was ready. Kalen and Mark moved swiftly, taking down the operatives with precision. Elara, still focused, helped cover their retreat, scanning the terminal data as they ran.

Finally, after what seemed like an eternity of firefights and narrow escapes, they reached an exit leading out into the surrounding wilderness. The storm outside had intensified, a wall of snow and rain slashing at their faces as they burst through the door.

Alex paused for a moment to catch his breath, looking back at the crumbling structure. It was only a matter of time before the entire base collapsed, but they had made it out. Barely.

Elara looked around, her face set in determination. "We need to regroup. The Syndicate is going to come after us harder now. This isn't over."

Alex nodded, wiping the rain from his face. "We've still got a long way to go. But we've got something they don't: knowledge. We know what they're planning. And we're going to stop them."

Kalen looked at him, his expression hard. "It's not going to be easy. The Syndicate has resources we can't even begin to imagine."

"We fight smarter," Alex replied, his voice firm. "We find their weak points. We destroy their plans. We give the world a chance."

They turned to face the storm ahead, knowing that the battle was far from over. The Syndicate had just shown their hand, but now they had the upper hand. And they would stop at nothing to see their mission through.

The future of the world hung in the balance, and the struggle had only just begun.

The rain lashed against them as they moved through the storm, their steps heavy and purposeful. The oppressive cold seemed to cut through their clothing, biting into their skin, but none of them flinched. The chaos they had just left behind was still fresh in their minds, but their resolve was stronger than ever.

Elara wiped her face, her breath visible in the frigid air. "We've bought ourselves some time," she said, her voice steady despite the adrenaline coursing through her. "But it won't be enough. The Syndicate won't just let us slip away."

Mark, walking beside her, kept his eyes on the horizon. "We can't stay on the run forever. We need a place to hide, somewhere they can't find us."

Alex looked at them both, his mind already calculating the next steps. "We'll need allies. People who know how to stay off the radar. But it won't be easy. The Syndicate's reach is everywhere."

"How are we supposed to trust anyone?" Kalen's voice was low, skeptical. "We're talking about a network that's practically invincible. Anyone could be compromised."

Elara glanced at Kalen, then back at Alex. "You're right. But we don't have much choice. We'll need to dig deep, find people with the right skills, the ones who can make things happen under the radar."

Alex nodded, his eyes narrowing. "We find the pieces, then we put them together. If we can't go head-to-head with the Syndicate's power, we'll find a way to dismantle it from the inside. Slowly. Methodically."

The journey ahead was uncertain, but it was their only option. They could either let the Syndicate win or fight back with everything they had.

As they made their way through the wilderness, their path obscured by the storm, a sense of urgency gripped them. They couldn't afford to stop. Not yet. The next move had to be perfect. It was no longer just about survival—it was about preventing something far worse from happening.

Elara adjusted her pack and looked at Alex. "Where do we start?"

"First, we get to the safehouse," Alex replied. "It's an old contact of mine. He'll know how to lay low. Then we figure out who we can trust. But no matter what, we don't stay in one place for too long."

They walked on, each of them lost in their thoughts, but united in purpose. The Syndicate's plans were vast, and every second they wasted could cost them dearly. But they were determined. They had seen what the Syndicate was capable of, and now they had to fight back with everything they had.

It wasn't just a battle for their lives anymore. It was a battle for the future.

The wind howled as they reached a small, hidden cabin deep in the woods. The flickering light through the windows was a welcome sight after hours of trudging through the storm. Alex knocked on the door in a specific pattern, then stepped back.

Moments later, the door creaked open, revealing an older man with a grizzled face and sharp eyes. He studied them for a moment, then stepped aside to let them in.

"Alex," the man said in a gravelly voice, his tone a mixture of surprise and suspicion. "I thought you were dead."

"Not yet," Alex replied with a small, wry smile. "But we need your help. And we need to move fast."

Inside, the cabin was modest but well-equipped. A small fire crackled in the hearth, and maps and equipment were scattered across a table. The man, whose name was Ivan, wasted no time in setting a fresh pot of coffee on the stove.

"Tell me what's going on," Ivan said, as they gathered around the table.

Alex explained quickly, laying out the events that had led them here and the plans the Syndicate had in motion. Ivan listened intently, nodding occasionally but offering no immediate comment.

When Alex finished, Ivan took a long drink of his coffee before speaking. "You're right to be worried. The Syndicate doesn't just control governments or corporations—they control the people. If they're working with the Russians, it's a game-changer. They'll stop at nothing to maintain their power."

Elara leaned forward. "What can we do about it? How do we stop them?"

Ivan studied her for a moment, then sighed. "You can't fight this with brute force. You need to hit them where it hurts the most—undermine their influence, destroy their networks. But that's going to take more than just you four."

"We've been building a team," Kalen interjected, his voice steady. "We know the risk, but we're willing to take it."

Ivan met his gaze, then turned to Alex. "This is bigger than I thought. You're playing with fire, but... I can help. I have contacts. People who owe me favors. But we need to move quickly. The Syndicate's spies are everywhere. And the Russians won't wait long before they realize you're still alive."

Alex stood up, his eyes steely with determination. "Then we move tonight. We get our allies, we hit them hard. And we make sure they never see us coming."

The storm outside continued to rage, but inside the cabin, a quiet resolve began to take root. They were no longer running. They were hunting.

And the Syndicate wouldn't know what hit them.

The night was thick with tension as Alex and the team prepared for their next move. Ivan's cabin had become a temporary base of operations, a safehouse, but it was only a matter of time before the Syndicate's forces caught up to them. The storm had provided some cover, but it was fleeting. They had to act before the window closed.

Elara leaned over the map spread across the table, tracing her finger over various points. "We can't waste time. Every minute we wait is a minute the Syndicate gets closer to tightening their grip."

Alex studied the map with her, his mind racing. "We've got three key objectives. First, we reach the safehouse in the city—our contact there can help us with the next step. Then, we need to track down the Russian asset the Syndicate's been working with. That's our ticket to getting them to pull back. We expose the deal, and we kill it before it can spread."

Kalen, ever the pragmatist, crossed his arms. "And what happens if they find us before we can hit those points? They'll be all over us like a pack of wolves."

Alex's jaw tightened. "Then we adapt. We do what we have to do to survive."

Ivan was quiet for a moment, his mind clearly turning over the options. Finally, he spoke, his voice low but confident. "I can get you out of here, but you'll need to move quickly. I've got an old network of contacts. They can help you get to the city, but once you're there, you'll be on your own. The Syndicate doesn't miss a thing. Be careful who you trust."

Elara looked up at Ivan, her eyes steady. "We don't have time to second-guess. If they're already onto us, we need to hit them hard."

"We will," Alex said, his voice sharp. "We need to stay ahead of them. No hesitation."

The group gathered their gear quickly, packing only what was essential. They knew the risks of staying in one place too long, especially in a world where betrayal was as common as survival. Each of them understood the gravity of what they were about to do. This wasn't just about stopping the Syndicate anymore. It was about fighting back against a system that had long held the world in its grasp, manipulating governments, economies, and societies to maintain its control.

As they stepped into the cold night, the wind howling around them, there was no going back. The mission was set. The stakes had never been higher.

---

The drive to the city was tense, the vehicle cutting through the slick roads as the storm raged on. Alex sat in the front, his mind whirring through possible scenarios. Every stoplight, every turn, felt like it could be their last. He could sense that they were being watched, the tension mounting with each passing minute.

Kalen sat beside him, looking out of the window, his eyes scanning the streets. "It's too quiet," he muttered. "Too clean. It's like they're waiting for us to make a mistake."

Elara, seated across from them, frowned. "We're being cautious. We stick to the plan, and we stay sharp."

They had agreed to go dark, avoid their usual routes, and keep off the grid. No phones. No digital footprints. They were ghosts, invisible to anyone who might be looking.

As they neared the outskirts of the city, Alex's phone buzzed, a signal cutting through the cold silence in the car. He glanced at the screen, his heart skipping a beat. It was a coded message from an old contact—someone who had helped them in the past. The message was brief, but the implications were clear.

"They've got a lead on the Syndicate's movements," Alex said, showing the others the message. "We meet them tonight. This is our chance to get ahead."

The group nodded, understanding the urgency of the situation. But as they reached the rendezvous point, Alex felt a prickle of unease. They were stepping into enemy territory. Their contact might be reliable, but the risk of a trap was always there.

They parked in an alleyway, out of sight, and exited the vehicle cautiously. The cold wind bit at their skin, and the distant sound of sirens added an eerie backdrop to the tension. Alex's eyes scanned the surroundings, his hand resting on the gun hidden beneath his jacket.

They moved toward a dimly lit building at the end of the alley, where their contact had arranged to meet. The door opened before they could knock, revealing a man in his late forties, wearing a nondescript jacket. His eyes flicked over them before he stepped aside, motioning for them to enter.

"You're late," he said in a low voice, his tone flat, as if he had seen far worse in his life.

Alex stepped in first, followed by the others. "We had to make sure we weren't followed."

The man closed the door behind them, locking it with a soft click. "You're being hunted. The Syndicate's already got eyes on you. But we've got a window. If you want to take them down, now's your shot."

He pulled a map from his pocket, laying it out on the table. "This is their main hub. If you can hit them here, you might be able to cripple their operations. But you'll need inside access. I've got someone who can help, but it's risky. You've got a very short window to get in and out before they shut down the entire network."

Elara studied the map carefully. "Inside access... how?"

The man gave a slight smirk, pulling out a small device from his jacket. "You'll need this to bypass their security. It's a one-time hack, so make it count."

Alex took the device, his fingers brushing the cold metal. "We don't have long. Get us in and out, and we'll take care of the rest."

As they prepared for their next move, Alex couldn't shake the feeling that this was their last chance. The window was closing, and if they hesitated even for a moment, it could be the end.

The Syndicate was everywhere, and time was running out.

The plan was simple, but as they made their way toward the Syndicate's headquarters, the reality of the operation began to set in. Every move, every decision would matter. Alex kept his focus on the road ahead, but his mind raced. This wasn't just a mission anymore. It was a fight for survival, for a chance to tear down the empire that had cast its shadow over everything.

They arrived at the rendezvous point—a nondescript building on the edge of the city. The air was thick with anticipation as they parked and moved quickly toward the rear entrance, where their contact awaited. The city was a maze of narrow streets and hidden corners, and every step they took felt like it could be their last.

Inside, the contact was waiting for them, his face hidden in the shadows. "I hope you're ready," he said, his voice low and urgent. "This is it. We hit them hard, and we hit them now. No second chances."

Elara was the first to step forward. "We don't need second chances. We just need to make it count."

The contact handed Alex a small, black box. "This is a direct link to the facility's mainframe. It'll give you access to their security systems. Once you're inside, you'll have a small window to extract what you need. No more than five minutes. After that, all hell's going to break loose."

Kalen took the box, inspecting it briefly before slipping it into his jacket. "Five minutes. Got it. Let's move."

They made their way through the dark, narrow corridors, their footsteps echoing in the silence. The further they went, the more the tension built, like the feeling before a storm. There was no turning back now. They were in enemy territory, and every corner could hide danger.

Finally, they reached the entrance to the Syndicate's main facility. The door was secured with a sophisticated biometric lock, but Kalen, ever the expert, wasted no time. With a few deft moves, he bypassed the security measures, and the door clicked open.

Inside, the air was cold, sterile. The hum of machinery echoed through the hallways, the silence broken only by the faint sound of distant footsteps. The team moved swiftly, staying in the shadows as they navigated the labyrinthine hallways. Each step felt like it was bringing them closer to something dark and dangerous.

Alex's heart pounded as they reached the central control room. The door was guarded, but it wasn't impossible. With a quiet nod, Elara signaled to Kalen, who began working on the next set of locks. As the door cracked open, Alex felt a rush of adrenaline surge through him.

Inside, the control room was filled with monitors, data streams, and a web of connections that spanned continents. This was the heart of the Syndicate's operations. Everything they needed to bring it down was right here.

Elara moved quickly, accessing the main terminal and pulling up the data they had been sent to find. As the information streamed onto the screen, she glanced over her shoulder, scanning for any sign of incoming security. Time was running out.

"We've got it," she said, her voice barely above a whisper. "This is the evidence we need to expose them."

But just as she was about to transfer the data, the warning alarms began to blare, a deafening sound that ripped through the air. The security was compromised.

"Shit," Kalen muttered, his hand flying to his weapon. "We're running out of time."

Alex's mind raced. They couldn't stay here. Not now. "Move. Now!" he shouted, already heading for the exit. The team followed close behind, adrenaline pushing them forward as they sprinted down the hallway. Every second counted.

But as they neared the exit, a group of armed guards appeared at the far end of the corridor, blocking their way. The doors behind them slammed shut, trapping them in a deadly standoff.

Alex gritted his teeth. This wasn't supposed to happen. They'd planned for everything, but there was no way out now.

"Make a path," he ordered, pulling his gun from its holster. "We fight our way out."

The sound of gunfire erupted, echoing off the walls as Alex and his team engaged the guards. It was a desperate, frantic battle, each shot taken with precision, each movement calculated to keep them alive.

In the chaos, Elara pushed forward, leading the way as the others covered her. They had to reach the exit. They had to escape with the data, with the evidence that could bring the Syndicate down.

But the guards were relentless, and the odds were stacked against them. Alex fought with everything he had, but he could feel the walls closing in.

It wasn't until they reached the final stretch—just as they were about to break through the door to freedom—that a bullet found its mark.

Elara's heart stopped as Alex crumpled to the floor, blood seeping from a wound in his side.

"Alex!" she screamed, rushing to his side.

Kalen and Ivan immediately took positions, covering the exit.

"Get him out of here!" Kalen shouted to Elara, his voice frantic.

But Elara didn't move. She knelt beside Alex, her hands trembling as she pressed against his wound. "Stay with me, Alex. Stay with me."

Alex groaned, his face pale, but he reached up, his hand weakly grasping hers. "Finish it," he whispered, his voice ragged. "The

Syndicate... it doesn't matter if I make it. You... have to bring them down."

Elara nodded, fighting back the tears. She didn't have time for grief. Not yet.

"We're not leaving you," she insisted, but deep down, she knew the truth. The mission came first. It had to.

With one final look, Elara kissed Alex's forehead and stood. She could feel the weight of his words pressing down on her—this was more than a battle. This was the fight to break the chains that had held the world in fear.

"Let's finish it," she said to Kalen and Ivan, her voice steady, determined.

The door exploded open, and the team raced into the night, leaving behind the body of a fallen leader, but carrying with them the hope of a shattered empire.

As Elara and the remaining team members sprinted into the cold night, their breaths visible in the frigid air, the gravity of the situation weighed heavily on them. Alex's death lingered like a shadow, an unbearable reminder that the price of their mission was steep. Yet, they couldn't afford to falter now. The Syndicate, a ruthless empire of corruption and control, still loomed large, and the evidence they had secured was the key to bringing it down.

They ran through the alleyways, staying low, hearts racing as they weaved between buildings. The streets were eerily quiet, as if the city itself was holding its breath. Kalen led the way, his eyes scanning the horizon, ever alert for danger. Ivan, the quietest of the group, kept a hand on his weapon, ready for anything. Elara moved quickly, but her mind kept drifting back to Alex. How could they carry on without him?

But there was no time for grief. Not now. Their mission was far from over.

They reached the safe house—a dimly lit warehouse tucked away in a forgotten corner of the city. Once inside, Elara locked the door behind them, her fingers trembling as she turned the key. The team moved swiftly, setting up a makeshift command center in the back of the building. Elara pulled up the data they had secured, her eyes scanning the files that Alex had fought so hard to get them. This was their moment to strike, but they needed to act fast.

As the minutes ticked by, Elara felt a growing sense of urgency. The Syndicate wouldn't take long to figure out they had been compromised. They needed to expose everything—every dark secret, every transaction, every corrupt deal. The data contained the names of high-ranking officials, corrupt businessmen, and the twisted web of power that had kept the Syndicate in control for so long.

"We need to get this out to the world," Elara said, her voice low, tense. "We can't just sit here. We have to move now."

Kalen nodded. "I'll set up the communication channels. We'll send it to every journalist, every outlet. Let them do the rest."

Ivan, standing by the door, watched for any sign of movement outside. "We're not safe here for long. They'll come looking for us."

Elara glanced at the screen one last time, her heart racing. The files were encrypted, but with Kalen's skills, they would be decrypted and sent out in minutes. The weight of the moment pressed on her—this was the beginning of the end for the Syndicate. They had the evidence. Now they just had to make sure it reached the right hands.

She took a deep breath and turned to Kalen. "Do it. Send it."

Kalen moved quickly, his fingers flying across the keyboard. A few seconds passed, and then the screen flashed green.

"It's done," he said, his voice flat. "It's out there."

Elara felt a surge of relief. But just as quickly, that relief was replaced with a deep sense of dread. They had completed their mission, but at what cost? How many lives had been lost, how many had been broken, just to get to this point? The Syndicate would not go down without a fight. The storm was far from over.

"We need to get out of here," Ivan said, breaking Elara's thoughts. "Now."

Without another word, they grabbed what little equipment they had left and moved out of the warehouse, keeping to the shadows. The city was still eerily silent, but there was an unmistakable tension in the air. The Syndicate's reach was long, and now that they had exposed the truth, there was no telling how far they would go to protect their empire.

As they navigated the streets, Elara couldn't shake the feeling that they were being watched. Every dark alley seemed to hide a threat. Every corner felt like it could be their last. But they pushed on, determined to stay one step ahead of their enemies.

They arrived at a safe house located miles away, a location so hidden even the Syndicate's best operatives would have trouble finding it. Inside, they collapsed into chairs, exhaustion settling in. The battle had only just begun, but they had done something that no one had thought possible—they had shaken the very foundations of the Syndicate.

But as Elara sat in the dim light, staring at the files on her laptop, she knew that they weren't done yet. The Syndicate wouldn't just disappear. They would regroup, retaliate, and they would come after her and her team with everything they had.

"Do you think they'll come for us?" Kalen asked, his voice low, tired.

Elara nodded slowly, her eyes hardening. "They'll come for us. But we're ready for them."

They had exposed the Syndicate, but the real fight was just beginning. The world would know the truth, but it wouldn't come easy. The shadows would move against them, and the cost of exposing an empire built on lies was yet to be fully realized.

As Elara looked out into the dark, stormy night, she knew one thing for sure—the world was on the brink of change. And whether they lived to see it or not, they had started something that couldn't be undone.

Elara stared out of the safe house window, her thoughts racing. The weight of what they had done, what they had started, was beginning to sink in. The Syndicate had been exposed, but at what cost? There were no guarantees, no assurances that they would survive the retaliation. She knew that the very people they had just taken down would stop at nothing to protect their empire, and now that the first shots had been fired, there was no turning back.

"We can't stay here long," Ivan's voice broke through her thoughts. His eyes were scanning the streets outside, ever watchful. "They'll trace the transmission back to us. It won't take them long."

Kalen, still hunched over his laptop, glanced up. "I'm securing the files in a secondary location, just in case. If they find us, at least they won't get everything."

Elara nodded, though her mind was elsewhere. What had they really accomplished? The Syndicate was vast, its influence like a dark cloud hovering over every facet of society. They had exposed a small part of its inner workings, but the true heart of the empire—the corrupt system that held everything together—remained intact. They needed to go deeper, uncover more, but how much could they afford to risk?

"We need to reach out to the people who can do something with this," she said, her voice firm. "Journalists, activists, anyone with the power to push this story to the forefront. We can't just sit back now. We've opened the door, but we need someone to walk through it."

Kalen nodded, his fingers flying across the keyboard again. "I'm making sure it's in the right hands, but we also need to find out where the Syndicate's next move is. They'll be regrouping. We have to stay one step ahead."

Elara stood up, pacing the small room. "We need to get in touch with our contacts. Get more intel. They're not going to take this lying down. If we're lucky, we've just set off a chain reaction, and now we just have to make sure it doesn't fizzle out."

Her mind raced through the possibilities, the numerous dangers they faced. The Syndicate was no ordinary organization—it was a shadow government in its own right, with fingers in every part of society: politics, business, law enforcement, the military. But exposing it could also mean tearing down the very fabric of the world they knew, a chaotic collapse that might leave nothing standing.

"Elara, we can't be everywhere at once," Kalen's voice interrupted again. He looked up from his laptop, his face weary but determined. "We need to divide and conquer. You take the contacts, get the media to push it. Ivan and I can dig deeper, see if we can find out who's pulling the strings."

She met his gaze, her mind already running through the plan. "Fine. I'll make the calls. But we all need to keep our heads down. This isn't just about taking them down anymore. It's about survival."

Ivan's eyes flickered toward the door, his hand tightening on his weapon. "They're not going to stop until we're all dead. We'll have to stay hidden for as long as we can."

Elara took a deep breath, the weight of their situation pressing down on her. "We'll stay hidden, but we'll also keep fighting. This isn't over yet. Not by a long shot."

The team moved quickly, their minds set on the task ahead. They had made their move, and now the pieces were in motion. The Syndicate would retaliate, but they would not be caught off guard again. They would find the truth, expose it, and bring down the empire that had long controlled their lives from the shadows.

But Elara knew that this war was far from over. It had just begun. And with every step they took, the danger would grow. The walls were closing in, and soon, there would be nowhere left to run.

As they prepared to move out, Elara couldn't shake the feeling that the storm they had unleashed was far more dangerous than anything they had anticipated. But it was too late to turn back now.

The world would know the truth. They just had to survive long enough to make sure the truth didn't get buried under the weight of the Syndicate's vengeance.

Elara adjusted her jacket and checked the small pistol tucked beneath it, her heart pounding with a sense of urgency. She had never felt the pressure of time so acutely before. Every second spent lingering in the safe house brought them closer to danger. The Syndicate wasn't a foe they could outlast by hiding—it was a beast that thrived on control and fear, and now they were in its crosshairs.

Kalen closed his laptop, his face a mask of concentration. "The files are in the right hands now," he said, standing up and heading toward the door. "We've done what we can, but we need to move fast. If they trace our location, we're finished."

Ivan slung a duffel bag over his shoulder, his movements precise, deliberate. "We've made a dent, but there's no time to rest on our laurels. The Syndicate will be looking for retaliation. We'll need to stay mobile, keep them guessing."

Elara nodded, trying to suppress the anxiety gnawing at her. "We can't just run. We need to disrupt their operation. If we can't expose their whole network, maybe we can take out their supply lines, their key players."

Ivan's eyes flickered toward her, a rare spark of agreement in them. "Disruption. It's not just about exposing them—it's about destabilizing them. We find their weak spots and hit them where it hurts."

They all fell silent for a moment, each of them aware of the risks they were about to take. They were no longer just fighting for truth—they were fighting for their lives.

Elara felt the weight of her decision pressing down on her. This was no longer just a matter of exposing corruption; it was personal. The Syndicate had taken too much already—too many lives, too much power. They could not let it continue. Not after everything they had risked.

"Alright," Elara said, breaking the silence. "We move out in five minutes. Kalen, keep monitoring their communications. Ivan, make sure the route is clear. We'll take the back streets to avoid surveillance. We have one shot at this—no mistakes."

Ivan gave a single nod. "Understood."

As they moved out, Elara's mind raced. The world outside felt suffocating. The city was alive with the noise of the unknowing—people walking through their daily routines, oblivious to the storm brewing just beneath the surface. But for Elara, the calm was an illusion. The calm before the storm. She felt every shadow, every movement in the peripheral of her vision. It was the only way to survive now.

The group moved swiftly through narrow alleyways, avoiding the main roads where Syndicate eyes would be watching. Every step was calculated, deliberate. They couldn't afford to slip up now. Their plan was in motion, and they had to see it through.

As they reached a secluded parking garage, Elara stopped for a moment, pulling her team close. "We need to get in touch with our inside sources," she said. "The ones who are embedded within the Syndicate. They'll be the ones who can give us actionable intel. If we can gain their trust, we'll have an edge. But we need to be careful. Trust is a luxury we can't afford."

Kalen glanced at his phone, tapping rapidly. "I've been in touch with a few of them. They're ready to move, but we have to be careful. The Syndicate has eyes everywhere. It won't be long before they figure out that we're making moves. We'll need to cover our tracks as we go."

Ivan let out a quiet, almost bitter laugh. "Cover our tracks? If they want to catch us, they will. The only question is how much damage we can do before they do."

Elara nodded solemnly. "Exactly. We need to hit them hard. Disrupt their infrastructure. Find the people behind the operations and eliminate them. We do that, and we'll start turning the tide."

Her words rang in the air, heavy with the gravity of what they were about to undertake. They were no longer just infiltrating a corrupt organization. They were waging a war—one that could either liberate the world or consume them in the process.

As they moved deeper into the darkened parking garage, Elara couldn't shake the feeling that this was just the beginning. The Syndicate had made its play, and now they were making theirs. The battle lines were drawn, and soon, there would be no neutral ground.

They had crossed the point of no return.

The world was about to witness the beginning of the end.

They descended into the labyrinthine depths of the parking garage, the sound of their footsteps echoing in the silence. Elara kept her senses heightened, aware of every shadow, every distant sound that could be a threat. Time was running out, and the city felt like a ticking bomb ready to explode.

"Move," Ivan whispered, his voice steady but tinged with urgency. He led the way, his eyes scanning the surroundings with the precision of a man who had been trained to anticipate danger at every turn. Elara followed, Kalen close behind, his fingers twitching over his phone as he monitored the flow of data from their contacts.

As they reached the far end of the garage, the sound of a car engine approached. Elara froze, her heart racing. It was too early for their extraction team to be here. They had planned for a quiet exit, not a confrontation. She motioned for them to take cover behind a nearby pillar, pressing herself flat against the cold concrete.

The car pulled into the garage, its headlights cutting through the darkness. The engine died with a low rumble, and Elara held her breath, waiting. She could hear the unmistakable sound of footsteps approaching—slow, deliberate. There was no mistaking it now. This wasn't a random patrol; it was someone who had been sent to find them.

She glanced at Kalen, whose eyes met hers with an unspoken understanding. It was time.

"Get ready," Elara muttered under her breath. Her hand slid to the small pistol at her waist, her fingers curling around the grip. She could feel the weight of the weapon in her hand, the cold steel a reminder of the stakes. It wasn't just about surviving now—it was about winning, about ensuring the Syndicate could never again harm anyone.

The footsteps grew closer, and Elara's pulse quickened. She nodded to Ivan, signaling him to move. Without a word, he slipped into the shadows, disappearing from sight. Kalen moved next, crouching low and using the cover of the car's frame to stay hidden.

The figure finally came into view—a tall man in a dark coat, his face partially obscured by a hood. He moved with the precision of someone who knew what he was doing, scanning the area as though he expected trouble.

Elara's heart beat faster, every instinct screaming that this was a dangerous man, someone who knew how to survive in the brutal world they had just stepped into. He stopped for a moment, scanning the parking garage, his eyes briefly resting on the spot where Elara had been standing. But he didn't see her.

She took a deep breath, steadying herself. This was their moment.

As the man turned, Elara moved swiftly, her feet silent on the concrete as she closed the distance between them. She wasn't fast enough to take him down with a single strike, but she was fast enough to make him regret not being more careful.

A flash of motion—Elara was behind him now, her pistol raised. The man's eyes widened in surprise, but it was too late. With a quick motion, Elara pressed the muzzle against his back, her voice cold and commanding. "Move. Slowly. No sudden moves."

The man tensed, but he didn't resist. He knew better. Elara's finger tightened on the trigger, just enough to remind him of the deadly seriousness of the situation.

"Where is he?" Elara demanded. "Where's your boss?"

The man remained silent, his jaw clenched in defiance. Elara pressed harder, pushing him toward a nearby storage room, the pressure of the gun against his spine the only language he understood. They had to move quickly—every second they wasted could bring more enemies.

"Talk," she said again, her voice low and filled with the threat of violence. "Or I'll make you."

The man's eyes flickered, but he didn't respond. Elara cursed under her breath, frustration mounting. She could feel the clock ticking down in her head—every moment bringing them closer to being discovered.

Without warning, the man moved. A sharp twist, a flash of movement, and Elara was forced to react. She sidestepped just in time, the barrel of her gun grazing his coat as he dove for cover. He was fast—too fast. But Elara was trained for this, and she was determined not to let him slip away.

Gunfire erupted in the confined space of the garage, the sound deafening. Elara's heart skipped a beat as she dove for cover, the shockwave of the blast rattling her bones. She had no idea if it was aimed at her or if the man had an accomplice, but she didn't have time to wonder.

She could hear footsteps—the heavy, deliberate sound of someone advancing. But it wasn't the man she had been confronting.

It was someone else.

The new footsteps were heavier, the sound more purposeful, and Elara knew immediately that this wasn't a coincidence. The enemy was closing in. She could feel the shift in the air, the tension rising like a storm. Her hand tightened around the grip of her gun as she peered from behind her cover.

Through the dim light of the parking garage, another figure emerged. Tall, broad-shouldered, moving with calculated precision. Unlike the man she had confronted earlier, this one wasn't fumbling or nervous—he was calm, controlled, a predator on the hunt.

Elara's mind raced. This was the one they had feared, the one who could bring everything crashing down. His reputation preceded him. He was the leader of the group that had been orchestrating the chaos in the city—the Syndicate's ruthless enforcer.

Ivan was still out of sight, and Kalen was too far to lend a hand quickly enough. Elara was on her own for now, but she had no intention of letting this man take control. She had worked too long and too hard for this moment.

Her eyes flicked to the shadows. The man was getting closer, his movements slow, deliberate. He knew how to approach without making a sound. He had no idea she was waiting.

But Elara wasn't about to let him gain the upper hand. She took a deep breath and, in one smooth motion, slid out from behind cover. Her body was a blur of motion as she approached from the side, staying low and quiet, her gun poised.

The enforcer's back was to her now. This was her chance.

Just as she was about to make her move, a sharp voice rang out behind her.

"Elara! Get down!"

She spun instinctively, barely ducking in time as the sharp crack of gunfire echoed through the garage. A bullet whizzed past her ear, the force of it so close that she could feel the heat of the passing air.

Kalen, his face set with determination, was standing at the far end of the garage, his rifle raised. He had acted just in time.

"Move! Get to cover!" he shouted, his voice firm and commanding.

Elara didn't hesitate. She sprinted toward Kalen, her heart pounding, adrenaline flooding her system. Behind her, the enforcer's growl of frustration reverberated in the concrete space.

The man's voice was low, menacing. "You think you can run, Elara? You can't escape what's coming."

But Elara didn't listen. She couldn't afford to. As she reached Kalen, she dove into the shadows beside him, narrowly avoiding another barrage of bullets.

"You alright?" Kalen asked, his voice steady despite the chaos. He was already reloading, preparing for another fight.

Elara nodded, though her eyes remained focused on the movements around them. "We need to get out of here, now."

"Agreed," Kalen replied. "The extraction team's in position, but we have to get to the car before they close the perimeter."

The sound of the enforcer's men growing nearer made Elara's pulse race. She knew they didn't have much time. The garage was closing in on them, the walls feeling smaller with every passing second.

"Can you hold them off?" Elara asked, glancing over her shoulder.

Kalen gave her a tight smile, his eyes alight with a grim determination. "I'll give you cover. Go."

She didn't hesitate this time. Elara took a deep breath and turned, sprinting toward the stairwell that would lead them out of the garage. She could hear the enforcers behind them now, their steps growing louder, closer. There was no time to waste. They had to make it out of the city, or everything they had fought for would be lost.

She rounded the corner, breath coming in ragged gasps. The stairwell door was just ahead, but she could hear them—her pursuers—closing in faster than she had hoped.

A gunshot rang out, followed by another. Kalen's voice echoed in her earpiece.

"Elara, move! We've got less than a minute before they trap us!"

The world seemed to move in slow motion. Elara reached the door, throwing it open just as she heard the unmistakable screech of tires. She didn't need to look—she could feel it in the air. The escape car had arrived.

But as she bolted toward the vehicle, a sudden realization hit her. The city was no longer a safe haven. The Syndicate's grip on it had only just begun, and the fight to reclaim it was far from over. This was only the beginning.

"Get in!" Kalen's voice was sharp, urging her forward.

Elara didn't need to be told twice. She dove into the car, slamming the door behind her just as the engine roared to life. The car shot forward, tires screeching as it sped toward the exit.

As they raced through the city, Elara glanced out the window. The lights of the city blurred past, but all she could see was the darkness that lay beyond. The battle was far from over, and the true cost of their mission was yet to come.

The collapse had begun.

# 11. Ashes of Empires

## ○ A Bitter Victory

The battle had ended, but the war was far from over. Alex stood amidst the ruins of what had once been a bustling city center, the heart of a world now broken. The air was thick with dust, the smell of burnt debris hanging like a grim reminder of everything that had been lost. The ground beneath his boots was scorched, cracked open by explosions, leaving jagged scars that mirrored the wounds of the world itself.

His team had fought valiantly, but victory had come at a great cost. Sophia's invention, the stabilizer, had been destroyed—her hopes for a new world, her dream of healing the earth, reduced to a pile of smoldering wreckage. The forces they had fought against, led by Victor Lynn, had been ruthless, but it wasn't just Victor who had made the sacrifices feel hollow. There had been moments when Alex had wondered if it was all worth it—if the price of freedom, of survival, was too high.

Emma stood beside him, her face pale and drawn. She had been with him through every step of this journey, her unflinching resolve a constant source of strength. But now, even she seemed shaken, as though the weight of the world had finally broken her. She looked out over the horizon, where the last remnants of daylight were fading into the blood-red sky, a sky that seemed to mirror the chaos they had just survived.

"We did it," Emma said quietly, her voice barely more than a whisper. "But at what cost?"

Alex didn't have an answer. The words she spoke were the ones that had been circling in his mind for days, weeks, since this war began. They had won the battle, but they had lost so much in the process—too much. The rebellion was now just a shadow of its former self, its members scattered, many lost. The loyalists to Victor had been decimated, but the power vacuum left in their wake promised more bloodshed, more conflict, before anything resembling peace could take root.

He turned away from the destruction, his eyes seeking the others. Danny had taken to sitting on the ground, his face buried in his hands, the weight of what they had done pressing heavily on his shoulders. The war had never been kind to him, and this victory felt like the culmination of a lifetime of regret. His redemption had been a hard-won prize, but it was one that seemed so insignificant in the face of what they had all endured.

Sophia was still in the distance, talking to a small group of survivors, her face hard to read. Despite the destruction of her work, there was something in her eyes that refused to break. She had lost so much—so much more than any of them—but she still stood tall. Her brilliance, her unwavering commitment to the future, had not been crushed by the bombs or the betrayal. There was a strength in her that Alex couldn't quite understand, but he knew it was the very thing that would carry them forward, even if the road ahead was uncertain.

A breeze stirred the air, carrying with it a faint, almost imperceptible sound—a whisper of something new, something yet to come. Alex wasn't sure what it was, but in that moment, he allowed himself to hope, just a little. A bitter victory it was, yes, but perhaps it wasn't the end. Perhaps, in the ashes, there could still be something worth rebuilding.

"Is it enough?" Emma asked, her voice soft as she stepped closer. She had always been the one to ask the hard questions, and this time, Alex wasn't sure he could answer.

"I don't know," he replied, his voice heavy with the weight of his own uncertainty. "But maybe it's all we can hope for."

The sun was gone now, the world swallowed by the shadows of night. But beneath those shadows, Alex saw the faintest spark—a glimmer of what might come next. The victory was bitter, the losses were too great, but as long as they were still standing, there was a chance. And in this broken world, a chance was all they had.

For a moment, the team stood in silence, the only sound the soft rustling of the wind, carrying with it the weight of their decisions, their sacrifices, and their future. There would be no easy answers. No clean slate. But there was still a world left to save, and somehow, they would find a way to do it.

It wasn't much. But it was something. And in the ruins, that was enough to start again.

## ○ Sophia's Legacy

SOPHIA STOOD AT THE edge of the ruined city, her eyes scanning the horizon where the last traces of civilization had been swallowed by the ravages of war. The wind tugged at her hair, carrying with it the scent of ash and decay, the final remnants of a world that had once been vibrant, full of promise and progress. Now, it was a wasteland—a reflection of what humanity had become in its quest for dominance, a quest that had shattered everything she had fought to protect.

She glanced down at the device clutched tightly in her hand—the stabilizer. It was a symbol of both hope and tragedy. Its potential to restore the earth's dying ecosystems was unprecedented. But with its power came the unbearable weight of responsibility. The world had failed to protect the environment before, and she feared it would make the same mistake again. She could feel the ghosts of the past—the scientists, the activists, the ordinary people who had warned the world of the coming collapse. They had all been ignored, and now the consequences were clear. The devastation was irreversible for many, but the stabilizer could still make a difference. It could be the salvation of those who remained.

The problem was, it was no longer just a scientific breakthrough—it had become a weapon in the hands of those who sought to control the future.

Victor Lynn had made it clear from the beginning that he had no intention of sharing the technology. To him, the stabilizer was a means of cementing his rule over what was left of the world. Sophia had seen the depths of his ambition, the cold, calculating nature of a man willing to sacrifice anything—and anyone—for power. He had betrayed her trust, manipulated her into believing they could work together for the greater good, and now he would stop at nothing to use her creation to expand his empire.

Sophia had made her choice. She had destroyed the original design, erased the schematics, hidden what remained of her work. The world didn't deserve to have the power she had unlocked. Not yet. Not until it could prove it was capable of change.

But that decision weighed heavily on her. Every day she had to live with the knowledge that the very thing that could save humanity was buried deep within her mind, locked away where no one could use it—not even her. And yet, she knew it was the only way. She had seen the corruption, the greed, the manipulation of every system, every hope for a better future, twisted into something ugly. To give the stabilizer to anyone now would be to condemn the survivors to a life controlled by the very same forces that had ruined everything.

It was a bitter truth, but one she could not deny. The world had to rebuild itself, piece by piece, starting with those who remained who still had the capacity for compassion, for community, for selflessness. The ones who hadn't been consumed by the greed and hunger for power that had led to this apocalypse.

But as she stood there, watching the last remnants of her hopes for a better future disintegrate in the dust, she couldn't help but wonder: Would they ever learn? Would they be able to rebuild not just their cities, but their souls? Or had the world gone too far, lost too much to ever return to the path of redemption?

Sophia's legacy wasn't just the stabilizer, though. It was the memory of those who had fought to preserve what little was left, the lessons learned through their failures. It was the quiet hope that, perhaps someday, humanity would rise from the ashes—not just to survive, but to truly live again.

As the sun dipped below the horizon, casting the sky in hues of red and gold, she turned away from the ruins. Her journey was far from over. She would continue to fight, not with the stabilizer, but with the small acts of resistance that could, perhaps, shift the course of history. The world was broken, but it was still breathing. And for now, that was enough.

## ○ The Survivors' Struggle

THE COLD WIND SWEPT through the crumbled remnants of what had once been a thriving metropolis, carrying with it the scent of decay and hopelessness. The survivors trudged through the debris, their faces etched with exhaustion, their movements mechanical as if they had become one with the desolation surrounding them. The city, once a symbol of human achievement and progress, now stood as a silent testament to the price of survival in a world that had descended into chaos.

Alex stood at the front of the group, his eyes scanning the horizon, always alert, always searching. He had become the reluctant leader, the one who bore the weight of decisions that could mean life or death for those who followed him. His hand rested on the hilt of a knife, not out of fear, but out of necessity.

It was a world where trust was as fragile as the walls of the ruined buildings they passed.

Behind him, Emma walked silently, her eyes focused on the ground, her mind a whirlwind of thoughts. She had seen the worst humanity had to offer in the last months, the betrayals, the power plays, the desperation. But it was the small moments of kindness, the brief flashes of hope, that kept her going. That was what she told herself, at least. She couldn't afford to dwell on the darkness that had nearly consumed her soul. Not now. Not when they were so close.

The rest of the group followed in a loose formation, some walking with their heads down, others glancing nervously at their surroundings. They were survivors. They had made it this far, and yet, survival in the aftermath of global collapse felt like a hollow victory. The world they had known was gone, replaced by a harsh reality where every day was a battle against not only the elements but also the other factions who roamed the earth, each one as desperate and ruthless as the next.

Sophia, the scientist who had once dreamed of saving the world, now moved through the ruins with the same steely determination as the others. Her work, her technology, had become the beacon of hope for the survivors, but even she knew that hope was a fragile thing. It could easily be snuffed out by the wrong hands, by the wrong choices.

"How much farther?" Danny's voice broke the silence, rough with fatigue. His eyes were bloodshot, his face drawn, but there was an underlying strength to him, a tenacity that had kept him alive when so many others had fallen. He had seen the horrors of war firsthand, had participated in them, and now, as much as he wanted to leave it all behind, he couldn't. Redemption wasn't something you found in the rubble; it was something you fought for.

"Not much," Alex replied, his voice steady but tinged with an undercurrent of uncertainty. They had been moving for days, avoiding the hostile remnants of civilization and searching for a place where they could regroup, a place where they could find something resembling peace, if such a thing even existed anymore. But every safe haven they found seemed to be just another illusion. A dead end. A place where their fragile existence could be snuffed out in an instant by the wrong person with the wrong intentions.

Sophia stopped for a moment, her eyes scanning the horizon with the same practiced gaze she had once used to examine data and research results. She knew what Alex was thinking. There were no safe havens left. Only survival. And even that was becoming increasingly difficult.

"We can't keep running," she said quietly, her voice barely audible over the howling wind. "There's only so much we can do before we have to stand and fight."

Alex turned to look at her, his expression unreadable. "We're not ready," he replied, his words carrying the weight of a man who had seen too much to believe in any easy answers. "We're not strong enough to face what's out there. We need more time."

"And how much time do we have?" Sophia countered, her gaze unwavering. "Time is a luxury we don't have anymore. The longer we wait, the harder it will be to make any difference."

Alex didn't respond immediately. He knew she was right, but he also knew the cost of action. Every decision, every move they made, could tip the balance in their favor or condemn them to a fate worse than death. The stakes had never been higher.

"We move forward," he said finally, his voice firm. "We'll find a way. We have to."

But even as he spoke those words, a part of him wondered if it was already too late. The survivors had struggled for so long, had fought against the elements, the factions, and their own inner demons. And yet, every step they took forward seemed to bring them closer to the precipice, a place where survival itself might become the greatest lie of all.

The survivors' struggle was far from over, but in their hearts, they knew that the hardest battles had yet to come.

## ○ A New Dawn

THE SKY, ONCE A TAPESTRY of chaos and smoke, now held the faintest trace of light—fragile, tentative, like a breath held too long. It was the first morning after the war's last breath, the end of an era that had ground civilizations into dust. The ruins of cities lay silent, their once-proud skyscrapers now hollow bones against a pale, bruised horizon. In this new world, hope wasn't something guaranteed. It wasn't promised with the sun's rise. It was something to be fought for.

Alex Novak stood at the edge of a crumbled balcony, his gaze drifting over the remnants of what was once a thriving metropolis. The world had changed, but it hadn't died. Not yet. Not if they had anything to say about it. His hands, calloused and worn from years of survival, gripped the stone railing with quiet determination. He didn't know what tomorrow would bring, but he knew what he couldn't afford to lose: the chance to rebuild, to find something worth saving in this broken world.

Behind him, Sophia Alvarez worked in silence, her fingers moving over the delicate circuits of a device she had promised would heal the planet. A stabilizer, she had called it—a miracle of science that could reverse the damage done to the environment, regenerate the soil, the air, the oceans. But Alex knew better than anyone that miracles came at a price. The world had been drained by greed and corruption, and no solution would come without its own sacrifice.

"We can't just build everything back the way it was," Alex said, his voice low but steady. "The old world, it's gone. There's no going back."

Sophia didn't look up from her work. Her eyes were focused, intense, as though the weight of her invention had anchored her to the task at hand. "I know," she replied quietly. "But we can make a new world. We can make it better than it was."

Alex shook his head slowly, his mind already racing ahead to the challenges that lay in their path. "Better?" he asked. "How do you measure that? What does better even look like in a place like this?"

She paused, her fingers stilling over the small, intricate machine. "Better is when we stop repeating the mistakes of the past," she said softly. "Better is when we don't let the same people who destroyed the world come back to control what's left of it."

Her words hung in the air between them, like the smoke of a fire long extinguished, lingering in the silence. They had both seen too much to believe in easy answers. The destruction had been deliberate. The war that had torn the world apart had been set into motion by those who had always held the power, and the remnants of that power still lingered in the shadows, waiting for the perfect moment to strike.

"I wish I could believe that," Alex murmured, turning his eyes back to the horizon. "But we're not the only ones who want to rebuild, Sophia. There are others—those who've thrived in the ashes of this world. And they won't give up what they've gained so easily."

Sophia finally looked up from her work, her expression unreadable. "Then we'll have to fight for it. Again. And this time, we won't let them win."

The weight of her words settled on him, and for the first time in what felt like forever, Alex felt a flicker of hope. It was small, barely a spark, but it was enough to remind him that there was still something worth fighting for in this broken world.

As the first light of dawn crept across the ruins, the world seemed to exhale, as though holding its breath for what was to come. It wasn't much, but it was a start. A new day in a shattered world. And maybe, just maybe, it could be the beginning of something better.

## ○ The Cost of Survival

THE WORLD HAD BEEN hollowed out by years of war, its bones shattered beneath the weight of greed and ambition. The once-thriving cities were now just broken remnants of their former selves, echoing the ghosts of lives lost and dreams crushed under the relentless march of time. Alex and his ragtag group of survivors trudged through this desolate landscape, their faces hardened by loss, their hearts weighed down by the grim reality of the world they inhabited.

Every day, they fought not just against the elements, but against something far more insidious—the gnawing, insatiable hunger for survival. The world no longer ran on politics, ideals, or moralities. It ran on the simplest, rawest instinct: the need to live. Food was scarce, water more precious than gold, and shelter nothing more than a fleeting illusion in the wasteland of what was once civilization.

Alex had never imagined he'd end up like this. He had spent his life as a diplomat, weaving intricate webs of alliances, navigating the subtle art of compromise, never once thinking the world could collapse so thoroughly. Now, as he stumbled through the ruined streets of what used to be a bustling city center, he realized how little the world had prepared him for this kind of war. There were no treaties to sign, no ceasefires to negotiate. Only survival.

"Any luck?" Danny's voice broke through his thoughts. The soldier had taken up the rear, always watchful, always alert. He was as broken as Alex, perhaps even more so. The things he had seen, the things he had done in the name of survival, had left him a shell of the man he used to be. But in this new world, that was often the only kind of man you could afford to be.

"No," Alex replied, glancing over his shoulder to meet Danny's hard eyes. "The last food stash we found was emptied days ago. If we don't find something soon..."

Danny nodded grimly, understanding the unspoken words. The group was running out of options, out of time. The last thing they needed was to become prey to the bands of marauders that roamed the desolate roads, searching for the weak to exploit or eliminate.

The sound of footsteps caught Alex's attention. He turned, his hand instinctively moving toward the knife sheathed at his side. Emma, the investigative journalist, approached with a bundle of scavenged supplies clutched tightly to her chest. Her eyes were dark with the weight of their shared struggle, but there was a fire in her that Alex admired. It was the same fire that had kept her going even after discovering the true cost of what had happened to the world—the corporate greed, the political corruption, the choices made by the powerful that had led them all to this ruin. She, more than anyone, understood how survival had become a currency.

"I found something," she said, her voice low but firm, like the calm before a storm. "Not much, but it should keep us going for a little while longer. But we need to think bigger, Alex. We're not going to survive just by scavenging scraps."

Alex nodded, but the weight of her words hung in the air, heavy and undeniable. She was right. Scavenging wouldn't be enough. The world was too far gone for such a small, temporary fix. They needed something more—something that could change the course of their lives and, perhaps, the world.

Sophia had been the one to offer that hope. The brilliant scientist who had, against all odds, developed the stabilizer—a device that could restore ecosystems, rejuvenate lands poisoned by war, and heal the planet's wounded veins. But there was a catch. The stabilizer was more than just a machine. It was a symbol of power, of control, and the moment the word of it got out, it would become the most valuable commodity in the world. The kind of commodity people like Victor Lynn, the powerful tycoon who had profited from the war, would stop at nothing to claim.

That was the true cost of survival. It wasn't just the fight to stay alive—it was the fight for control over the future. The fight to possess the one thing that could reshape the world, even as it threatened to break it further. The fight to protect the fragile hope they had left, no matter the cost.

Alex felt the weight of that responsibility settling on his shoulders, like a boulder poised to crush him. The cost of survival had never been this steep. They had come too far to turn back now, but the road ahead was fraught with peril—betrayal, bloodshed, and the very real possibility that their fight for survival would come at the ultimate price.

As the sun dipped beneath the horizon, casting long shadows over the ruined city, Alex made his choice. They would move forward. But survival, in this broken world, would no longer be a matter of simply breathing—it would be about deciding who would live, and who would die.

The darkness crept in quickly, swallowing the last remnants of light as the cityscape became a maze of twisted metal and decaying concrete. The cold wind began to bite, and Alex pulled his worn jacket tighter around his shoulders, trying to stave off the chill that gnawed at his bones. It wasn't just the weather that was unforgiving—it was the constant, suffocating weight of uncertainty. In the ruins of the old world, every step was a reminder that survival was no longer guaranteed.

"Night's coming fast," Emma murmured, her voice barely audible above the wind. She had returned to the small fire they'd managed to start, her face illuminated by the flickering flames. "We can't keep moving at night. We'll burn through what little we have left if we don't rest."

Alex nodded in agreement, though the thought of staying in one place, vulnerable and exposed, filled him with unease. They couldn't afford to waste time. Victor's men were likely still searching for them, and each moment spent in the open was another chance for the enemy to close in.

But he knew Emma was right. They had to rest, if only for a few hours. They couldn't afford to push themselves beyond their limits. The consequences of exhaustion would be more lethal than any enemy they could face. Survival wasn't just about fending off threats—it was about knowing when to yield, when to retreat into the shadows and let the world pass by.

Alex took a deep breath, the familiar smell of burning wood filling his lungs as he crouched beside the fire. It wasn't much, but it was warmth, and warmth was a luxury now. He watched as Emma dug through the supplies she'd scavenged, pulling out a few cans of food and some dried meat. It was meager, but it would sustain them—for now.

Danny sat off to the side, sharpening his knife with slow, deliberate strokes. His eyes were fixed on the blade, but Alex could see the storm behind them. The soldier was a man broken by war, yet somehow still alive, still fighting. It was hard to tell which was harder to survive: the war itself or the aftermath. The war had stolen everything from him, and now the world was taking its toll in a different way—slowly, insidiously, like a cancer eating away at his soul.

"You think it'll be enough?" Danny spoke, his voice gruff, as if the words had been buried for too long. He wasn't asking about the food, but the bigger question. They all knew what was coming.

Alex looked into his eyes, and for a moment, there was no need for words. They both understood the stakes. The stabilizer, the device that could change the world, was a double-edged sword. It could heal the land, restore balance—but it could also become a weapon. Those who controlled it would hold unimaginable power, and that power could crush the last flickers of hope for a peaceful future.

"I don't know," Alex said quietly, more to himself than to anyone else. "But we can't stop now. Not when we've come this far. We have to take the risk. We have to try."

Emma met his gaze across the fire, her eyes hard with determination. She was no stranger to risk—she had been in the game long enough to understand that survival meant more than just avoiding death. It meant making impossible choices, facing the abyss, and still walking forward.

"Then we move at dawn," she said, her voice steady, though her hands trembled slightly as she handed out what little food they had left. "And we make sure we stay ahead of Lynn. We can't let him get to it first."

Sophia's discovery had brought them this far, but they knew the hardest part was still ahead. They couldn't afford to trust anyone—not even each other, not fully. In this new world, alliances were as fragile as the earth beneath their feet, and betrayal was never far behind.

As Alex settled down on the cold, uneven ground, he found himself staring at the fire, watching the flames dance and flicker in the wind. There was something mesmerizing about it, something hypnotic. Perhaps it was the way it burned—fierce and wild, like the world itself—but always fading, always fleeting. He thought about the future, about what kind of world would rise from the ashes of the old one. Would there even be a future? Or would they all be consumed by the fire, as so many others had been?

Sophia's stabilizer might offer them a way out, but at what cost? Could they really reshape the world, or would they just end up fighting over the remnants, scraping for survival like everyone else?

His eyes closed, exhaustion settling into his bones. The fire crackled in the silence, the sound of the world coming apart around them. Tomorrow would bring another challenge, another battle. But tonight, for a brief moment, there was peace. And for Alex, that was enough to hold on to.

The night stretched on, long and restless, the fire flickering like a dying heartbeat in the cold dark. The wind howled through the broken windows of the nearby structures, sending sheets of debris tumbling across the desolate streets. Alex lay awake, eyes wide open, staring at the flickering shadows cast by the flames. His thoughts were a chaotic jumble—fragments of conversations, strategies, and fleeting memories. But most of all, it was the question of survival that gnawed at him.

He couldn't escape the thought that no matter how far they ran, no matter how hard they fought, they were always just a step away from being swallowed by the world around them. The consequences of their choices, the weight of their actions, were too heavy to ignore. They had already gone beyond the point of no return.

"Can't sleep either?" Danny's voice broke through the silence, low and hoarse. Alex turned his head to see the soldier sitting up, his back leaning against a pile of rubble.

"Not yet," Alex replied, rubbing his eyes. "You?"

Danny grunted in response. "Too much on my mind. I keep thinking about what's waiting for us. The Stabilizer... if we find it, what then? What happens when we've won the battle, but we can't control what comes after?"

It was a question Alex had asked himself more times than he cared to admit. The power of the Stabilizer was undeniable—it was a force that could shift the balance of power on the planet, but what if that power fell into the wrong hands? What if they were wrong to trust Sophia and her vision? They had no guarantees, no assurances that they wouldn't end up just like the forces they were fighting against.

"I don't know," Alex said quietly. "But we don't have a choice, Danny. If we don't act, then all of this—everything we've been through—was for nothing. We have to try."

Danny snorted softly, the sound bitter. "Trying won't fix the world. Hell, I don't even know if the world can be fixed." He paused, running his hand over his face. "We're just buying time. That's all we've been doing. Buying time before it all falls apart."

Alex didn't have an answer for that. He wished he did. He wanted to believe that they were doing something meaningful, that they were fighting for a better future. But the harsh reality of the world they lived in made it hard to hold on to hope. Every decision felt like a gamble, every choice a step closer to ruin.

"I guess we'll find out," Alex said after a long silence, his voice carrying a certain finality. "One way or another."

The wind picked up again, howling through the broken streets, a reminder of the chaos that awaited them outside the relative safety of their small encampment. Tomorrow would bring its own challenges—more obstacles, more enemies. They had no illusions about what they faced.

But for tonight, there was something comforting in the quiet, in the stillness between the gusts of wind. Tomorrow would come soon enough, and when it did, they would face it together.

The fire died down to embers as the last traces of warmth faded into the night. Alex finally closed his eyes, but sleep was elusive. Instead, his thoughts raced, chasing shadows of what lay ahead.

At first light, they gathered their things and prepared to move. The quiet of the night gave way to the tense anticipation of the day ahead. They would leave behind their makeshift camp and continue the journey toward the unknown.

Alex glanced around at the small group—Emma, Danny, and himself. They were a fractured team, united by necessity, but bound by the shared understanding that survival was the only thing that mattered. Trust was a luxury they couldn't afford, but there was a common bond between them: the will to survive, no matter the cost.

As they began their trek through the ruins, the weight of their mission hung heavy in the air. They were headed toward the last hope for a better world—or perhaps the final nail in the coffin of what remained.

The cost of survival was more than just the risk of death. It was the toll on their souls, the price they paid with every choice they made. Every step forward took them deeper into the heart of the storm.

The world outside had become an unrecognizable place, a battleground of shattered dreams and broken promises. It would take more than hope to rebuild. It would take something much stronger—a force that could move mountains, that could reshape the very fabric of the world they had known.

But as they walked through the wasteland, Alex couldn't help but wonder: when the dust settled, would there even be a place for them in this new world? Would they have the strength to survive what came next?

As the group moved forward, the landscape around them seemed to stretch endlessly, an unbroken sea of rubble and ruins. The roads, once bustling with life and movement, were now nothing more than cracked, dilapidated remnants of a time long past. Buildings, stripped of their purpose and identity, stood like hollow sentinels, their windows broken, their walls scarred by the violence of war. Yet, despite the destruction, there was something eerily beautiful about the desolation—a quiet, haunting stillness that clung to the land as if the earth itself was holding its breath.

They walked in silence, each lost in their thoughts, each carrying the weight of the unknown future. The tension between them was palpable, but it was a tension borne out of survival rather than distrust. They were bound by the same goal, driven by the same desperation to escape the grip of their fractured world. But as the days passed, Alex couldn't shake the feeling that something deeper, more insidious, was at play.

It was Emma who spoke first. Her voice was soft, almost hesitant, as though she too was trying to break free from the unspoken thoughts that held them captive.

"I know we don't talk about it much," she began, her eyes scanning the horizon as if she were searching for something beyond the emptiness. "But what happens if we find the Stabilizer? What happens after we fix this?"

Alex didn't respond immediately. He hadn't allowed himself to think that far ahead. The mission—stopping the remaining factions from harnessing the Stabilizer's power—had been his focus, his obsession. But Emma's question forced him to confront the uncertainty that lurked beneath the surface.

"We'll do what we can," he said, though even to his own ears, his words sounded hollow. "We'll make sure it doesn't fall into the wrong hands."

Danny snorted bitterly, his boots kicking up the dust of the road. "Right. Like we're going to be the ones to fix all this. You saw what's left of the world. Power's all anyone cares about now. If we find it, we'll be fighting a war for control. And it'll be just like all the other wars. Only this time, it won't just be people fighting for land or resources. It'll be something worse—something that can literally change the course of history."

Alex knew Danny was right. The Stabilizer wasn't just a tool; it was a weapon—one that could alter the very fabric of reality itself. And in the hands of the wrong people, it would be the ultimate means of control. He couldn't allow that to happen. They couldn't allow that to happen.

But what if they were the wrong people?

The thought chilled him to the core.

"You really think we're better than the others?" Danny's voice broke through his thoughts, a harsh edge to it. "That we can make the right call when we get our hands on something like that? I don't know, Alex. I'm not sure anyone can."

Alex paused, staring at the ground beneath his feet. He had no answer. He wasn't sure they were better—or if they even had the luxury of making the right call. Survival was the only thing that mattered right now.

"Maybe we're not better," he finally said, his voice low. "But we're the ones still standing. And that has to count for something."

For a moment, there was silence again, broken only by the wind, which howled mournfully through the ruins. Then Emma spoke, her voice calm but resolute.

"We can't keep thinking about what we might become. We have to focus on what we need to do now. The world will keep spinning, no matter what we do. But if we stop, if we hesitate, we'll lose everything."

Alex turned to her, meeting her gaze. She was right, of course. The world would keep spinning. Whether they were ready for it or not, the forces at play were bigger than any one of them. And the only thing that could save them now was their willingness to move forward, to keep fighting, even when the cost was unclear.

"Let's keep moving, then," Alex said, his voice firm, more to himself than anyone else. "We'll deal with the rest when we get there."

They walked on, the steady crunch of their boots against the broken earth the only sound in the oppressive silence. With every step, the weight of the unknown grew heavier, and the threat of failure loomed ever closer. But there was no turning back now. They had come too far.

The wind began to pick up again, carrying with it the scent of dust and decay. Alex glanced up at the sky, where the clouds were thickening, darkening with the promise of a storm. The landscape ahead was shrouded in shadows, a fitting mirror of the journey they were on.

They didn't know what awaited them at the end of the road, or what price they would have to pay for survival. But as the first raindrops began to fall, mixing with the dust of the earth, Alex felt the weight of the world on his shoulders. And in that moment, he understood the true cost of survival. It wasn't just about staying alive. It was about what they would lose along the way—and whether it would be worth it in the end.

As the rain began to fall in heavier sheets, the group quickened their pace, seeking shelter where they could find it. A crumbling structure loomed in the distance—one of the few remaining buildings still standing with a semblance of its former purpose. It was an old factory, the kind that used to churn out goods for a thriving economy before it all came crashing down. The rusted skeleton of machinery within the walls reminded them of how far everything had fallen.

Inside, the air was musty and thick with the scent of mildew and decay. The windows were shattered, allowing the rain to penetrate the interior, but at least it offered them some reprieve from the storm outside. The group huddled in a corner, pulling out the last remnants of their rations as they tried to gather strength.

They spoke little, each lost in their own thoughts, aware that the world outside was closing in. The silence between them was not uncomfortable but necessary, a way to give space for the grim reality of their situation to sink in. The weight of what they had set out to accomplish was settling heavily on Alex's chest, and he could feel his body and mind fighting against exhaustion.

"How much further?" Danny asked, breaking the silence. His voice was gruff, wearied by the relentless strain of survival.

Alex glanced at the map again, studying the faded markings that seemed to blur with each passing day. They had come far, but there was still much to be done, and every step forward felt like a gamble. The world had fractured into so many unpredictable pieces that even a single wrong move could lead them straight into a trap.

"Hard to say," Alex replied. "But we're getting close. I can feel it."

Emma, ever the optimist, offered a slight smile, though it didn't quite reach her eyes. "I'm sure we'll make it," she said softly, her voice carrying a sense of quiet determination. "We've come this far. We can't stop now."

But even as she spoke, a shiver ran through Alex. The odds were never in their favor, and the path they had chosen was fraught with peril. He had been hoping for some sign, something to show them they were on the right track. But the further they journeyed, the more it seemed like they were walking into a storm that no one could survive.

The quiet hum of the storm outside reminded him of a distant, terrible memory. It had been years ago, when the first waves of conflict began to tear apart the fabric of society. People had fought over resources, over power, over survival itself. Governments had crumbled, and alliances had shattered. And through it all, the Stabilizer—the key to it all—had been the thing that everyone wanted, the thing that could reshape the world.

And now, it was in their hands.

For better or worse, they were the ones who had to decide its fate. Alex had hoped that by finding it, they could end the madness, restore some semblance of order to the chaos. But now, with each passing hour, doubt was beginning to creep into his mind. What if they weren't meant to be the ones to fix it? What if they were just as much a part of the destruction as the people they were trying to stop?

"Do you ever wonder if we're doing the right thing?" Alex asked, his voice barely above a whisper.

Emma looked up, meeting his gaze with a knowing look. "Every day," she said. "But sometimes, doing the right thing doesn't mean we get it right every time. We just have to keep moving forward."

Her words were a balm to his weary soul, but even they couldn't erase the nagging doubt that lingered in his mind. They were standing on the edge of something far bigger than themselves, a force that had the potential to either save or doom the remnants of humanity.

A loud crack of thunder echoed through the ruins outside, a reminder that nature, like the world itself, was unpredictable and unforgiving. They were running out of time.

"You're right," Alex muttered, shaking his head as if to clear away the fog that had settled there. "We can't afford to hesitate. Not now."

The sound of rain intensifying outside seemed to mark the turning point. They would face the rest of the journey, for better or worse, no matter the cost. The weight of their mission was not something they could shed. It was a burden they would carry to the very end.

As the storm raged outside, they prepared to leave the shelter, knowing that the path ahead was uncertain. There would be more obstacles, more choices, and more sacrifices to come. But for now, they had made it through the worst of it. They had survived the night.

And in this broken world, survival was everything.

• • • •

## ○ Echoes of Hope

THE CITY LAY IN RUINS, its once towering skyline now nothing more than jagged silhouettes against a darkened sky. The air, thick with dust and ash, clung to everything it touched. Buildings crumbled into heaps of concrete, steel, and forgotten dreams, a testament to the devastation that had torn through the world. Once, this place had been a bustling metropolis, teeming with life, ambition, and possibility. Now, it was a hollow shell—an empty, breathing wound on the earth.

Alex Novak stepped cautiously through the wreckage, his boots crunching against the remnants of shattered glass and twisted metal. His gaze was fixed forward, focused on nothing but the path ahead. He had long stopped searching for things he could never find—homes, families, hope. Yet, there was something in this desolate landscape that made him feel alive. It was the smallest of things: the soft rustle of wind through broken windows, the fleeting glimpse of a flower blooming defiantly amidst the decay, or the way the sun slanted through the smoke clouds in the distance, casting long, eerie shadows across the rubble. In this place of death, there was still a trace of life.

The survivors moved in a tight group behind him, their eyes darting from side to side, always watchful. Trust was a luxury none of them could afford. But Alex had earned their respect, if not their trust. He had once been a diplomat, someone who understood the delicate balance of power and negotiation. Now, he was the leader of a ragtag crew of scavengers, trying to survive in a world that had long since forgotten what it meant to thrive.

"Over there," Emma Carter whispered, pointing to a structure in the distance. A flicker of something that might once have been a library, now a skeletal framework, its walls scarred with the markings of battle. It was a faint glimmer of what the world had been—a reminder that there had been something worth saving.

Alex nodded. He didn't need to ask why Emma had chosen that spot. They'd all seen the same thing: Sophia's device, the one that could reverse the slow death of their planet, lay somewhere within those crumbling walls. But getting there wouldn't be easy. The city was still crawling with survivors who weren't interested in peace or hope. They wanted control. They wanted power. And in a world where survival was a game of ruthlessness, they'd do anything to claim what little was left.

"Stay close," Alex muttered, his voice low but firm.

As they made their way through the desolate streets, Emma walked beside him, her sharp eyes scanning every corner. She was more than just an observer—she was a vital part of the team, her journalistic instincts constantly seeking the truth, even when it seemed too dangerous to uncover.

"I know you're holding something back, Alex," Emma said quietly, her voice cutting through the silence like a blade. "You're not just after Sophia's invention. There's more to this, isn't there?"

Alex's jaw tightened, but he didn't look at her. "It's not just about technology, Emma. It's about the future. About making sure we don't repeat the same mistakes."

"I don't think we're capable of that," she replied with a bitter laugh. "Look at us. We're scavengers in a world that's been burned to the ground. We can't fix what's broken."

"Maybe we can't fix it," Alex said, his voice distant, as if he were talking to himself more than to her. "But we can try. And that's all we've got left. Trying."

He felt her eyes on him then, but didn't look back. The weight of her gaze lingered, and for a brief moment, he wondered if she saw through the walls he'd carefully built around himself. He had always been good at hiding the parts of himself that were too raw, too vulnerable. But something about this place—this wasteland—brought out the things he had buried.

Ahead, the library's skeletal frame grew larger, the space between them and it shrinking with every cautious step. The wind picked up, sending dust swirling through the air, carrying with it the scent of decay. There was no telling how much longer Sophia's work would last, how long they could afford to chase this fragile dream of hope. The device could save them—or destroy them.

When they reached the building, Alex didn't hesitate. He motioned for the group to spread out, weapons drawn, ready for anything. Inside, the air was thick with dust, the remnants of books and papers scattered on the floor like forgotten memories. But there, amid the chaos, Sophia's invention stood untouched. The stabilizer, small but powerful, pulsed with a faint glow, its blue light cutting through the dimness.

For a moment, Alex just stared at it, the weight of their journey settling over him. They had fought to get here. Lost people, lost time, lost hope. But this—this was the answer.

Then, from the shadows, a figure stepped forward, tall and menacing. It was Victor Lynn.

"I knew you'd come for it," Victor said with a grin that didn't reach his eyes. "But it's too late, Alex. Everything's already been decided."

A chill ran down Alex's spine. He had been expecting this, but the finality of Victor's words hit harder than he had anticipated. The battle for the future, for hope, was about to begin.

As the group braced themselves, Alex took a deep breath. No matter what came next, they couldn't afford to lose. Not now. Not when the last echo of hope had finally been found.

# 12. The Fragile Future

## ○ Lessons from the Past

The wind howled through the broken remnants of what once had been a thriving city, now a ghost of its former self. Buildings stood as skeletal frames, their walls crumbling from years of neglect and violence. In the distance, the faint hum of machines echoed—reminders of a world that had come and gone, leaving only fragments behind. The survivors, those few who had managed to cling to life in the aftermath of the war, gathered in the shadow of this forgotten city, their faces marked by the scars of the past.

Alex stood at the edge of a rooftop, staring out at the horizon. He could almost see the world as it once was—a place of power, wealth, and ambition. But those days were gone now. The empire of nations had crumbled under the weight of greed and desperation. The lessons of the past were clear to him now, though he had ignored them for so long.

The wars had started like any others—small conflicts, hidden motives, and the ever-present thirst for more. It had been about resources at first, and then about control. Nations had fought not just for survival, but for dominance, their leaders driven by a hunger that knew no bounds. The technology that had once promised to elevate humanity had instead become a tool of destruction. And in the end, it had all collapsed.

Alex remembered the meetings, the secret deals in back rooms, the whispers of politicians and businessmen scheming for power. They had believed they were invincible, untouchable. But in their pursuit of greatness, they had destroyed the very thing that made civilization worth protecting—trust, integrity, and the shared belief in something greater than themselves.

He turned from the edge and walked back into the darkened interior of the building. Inside, Sophia was hunched over a makeshift table, her eyes focused on the blueprints scattered in front of her. She had been working tirelessly on her stabilizer, a piece of technology that could potentially reverse the damage that had been done to the planet. But Alex knew that even if she succeeded, it might be too little, too late.

"The past is dead," Alex muttered, more to himself than to anyone else. "And we're the ones who have to live with the consequences."

Sophia looked up, her tired eyes meeting his. "The past may be dead, Alex, but the future is still ours to shape. We can't keep blaming the mistakes of others. We have to learn from them. If we don't, we'll just repeat the same cycle."

She was right, of course. The lessons of the past were there for all to see, if they were willing to look. The greed that had fueled the wars, the arrogance of those in power who believed they were above the law, the disregard for the environment that had led to the collapse of ecosystems—all of it was a cautionary tale. But the question remained: would humanity heed those lessons, or would it continue down the same path of destruction?

Alex thought about the people who had come before him—the leaders, the visionaries, and the everyday citizens who had once believed in a better world. They had all failed in their own way. They had believed that power could be controlled, that technology could be harnessed for good, but they had been blinded by their own ambitions. And now, those who remained were left to pick up the pieces.

His thoughts were interrupted by a sudden noise—a series of sharp knocks at the door. He turned to Sophia, and for a moment, they both stood in silence. Whoever was knocking, they weren't here to deliver good news. The world outside was as unforgiving as ever.

Alex walked over to the door and swung it open. Standing in the doorway was Danny, his face grim, his uniform dirty from the journey. Behind him, the sound of distant gunfire echoed through the streets.

"We need to move," Danny said. "Victor's men are closing in. They've found us."

Alex's mind raced. There was no time for hesitation. No time to dwell on the past. The future was now, and every decision made from this point on would be a reflection of the lessons learned—or ignored.

Sophia stood and grabbed the blueprints from the table. "Let's go. We can't waste any more time. The stabilizer is our only hope."

As they gathered their things, Alex felt the weight of the past bearing down on him, but he pushed it aside. The past had already been written. It was the future that needed their attention. The mistakes of the past had created a world of ruin, but it was in the ashes that the seeds of a new world could be planted. They could still make a difference.

They had to.

As the trio moved swiftly through the crumbling building, Alex's mind buzzed with the weight of their mission. Every step felt like an echo of something that had been lost, something that could never truly be regained. The world they had known—full of cities and nations—was gone, shattered by the very same hubris and greed that had driven humanity to the brink. But still, they moved forward, their purpose stronger than ever.

Sophia had always believed in the possibility of change, even when the odds seemed insurmountable. She was the reason they were still fighting. Her stabilizer was not just a piece of technology—it was a symbol of the last hope for a world that had forgotten its way. If they could get it to work, they might just have a chance to repair the damage that had been done. But first, they had to survive the chaos closing in on them.

Danny led the way down a narrow staircase, his senses heightened, constantly on alert. He had lived through the wars, seen the worst humanity had to offer. He was no stranger to violence, but something about the world they now lived in felt even more perilous. There was a sense of unpredictability in the air—every corner held danger, and no one could be trusted. The remnants of power, like Victor and his mercenaries, were ruthless, and they would stop at nothing to maintain control.

"How close are they?" Alex asked, his voice low.

"Too close," Danny replied. "We need to keep moving."

They reached the bottom of the stairs and slipped into a dark alley, where the remnants of the old world were barely visible. The buildings had been stripped of anything valuable, leaving behind only skeletal structures and the lingering smell of smoke and decay. It was a world where the past had been erased, leaving only the desperate scramble for survival.

The sound of gunfire grew louder, echoing through the empty streets. Victor's men were coming—closing in, just as Danny had warned. The city that had once been a hub of commerce and power was now a battleground, a place where the rich and the powerful fought to maintain what little they had left. And at the heart of it all, the stabilizer that Sophia had created held the potential to change everything.

They ducked behind a pile of rubble, watching as armed men in dark uniforms moved past them, searching for any sign of life. Alex's heart raced as he glimpsed their figures in the shadows, their weapons gleaming in the dim light. It was only a matter of time before they were discovered.

"Where are we going?" Sophia whispered, her voice tight with urgency.

"To the safe house," Danny replied, scanning the area for any sign of movement. "It's the only place we'll be able to hide for now."

They moved quickly, staying close to the shadows, avoiding the main streets and the prying eyes of Victor's forces. The city had once been full of life, a place where people walked the streets with purpose. Now, it was a ghost town, haunted by the choices of the past.

As they reached the edge of the city, the atmosphere grew even more oppressive. The air was thick with dust and the remnants of destruction. The safe house was just a few blocks away, but Alex felt as if every step took them deeper into the abyss. There was no going back, no undoing the choices they had made. But the stabilizer—their only hope—was still within reach.

They arrived at the safe house just as the first rays of dawn began to break through the horizon, casting an eerie glow over the ruins. It was a small, nondescript building, tucked away in a forgotten corner of the city. The door creaked open, and they slipped inside, safe for the moment. But they knew their time was running out.

"We need to get to work," Sophia said, her voice steady despite the chaos around them. "We can't afford any more delays."

Alex nodded. He had no illusions about the difficulty of the task ahead. The stabilizer was their last chance, and even then, the odds of success were slim. But it was the only chance they had. If they didn't act now, the world they had fought to protect would be lost forever.

As Sophia set to work on the stabilizer, Alex and Danny stood guard, their eyes constantly scanning the streets outside. They knew it wouldn't be long before Victor's men found them. But for now, they had a moment of peace—just enough time to prepare for the next fight.

And as the first light of day broke over the horizon, Alex couldn't help but wonder: Could they really undo the damage of the past? Or was the future already written, and they were simply playing out the final chapter?

The answers would come soon enough.

Sophia worked in silence, her hands moving with practiced precision as she adjusted the delicate components of the stabilizer. Her mind was focused, each connection she made a step closer to the answer they so desperately needed. Outside, the world seemed to hold its breath, the distant sounds of chaos growing faint as they sought refuge in the crumbling remnants of what had once been.

Alex sat on the edge of a broken chair, his gaze fixed on the window. His thoughts were a whirlwind, torn between the looming danger and the fragile hope that Sophia's work would succeed. He had seen so much destruction, so many lives lost, but the stabilizer was something different. It was a bridge to the future, to the possibility of change—a change that could alter the course of history, or at the very least, provide a chance to rebuild.

"Do you think we can really fix it?" he asked, his voice barely a whisper.

Sophia didn't look up from her work. "It's the only shot we have left," she replied, her tone steady but tinged with uncertainty. "We either try or we let it all fall apart."

Danny stood by the door, his back to the wall, eyes alert. He was no stranger to uncertainty, but this felt different. They were playing with something far beyond their understanding—something that could change everything or leave them in ruins.

"I've been in situations like this before," he said, breaking the silence. "Where the odds are stacked against us, and the only choice is to keep going. We're not dead yet."

Alex nodded, though his mind was far from reassured. The stakes had never been higher. Victor's men were closing in, and the tension in the air was palpable. They had no time to waste.

A soft beep from the stabilizer interrupted their thoughts, a small but hopeful sound. Sophia's face lit up with a faint smile as she made a final adjustment.

"It's working," she said, her voice tinged with both relief and exhaustion. "The stabilizer is online."

Alex stood up, walking over to her side. He peered over her shoulder at the device, a jumble of wires and screens, its soft glow now pulsing steadily. It was far from perfect, but it was something. It was a chance.

"We need to move fast," Danny said, his voice low but urgent. "They'll be here soon."

Sophia nodded, gathering the stabilizer carefully, as though it were the most fragile thing in the world. "Let's go," she said. "We'll make it work. But first, we need to get to the transmitter. It's the only way to broadcast the signal and make sure this works for everyone."

The group moved quickly, slipping out of the safe house and back into the streets of the city. The familiar sense of danger returned as they navigated the narrow, ruined alleyways, constantly on the lookout for any sign of Victor's men. Every corner they turned seemed to hold new threats, and every shadow felt like an enemy lurking, waiting for the moment to strike.

As they neared the transmitter's location, a faint but unmistakable sound reached their ears—the rumble of approaching vehicles, the unmistakable hum of armored trucks and jeeps. Victor's men were closing in, and fast.

"Shit," Danny muttered, taking cover behind a broken wall. "They're here. We don't have much time."

Alex's heart pounded in his chest as he scanned the street, his thoughts racing. They couldn't afford to be caught now. If they did, everything would be over. But there was no turning back. They had come too far to fail now.

Sophia's voice cut through the tension. "We need to push through. I'm almost there."

They made a break for it, running as fast as they could, the sound of footsteps and gunfire echoing behind them. The transmitter building loomed ahead, a decrepit structure that had once been a hub of communication. Now, it was little more than a hollow shell, but it was the only place that could amplify the stabilizer's signal to the rest of the world.

They reached the door, but just as they were about to enter, the first shot rang out. It was a warning. The game had begun.

"Go!" Danny shouted, throwing open the door and rushing inside.

They dashed up the stairs, the sound of pursuing footsteps growing louder. Alex's muscles screamed in protest as they pushed themselves harder, knowing there was no time for hesitation.

Sophia reached the control panel, her hands trembling as she began to input the necessary commands. The stabilizer hummed to life, its screens flickering with data, signaling that the broadcast was about to begin.

Outside, the roar of engines grew deafening as Victor's men closed in. The building shook with the impact of explosions, the sound of war closing in on them with terrifying speed. But Sophia's focus never wavered. This was it—the moment of truth. The world's fate was hanging by a thread, and the stabilizer was the only thing that could stop the spiral of destruction.

"Almost there..." she whispered, her fingers flying across the keys.

Suddenly, the lights flickered. A sharp, metallic clang echoed from below. They weren't alone anymore. Victor's men had arrived at the building.

"Move!" Danny yelled, grabbing Alex by the arm. "We don't have time for this."

With one final keystroke, the stabilizer activated, its hum now filling the room with a steady, vibrating energy. The broadcast was live. The signal would spread, reaching every corner of the earth.

But at that exact moment, the door to the room burst open, and a figure stepped into the doorway. Victor.

"Did you really think you could stop this?" Victor sneered, his gun aimed at them. "You've already lost."

Alex's heart raced. They had done it. The stabilizer was working. But it wouldn't matter if they didn't survive the moment.

## ○ The Birth of a New World

THE WORLD, OR WHAT remained of it, had always been on the edge of collapse. But as the last fragments of the old order crumbled, something new was beginning to stir beneath the ruins. It was hard to say whether it was hope or desperation, but one thing was clear—humanity had learned to adapt. The survivors had no other choice but to rebuild, and in doing so, they began to forge something entirely different from what had come before.

Alex stood at the edge of the makeshift settlement, looking out over the barren landscape. The once-vibrant cities now lay as empty husks, ravaged by war, by greed, by the insatiable need for resources that had led to the war that had nearly destroyed the planet. But in the midst of the devastation, life had begun to find its way back. Tiny shoots of green pushed through the cracked earth, stubbornly refusing to die. It was a symbol, small but significant, of the possibility of rebirth.

In the distance, a figure approached—Emma. She had been one of the few to witness the final moments of the war, the shifting tides of power, the desperate last attempts by the elites to cling to control. Her eyes, though tired, burned with the same fierce determination that had carried her through the darkest days of the conflict. She had watched the birth of a new world before, in the pages of history, but this time it felt different. This time, the survival of the human race wasn't just a matter of history repeating itself. This time, the survivors were the architects of their own future.

"Is it ready?" Alex asked, his voice thick with both hope and uncertainty.

Emma nodded slowly. "We've secured enough resources to begin. The stabilizer works. It won't be easy, but it's a start."

Behind her, the hum of machines echoed faintly—a stark reminder of the fragile progress they had made. The stabilizer, a device Sophia had created, was their only hope for restoring some semblance of order to the planet. It could purify the air, replenish the soil, and begin to reverse the ecological damage caused by decades of exploitation. It was the beginning of a long journey, one that would take years, maybe even decades, but it was the first real step toward the future.

"We'll need to move quickly," Alex said, his gaze shifting back to the horizon. "Victor's people are still out there, and we both know they won't give up easily."

Emma's expression hardened. "They'll have to fight for it. Just like the rest of us."

Alex knew she was right, but even as they spoke, a sense of foreboding lingered in the air. It wasn't just Victor who posed a threat anymore. There were factions, individuals, and groups scattered across the planet, each with their own agenda, their own vision of what the world should look like. Some of them were ruthless, driven by power and profit, while others—like Alex and Emma—were driven by something far more fragile: hope.

But hope was a dangerous thing in a world so deeply scarred by betrayal and greed. It could heal, or it could destroy. It could unite people, or it could tear them apart.

The sound of footsteps interrupted their thoughts, and they both turned to see Danny approaching. He had always been the quiet one, the soldier with a past too dark to discuss, but over time, Alex had come to trust him more than anyone. Danny's struggles mirrored their own, and his scars—both physical and emotional—were reminders of the price that had been paid for survival.

"We've cleared the way for the first convoy," Danny said, his voice steady despite the weight of their situation. "The first shipments of supplies are on their way. We'll need to get the stabilizer into position within the next few days, or we risk losing the momentum."

Alex nodded. Time was not their ally, but it was all they had left. The world was moving on, for better or worse, and every moment they hesitated could be a step closer to the end.

"We'll be ready," Alex said firmly. "This is our chance to make things right."

The wind howled as it swept across the desolate plains, carrying with it the scent of dust and decay. But beneath the weight of the past, something new was beginning to grow—something born from the ashes, something fragile, yet unyielding.

It was the birth of a new world, and with it, a chance for redemption. But redemption would come at a cost. The question was not whether they could rebuild—but whether they were willing to sacrifice everything they had left to do so.

As the sun began to set on another day in the wasteland, Alex turned his gaze to the horizon once more. Somewhere out there, the future awaited. It was unclear, uncertain, and dangerous—but it was theirs to shape.

And they would fight for it, no matter what it took.

As night began to fall, the settlement seemed to pulse with life, albeit a fragile, tentative life. The glow of campfires flickered in the distance, casting long shadows over the survivors who had found their way here, to this small corner of a dying world. There was an uneasy quiet in the air, the kind that always came before the storm. In the midst of this stillness, the weight of their mission settled heavily on Alex's shoulders.

He knew the dangers they faced, both from external threats and from within. The stabilizer might hold the promise of a new world, but its creation had come at a cost. Many had died during its development—brave men and women who had sacrificed their lives for a future they would never see. And now, the device was their last hope. If it failed, all would be lost, and they would be left with nothing but the dust and echoes of a broken civilization.

Yet, in his heart, Alex couldn't help but feel a flicker of something—something far more elusive than hope. It was a mix of desperation and determination. Desperation for the world that had already been lost, and determination to ensure that the next generation, his children if he had them, wouldn't inherit the same fate.

"Alex," Emma called out softly, her voice cutting through the night air. He turned to face her, the faintest of smiles crossing his face as she approached.

"Everything ready?" he asked.

She nodded, but her expression was heavy. "We've secured the first shipment of supplies, but we'll need more. It's not just the stabilizer that's our problem anymore. The infrastructure we've built here is still fragile. Without proper resources—fuel, materials, manpower—we won't be able to maintain it."

Alex's heart sank. He had known the risks of this mission, but hearing them out loud, seeing them in Emma's eyes, made the reality all the more real. They were on the brink, but the edge was a long way down.

"We'll find a way," he said, more to reassure himself than her. "We'll make it work. We have to."

She didn't respond immediately, but her gaze lingered on him for a moment longer than necessary. There was something in her eyes, a silent acknowledgment of the uncertainty that they were both trying to ignore. And in that brief moment, Alex felt the weight of everything they were carrying—everything they were trying to build—from the ashes of the old world.

"We will," Emma finally said, her voice steady, though her lips trembled slightly. "But we have to be prepared for the worst."

Alex nodded. They had already seen the worst. The question was whether the world they were fighting for was worth saving, or whether it would all fall apart again, as it had so many times before.

As the night deepened, Alex retreated into his thoughts. The stabilizer was their beacon, their only chance to heal the planet, but there was something else, something nagging at him. In every corner of the world, there were still men like Victor, men who would stop at nothing to maintain their control, their power over the few remaining resources. And if they didn't act quickly, the new world they were trying to build would be nothing more than another puppet of those who had caused the destruction in the first place.

The moon cast a pale glow across the barren landscape, reflecting off the scattered ruins of a once-thriving city. In the distance, the faintest glow of a fire signaled that the rebels were gathering, preparing for the next step in their fight. The silence between Alex and Emma grew as they watched the lights flicker and shift, like the last embers of a dying fire, struggling against the dark.

"The world is still broken," Emma said quietly. "But we can fix it."

Alex didn't have an answer. The weight of her words pressed down on him, but there was something in them that made him feel like they could, somehow, defy the odds. They were fighting for more than survival now. They were fighting for something they could barely comprehend, something worth the pain and sacrifice.

And as the first light of dawn began to break over the horizon, casting long shadows across the earth, Alex knew that no matter the cost, they couldn't give up now. There would be no turning back. There would be no second chances.

The new world had already begun.

As the first rays of sunlight pierced the darkness, Alex stood at the edge of the settlement, his eyes scanning the horizon. The world before him seemed as though it had been carved from stone—silent, desolate, but holding a strange, fragile promise. The stabilizer was their last shot, but it would only work if they could maintain their grip on it. The resources they had were scarce, and every day that passed without progress felt like a step closer to ruin.

"Alex," Emma called again, this time with a note of urgency in her voice. She approached from behind, her footsteps muffled by the dust-laden earth. "We've received a transmission from the East. It's the rebels—they've found something."

His heart skipped a beat. The rebels had been a constant source of concern, a reminder that even in the ruins of civilization, there were those who sought only chaos. He turned to face her, his expression hardening.

"What did they find?"

"Unknown," she said, her voice tight with uncertainty. "But they're asking for our help. They claim it could lead to something we've been searching for—something that might tip the balance in our favor."

Alex's thoughts raced. The idea of trusting the rebels was dangerous; they were unpredictable, often working in their own interest, but they knew the land, the remnants of the old world, like no one else. Could they truly have discovered something that could change the tide of their struggle? Or was it another trap, another attempt to lure them into a dangerous game they could never win?

"What kind of help?" he asked, already knowing Emma didn't have all the answers.

"They want us to send a team," she replied. "They've located a source of energy, something buried deep in the ruins of the old world. They believe it could be the key to powering the stabilizer indefinitely."

Alex's mind snapped back to the task at hand—the stabilizer. The idea of extending its life was both a blessing and a curse. If they could harness this new source of power, they could build something lasting, something capable of restoring the world. But the risks were monumental. The rebels had their own agenda, and trusting them would mean venturing into uncharted territory, into the heart of the very chaos they were trying to escape.

"I'll gather a team," Alex said finally, his voice low. "But we're not going in blindly. If this is a trap, we'll make sure we're prepared."

Emma nodded, though her expression remained doubtful. "I'll make the arrangements. But be careful, Alex. Whatever they've found, it's bound to be dangerous. We're not the only ones who want it."

As Alex turned away to prepare, the weight of the decision pressed down on him. Every choice they made now could mean the difference between life and death, not just for them, but for the future of humanity. The stabilizer was their only hope, but if they were to fail, it wouldn't just be a loss—it would be the final nail in the coffin for the world as they knew it.

The journey ahead was uncertain. It always had been.

The days leading up to the mission were filled with tension. As Alex and his team gathered their supplies, the air around the settlement seemed to grow thicker, as though the very earth itself was holding its breath. Every step felt heavier, as if the weight of the past—of the world's collapse—was pressing down on their shoulders.

Alex stood in the center of their makeshift command tent, maps and data scattered across the table before him. His eyes flickered over the terrain, tracing routes and potential hazards. The rebels had promised they would guide them to the energy source, but Alex knew better than to trust a promise from people who had their own hidden agendas.

"I've got the coordinates," Emma said, stepping into the tent with a tablet in hand. "It's a two-day journey. There's a cave system near the old industrial district they've identified as the location. But we'll need to move fast. The weather's turning."

Alex frowned. The weather had always been a variable they couldn't control, and it had become even more unpredictable in recent years. Harsh storms, sudden temperature drops, and dangerous shifts in wind patterns had made travel increasingly perilous. But they had no choice. If this energy source truly existed, it could be the key to securing their survival. They couldn't afford to let the rebels—or the elements—stop them.

"Any sign of other groups in the area?" Alex asked, his voice sharp.

"Nothing solid yet," Emma replied, her eyes scanning the map. "But we've seen more movement from rival factions in the past few days. Whoever controls this energy source will have power—real power. We can't afford to let anyone else get there first."

Alex nodded. The stakes were higher now, not just for their settlement but for everything they had fought for. If the rebels were telling the truth, this was the moment they could seize control of their future. If not, they could lose everything in the blink of an eye.

The team was ready. Packed and armed, each member was prepared for the harsh realities of their journey. The wind howled outside the tent as they finalized their preparations, the last of the daylight fading into the cold, unforgiving night.

Alex stood, his gaze shifting to each member of the team. Their faces were hardened, worn by the years of survival. There was no room for fear here, only resolve.

"We move out at first light," he said, his voice firm. "Stay sharp. We're not just after energy—we're after our future."

The next morning, as the first light of dawn broke over the horizon, Alex and his team began their journey. They moved quickly, cutting through the dense underbrush and navigating the remnants of the broken cityscape that had once been the heart of a thriving metropolis. The streets were empty now, save for the occasional scavenger or pack of wild animals. The destruction that had swept across the world was palpable, each ruined building, each shattered streetlight, a testament to the devastation that had claimed it all.

The deeper they ventured into the industrial district, the more the air seemed to shift. There was an eerie stillness, broken only by the crunch of their boots against the debris-laden ground. The energy source, whatever it was, had to be hidden beneath layers of collapsed infrastructure. But the rebels were confident it could be found, and Alex needed to trust them—at least for now.

As they approached the cave system, the ground beneath their feet began to tremble slightly, a low hum vibrating through the earth. It was faint at first, almost imperceptible, but it grew stronger with each step. The air seemed to thicken, filled with a strange, static energy that made Alex's skin prickle.

"This is it," Emma whispered, her voice tight with awe.

The entrance to the cave was hidden beneath the remnants of a collapsed building, the massive stone and concrete slabs twisted and broken, but still standing guard over the unknown. They would have to climb over the debris to reach the opening, a narrow crack in the stone that led deep into the earth.

Alex glanced at his team, then motioned for them to follow him. One by one, they scaled the rubble, their movements careful and deliberate. As they reached the cave's entrance, the humming sound intensified, vibrating through the air around them.

Inside, the cave was dark and cold, the air thick with the smell of damp earth and metal. Alex activated his flashlight, cutting through the darkness. The beam illuminated the walls, revealing strange, metallic symbols etched into the stone—symbols that seemed out of place, like remnants of a forgotten civilization.

"We're not alone," Alex muttered, more to himself than anyone else.

The humming sound grew louder as they descended into the depths of the cave, the tunnel twisting and turning, leading them deeper into the unknown. It was as though the very cave was alive, breathing with the power of whatever lay hidden within its walls.

Suddenly, the tunnel opened up into a massive underground chamber, its size impossible to comprehend in the dim light. In the center of the chamber, surrounded by old machinery and crumbling infrastructure, stood a towering structure—an enormous, pulsing energy core.

Alex's breath caught in his throat. The source of power they had been searching for was right in front of them.

But even as he stepped forward, the hairs on the back of his neck stood on end. He could feel it—the presence of something watching them, something waiting. The rebels had been right about one thing: this place was powerful. But it was also dangerous, and he knew they were not the only ones who had come looking for it.

The cavern seemed to pulse with energy, the strange hum vibrating through Alex's chest as he stepped closer to the massive structure. The air was thick with anticipation, and a sense of unease settled over him. It was too quiet, too perfect in its stillness. The energy core, though ancient, seemed to draw all the attention, its cold metallic surface glimmering faintly under the light of their flashlights.

Emma moved cautiously beside him, her eyes scanning the room for any signs of danger. "Do you think it's stable?" she asked in a whisper, her voice low, almost reverent.

Alex didn't respond immediately, his gaze locked on the core. The machine appeared untouched by time, as if it had been waiting, dormant, for someone to come and wake it. The question of stability was a difficult one. If this power source could be harnessed, it could revolutionize their survival efforts, but if it was unstable, it could lead to catastrophic consequences.

"I don't know," Alex finally replied, keeping his voice steady. "But we're not leaving without it."

His decision was firm, but a nagging feeling in the back of his mind told him they weren't alone. He could sense it—movement at the edge of his perception, shadows shifting just beyond the beam of his light. He glanced at his team. They were all on edge, aware of the same unease, but none of them dared to speak it out loud.

Suddenly, a loud crash echoed through the cavern. A group of figures emerged from the shadows, their weapons raised, their faces masked by the hoods of their cloaks. Alex's heart skipped a beat.

"The rebels," Emma muttered, her hand instinctively going to the sidearm at her belt.

But Alex shook his head. These weren't the rebels who had led them here. These were different—organized, military-like, and dangerously well-equipped.

"You knew we'd find it," one of the newcomers spoke, his voice calm but carrying an unmistakable edge. He stepped forward, his eyes glinting under the dim light. "We were just waiting for you to uncover it. You see, this power source is ours, and you're trespassing."

Alex's grip tightened around the handle of his own weapon, but he didn't draw it yet. The situation was precarious. A direct confrontation could turn the whole place into a war zone, and if they caused any significant damage to the core, it could trigger a catastrophic failure.

"We don't want trouble," Alex said, his voice cold and measured. "We only came to secure this power source for our people."

The figure in front of him laughed, a low, hollow sound. "Your people?" He scoffed. "You think the future of this world belongs to you? You don't even understand the technology you're standing next to. It's not just power—it's a weapon, one we've been trying to unlock for years."

Alex's mind raced. A weapon? Was this why the rebels had been so secretive? Why had they sent them to retrieve something that had such dangerous potential?

"What kind of weapon?" Alex asked, his voice low, his eyes never leaving the stranger.

"An energy weapon," the man replied with a grin, his eyes narrowing. "A weapon that could erase entire cities, wipe out any enemy. It's a key to control—control of the future, control of everything."

Alex felt a chill run down his spine. This wasn't just about survival anymore. It wasn't even about rebuilding. The core had the potential to destroy everything—something they couldn't let fall into the wrong hands.

"We can't let you have it," Alex said firmly, stepping forward. "We've fought too long to let it be used as a weapon. It's for the future of the human race—not for power."

The stranger tilted his head, amused. "You think you can stop us? You don't even know how to activate it."

"We'll figure it out," Alex said, his resolve solidifying. "We always do."

The tension in the room thickened, the two groups sizing each other up. The unknown enemy stood between them and their goal, but Alex wasn't backing down. The core, this powerful energy source, was the key to everything they had been fighting for. If it fell into the wrong hands, it would tip the scales in favor of those who sought to control the remnants of the world for their own gain.

"You're right," the man said suddenly, his voice changing, becoming more calculated. "You'll need to figure it out, and you'll need our help. But it's going to come at a cost."

Alex's pulse quickened. What did they want from him? What was this new game they were trying to play?

"Tell me what you want," Alex demanded, his voice steely.

The stranger smiled, a cold, calculating smile. "Your allegiance. We can help you activate the core, but only if you swear loyalty to us. Only if you pledge to join our cause. Together, we can reshape this world. Together, we can reignite the flames of civilization."

Alex's mind spun. What was this man proposing? An alliance with the very people who were threatening the future of humanity? They were the enemy—people who believed in control, in domination, not in the survival of all.

But the core... could it truly hold the power to rebuild? Or was it already too late?

"Think about it, Alex," the man continued, sensing his hesitation. "You're fighting for survival, but it's more than that now. This isn't just about food or shelter. It's about power. Power that you can't even begin to comprehend."

Alex's eyes flicked to Emma, who stood nearby, her face unreadable. He could see the uncertainty in her eyes, the same doubt that gnawed at him.

"I won't be your puppet," Alex said finally, his voice low and dangerous. "And I won't let you use this power to destroy what's left of the world."

The man's expression darkened. "Then you'll have to die for it."

The words hung in the air like a death sentence. Alex's muscles tensed, ready for action. But the moment he reached for his weapon, the man's voice cut through the tension with a calm that made the threat feel all the more chilling.

"Not yet," the stranger said. "You're not in control here."

Alex felt the shift in the room, the oppressive weight of the stranger's presence sinking deeper into the cavern's cold stone walls. The sound of footsteps echoed behind him—more of the stranger's group, no doubt. Their weapons were trained on him, silent but unyielding. There was no way out without a fight.

"Leave us, now," Alex growled, his tone unwavering. His eyes darted quickly to Emma and the others, trying to gauge their next move.

But Emma spoke before anyone could act. Her voice was sharp, cutting through the standoff.

"We won't let you use this to conquer what's left of this world," she declared, stepping forward beside Alex. "This isn't a game of power for us—it's survival. We'll fight until the end."

The man smiled again, but this time there was no humor in it—only a deadly calm. "I admire your spirit," he said. "But there's no room for sentiment in this world anymore. You've seen it. Everything's crumbling. Power is the only thing that will allow anyone to survive. It's the new currency."

The room fell silent as the others considered his words. Alex could feel the weight of the choice hanging over them—join them, or fight and risk losing everything.

"Power won't rebuild humanity," Alex said, his voice low but fierce. "It'll destroy what's left of it. You want to control it all, but all you're doing is feeding the same cycle of destruction."

The man's eyes narrowed, his hand hovering near the holster of his weapon. "Then it seems we're at an impasse, don't we?"

Suddenly, the silence was shattered by the unmistakable sound of weapons cocking, echoing throughout the cavern. There was no turning back now. This wasn't just a battle for the core—it was a battle for the future of everything they had fought for, everything they believed in.

Without warning, Alex's team sprang into action. Emma dove behind a nearby pillar, drawing her weapon as she fired a shot toward one of the approaching figures. The explosion of sound and the sharp crack of gunfire broke the stillness of the underground chamber, and all hell broke loose.

Alex ducked, the cavern's walls vibrating from the sudden eruption of violence. Bullets whizzed past him, and the enemy reacted quickly, their precision honed from years of training. He knew they were outnumbered, and their chances of surviving without significant losses were slim. But there was no other choice. They had to protect the core at all costs.

He moved swiftly, dodging incoming fire and taking cover behind a large metal structure that had once been part of the old machinery. His mind raced, searching for a way out, a way to turn the tide. Emma's voice rang out in his earpiece, sharp and clear.

"We need to make it to the core! If we can deactivate it before they get to it, we stand a chance!"

Alex nodded, his grip tightening around his weapon. They had to act fast. There was no room for hesitation. He motioned for the others to follow as they sprinted through the chaos. The core was their only hope, their last line of defense.

But as they neared the heart of the chamber, they were met with resistance. The enemy had anticipated their move, positioning themselves strategically between Alex and the core.

"Move!" Alex shouted, pushing forward despite the gunfire that continued to barrage them from all sides.

The others moved with him, synchronized in their determination. Every step closer to the core felt like a victory, but the danger was far from over. Alex could see the glint of the weaponized energy source just beyond the shadows, an almost hypnotic glow that promised both hope and destruction.

They were running out of time.

Alex took a deep breath, blocking out the chaos around him. They had come too far to fail now.

And then, as if the universe itself was testing their resolve, a massive explosion shook the cavern. The ground beneath their feet trembled, throwing them to the ground as the air filled with dust and debris. For a moment, the world seemed to stop, the sounds of battle fading into a deafening silence.

When the dust cleared, Alex could see it—an opening in the wall, a passage they hadn't noticed before. It was the only way forward.

"Get to the passage!" Alex yelled, rallying his team. They had no choice but to move toward it.

But as they began to scramble toward the new escape route, Alex felt a sharp pain in his side. He glanced down—blood was staining his shirt, but he couldn't afford to stop. He wouldn't stop. They were so close.

The enemy regrouped quickly, their leader's voice ringing through the cavern. "We will not allow you to take the core. You will pay for your defiance."

But Alex didn't look back. There was no time for words. They had to get out, and they had to stop the enemy from taking the core at all costs.

And in that moment, Alex realized—this wasn't just a fight for survival anymore. It was a fight for the soul of humanity.

・・・・

## ○ Alex's Final Choice

THE WIND HOWLED THROUGH the cracks in the old concrete walls, sending a chill that seemed to freeze even the most desperate thoughts. Alex stood at the edge of the makeshift balcony, his eyes scanning the desolate cityscape below. Ruins were scattered everywhere, remnants of a world that had once thrived. What had been vibrant streets and marketplaces were now nothing more than skeletons, empty and broken. His mind was consumed by the weight of the choice that lay before him.

Behind him, the flickering light from a nearby lamp cast long shadows across the room. It illuminated Sophia's tired face, her eyes reflecting the uncertainty of the moment. She had put everything into the creation of the stabilizer, the device that could heal the earth. It was the last hope for humanity, a fragile spark of salvation in a world on the brink of complete collapse. But there was a price—Victor Lynn had already set his sights on it, and he would stop at nothing to control it.

"You don't have to do this, Alex," Sophia's voice broke through his thoughts. She had been pleading with him for hours now, her hands trembling as she reached out to him. "We can still find another way. There's always another way."

Alex turned slowly, meeting her gaze. Her face, usually so strong and resolute, now appeared fragile, worn by the burden of their choices. He could see the fear in her eyes, the same fear that had haunted him for days, creeping into his every thought. But there was no other way. He had known this moment was coming, had felt its inevitability growing ever closer. The world had broken, and with it, the hope of rebuilding it. This was his responsibility now.

"I don't have a choice," Alex said quietly, his voice tinged with a resignation he could no longer hide. "Victor will use the stabilizer to cement his control. He'll turn it into a weapon, Sophia. He doesn't care about healing the world—he cares about power. And we know what that means."

Sophia shook her head, a tear slipping down her cheek. "But we can't fight him forever, Alex. If we're going to stop him, we need to act quickly. Time is running out."

He knew she was right. Every moment spent debating felt like a moment lost. The longer they waited, the more power Victor gained. The more lives were lost in the chaos he had already unleashed. Alex had always believed that change could come through diplomacy, that there was always a way to find common ground. But now, after everything, he understood that not all battles could be fought with words.

"Alex, please," Sophia urged, her voice breaking. "You don't have to become like him. Don't give in to the darkness."

He stepped closer to her, the weight of his decision pressing down on his shoulders. She was right. Every part of him screamed to find another path, to not lose himself in this fight. But the world had changed. The old ways were gone, and in their place stood a harsh reality where survival meant making impossible choices.

"I can't," Alex said, his voice steady, though his heart was heavy. "I can't let him win, Sophia. Not after everything. We've come this far. We have to finish this, or everything we've fought for will have been in vain."

A long silence fell between them, the air thick with the gravity of his words. Finally, Sophia nodded, her shoulders slumping in defeat. "Then we do what we must. For the world."

Alex's gaze shifted back to the ruins outside. The city, once teeming with life, was now nothing but a hollow shell of its former self. The decision before him was not just about fighting Victor. It was about the future, the world that could rise from the ashes or be consumed by them.

"I'll do what I must," he said, more to himself than to Sophia. "But I won't be the one to become the tyrant."

The room was silent, save for the distant sound of wind whistling through the broken windows. Alex had made his choice. There would be no turning back now. The battle ahead would demand everything from him—his strength, his will, his very soul. But as he stood there, staring at the broken horizon, he knew this was the only way to stop Victor and save what little was left of the world.

The future would be built on the choices they made today. And Alex had chosen to fight, even if it meant sacrificing everything he had left.

## ○ Emma's Unfinished Story

EMMA SAT ON THE EDGE of the makeshift campfire, the flames casting shadows on her tired face. Her hands trembled slightly as she scrolled through the old tablet, the last remnant of the world before it all fell apart. She had become so used to silence that the hum of the device felt jarring, almost unnatural. But this silence... it was different. The kind that filled the gaps between words, the kind that hinted at secrets she had long buried but never quite let go of.

The war had taken so much from her, and even now, as the world crumbled in ways she had once predicted, she couldn't escape the feeling that her story was unfinished. That her journey—her search for the truth, the truth that could end all of this—was somehow still incomplete. She had spent years chasing answers, piecing together fragments of a broken narrative, and all that remained was a shadow of what could have been.

When she had first started as a journalist, she had dreamed of writing stories that mattered—stories that could change things, challenge the powerful, expose the corruption festering beneath the surface of society. But that dream had faded as the world around her crumbled, leaving only the harsh reality of survival. Her investigations, once full of passion and fire, had turned into something colder. She had learned to hide behind facts, to hold back her emotions, to shield herself from the horrors she uncovered.

But now, with the world's last hope resting in the hands of a handful of survivors, Emma knew she couldn't remain distant any longer. She had to finish what she had started. She had to tell the truth, even if it meant exposing her own vulnerabilities in the process.

The device buzzed in her hand, a new message blinking on the screen. It was from Alex. Her heart skipped a beat. She had never expected to care for him—he was, after all, a politician by nature, one who thrived in the art of negotiation and diplomacy. She had always been cynical about people like him. But through the months of struggle, of survival, she had come to see him differently.

Emma glanced down at the message, her eyes scanning it quickly. "We've got a problem. Lynn's making his move. We need you."

She closed her eyes for a moment, taking a deep breath. She had been waiting for this. It was never going to be easy, but it was necessary. The plan had been set into motion long ago, the pieces were in place. But the time for waiting was over. Emma knew this was her moment to act, to do what she had promised herself she would do: expose the truth.

The shadows of the fire flickered around her, their dance a haunting reminder of how far she had come—and how much she had lost along the way. But for all the destruction that had ravaged her world, for all the betrayals she had endured, Emma wasn't ready to give up. She wasn't ready to let it end this way.

The unfinished story wasn't just hers anymore. It was everyone's. She had a duty now, to herself, to the survivors who were clinging to whatever remnants of hope they could find. But more than anything, Emma had a responsibility to the truth. No matter the cost.

She stood up, her legs stiff from sitting too long. The cold of the night air bit into her skin, but it also cleared her mind, sharpening her resolve. She had a purpose now, a purpose that no amount of fear could extinguish.

As she walked toward the others, her mind raced. Lynn was a dangerous man, ruthless in his quest for control, and he wouldn't hesitate to do whatever it took to maintain his power. But he underestimated the power of those who had nothing left to lose. And Emma knew this better than anyone.

She approached the fire, where Alex and Danny were already gathered. The moment she stepped into the circle of light, Alex's gaze met hers, and for the first time, she saw something in his eyes that was more than just determination. There was something like understanding, a shared recognition of the weight of what they were about to do.

"We're ready," she said, her voice steady, despite the storm raging inside her.

Alex nodded. "It's time."

And with that, Emma knew the story would finally be told. Not just her story, but the story of the world they were fighting to rebuild. She wasn't just a journalist anymore—she was a witness, a part of the history that was being written in the ashes of the old world.

Her unfinished story would be completed. Not in words alone, but in action. And it would change everything.

Emma glanced at Danny, whose face was a mask of stoic determination. He had been through more than his fair share of battles, both on the front lines and within himself. But there was a cold edge to him now, a hardness she had seen take root in him over the past few months. War had a way of erasing the humanity from people, even the ones who fought for what they believed was right.

"Do you have the data?" Alex asked, his voice low but urgent.

Emma nodded.

She reached into her bag, retrieving a small, encrypted drive. It had been the key to everything. She had risked her life to get it, and now it felt as if the weight of the world rested in the palm of her hand.

"I've got it," Emma said, passing the drive to Alex. He took it without hesitation, his fingers brushing hers for the briefest moment. She didn't let herself dwell on it. There were bigger things at stake now.

Victor Lynn's name had been whispered like a curse among the survivors. His empire, built on manipulation and deceit, had cast a long shadow over what was left of civilization. He had the power to destroy them all, to wipe out any hope of rebuilding. His reach extended far beyond the borders of any nation now; he had allies in places Emma had once thought safe. But she knew his days were numbered. If they could get this information to the right people, they had a chance to take him down.

Alex's expression tightened as he plugged the drive into a makeshift terminal, his eyes scanning the data as it loaded.

"Are you sure this is going to work?" Danny asked, his voice full of skepticism, but with a trace of hope.

Emma's heart raced, but she forced herself to stay calm. "It has to," she said. "This is the only leverage we've got."

The screen flickered to life, revealing encrypted files, data leaks, and confidential communications that exposed Lynn's plans in grim detail. Plans to manipulate global supply chains, to create false narratives through the media, and worst of all, a vast network of political puppets who answered to him.

Emma couldn't help but feel a surge of disgust as the screen filled with the evidence. For years, Lynn had been playing a game no one even knew they were part of. And now, they had the proof to end it.

"We're in position," Alex said, breaking her momentary reverie. "This is it. We send it out, and we expose him."

Emma swallowed hard. The moment of truth had arrived. She had always known that this was what she was meant to do, but now the weight of the decision felt crushing. Exposing Lynn could ignite a firestorm. It could lead to wars, to unrest, to chaos. But the alternative was worse—letting him continue to pull the strings from the shadows, ensuring the downfall of every last hope for a new beginning.

"Do it," she urged, her voice steady.

Alex nodded and pressed a few keys. The files began to upload, traveling through the encrypted channels Emma had set up, her heartbeat matching the rhythm of the progress bar.

It was done.

She exhaled, but the tension in her chest didn't loosen. There was still so much to do. They couldn't wait for the world to catch up to them; they had to act, and fast.

"We've done our part," Alex said quietly, closing the terminal. "Now, we wait."

Emma didn't feel any relief. The danger wasn't over. In fact, it was just beginning. Victor Lynn would not go down without a fight. And the information they had just sent out would send shockwaves through the already unstable power structures.

"We need to get out of here," Danny said, looking over his shoulder as if expecting danger to materialize at any moment. "Now that we've exposed Lynn, we're marked."

Emma nodded. "We leave at dawn. No one knows we were here."

It wasn't just their survival they had to think about now; it was the survival of everyone who depended on them. The revolution that was brewing wasn't just about fighting for freedom—it was about ensuring a future for those who had nothing left but hope.

As they moved out, Emma couldn't shake the feeling that she was finally living the story she had spent years writing in her head. But this wasn't fiction. The stakes were higher than she could have ever imagined. And as the flames of the fire flickered behind them, she knew one thing for certain: the story she had begun all those years ago was no longer unfinished.

It was about to change the world.

## ○ The Stabilizer's True Power

THE WIND HOWLED THROUGH the broken windows, rattling the remains of the glass. Inside, the once pristine laboratory now stood as a shell, its walls scarred by time and neglect. The faint hum of machinery was the only sound that remained, a reminder of what had once been—the heart of a dying world's last hope. Sophia Alvarez stood at the center of the room, her hands trembling as she adjusted the final calibration of the stabilizer.

The device, small yet impossibly complex, sat on the table before her. Its metallic surface gleamed under the dim light, and its intricate web of wires and circuits seemed to pulse with life. It was supposed to save humanity, to reverse the environmental collapse that had torn the planet apart. But Sophia had always known that its true power went beyond simple restoration. It was something far more dangerous.

She glanced at the stack of blueprints beside her, the same blueprints that had led to her exile from the scientific community. They had called her mad. They had called her a fool. And maybe, in some twisted way, they were right. But as she ran her fingers over the edges of the device, the hum seemed to grow louder, more insistent, as though the stabilizer was alive, waiting for her to make the final decision.

It wasn't just a tool for restoring ecosystems. It could alter the very fabric of reality itself. It could bend the rules of nature, reshape the environment in ways no one could predict. And with that power came unimaginable consequences.

Sophia had always known the risks. The technology was too potent, too volatile. In the wrong hands, it could mean the end of everything. But in the right hands... it could create a new world. A world where nature healed, where humanity learned from its mistakes and embraced the delicate balance that had been lost.

Her fingers hovered over the final switch. There were only minutes left before Victor Lynn's forces would arrive, and once they did, it would be over. They would take the stabilizer, use it for their own gain, and everything she had worked for would be twisted into something unrecognizable. Sophia had no illusions about Victor. He didn't care about saving the world. He cared only about consolidating power, using whatever means necessary to hold onto control. The stabilizer was just another tool for him.

But it wasn't just about the stabilizer anymore. It was about the future. The future of those who had fought beside her—Alex, Danny, Emma—and the countless others who had no voice in this fight. She thought of their faces, their unwavering trust in her, and for the first time in days, she felt the weight of her decision.

She had never believed in fate, but now, as she stood on the precipice of a decision that could change everything, she felt its presence. It wasn't just the world that was in her hands. It was something deeper, more profound—a chance to redeem humanity, to set things right before it was too late.

Sophia's breath caught in her throat as the door to the lab creaked open. She knew they were here.

But she couldn't turn back. Not now. Not when everything hinged on this moment.

She pressed the button.

The stabilizer hummed louder, its core glowing with a brilliant light. A surge of energy rippled through the air, and for a brief moment, the room seemed to come alive, as though the very walls were breathing. Sophia's heart raced as she watched the machine pulse with energy. The ground beneath her feet vibrated, and she staggered back, her breath shallow, but she couldn't tear her eyes away from the machine. It was working. It was... alive.

For a fleeting second, Sophia allowed herself a breath of relief. But it was short-lived. She could feel the presence of Victor's men in the hallway, the door already beginning to buckle under their weight. They would come, they would take the stabilizer, and everything she had done would be for nothing.

Her mind raced as she grabbed the device from the table, clutching it to her chest. The power surged within her, a newfound strength she didn't understand. She didn't know if it was the stabilizer, or something else—something deeper, something ancient—but she felt its grip on her, driving her forward.

The door burst open.

Victor Lynn's figure filled the doorway, his face contorted with rage. His men flanked him, their weapons raised, but they hesitated as they saw the power coursing through Sophia. The light from the stabilizer illuminated the room, casting long shadows on the walls. It was a light unlike any other—a light that seemed to defy the very laws of nature.

Sophia stood her ground, her body trembling, but her resolve firm.

"This is where it ends, Victor," she said, her voice steady despite the fear gnawing at her insides. "You can take this, but you'll never control it. No one can."

Victor smirked, stepping forward, his eyes filled with a dangerous mixture of greed and admiration. "You're too late, Sophia. You've already lost. You're nothing but a relic of the past."

Sophia's fingers tightened around the stabilizer. She didn't need to explain herself. The machine had already chosen. She had made the decision, and now there was no turning back.

As Victor took another step forward, the stabilizer flared to life, its energy rippling through the room, and the world around them shifted.

## ○ A World Reborn

THE AIR WAS DIFFERENT now—not cleaner, not freer, but undeniably changed. The ruins of the old world still cast long shadows, their broken spires stretching toward a sky that no longer wept acid rain. Alex Novak stood at the edge of what had once been a bustling metropolis, now a skeletal reminder of humanity's hubris. The wind whispered through the shattered glass and steel, carrying with it the faint scent of earth being reborn.

He watched as a small group of survivors worked in the distance, clearing debris to make way for a communal garden. Sophia's stabilizer had done more than just halt the decay—it had sparked a fragile hope. The technology, once fought over like a mythical artifact, was now the cornerstone of their collective survival. But the cost of its activation lingered in Alex's mind like an unhealed wound.

"Are you just going to stand there, or will you help?" Emma's voice cut through the moment, her sharp tone softened by a rare smile. She carried a bundle of tools, her once-pristine journalist's hands now calloused from weeks of labor.

Alex turned to her, his own smile faint but genuine. "Supervising is an important job," he quipped, though he stepped forward to take the tools from her arms.

"You're terrible at it," she shot back, glancing at the horizon. "But at least you're here."

The "here" she referred to was more than just a place. It was a fragile sense of togetherness, a shared purpose that had been forged in the crucible of loss and sacrifice. For every life saved, they had buried another. For every victory, there had been a cost. The weight of those sacrifices hung heavily on all of them, but none more so than Alex.

Sophia Alvarez emerged from the makeshift lab she had set up in what used to be a public library. Her face bore the weariness of someone who had carried the fate of the world on her shoulders, yet her eyes still held a spark of determination. She approached Alex and Emma, holding a small device.

"This," she began, holding up the object, "is the next step. It's not perfect, but it's a start."

Alex took it from her hands, examining the intricate circuitry. "What is it?"

"A soil rejuvenator," Sophia explained. "It'll take time, but it should help restore arable land faster than nature could on its own. If we can deploy a few of these strategically…" She trailed off, her voice tinged with both hope and doubt.

"You're a miracle worker," Emma said, though her expression remained cautious. "But will it be enough? There's still… him."

They didn't need to say Victor Lynn's name aloud. His shadow loomed large even in his absence. Though his empire had crumbled, his network of loyalists and mercenaries remained a threat. Rumors of his whereabouts were as elusive as the man himself, but his ideology—his belief that survival belonged to the ruthless—was harder to extinguish than his physical presence.

"Do you really think we can rebuild?" Alex asked Sophia later that evening. They sat by the fire, its warmth a small comfort against the chill of the night.

Sophia hesitated, then nodded. "Rebuild, yes. But not as it was. The old world is gone, Alex. Maybe that's not entirely a bad thing."

"Tell that to the millions who died," he replied, his voice low.

"I think about them every day," Sophia admitted. "But if we don't learn from this, if we don't do better, then their deaths mean nothing. We have a chance to start over, to build something more sustainable, more just. That's why I keep going."

Alex looked at her, his eyes searching for something he wasn't sure he'd find. "And if we fail?"

"We won't," Sophia said firmly. "Because we can't afford to."

The next morning, Alex called a meeting of the community. Survivors gathered in what had once been a park, now cleared of rubble and tentatively dubbed "Hope Square." People of all ages, backgrounds, and beliefs stood together, united by necessity and something more fragile: trust.

"We've been through hell," Alex began, his voice carrying over the murmurs of the crowd. "We've lost more than I can put into words. But we're still here. And as long as we're here, we have a responsibility—not just to survive, but to make sure what happened to us never happens again. That starts with us, today, right here."

There were no cheers, no triumphant applause, only a quiet resolve that rippled through the crowd. In that silence, Alex saw the first true signs of a world being reborn—not in grand gestures or declarations, but in the collective will to keep moving forward, one step at a time.

The past was ash, but from it, something new was beginning to grow.

# Epilogue

The sun rose over a world transformed. The jagged ruins of the old cities still stood as solemn reminders of what had been lost, but amidst them were signs of renewal. Where desolation once reigned, green shoots now broke through cracks in the concrete. In the distance, the hum of activity echoed—a people not just surviving, but rebuilding.

Alex stood on a hill overlooking the settlement that had become their beacon of hope. It wasn't much, but it was theirs. Roads were being cleared, fields tilled, and homes erected from the remnants of a shattered age. Each structure, no matter how rudimentary, carried the weight of determination—a promise that they would not repeat the mistakes of the past.

Behind him, Sophia approached, her steps purposeful but unhurried. She carried a small tablet displaying data from the latest soil rejuvenation tests.

"It's working," she said, handing it to Alex.

He glanced at the figures, understanding little of the technical details but trusting in her brilliance. "You've saved the world, you know."

Sophia shook her head, a bittersweet smile on her lips. "Not saved. Given it a chance. That's all any of us can do."

Alex nodded, his gaze returning to the settlement below. "Do you think we'll get it right this time?"

Sophia paused, her eyes distant. "Maybe not in our lifetime. But we've planted the seeds. It's up to them—those who come after—to nurture it."

---

Emma sat under the shade of an old oak tree, scribbling in a weathered notebook. Her journalist instincts had never left her, even when the world seemed beyond repair. She chronicled everything—the losses, the triumphs, the moments of quiet humanity that had carried them through the darkest days.

One of the children ran up to her, a small bouquet of wildflowers in hand. Emma laughed, accepting the gift with genuine warmth.

"What are you writing, Ms. Emma?" the child asked.

"A story," Emma replied, ruffling the child's hair. "About us. About how we made it through and what we're building now."

The child tilted their head thoughtfully. "Will people read it one day?"

Emma smiled. "I hope so. And I hope it helps them remember."

As the days turned into weeks, then months, the fragile new world began to take shape. The stabilizer technology became a cornerstone of the rebuilding effort, its reach spreading beyond the small settlement. Word of their progress traveled, drawing other survivors who carried their own skills, stories, and burdens.

Victor Lynn's name faded into legend, a cautionary tale of power unmoored by morality. His empire of greed and violence became a distant memory, overshadowed by the collective determination to forge a better future.

Years later, Alex found himself walking through a thriving community where children laughed, gardens flourished, and the air buzzed with possibility. He passed a mural painted on the side of a building, its vibrant colors depicting the journey from chaos to renewal.

The past would never be forgotten—nor should it be. The scars were too deep, the losses too great. But the survivors had chosen to look forward, to embrace the chance they had been given, however tenuous.

As Alex stood beneath the mural, a young woman approached him, a child on her hip. "You're Alex Novak, aren't you?"

"I am," he said, his voice steady.

"My grandmother told me about you," she said. "About everything you and the others did. She said you gave us a world worth fighting for."

Alex met her gaze, his expression softening. "No," he said. "We just made sure there was something left to fight for. The rest is up to you."

The woman smiled, nodding before walking away. Alex turned back to the mural, its vibrant hues a testament to resilience.

The world was not what it had been, but it was alive. And for the first time in a long time, it felt full of promise.

Milton Keynes UK
Ingram Content Group UK Ltd.
UKHW040352111224
452348UK00001B/99